THIRTY-ONE SECONDS

Also by this author:
Dark Time, 2014
Absolute Truth, 2015
Flood Moon, 2017
Northward, 2018

THIRTY-ONE SECONDS

BY

CHUCK RADDA

Cover designed by Cindy Satagaj-Radda.

Author photo by Lindsay Vigue Photography.

Published by Lefora Publishing LLC. www.leforapublishing.com

Visit the author's website at www.chuckradda.net.

Printed in the United States of America.

Eagles song lyrics used by permission.

ISBN 978-1-7336963-4-0

For Deanie

Time past and time future
What might have been and what has been
Point to one end, which is always present.

T. S. Eliot, from *Four Quartets*

CHAPTER 1

In a brown shoebox half-filled with loose photos, there's a small, slightly faded color print of my sister Eveline and me. It's curved slightly, having been secured with others too enthusiastically by a wide rubber band, long since deteriorated and crumbled nearby. Eveline and I are at Saylorville Lake, but I'd know that without even looking. It was where we went—it was where most of central Iowa went nearly every summer Sunday. And my uncle took the picture—I know that too: my aunt always said she hated cameras and left all that mumbo-jumbo about shutter speeds and f-stops to her husband, Thomas.

He's the photographer in the family, a responsibility he inherited when my mother died some forty years ago. Susan Blaine was someone I never knew—I was a year old when she died—but her photos are scattered about. They're in brittle newspapers and faded magazine, many of which have vanished over time or whose very existence might be unearthed by only the most thorough Internet search. **Susan Blaine–Chicago–photography.** For me she was never more than a name on a business card.

Uncle Thomas is her brother-in-law. It's not an explanation, but it's something. We're not together, Eveline and I, in that photo. She stands about five feet away and holds a blue beach pail in a threatening position. I know it's filled with water and I can tell by her grin what she intends to do with it. I even remember how furious my uncle was because (1) those were my only dry clothes, and (2) he had been an accessory to the action in the photo. He had posed it—told Eveline to hold the pail and make believe. She heard only half the request.

She was mischievous but never malicious. I got wet. I dried off. We went on with the day, and with our lives, but we seldom stood together.

For one, the seven years' difference in our ages ensured the fact there would always be a separation. Even our outfits in the photo illustrate it. That day at the lake Eveline wears a strawberry colored halter top which lies flat on her undeveloped breasts. A pair of bright-white shorts reach to the knees of her bony legs. On her face is a pair of oversized sunglasses, purchased with her allowance after a boy told her that people with fair complexions need to protect their eyes. (She did not possess a fair complexion, but she liked the boy.)

My outfit: red shorts and a Hulk t-shirt.

She already looks like a young lady; I, a goofy first-grader.

Those sunglasses notwithstanding, Eveline had beautiful eyes—large, almost teal, deep-set. She once told me they were too close together for her to be considered pretty, but I was seven: eyes were eyes, functional and handy, nothing more. I don't know when I stopped looking at those eyes, looking at her, talking to her, recognizing her very existence. Our falling out—our gradual descent from that day at the lake—was thorough, unremitting, ineffable. We disappeared from each other's lives so completely, that not even the variable politics of families, complex and erratic as they can be, could reunite us.

Even the best relationships seem to comprise moments of turbulence interspersed with calm. For Eveline and me, however, there were no moments. Our estrangement grew, became absolute: I never even paid attention to where she was living or how. At the end…at the very end… there was no phone call in the night, no ominous knock at the door. There was, instead, only a letter carrier on the front stoop, holding a packet addressed to me, asking me if I knew people in Connecticut.

I had spoken to the man only once before. That time he actually rang the bell and found me, laid up with the flu. I stumbled to the door, shivering and coughing, to hear his apology for a bill that had fallen into a puddle. He made sure I knew his name so that, if I had a complaint to make about the wet envelope, I would mention him specifically. It seemed like a lot of trouble to go through to make sure he earned a reprimand, but I agreed that, if a complaint were forthcoming, I'd mention him by name.

I never made a complaint—not for a damn cable bill—nor did I make note of his name.

When he came by last Friday, I had gifted myself a day off from work and extended my weekend. I was in the front yard, half-stoned from a can of spray paint which I was using to "fix up" a badly chipped Windsor chair. The day was sweltering, I felt woozy, and my head was spinning. I took some breaths of fresh air upwind from the spray and tried to clear my head.

"No," I said to him, trying to remember his name. Spanish. "No relatives or friends in Connecticut."

He pointed to the return address, then handed me the packet. It was from Eveline.

That's my sister," I said. "She moves around."

"*Sí*, I do that too. From Peru to Connecticut to Chicago."

"Where next?"

"Someplace cooler," he said.

"*Muy caliente*," I said, fairly exhausting my Spanish vocabulary.

It was more than *caliente*—it was suffocating—not late enough in fall for Indian Summer, though the North Avenue Beach crowds had long since thinned out, and there were no longer struggles or bribes involved in seeking a seat at an outdoor café. A few days earlier we'd endured our first-of-the-season day-long drizzles, blowing in—sideways of course—off the lake. The pathway to Chicago winters is circuitous, fits and starts, but like everyone else, I was preparing—while the A/C blasted in the background.

He pointed to the chair. "You do this as your job?"

"Oh, no," I laughed. "If I did, I would not eat. I work in the city—a financial management company."

"Good. You do not want to work in this sun."

He knew what he was talking about. Despite his government-issue Bermudas and a short sleeve shirt, he was wilting: I got him a glass of ice water. We talked about Peru—he'd lived in the mountains where it was cooler; we talked about Chicago winters and how he had struggled through the first few; we even talked about his job and how long he hoped to work before he could retire. I was in no great hurry to open the packet, but at least my head was clearing.

"I am not nosy," he said, "but my sister's family still lives there. When they came up from Peru, I gave them the house and moved here."

"You *gave* it to them?"

"There is a bill of sale and it is all legal, but yes. My sister did not have much so we shared."

"You are very generous."

"You have family, Mr. Blaine?"

"In Iowa. An uncle and aunt. But my sister—we don't keep in touch."

"*Sí*," he said, as if he knew what I meant—as if it made perfect sense to a man who gave his sister a house that I would have a sister whose whereabouts I didn't even know. I was weary of the conversation. I think he knew.

"I will let you finish," he said. "Looks good."

It didn't. The paint was uneven and there were drips here and there. I was beginning to regret my decision not to toss the thing in the first place. But I thanked him, and admitted finally that I'd forgotten his name.

"Miguel," he said. "Miguel Martinez. There are so many names we have to remember."

He was making an effort to save a total stranger from embarrassment: he *was* the kind to give his sister a house. Our approach to life had apparently diverged somewhere.

"My sister and I, we don't keep up. We are—do you know the word *estranged*?" He didn't.

"Apart?"

"*Distanciado*," he said. "I am sorry for that."

"Families," I said with a smile, then remembered again that his life was the antithesis of mine.

He finished the water, thanked me, and left. I made a few more attempts to salvage my project, then did a quick cleanup and headed for the refuge of my air-conditioning. Once inside I drank down a beer a little too fast, took a shower, even shaved though I had no place to go, and then finally decided I had exerted enough autonomy to allow me to open the packet.

I looked for a letter first, anything with "Dear Daniel" on it. There was nothing but pages and pages of scanned newspaper articles, most of them about airplanes and airports, there were some poorly photocopied pictures from my childhood, some of which I remembered. There was an informal snapshot from my parents' wedding, a promotional brochure from the company where I worked that included a picture of me in a large group; and then there was *stuff*—not definable, not categorizable, not noteworthy. Just *stuff* that used to be hers but now was mine.

I wracked my brain, using the cells not destroyed by the paint fumes. Was this her birthday? Some dismal anniversary or commemoration? Our parents' birthday? Wedding anniversary? Anything?

I wish I could say I had an inkling or a premonition, but it was clearer than that. I just knew. Found a list of recent obituaries in Connecticut and there it was: Eveline Blaine, 47, after a long illness, born in Chicago, leaves a brother Donald....

If that was her last joke at my expense, it was a good one.

Donald. First I'd disappeared from her life, then from her death.

Or maybe the last joke was that a letter carrier had brought me the news. Eveline would have roared at the irony. She'd have remembered how all us kids were warned about strangers at the door, except for Ed the mailman.

Since he wasn't family and he wasn't a friend, he thus fell into that broad category of people who probably wouldn't do us harm, but could potentially kidnap us. Or kill us. Or commit crimes whose definitions remained nebulous but whose intent did not. We had been warned. But Ed was the exception.

At six and a half feet tall, Ed was capable of peering through the three small windows near the top of our front door if he chose to. We never saw him do it, never saw anything untoward in him at all, but uniform or not, he was a stranger.

One time—it was late afternoon but the kids were alone—Ed rang the bell. We knew it was him—had seen him coming up the walk. One of my cousins said we should all be quiet, but Eveline said it was stupid and opened the door. We were aghast, but she seemed to relish the risk. At least a half-dozen times she broke the rules, then one day she announced she would open the door to Ed no more. She had overheard a conversation between the mailman and my uncle—they often spoke about the state of the world, sometimes about sports, often about nothing in particular. But on this one particular day Eveline heard Ed ask my uncle how long those kids were going to be staying there. Those kids: Eveline and me. It was not an impertinent question; after all, my uncle and aunt had signed up for three children, bought a house for three children, planned to buy food, provide utilities, clothe and shelter three children. Eveline and I were add-ons. We were *staying* there.

All I cared about was the answer, but she said she didn't hear.

"You did and you won't tell me," I said. "Do we have to leave? Where will we go?"

"We're not going anywhere," she said, with the authority on which I had already come to rely.

We stayed.

My uncle could shrug his way out of difficulties, and maybe that day a shrug was a sufficient answer. But if so, was it in willing acceptance or frustrated obligation? At the time I knew we were visitors, that we'd been taken in. But when Ed put a kind of termination date on our so-called visit—*how long are they staying?*—our viewpoint changed. We weren't visitors. We were interlopers. Of course at the time that word was not part of my lexicon. Nor was *lexicon*, I suppose. As we grow words tend to fill in the blanks for us. I suppose I became an English major to fill up that lexicon faster, to know who I was and maybe who I would become.

Maybe we all battle words as much as we accumulate them. Eveline and I didn't want to be interlopers, we didn't want to be orphans, our mother never wanted to be a widow; nor my father, a name on a casualty list. Maybe words use us more ably than we use them.

Ed's assault on my childish insecurity would have passed without notice had I known concepts like loyalty and steadfastness and applied them to my uncle and aunt, though I still—in all those years—had not acquired the words to make my sister's passing any easier to accept.

*****

On Saturday, the day after Miguel's visit, I waited for him, even though I know fill-ins often handle weekend deliveries. Shortly before noon, however, he came up the walk and ascended the steps. I met him with a bottle of water—the heat had not broken yet.

I was going to ask him if he needed *agua*, but speaking a foreign language when one's entire vocabulary comprises a half-dozen words does seem pretentious.

"Water?"

"No thank you." He showed me a water bottle in his mailbag.

"Uno momento," I said, holding up my index finger and forgetting I didn't want to sound pretentious. I showed him the photograph of Eveline and me.

"This is my sister," I said, "many years ago."

"*¿Cuántos años*? How old?"

"She is 13."

He held the picture away from the sun. "*Hermosa. Hermosa.*"

"English?"

"Beautiful."

"Yes. What you brought yesterday—the packet—it was mailed by someone else."

"Oh?"

I think Miguel thought I was complaining. He seemed ready to apologize, for what I don't know.

"It's all right," I said. "Someone was helping her. She was very sick and…she did not recover."

He stood open-mouthed.

"She was very sick," I repeated, as if were a legitimate excuse. "He shook his head. "I am so sorry that has happened."

He shook my hand—held it for a long time. I didn't doubt his sincerity, but something in his voice—or maybe in my soul—turned his expression of sympathy into an accusation. I had *let* my sister die, then left it to him to tell me.

"Mr. Blaine," he said, gathering himself, "you will want me to stop the mail while you attend to her?"

"Yes, please." I hadn't thought of it. "For a week?"

"Yes," I said, though I was really thinking a day or two. Of course that would have made me look even more callous than Miguel imagined I was.

"And call the post office if you return early.

Yes, thank you."

He was still holding the picture. He held it up once again, seemed to examine it even more closely.

"*Que hermosa era*," he said. "*Era?*"

"*Was*. How beautiful she…was," he said, his eyes lowered.

CHAPTER 2

Twenty-some-odd years ago, still in college and grinding through a course in Victorian literature, I discovered (later than most, I guess) *Great Expectations* and the venomous Miss Havisham—jilted at the altar, never to have another positive thought in her miserable life, and little Estella, her icy protégé who followed in lockstep. There were classroom discussions and debates over whether the pair of them should be pitied or reviled. I wrote a paper about the absurdity of wasting the one life you have on something that cannot be undone. I earned a B- and a written comment about my seemingly having an axe to grind and the importance of keeping personal biases out of analytical papers. Pretty insightful.

And that was before Bethany Mallin and I were engaged to be married, and then weren't. That's the past from which I have not been able to run entirely, a past I've tried to replay even though I know—as Eveline did—the past is not replayable. If my sister felt that her childhood had been stolen from her and surrendered her adulthood trying to fix it, maybe I blame Bethany for stealing time from me.

Maybe that was the intersection of our lives, Eveline's and mine, the one I failed to recognize—or refused to accept—of paralyzing regrets and tedious laments. Or maybe they gave our lives meaning, like Ahab's whale, or Gatsby's Daisy, or Shackleton's Pole, or the Grail itself. That B- I received for berating my sister? I probably wouldn't write the same paper today.

But with all that, what if, on a sunny Friday in 1979, there had been no flight to L.A. with my father in row 33? Or if there had been a flight, what if it had soared uneventfully into the skies over O'Hare and onward to California, and then back again? What would my life mean today? What would Eveline's? I never sympathized with that wretched Miss Havisham and her self-induced misery, but I understood it.

A little.

I probably should have tried harder to understand Eveline.

*****

My newlywed starter home—the one I bought for Bethany and me and has been officially a "single-occupancy domicile" for a long time—lies a half mile from the spot where the north branch of the Chicago River bends around Horner Park. A shorter distance away in the other direction is the venerable Wrigley Field. I should be a Cubs fan, but I suffered through their World Series in 2016 and I don't care if they never win another game, let alone a championship. My father rooted for the White Sox, and while it's true that sons often go their own way and piss off their parents, I had no reason to piss off someone I'd never met. I'll admit though that there may be some misplaced anger or resentment at play: I hate the Bears who were also his team.

I grew up idolizing the White Sox's Frank Thomas—the Big Hurt. Some say he got that nickname because he hurt the baseball when he hit it. Others that he hurt the other team at the same time. The *big* was never debatable. Most of all he wasn't a Cub. If my sports biases separate me from my parents, my home does the opposite.

Stand near the North Branch and it's hard to believe it's the same congested waterway that splits downtown—the one that is famously dyed green on St. Patrick's Day purportedly to honor the large Irish population in the city. The true story of the green dye is less ethnic than functional: sixty years ago the Chicago was "the dirtiest river in the world," the clean-up chemical was green, the project worked, the tradition continues.

It's the same river that runs under the bridge on Michigan Avenue, one that I have traversed countless times—but then so has everyone else who lives in, works in, or visits the city. That drawbridge is as iconic a landmark as the Empire State Building, the Washington Monument, or the Gateway Arch; and visiting it, treading on it, touching it are all free. Purists will insist it's the DuSable Bridge, but nobody calls it that; it's the Michigan Avenue Bridge, or just "the bridge," and it probably has special significance to thousands. For better or worse, I'm one of them, for on a January evening in 1981, Susan Blaine—Eveline's mother and mine—jumped from that well-traveled landmark and drowned.

I could enhance that story with a lot of added drama, but it's a simple fact. Her body was found a day later, floating near some pack ice near what was then called the Sears Tower, and witnessed by untold numbers of curious and horrified onlookers. And even though the ubiquitous cell phone camera was still three decades in the future, I have no doubt that pictures of "a dead woman in the river" exist somewhere. Worse, the Chicago River famously runs backwards, away from the lake, so instead of her body having disappeared into wintry Lake Michigan never to be discovered, my sister lived with the memory of our mother's body on display for all to see, and I lived with the story.

Susan Blaine's suicide wasn't much of a shock to anybody. She had been devouring antidepressants and supporting a covey of grief counsellors—a profession that was, at the time, just catching on. I'm still a skeptic. Sometimes people have to grieve without assistance, though going it alone and denying support never seem like the best paths either. My sister used to tell me that Mom had good days and bad. I was so young I wouldn't have known a good day from the apocalypse. And even when our mother died, the whole sequence was lost on me, a child hardly past his first birthday. As I grew older, I learned the story, but it was always just a story to me—it was a lived experience to Eveline. She was in the second grade that day the plane crashed.

The *ill-fated* plane—that's newspeak for incidents like that. In retrospect I would use the adjective *defective* for the plane or *shoddy* for the workmanship that was supposed to make it airworthy, but a journalist would have to prove that…so…it's ill-fated. And the fates were especially duplicitous: a flawless day in May. Eveline had gone to a friend's house after school for a play date—a friend with a pool, no less, and not even summer yet. It did seem flawless, but it wasn't. No day ever is.

My mother spent that afternoon in Grant Park taking photos for a project she'd begun for some publisher—a picture-and-text book on Chicago architecture. Enthusiastic as she was, however, finding blocks of time to put it together, even with her daughter in school all day, seemed more and more difficult. And there was added pressure to get it done: she was pregnant, expecting later in the year. Eveline had been a difficult delivery, and she knew that once the cold weather set in, she'd be housebound if not actually bedridden. So that day, with my father having left for the airport and my sister at school, she was free. With her portable typewriter on the dining room table and a packet of erasable bond, she started to sort through some of the 500 photos she had already taken, typing the accompanying text as she went along. There's a picture of her doing that, a pre-selfie photo via tripod and self-timer—one that I think she'd planned to use for her author's bio when the book came out. It's backlit so she's almost in silhouette—she had a great eye and knew what the finished photo would look like. You can see individual strands of her light brown hair—Eveline's shade, and glints of reflected room light in her eyes—again, Eveline's. My aunt and uncle still have the tentative beginning of that project—words and *the* photo.

Quaint to be using a typewriter, even in 1979. Businesses were already discarding them, and my dad was touting the word processor at the office. There was even a computer at home, an old Apple—bulky and primitive—but Susan Blaine always preferred the clicking and tapping of the portable—the keys moving the hammers and striking the platen and the little *ding* of accomplishment when one reached the end of the carriage. I'm not projecting here—she actually wrote that somewhere. Even said it once or twice to Eveline.

On that Friday while she worked, Louis Blaine called home just prior to boarding the plane. I would imagine they spoke briefly, but whatever passed between them was the last thing that ever did. Eveline always said there was no final farewell or expression of eternal love—she knew them both. I'd like to think there was, but I'm projecting without any rationale.

In 1979, when the digital age was in its infancy, teleconferencing was more an excuse than an innovation. As bothersome and expensive as it was to fly 2,000 miles to Los Angeles for a one-hour meeting, then immediately afterwards take a cab to LAX and return, businessmen did it all the time. My father's call home that day may have been thoughtful and, in retrospect, poignant. Or it may have been a complaint. I only know it was unnecessary: Susan Blaine was one of those people who knew schedules and itineraries. She also knew her husband had been grumbling about this flight to Los Angeles for the better part of two weeks. A meeting in L.A. on the Friday of Memorial Day weekend? What level of insensitivity and thoughtlessness goes into planning like that?

In his position and with his stature, he could easily have tabbed an assistant to take his place. I work in the business world: I know how it operates. The meeting that day in 1979 involved no negotiations, just some review, clarification, and witnessed signatures—but there was a major acquisition involved, and if something were to go wrong—some *t* not crossed, some sequence not followed—it would be Louis Blaine's ass on the line. Worse, it would be Louis Blaine's paycheck—the one that provided the salary that made the world comfortable for Susan, for Eveline, eventually for me, and for himself.

Something else. May of 1979 in Chicago was not just another spring month. The previous winter had been dreadful. Hundreds had died from exposure, from hunger, from malfeasant neglect. Residual anger over unplowed streets and neglected poor and homeless had threatened the future of many local politicians. Chicagoans who had survived it could hardly be faulted for rushing summer a bit that day.

Susan Blaine, too, eventually gave in. Maybe it was the first fragrances of summer blooms wafting through the open windows, or the view of sundresses and t-shirts below. Whatever the motivation, she eventually convinced herself this was no day to be stuck inside somewhere. She grabbed her old Minolta, stuffed her pocketbook with the ubiquitous Ektachrome, looped the camera around her neck, and left.

Eveline knows the whole story from there. A bus ride south on Michigan to the museum, then the urban prairie of Grant Park where Buckingham Fountain was already ringed with hundreds of spectators, then across Lake Shore to the harbor packed with bobbing watercraft of all sorts crowded in for the weekend. She pointed the lens toward the lake, toward the park, and upward to capture the skyline she loved. There remains a dated and numbered record of the day, courtesy of the pharmacy (long since closed) where she dropped off her film to be processed. The slides were retrieved after numerous inquisitive phone calls weeks later.

In a macabre way we have a depiction of the world on the day my father died and the day my mother's world dissolved—preserved carelessly in shoeboxes and manila envelopes and desk drawers—the family history of a family's last day.

I don't know how long my mother remained near the lake, or if, like so many spring days in Chicago, a chilly wind blew in off the water and brought everyone back to reality. I do know that on the bus ride home she heard murmurs and felt something was wrong. Then, gradually, details, sketchy and incomplete. There'd been a plane crash in Los Angeles, then later it was a flight *to* Los Angeles. I can imagine what she told herself, that a dizzying number of planes left O'Hare daily, many of them bound for the west coast. Louis could not possibly have been on *that* one.

But surely the details accumulated. American Airlines.

To LAX.

Finally, the flight number: 191.

At home she spent the late afternoon in silence, answered only one phone call: Louis's secretary. Was Louis at home? Did he miss the flight? No. And no.

In the evening a friend, aware of the crash but not of Louis Blaine's death, brought Eveline home from her play date. It was my sister who found her mother standing in the kitchen in only a towel that draped her shoulders, still wet, her belly barely showing the indication of…me. At a loss for an explanation and, by her own admission terrified, Eveline chased down the friend, who helped clean some of the puddled water from the floor, got her straightened out and dressed, then made arrangements for the airline to send someone to the house. Some of that is hearsay and second-hand knowledge—told by someone to someone—and after forty years the truth is all mixed up with conjecture. But Eveline was there, trying to reconcile the woman who had sent her off to school that morning with the one standing before her naked and frail.

An airline official arrived and called 9-1-1. PTSD was not the everyday expression it is now and, no doubt, she was treated for shock. But shock fades, a syndrome doesn't.

Several months later I was born. That part I do know.

A mile past the end of the runway, at the perimeter of O'Hare that Friday in May, 1979, 273 lives ended, the bodies burned beyond recognition. Pilots talk about souls on board—I have little interest in what became of those souls. After all this time, only Louis Blaine the person matters to me.

In the months to come the investigation and the lawsuits would drag on, punctuated by accusations of faulty maintenance and negligence, and degraded further with abhorrent estimates of each victim's monetary worth. For my mother the settlement, if and when it came, would mean nothing. Life insurance would guarantee her children's future, ensure the fact that the rent would be paid, but money would never separate her from the world she entered into on that warm Midwest afternoon.

And that money—as a macabre bonus it even covered the cost of a tasteful and discreet funeral for her, so that on a frigid January evening twenty months later, with a stiff lake wind driving the sleet against the framework of the "the bridge,"

Susan Blaine could jump from Michigan Avenue into the river below and make that separation final.

CHAPTER 3

I kept poring over my sister's obituary which, since everything electronic lives forever, will consider me Donald for just as long—even after old Donald passes on.

And apparently she had died away from one of her "Q-phases." Eveline's middle name was our mother's maiden name—Quilling. Eveline had gone through several periods when her signature always included a prominent and somewhat flamboyant Q swirling about in script, but whether it was homage or ostentation, I never knew.

Of greater significance, the obituary said she died after a long illness. Women that age can have heart attacks, and strokes, but there's no strong history of it in the Blaine family. Opioid deaths are rampant these days, and with the death of every young person, that cause crosses my mind. But, as much as I'd lost track of her, that doesn't sound like Eveline. She was always in control, always focused, though never (I thought) on the right thing. Could a simple medical procedure have gone wrong? An anesthetic that stopped her heart? Was it suicide like her mother?

I scoured the Internet but found no highway fatalities that could have involved her; of course, I couldn't discount the possibility of the accident having occurred long before and the injuries eventually taking their toll, or even that she was a victim of a less dramatic accident: a fall down a flight of stairs, a carbon monoxide leak, choking alone, even a discharged weapon. I found nothing. There were police I could call, I guess. Hospitals? Town halls? Places where records were kept? But I was not an investigator and felt quite sure I'd make a fool of myself with any further pursuits, especially ones that began "I just learned my sister was dead

And I could have phoned Lon Taggart—a prospect that would have been incredibly uncomfortable since I had no inkling there even was a Lon Taggart until I saw him named as her companion. She may not have been married, but she had broken free of that connection of failed relationships that had bound us together. I felt more desolate than at any other time since I'd received the news. She'd had had a life, not just an existence. I let self-pity and regret battle it out in my mind, never quite sure what was less appropriate.

No calling hours or wake. Eveline told me once she wanted her boy cremated when the time came, and though people frequently waver about such things, I had no reason to doubt that her ashes lay scattered somewhere. Even so, the line reading *burial will be at the discretion of the family* seemed odd. I was her family. Her uncle, aunt, cousins, then—they all knew.

My Uncle was not surprised to receive my call.

"We were going to tell you," he said. He sounded defensive—not a good beginning.

"Why didn't you?"

Before he could answer I backed off quickly—no sense adding hypocrisy to my sins.

"I just mean," I said with less accusation, "you know, I wish I'd known. Did she ask you not to tell me?"

"Yes," he said, without hesitation. "She didn't want to complicate things. I told her she was wrong, but we also thought she'd get better. Then we got a check. $10,000. Expenses."

"You were there at the end?"

"No. We would have been, but she took a sudden turn and it was over before we could move."

"The paper said a long illness. What was it?"

"It was a brain tumor. They thought they had it stopped, resected, whatever they call it. But it got ahead of them."

"Was she, you know, cogent at the end?"

"Cogent?"

"Sometimes those tumors can affect thinking, speaking."

"I think her final week was tough, but before that there were so many times she seemed to have licked it."

"She sent me packets of information. When did she do that?"

"Information on what?"

"On her life," I said. "One more chance to call me Donald."

My uncle laughed. "Did she do that? She was something, Evie. I wish she had done more with her life, but it was her life."

"I never saw it that way."

"I know, and what did it prove? Listen, Danny, she said the reason she didn't want to tell you is that you'd held fast all that time—why waver at the end?"

"Because it was the end."

"She didn't want you to pity her, to be uncomfortable when people asked about her. You know, all those years of…I don't know…separation? anger? Look, I don't know if she was right, but we honored her wishes."

She had placed them in an untenable situation. I let it go, asked about the services. They were simple, he said, but nice. He laughed when I asked if there had been a mass or church service.

"Eveline? Really?"

"Just kidding."

"A closed casket, but the family was able to…view her. She looked nice. She was a pretty girl, always had been."

"Like her mother. I thought she wanted to be cremated."

"Her partner said she had changed her mind. Did you know she had a partner?"

"The obituary mentioned a companion."

"Yes, companion, Lon Taggart. I liked him a lot, just an easygoing guy, but he was devastated."

"I'm glad she found someone to care that much."

"I thought the same thing, Danny" he said. "It made me feel good for her, but you hate to see anybody hurting like that for so long."

The solemnity evolved into some small talk—my aunt was doing well, the house had just had a makeover of paint and landscaping, their own two kids were working and apparently had stopped providing grandchildren, but he admitted there were enough of them. There had also been a third child, a daughter, whose death and aftermath helped deepen the antipathy between Eveline and me, but broaching that topic again would have benefited nobody.

"How about you, Danny? Any chance?"

"Of what?"

"Of children. Time's passing, you know."

"First, if I actually learned anything in high school biology, I'd have to convince some woman to go along with it. I don't think an adoption agency would provide a child for a single parent who works sixty hours a week, then comes home and does more work."

"Gotta change that lifestyle, Danny. That Bethany girl—she still in the picture?"

"You're the photographer. If you're using a really wide-angle lens, yes, she's in the picture—way out on the edge. Far as I know she hasn't married anybody yet, but we don't see each other much."

"You know best, but maybe give her another try. It's not the race thing is it?"

"Wait, is Bethany black? I never noticed."

"You know we don't care," he said. "But sometimes there are pressures…"

"It's not a race thing, not for either of us. It just wasn't happening."

"Well if it starts again…."

"You'll be the first to know."

"We'll be waiting. And listen, what she sent you, maybe it isn't supposed to be news, or some kind of puzzle. Maybe it's a memento, like a yearbook or a scrapbook—what was important to her. You just look at it and remember."

"Like Saylorville. You two still go there?"

"Not so often, but yes, we still do."

"You two did all right by each other, and by us."

"Nothing any good midwestern Christian wouldn't do," he said.

"Christian huh? When's the last time you saw the inside of a church?"

"No connection between that and being a Christian, Danny. When are you going to come visit us?"

"I think I'm heading east, gonna see what's happening, what happened, all that."

"Come for Thanksgiving. See your cousins, we'll all get drunk."

I could hear my aunt laughing in the background, issuing half-hearted denials, telling my uncle to stop exaggerating. They sounded very much okay and it was easy to play along.

"We'll all get drunk? Who is this anyway?"

"We set a good example for a lot of years," he said, "Lucille and I, now we can let loose."

"I'll be there just to see that."

We hung up on good terms—no reason not to.

I still wondered what my responsibility was in a situation like this. There was no one to console, likely no financial loose ends to tie together, only a grave to visit. I went online, looked at some flights from O'Hare to Connecticut. There were six or seven a day and they weren't terribly expensive, not that money was an issue. I do pretty well, and what I said about one living as cheaply as one is inarguable at this point.

I could easily take a day or two from work—I had plenty of vacation days built up—fly out, check up on things, and be back the next morning. But I remembered a poem I'd read in college by William Carlos Williams. Everyone knows he wrote the "Red Wheelbarrow," but they don't know he was a family physician with a keen awareness of life and death and the hair's breadth that separate them. In another darker poem about death and burial, he said that we survivors were supposed to be inconvenienced by others' deaths—by death itself. I liked the poem, couldn't remember the title, but decided that my closest blood relative deserved at least a few days of my being inconvenienced.

I made some calls. The hospital was reluctant—probably legally bound—not to give out information over the phone, but the funeral home that handled the arrangements was a little more forthcoming, though I could not wheedle Taggart's phone number out of the man. Eventually an Internet research gave it to me. For the remainder of the day I tried to reach him, but either he was screening his calls or he had shut down his landline in favor of a cellphone.

And then another package came, maybe from Miguel, maybe from a fill-in, definitely from my sister—a fairly heavy package, about the size of a coat box. If it was important, it was well disguised—a flimsy carton taped and re-taped in a myriad of directions, sent cheaply and slowly. Even the label looked as though it had been reapplied by some good Samaritan in a post office somewhere. I laid it on the kitchen table, then found a dust pan and gathered up the scraps of tape and packaging that flew everywhere. Inside there were papers, kept neat and organized by a food storage bag. *Papers* here is more generic than precise, though there were in fact sheets of typing paper and some others torn from a legal pad and folded haphazardly. But also there were Post-it notes and note cards, newspaper clippings in envelopes, a copy of an airline magazine. In many ways it was a repeat of the first, though there were some greeting cards, some official-looking documents with a government stamp on them, a slew of photos, and several maps and diagrams including, inexplicably, one of South America with something circled in Brazil. The package was, to be honest and succinct, a mess. It was like the first envelope, but there was more of it.

There were photos I didn't recognize, including a few with Eveline and another couple—an older man and a young woman. On the back was scribbled "Kasi, Jake, me." Just the kind of cryptic message I was not looking for, and what made it even more confusing was that Eveline looked no older than thirty. My uncle had called her a pretty girl: she was freaking ageless.

And of course there was a separate portrait gallery for Kenneth Mullins, current airport executive and—rightly or wrongly—the embodiment of all things destructive in the lives of the Blaine family, at least from Eveline's perspective. It had been no surprise to learn my sister had moved to Connecticut, not with Mullins in the vicinity. Windsor, it turned out, was a short distance from Bradley International Airport where Mullins served as CEO. The photos didn't tell the story, but they told his story—from a young rising star exuding youthful energy to an older, graying, more sedate airport executive.

My sister had done a creditable job compiling the dossier—which was really little more than a scrapbook, but it had been mailed from Chicago only a day before, well after her death. Considering that fact, maybe I shouldn't have been surprised when my doorbell rang again a while later.

It was Bethany—my former-almost-wife Bethany.

"Surprise," she shouted, without any real joy. I immediately searched my brain for the perfect greeting—it had to be good in case this was another last chance— but I could come up with only "is the wedding on again?"

She laughed, so I guess the response passed some sort of scrutiny.

The drop-in from Bethany, though not something I'm accustomed to, is not that terribly unusual either. She still has a key for the place—I didn't need it back. I'm not sure what that says about me, but I'll leave that sort of analysis to a competent psychiatrist someday.

"Come in," I said, even before I saw the crazily taped package under her arm. "Wow," I said, "you too?"

She nodded. "Where can I put this? Fuckin' thing weighs a ton."

"It weighs a pound."

She ignored the response, then shifted past me and into the living room. "Place looks the same," she said.

"Don't fix what ain't broke," I said, pointing to her package. "Toss that on the coffee table. I'll throw them both out at the same time."

"No can do, pal. Gotta get this right. Sit down."

"Gotta get *what* right?"

"If you would sit down, I'd fucking tell you."

I shook my head. "Oh, Bethany, I thought you were going to clean up your language. You promised."

"I promised to try," she said, "but when I broke my promise to marry you, I figured, fuck the rest."

"So it's officially off then, the wedding? I've been clearing my weekends for so many years. And all that time you've just been studying the dictionary of vulgar slang."

"I never had to study."

I shook my head in mock disgust.

"Okay, okay," she said. "You don't like it when I swear. You liked it when I talked dirty.

"During sex, maybe, not when you're ordering Chinese."

"That was only once. You lit majors—you think there's one dictionary for people like you and one for everybody else, and yours has all the good words in it."

"No, I think the people who actually speak English have that dictionary."

"You're a dying breed, English majors, you know that, don't you? Last year in

the United States there were only three. In the whole fucking country. "That might be a bit of an exaggeration."

"Not by much. Not many of you around anymore. What will we ever do without word snobs?"

"Swear more."

"Fucking right. Now sit down and let me do my…effin' job."

"Better, though you didn't really need any adjective. *Let me do my job* would have been sufficient."

"Here's an adjective for you," she said, extending a middle finger as I sat down. "You used to be a Dickens guy, right? *David Copperfield. Nicholas* something-or-other?"

"*Nickleby.*"

"Well now you, Daniel Blaine of somewhere in Iowa…."

"DesMoines."

"Whatever, white guy from the great white Midwest who almost married a black woman, you are *in* a Dickens novel. Want me to leave until after your orgasm?"

"I never asked you to do that before."

"I figure you're going solo a lot these days and don't want an audience."

"Or maybe I'm seeing someone."

"Look around," she said. "This house doesn't show a woman's hand, or many a woman visitor either. No, I figure it's you and your laptop, no pun intended. So I have this letter."

She waved a stamped and sealed envelope. "What about Dickens?"

"You said Dickens always had important letters in his novels and they were always the turning point."

"In many Victorian novels. But I wouldn't have said turning point. Maybe I…."

"Stop. I don't care. Now you're in a Dickens novel, Danny boy."

She pulled a sheet of paper from the envelope and unfolded it. "Not to interrupt this…ceremony," I said, but coffee? Wine?"

"No," she said, "this is hard enough."

For all her well-practiced insouciance, Bethany had always presented a singular combination of toughness and sensitivity. It wasn't unusual to see both qualities contesting for dominance. Back when we were together, it was always wise for me to steer clear of these internal struggles—the kind she needed to work out for herself—but that option was not available this time, so I prepared to be an innocent bystander, aware that the tactic had never worked before.

She was silent for another moment, then laid the letter on her lap. And I remembered the name of the poem about funerals. "Tract."

Go with some show

of inconvenience; sit openly— to the weather as to grief.

Or do you think you can shut grief in? What—from us? We who have perhaps nothing to lose?

Miguel Martinez may have initiated my inconvenience; Bethany had arrived to enhance it.

CHAPTER 4

I met Bethany Mallon at my tenth high school reunion. We had had a good number of black students in my graduating class—some I hung out with, some I never actually met. Bethany I would have met—or tried. She was strikingly beautiful. She had also, however, attended a high school across town. A rival. It was possible I had seen her at games, but I always think I would have remembered.

Mixed racial couples were not the norm, but neither were they a scandal. That notion of the white Midwest just isn't true—it's just a political shortcut for people who like their lives simple. We were raised, Eveline and I, by people whose family comprised whites only, but I never heard a hint of bias or racial animus from any of them. I doubted that the prospect of dating a black woman would bother them; my only hesitancy was horning in on whoever brought her to the reunion. She had come with Buddy Simms—a former soccer star on the team where I served primarily as a cheerleader. He was always a good guy— bigger, stronger, better-looking, and—since he was our class salutatorian— probably smarter. Add to that the fact that he was black, and it seemed there were many variables beyond my immediate capacity to change. I did know him, though, and since I'd decided to attend stag, waited for a chance to speak with him alone. I was patient, aware that he'd have to take a leak eventually. When he finally headed for the bathroom, I nonchalantly sprinted after him. I wonder what that looked like.

One feature of a urinal conversation is there's no mandatory handshake. Just talk.

"Don't have to ask how you're doing, Buddy," I said. "Who's the wife?"
"I'm not married," he said. "Beth and I work together. I needed a date. Want her number?"

"Really? She's available?"

"I'm not her pimp," he said, smiling. "I'd like to see her date someone who isn't an asshole."

"I'll take that as a compliment."

"Hey I see your name in the paper once in a while. Corner office, dude?"

"Corner parking spot."

He laughed. "You were always funny, Dan. Beth is gonna get a lot of phone calls after tonight—you might as well be one of them. Make her laugh."

I tried.

I called her the next day. Maybe others did too, but if it was some kind of lottery, I made her laugh more.

There was never any racial divide, never any meddlesome adults interfering. Her folks did have misgivings about their daughter settling down with a white person. They liked me well enough, but told me flat out they weren't sure I could adjust to prejudice. I made the typically facile response one would expect from someone who had been white all his life and for whom prejudice was something he'd read about in Baldwin or Ellison or, sadly, in the Chicago papers too often. Still, you say those things when you're in love and want the girl's parents to like you. Maybe I wasn't convincing when I said it would never be an issue, but it never was.

Our issues were always more subtle, maybe more profound, certainly more inherent. She never once told me she didn't love me anymore or had fallen for someone else, nor were there any violent explosions or passive-aggressive silences. The only arguments we ever had centered on Eveline and my unwillingness to be, as Bethany said, a "faithful brother." We just cooled, she more rapidly. Now I'm living as cheaply as one…and not enjoying it very much. And Bethany has become my surprise drop-by—never an unpleasant one.

"Maybe I'll have a little wine after all," she said. "A small one."

"Of course," I said.

I stood up and moved toward the kitchen. "What would you like?"

"You never were much of a wine guy so…."

"*Au contraire, mes amie,* I always keep a bottle of Chardonnay in the refrigerator just in case you dropped by."

"It's *mon amie*. And if that's a French accent, it's terrible. It sounds…I don't know…Romanian."

"And the wine, Madame? Shall I uncork?" I said, retaining the accent. "Now it's just annoying. How old is the bottle?"

"Let's see, I bought it to celebrate Clinton's election—he was our first black president, you know."

"You were ten."

"Almost twelve. And it has been refrigerated. Unopened. And there's no use-by date so it's good forever."

"If that's true, none of us will ever die" she said. "Uncork."

It turns out I unscrewed—it worked equally well—then returned with two glasses and the bottle under my arm.

"Not awful," she said, after her first sip.

"Succinct and heartfelt, and yet spot on—you're the same Bethany Mallin I fell in love with."

"Let me finish reading," she said, "before I get all…let me finish." We put the glasses down.

"Dear Daniel," she said, then looked at me. "Meant for you but in my package."

"I'm not surprised. Is there more?"

"There is."

"*I knew,*" she read, "*that if I wrote to you, you'd shred the letter. Remember how you said you'd shred whatever I sent?*"

Bethany glared at me. "Is that true? You said that to your sister?"

"I may have."

"You really do suck. Anyone ever tell you that?"

"I inferred it from our unwedding."

"Take it to heart then," she said, then sipped at the wine again. I waited for her to start, but she shook her head and waved the letter at me.

"What an awful thing to say," she said. "What if she wanted to square things at the end and you just said fuck you—I'm not interested? How would you feel now?"

"The exact way I do feel now. Shitty. Awful. You knew about Eveline and me. It was no secret."

"It's worse when you see it in black and white."

"Or hear it."

We were silent for a moment. I think she was judging whether I'd given her the response she wanted. I wasn't sure myself, but it was honest. I'd spent too many years ignoring my sister, or apologizing for her, or ostracizing her. Bethany gathered herself, then lifted the wine glass.

"This isn't bad," she said, an obvious but effective diversion to lessen the tension. "Let me see the bottle."

I showed it to her. "They probably don't make it anymore," I said. "Out of business after all these decades."

"Only 2015. It isn't that old."

"Maybe that's the use-by date."

Her voice had lost its edge: I poured a little more into her glass. "I'm driving," you know. "I didn't walk over here."

I poured some back into mine.

"Better," she said. "Let me finish this…letter."

"The Dickens letter."

"Yes, that one." She held it up at eye level.

I'm sending this part of the package to Bethany. I liked her.

"Good taste," she said, "obviously."

"Obviously. Go on."

She would have been a good sister-in-law. Maybe she still will someday.

She looked me straight in the eye so that there would be no uncertainty. "Not happening."

"Didn't think so. Is that all?"

"Almost." She took another deep breath, then continued.

You always thought I was wasting my life trying to get even. But you never knew Mom and Dad, not really. You don't feel you owed them anything and I get that. I understand how my obsession—and yes, it is one—even deprived me of a brother. So I did lose everything. But I wasn't wrong.

The words intended for me were having an effect on Bethany. She finished the wine.

"Whew." And she settled back. "Just a little more."

If you're reading this, I'm certainly gone. Daniel, I don't know how our lives got so out of control. If I could rein them back in, I would. And now what's worse— I'm leaving everything undone. Maybe everybody dies feeling that way. Cheated. Frustrated. If I had one more day, week, month…if I could live my life again…. And while we're wishing, we waste the one we have.

But being sick like this, I think I know what death is. It's nothing. Not dark or light or quiet or noisy or warm or cold. Just nothing. I look at the crash pictures and see charred earth and what has to have been people. Dad's in there somewhere, but he's not anything. And Mom adrift in that icy water. Nothing. That's death.

She folded up the letter.

"The rest is just, you know, take the information enclosed and see what you can do with it."

"Do? Like what?"

"Like…she never felt she avenged your folks' death."

"No," I said. "Don't even imply that. That's not going to be some quixotic quest that I take over. My life may not be perfect, but it's a whole lot better than trying to make up for something that happened forty years ago."

"Quixotic?"

"Idealistic."

"I know what quixotic means you snob, what makes a quest quixotic to you?"

"The impossibility of it."

"For someone who knows the word and the person it came from, you certainly don't get it."

She handed me the letter "Read the last line."

"I thought you'd finished."

"Read the last line."

"Only for you, my dear," I said in my most dismissive tone, and took the sheet. "Aloud," Bethany said. "Read it out loud."

"Fine," I said, but I was hesitant. Bethany had already read most of it. If she wanted me to do it aloud, there was something incriminating or embarrassing ahead. But I'd agreed.

"Don't be mad at Thomas and Lucille," it said. *"I begged them not to tell you because I wanted to be the one. To be honest, Danny, I love Lon—I hope you meet him and that you feel the same. He's my husband in every imaginable way, but beyond that I don't know if I ever loved anyone but you. I just never knew how to show it."*

I stopped. Bethany knew there was more.

"Finish it," she said, her eyes glassy, and not from the wine.

"One last favor—don't think of me dead. Think of me in some photograph you like, maybe when we were kids. That's me. That will always be me."

I'm not sure how long we were both silent after that, but Bethany began dabbing at her eyes with a wrinkled tissue.

"I knew that would happen," she said. "Again. Every time I fucking read that…"

"Hold on," I told her, got her a paper towel from the kitchen, and handed it to her. She stared in astonishment.

"What is wrong with you, Daniel? Is there a chemical spill I'm supposed to take care of? You got me a paper towel?"

"I just thought, you know, the kitchen was closer than the bathroom…so… would you rather have a Kleenex?"

"No, I'll just scratch my cornea with this finely shredded wood pulp. Unless you have a Brillo pad I can use."

And I started laughing. The image was absurd, yes, but there was an element of hysteria in the laughter—that point you reach when the sadness is so extreme that there's no way forward and all bets are off. She was laughing too, her eyes red from the tears.

I got her a Kleenex. We settled down again.

"I cried when she called," she said after she had dabbed away the moisture. "She called? When?"

"A while back. A month or so. It was supposed to be between us."

"Why?"

"Because she said so."

"You mean she specifically said don't tell Dan?"

"Yes."

"But you didn't have to listen to her. Didn't you owe it to me to tell me?"

The question just flowed out as if it made perfect sense. Bethany interpreted it differently.

"What's all this *owing* shit? You and I don't owe each other anything."

I could have said she owed me a wedding and maybe some kids—a clever retort, but one which under those circumstances would have been dumb, even by my variable standards.

"And as for your sister, Mr. Shredder," she continued, "what did you care about what she had to say?"

"I misspoke."

"Politicians misspeak. You fucked up."

"You're right," I said. "You are. How did she reach you?"

"Easy to find people these days."

"My uncle said it was a brain tumor."

"I'm short on detail, but it had been something of long duration. Your uncle is probably right."

"But it was a disease, right? I mean lots of young people are dying of opioid addiction, or fentanyl overdoses."

Bethany wasn't buying that. "That doesn't sound like Eveline. She was purposeful. She just called one day—even bought me an airline ticket."

"You went to Connecticut?"

"It's two hours, Daniel. It's not New Zealand, for chrissake. She was two hours away. Where'd you think she was? No, don't answer. You didn't think of her at all."

"You're right, I know. But still, you could have told me. She *was* my sister."

She folded her arms. "Don't listen to yourself, Danny boy, you'll just be disappointed. You're not the first jerkoff who planned to reconcile *one of these days* but waited too long. You feel bad, and you should. But it happens."

"I know, and I'm glad you went. Patients get better treatment when people are watching."

"They loved her there. I'm not just saying that to…."

"…rub it in. I know. Did you help her put this information together?"

"That was Lon."

"You met him, too?"

"And you should too. He's just…nice. I suppose that's damning with faint praise, but it's true."

I was going to tell her that my uncle had made much the same assessment, but by then I was beginning to realize I'd be meeting this companion of my sister's soon enough and could make my own decisions.

"Look, Daniel," she said, pressing her hands together as if praying, "I understand guilt, and you're going to have some. But now you have work to do."

"Me? Not us?"

"I don't think you and I make an effective team," she said. "Didn't we already establish that?"

"Maybe as business partners…."

"You don't even know the business yet, Daniel."

"I do. It's the same business she ran for forty years: make someone pay for killing our parents. I don't want to sound callous, but I think the business is out of business."

"Eveline didn't think that. She paid for my plane ticket to make sure you got this. She sent two packages to different addresses."

"Like I said…wait…*two*?"

"You have two. I have one. The other will appear in good time, I suppose. Like the ghost in *A Christmas Carol*."

"Dickens again? I must have made a huge impression…."

"Don't flatter yourself. I saw the cartoon."

She pulled a piece of paper out of her handbag. "Do you know a Kasi Brennan in Urbandale?"

"Iowa?"

"Yeah, where is that?"

"Near DesMoines, part of the metropolitan area. Who's Kasi Brennan?"

"If I knew," she said, letting the sentence trail off before adding, "didn't you grow up there?"

She didn't wait for an answer she already knew, just handed me a scrap of paper with a street address and a zip.

"A phone number would have been handy," I said. "It's all I got."

She zipped up the leather coat she'd never removed.

"Too hot for leather," I said. "Come on, Beth, help me finish the wine. You can stay and sober up."

She gave me a sidelong glance. "You want to have sex, right?"

"I could be convinced," I said.

"We both could. That was a good piece of our life together, but that can't be all a couple has."

"It can for a short period of time."

"Like what, ten minutes?"

"I suppose I could stretch it out to ten."

She laughed. "Remember Buddy Simms? My reunion date?"

"Of course."

"He said you were funny. He was right. But there has to be more."

"Bethany, that's why there's sex."

"See? That's why I thought I loved you."

She smiled again, but she wasn't staying and I wouldn't have wanted her to, not under those circumstances. It would have been exploiting my sister's death. "Gotta run," she said. "I told Terry I'd be home at a reasonable time."

"Terry? I suppose that's your…terrier?"

"Terry is my roommate."

"People have dogs as roommates."

"Not you. You hate dogs."

"Not true. I just find them needy. Terry as in Terrence?"

"Now that's a better question. Maybe it's Terri with an 'i.' There's a fantasy for you."

"Come on, Bethany. If I were gay, I'd tell you."

"If you were gay you'd send out fucking announcements. No, it's a woman—black, in case you have to refer to her—and we share an apartment. Two-bedrooms."

"You could have ten bedrooms and still be gay."

"We like each other, we both date men, sometimes we walk around naked."

"What does that have to do with anything?"

"Just planting an image. You and I, are we good? Sober? Friends? No sex?"

"You only *thought* you loved me?"

She smiled. "Fuck. I knew it when I said it. I could have phrased that better."

"I have time. I'll wait."

All I meant was that I did love you—I still do. Once you love somebody, you don't stop. Before I go, do you have a picture?"

"Of you?"

"Of your sister. She wanted you to find one."

"I have one."

"Where is it? Why isn't it out?"

"It's in a drawer. I'll get it."

"Wait until I leave," she nearly shouted. "I'm not going to cry again." She reached the door, then turned back.

"Days like this—you and I here—this is forced. Artificial. We both look better to the other than we are. Maybe we're lonely, a little down. Death can do that. It's not a good time for—I'll use one of your fancy lit words—an epiphany."

She was right. Loneliness, regret, heartache—those aren't the conditions under which we make valid choices.

"So are we good?" She repeated.

We were, or would have been, except the image of a naked Bethany kept flitting through my brain. Believe me, it was not an unpleasant image.

"I'll be undressing you with my eyes as you leave," I said. "I hope you don't mind."

She smiled. "Whatever works for you."

"Feel free to do the same."

"Daniel," she said, "If I could do that, I wouldn't be leaving."

CHAPTER 5

Bethany wasn't with my sister at the end, not if my sequence of events is accurate. But she told me about my sister's change of heart, how she had wanted her ashes sent to the aunt and uncle who had raised us. Then another—claimed she'd become an Easterner and had no great affection for the Midwest that had orphaned her and preordained her life. She was buried in Connecticut. But the other remains—the boxed "autobiography"—that was shipped to Chicago and points west.

Bethany was right about the letter and its effect on me…on her. But everything else was a compendium of Eveline's life, her quest, her successes, her failures—in short everything I knew and everything that had separated us. My uncle had called it a yearbook. It was.

That uncle—Thomas Dorsey (yes, the same name as the forties bandleader—to his everlasting pleasure) —was an outgoing guy, comfortable at any gathering. He would always assume the responsibility for keeping things moving, sometimes by refreshing a drink, usually by relating some anecdote he had committed to memory from his thirty-odd years of managing a building supply outlet in farm country. He was in no way a confessional sort —not the kind of person Eveline and I would corner for a heart-to-heart and ask how he really felt about being forced to double the size of his family overnight. He just went along. Eveline and I never took him for granted, but then again my sister and I never intimated to each other how lucky we were not to have been tossed into some system that might have produced less favorable results. The negative connotation of the word orphanage has never really disappeared, but even so, we were less likely to thank our modest good fortune than to lament the loss of our real parents. I think we were grateful in the way most kids are grateful—with plenty of privilege added in— but in retrospect, we owe them everything. Same with my Aunt Lucille whose bad fortune it was to have a sister who married Louis Blaine, whose bad fortune it was to board that plane on Memorial Day weekend forty years ago.

Maybe by witnessing the stoic cordiality of my uncle, I became a little like him—comfortable in social situations but loath to share any intimacies. Of course my being so unceremoniously uprooted affected me, but everything was worse for

Eveline. Not only had she been uprooted, she was also saddled with the unspoken, undefined responsibility of tending to her little brother. There were topics I never broached with my sister—maybe that was one I should have.

My Aunt Lucille would not have missed the opportunity. She was the heart-to-heart person, one who many times I thought was reaching out to see how I felt about life in general. (She'd probably made the same overtures to Eveline, who was probably more forthcoming.) I always said I was fine, and I think I was. What criteria did I have to go by? What criteria do any kids have to go by other than the superficial observations of their friends, classmates, relatives, and artificially, at least, perennially maladjusted television characters who always come through?

I hadn't planned to see the Dorseys when I sought out Kasi Brennan, but I couldn't very well wind up in Urbandale without visiting my closest relatives a few miles distant. When I let Uncle Tommy know I was driving, his response was typical.

"If you're strapped for money," he said, "we have some put aside."

Always the caretaker or care*giver*, this time worried that I couldn't afford a plane ticket. My reason for driving was more pragmatic than financial. On the one hand a half-hour, fifty-dollar cab ride drive to O'Hare and a two-hour wait for the one-hour flight to DSM, then a half-hour drive to their house in a rental I would probably hate. Four hours of misery and inconvenience. Or there was five hours on I-80 in a comfortable rental with good music, and the possibility of food that didn't come in a foil bag marked "peanuts." When I explained that to him, he agreed.

"Come anytime," he said. I picked the following Saturday.

I didn't tell him my trip would serve a dual purpose, but it did provide me with a day or two to locate Kasi Brennan. I had her phone number—a landline—and called. These days I never expect to reach anybody not on a cell, but she picked up right away. Surprised, I fumbled through my greeting so poorly that I expected to hear a click when I was finished. I didn't.

"I wondered if you would call," she said. "Eveline wasn't sure."

I'm sure she did not intend for her words to sting, but they did. Even strangers knew the distance I'd scoured out between my sister and me.

"No, I…Eveline and I…."

"Mr. Blaine, yours is not the only family with ongoing disputes."

"Was," I said. "*Was* the only family."

"Oh," she said, the airiness gone from her voice. "I was afraid of that," she said. "Of course the package—I figured she knew the end was close. When did she pass?"

"A few days ago," I said. Not a major lie, just a slight understatement. "Did you know each other from high school?"

"No, we were many years apart. We met…it's a long story. How much time do you have?"

"I have relatives in DesMoines and I'm driving out to see them this weekend. Maybe we could meet for coffee? You can give me the package too, if it's convenient."

"You don't mind driving 300 miles for a latte?"

"Not a bit. What about Friday? I'm staying with my uncle and aunt."

"The ones you lived with."

"You even know that?"

"Was I…not supposed to? I don't mean to be a smartass."

"Not at all. It's just…odd I guess. Friday afternoon, then? Maybe after work?"

"I'm in Urbandale. There's a coffee shop on Merle Hay."

I laughed at that. Everything in Urbandale is on Merle Hay Road—a sea of strip malls and car dealerships. Still, as I remembered it, up past I-35 there were some interesting little places. She used a cellphone to text me the name and address of the Twisted Bean.

"It's your basic coffee and Wi-Fi place," she said, "where people spend five bucks and treat the place like they live there until closing time."

"Then return the next day. The Starbucks model."

"Yep. How about two o'clock Friday," she said. "Look for the floral hat."

And she also corrected me on her name, which rhymed with Cassie, not Casey or Cazzie or any of my other attempts.

"No way you'd know that," she said. "When I'm too old to have a cute name, maybe I'll change the spelling, or go with something more age-appropriate."

She suggested Martha or Judith, repeated *Friday at 2:00*, and hung up.

Rhymes with *classy*, I told myself. A simple mnemonic. These days a person's name isn't the identifier it used to be, but I was grateful that my mother had loved the story of Daniel in the Bible, and not Esau or Jedediah.

I was on the road Friday at dawn, having informed Aunt Lucille that I'd be a boarder for a night or two. I outraced the commuters out of the city, and let the fog on I-88 burn off behind me. I had pancakes at a diner near the Mississippi River, got a coffee to go, then finished the second half of the drive at a fairly leisurely pace. Even so, I arrived at the Twisted Bean a half hour early and found a woman seated at a corner table right next to the meeting room…and waving a black baseball cap furiously. As I got closer I saw a sunflower stitched on the front of it. Not what I pictured when she said floral hat, but she hadn't lied.

"I knew it was you," she said, then stood and shook my hand. "You look like your pictures, and Eveline had her share. I'm Kasi."

"Pleasure," I said and sat across from her at a table the size of a small pizza. "Getting crowded in here—I thought you might miss me."

"The floral hat gave you away."

"Bought it about an hour ago. Got a million hats and not one with a flower. Got a spider, a collie, a semi…you would think…."

"I would have found you," I said.

"Can't be too careful. Some table, huh?" She pointed to the meeting room. "I could have reserved that. Who knew that a wannabe Starbucks would have an actual meeting room? And you think people overstay their welcome now! How was your trip?"

"Uneventful. Listen, thanks for meeting me. I know I'm early."

"Gets me out of the house," she said, then handed me a gift card. "Get yourself something to drink. My Mom got me this for Christmas but I never come here. I'm trying to use it up. Go big if you want. God knows how much credit is still on here. Could be a thousand dollars. My mom tends to overspend."

I didn't go big. No latte, nothing exotic, coffee black, as usual. Same as hers, it turned out. And I paid cash—I didn't want to embarrass her or myself when the card was rejected—or I was told that $995 remained.

"You have trouble getting out of the house?" I asked when I returned. "You said before…."

"Sometimes a retiree needs motivation," she said.

She took off the hat now that she'd been ID'd, exposing the rest of the streaked straight blond hair that fell just short of her shoulders. It was what some might call a "cute" haircut, and on a three-year-old it would have been charming. Kasi wasn't three. But she was nowhere near retirement age. I pointed that out in the most innocuous terms I could think of, but trapped myself anyway. "How old do you think I am?" she asked.

"Uh uh," I said. "That's not the question we open with. Not much can go right after whatever answer I give."

"Thirty-nine," she said. "I'm not fussy about personal information. You can have my height and weight, too."

I held up both hands, declining both. Of course my brain was working. Five-six maybe? One-twenty-five?

"Besides," she said, I couldn't dress like this for work."

"Not even on casual Friday? It's kind of a dressy hat."

"And new. No sweat marks. Anyway, let's say I'm between jobs but not looking. What do you do, Dan? They call you Dan?"

I went through my usual truncated biography. She was less impressed with what I did than how long I'd been doing it. Twenty years was five more than she'd ever held a job. She didn't seem regretful of her abbreviated career, whatever it had been.

"It's my generation," she said. "We're supposed to be more mobile, you know, job to job, condo to condo, partner to partner? Good for you, hanging in there."

"Aren't we kind of the same generation?"

"You're a year older than I am, so yes, I guess we're about the same."

"You're between jobs?"

"If I work again, yes, semantically. If not, retired."

"Who'd you work for before?"

"National Transportation Safety Board. Know what that is?"

I would have laughed, but the whole thing was so unreservedly sad that I couldn't. Of course I knew what the NTSB was…and what they did. There's never a news report of an aircraft incident, train wreck, refinery explosion, even truck or bus accident that doesn't have an NTSB team on site or en route. I can't even count the number of times my sister referred to them, even considered becoming a field worker or agent so that she could gather even more minutiae about "the crash." Go online, I used to tell her. It's all there. But by that time I was probably so frustrated with her monomania that I stopped listening or suggesting.

Yes, I knew the National Transportation Safety Board—knew their locations, protocols, even the names of some of their investigators.

"You must have been the answer to Eveline's prayers," I said. "How did she find you?"

"She wrote me a letter. A real letter, not even an email. She'd seen my name on some reports in the previous year or two and got in touch."

"Is that normal? I mean I sometimes I hear 'a spokesman said' as opposed to a name."

"The investigator-in-charge sometimes becomes a celebrity of sorts."

"Like Greg Feith? John Cox?"

She was impressed. "You really are your sister's brother. I'm not quite that well known, but I was investigator-in-charge a few times."

I waited for the rest of her story, how she made the news, but she skipped ahead…or back…to Eveline. They had met three times, always in the DesMoines area. There's no direct flight from Hartford—everything goes through Chicago—so it was an effort. Of course not stopping by to say hello to her brother perfectly depicted her feelings toward me; and my not caring depicted mine.

"She always came with somebody," Kasi said, "a man."

"Lon Taggart—her boyfriend, or husband."

"I know Lon," she said. "Lon is white. That's not the man she traveled with." She took out her phone and swept past a few pages.

"Marty Hendricks," she said, "c-k-s, not like Jimi." The spelling didn't help. I'd never heard of him.

"She always introduced him as a friend," she said. "I tried not to read too much into things."

"This black man she traveled with—you think they were lovers?"

"A quaint term," she said. "Maybe former lovers, though that would still make it weird to be traveling together. He never looked me in the eye. Maybe he knew that I knew he was…hey listen, I feel a little weird talking about your sister this way."

"If you knew her, you knew about our relationship. You said maybe you knew he was…what?"

"Eveline would pull away from him whenever he, you know, invaded her space.

I wasn't imagining things: I'm pretty observant."

"You think he was abusive?"

"No, just nutty, scattered. He said things that made me laugh but they weren't funny. Hard to describe."

"Was he another NTSB expert?"

"Not at all. Whatever wavelength they shared, that wasn't it. Eveline, though, I was pretty sure she knew more than I did, and I actually studied the case history when I was training. Did you know there was another Flight 191 that crashed in Dallas six years later."

"Delta, yes. Microburst. There were survivors."

"Not much fire, slower speed. You know your stuff."

"I'm *married* to the history of air crashes."

"Marriage can be difficult. Tried it once—didn't work out. How about you?"

"I have a wedding pending."

"With Bethany," she said, then apologized. "Sorry if I know too much, but Eveline and I…you know…talked."

"More than she and I did probably. Did Eveline think you had secret information that the public wasn't aware of?"

"After forty years? Unlikely. That usually happens when there are survivors, you know, somebody remembers something and one thing leads to another. But with 191, no crash was ever as publicly and openly investigated as that one. What I do think is that I gave her crusade a kind of credibility, as if I had somehow been there to witness it. At times I thought it was maybe cathartic to talk with me. I guess it wasn't."

"She was well past catharsis," I said. "Revenge is the emotion that never dies."

"That's a pretty depressing observation. What about love? The world is full of stories of love enduring hardships and surviving."

"Most of those involve dogs," I said.

I don't think she was partial to sarcasm, but she forced a smile. Of course if that had been Bethany sitting across from me, I might have been wiping coffee off my face, and my clothes, and my shoes, while some polite manager escorted us to the door.

"I don't mean to sound cynical," I said, "but couples fall out of love; enemies become friends, respect becomes disdain—and revenge just hangs on forever."

Kasi didn't respond. "Sorry," I said. "Preaching."

"Not at all," she said, "but I disagree."

She picked up Eveline's packet of information from an empty chair and laid on the table.

"I haven't really looked at it because…you know…."

"You knew it already?"

"Inside out."

She drank the last of her coffee. "This was a mistake," she said. "Thanks," I said, feigning insult.

"Not meeting you, just…I only miss the investigative work when I talk about it. Like now."

"Then go back to it. You must have one or two good months left before the doddering senility sets in—at forty."

She smiled, put the cover on the empty cup, and slipped on her sunflower hat. "It was nice meeting you, Daniel, but sad too. I'd always hoped Eveline would make it. I liked her."

"I did too, once" I said.

"Don't say that," she said. "It's unbecoming."

It was a presumptuous statement to make to a person she'd met mere minutes before, but she was right.

"The last time you saw her," I said, interrupting her departure, "was she very sick?"

"She looked worn out. Treatments? Meds? I think the repetition was getting her down. The improvement, the relapse, the treatment, the recovery, the improvement, and on and on. I don't know what her thoughts were—she never struck me as the kind who would give up. But there's a point where the struggle becomes untenable, where you give up and don't even know it."

"Is that what happened?" She raised both hands.

"We'll never know. Look, I have to run."

If anyone did not have to run, it was Kasi Brennan. I don't think she liked me much—she didn't know I was more than just a lousy brother—that I had good qualities too. Or maybe the lousy brother hid everything else, especially from people who knew Eveline…and liked her. At least I made sure Kasi had my cellphone number—in case she remembered anything else—I was sure I would never hear from her again.

I left the Twisted Bean to find my relatives, and she went back to whatever she wasn't doing.

CHAPTER 6

Over the years I have pieced together the seconds that preceded my father's death using a combination of conjecture, surmise, common knowledge, official transcripts, and even courtroom testimony. It has led me, by a route not so much circuitous as circular, back to square one. I know for instance, that Louis Blaine preferred to sit in the rear of the plane. On a DC-10 that meant 200 people deplaning before you. An annoyance, of course, but he had once explained to Eveline that crashes were more survivable in the rear of the plane, and so he chose accordingly. I don't know if he also realized that the rear engine of the plane, right behind and above him, was fed by the two fuel tanks on the wings' interior. An aborted take-off, one in which the plane slammed into something, would almost certainly rupture the tanks and send the fuel, likely ignited, careering back toward the rear-seat passengers. Of course being far back in the middle bank of seats on the aisle allowed a minute amount of extra leg room, as long as one didn't trip a person walking by to use the lavatories behind him.

From that seat on that day, if he had glanced out a port window on takeoff, he might actually have seen number one engine streak by after coming loose from the left wing. Even if he hadn't seen it, he would have felt the plane bank to the left too soon to be merely setting a course. He might even have felt the pilot's attempt to correct it, momentarily successful, then the more drastic and fatal descent. Fifty-two seconds comprised the entire event. Twenty-one of them to get airborne.

One thousand one, one thousand two—there has never been a flight I've taken when I haven't counted off those fifty seconds. Other passengers ignore me—the noise of the engines masks my whispering. When I get to the 21-second mark, I play out the next 31 in my head. Twenty-nine seconds of flight, only nine or ten of them level—then the banking, too deep to support lift, the nose down, and the call from the controller of a "strike on the field." Flight 191 was down.

The imagined terror would have been fleeting. In the time it took those passengers to realize what was happening, they were already dead. Some say that was merciful: they are welcome to that opinion. And some passengers knew more than others. In the airlines 'nascent but ongoing efforts to make flying fun, American had installed in that particular DC-10, some TV screens that displayed the pilot's view of takeoffs and landings. Anyone with the equanimity to be watching would have seen the picture tilt crazily, then seen tarmac and airport grass overtaking the left half of the screen. Three, maybe four seconds would have elapsed between the time experienced air travelers saw something wrong and when they took their final living breath. They would have held out as much hope for a positive resolution as the cockpit crew did. I always wondered when the moment of realization occurred, when it became clear that there was no recovery possible, that being strapped into a 300-ton airplane, fully fueled and no longer flightworthy, was not survivable. (There was some talk afterwards that the destruction of the wing reduced power and terminated the closed-circuit picture for the passengers. I hope that's true, but it's just another facet of those final seconds about which we know nothing.)

In any crash the impact kills most airline passengers. Hitting the ground—or the water for that matter, at 300 knots, sometimes more, is not survivable. But Flight 191 had climbed to only 350 feet and was struggling to gain altitude with an engine lying on the tarmac a mile away. Its speed could not have been more than 150 knots when it hit the ground, and the impact may have been less than direct: the plane slid a good distance. The mercy of an instant death from impact was probably not granted; and though my brain can imagine the next few seconds, my soul recoils at verbalizing it.

Maybe that far back in the plane, Louis Blaine was provided a millisecond longer to accept his destiny, a millisecond in which he might have felt the impact and seen a flash of flame streaking toward him, probably faster than the mind could comprehend. But such trivia and emotion lie outside the province of investigators. In the end 271 passengers and crew died. Two fatalities occurred on the ground. Even forty years later, as I sorted through the pieces of my sister's life, American-191 retained its undesirable position as America's worst airline crash. Nothing in Eveline's scrapbook of information could alter the results or the inevitability.

*****

I spent most of Saturday with my uncle and aunt. They liked to putter around outside, so I helped where I could, usually by performing the least thought-intensive jobs—bringing out empty trash bags and moving full ones. The few conversations we had were superficial. Eveline's name probably came up once or twice, but then only to recount some childhood anecdote. By mid-afternoon I sensed that, by and large they'd forgiven me for letting Eveline be what she wanted to be—another Job screaming out complaints to a God who seemed not to be listening. I did not share that definition with them.

Late in the day, just as the three of us were about to leave for some new Italian restaurant, Kasi Brennan called.

"I was out of line when I said your comment was unbecoming. It wasn't my place."

"You were right," I said. "I was critical of Eveline for so long that it's second nature now. But it *was* unbecoming." I said.

"You'll work through everything," she said. "It takes time."

She told me to have a safe trip home, wished me luck back east, in short prepared to part company on a positive note when my uncle walked by.

"She can meet us at the restaurant," my uncle yelled in a volume appropriate for yelling across the street that a neighbor's house was on fire, "then you two can take off if you want to."

I had of course told them about my meeting with Kasi, upon which they put two and two together and got another grandchild, grandnephew, grandniece—I don't think the nomenclature was an issue.

All I could envision was my Uncle Thomas in his shirt and tie and Aunt Lucille in some conservative dress, me in khakis and a sport shirt all dutifully representing Middle America…and Kasi Brennan in a "floral" baseball cap, a ripped t-shirt, and a pair of jeans from her Saturday-yard-work collection. But my uncle—still envisioning me with…with anybody—insisted, and so I invited her. She accepted.

"I'm not sure what the dress code is at this place," I said, just feeling her out. "I have sloppy baseball caps and dressy ones," she said. "What time?"

I was pretty sure she was goading me, but I didn't feel comfortable until she showed up—no baseball cap, just black pants and a short-sleeved ruffly orange top and some tan sandals with straps, which I'm sure have a name other than sandals with straps. She looked a bit summery, but with the weather still warm, the outfit was perfect. My uncle—getting older but with his vision still intact—did a subtle double-take when he saw her, but not so subtle that my aunt didn't feel she had to poke him. I won't lie—Kasi Brennan looked really pretty—and it's not that I can't still appreciate a pretty girl, but thoughts of Bethany always put a cap on that interest.

That particular obsession aside, Kasi was fun, maybe for all of us. She's one of those people who know how to engage everyone, to make everyone feel important. Lucille even seemed to tolerate her husband's flirting. It was one of the few times in my life when I'd seen him…well…smitten.

That evening we spoke very little about Eveline. It wasn't by design, it's just that we were all locals reuniting and there was a lot to talk about—changes good and bad. DesMoines has one of the world's great newspapers, but when the *Register* entered into the conversation, I knew that politics was not far behind. Thomas and Lucille, neither of them bashful, wanted to make sure Kasi knew that, Iowa may have been a red state, but the Dorsey's house was deep blue.

Kasi, more circumspect, said only that her mother had hoped to live long enough to see a woman president but now in her seventies, wasn't so sure. Personalizing it like that took the edge off any possible salvos Thomas and Lucille were ready to launch, and she further defanged them when she complimented my uncle on his willingness to talk civilly about the subject. He's never done that in his life, and I almost laughed out loud; but then I remembered who had volunteered to pick up the check and held back.

Only once did the conversation become strained, and it had nothing to do with Washington. Apparently on one of her visits home, my sister had brought Martin Hendricks with her. Kasi had pegged him as creepy, but that assessment was mild compared to my Uncle's.

"Psychopath," my uncle said with little provocation. "I looked in his eyes," he said, "or tried. Nothing. If he wasn't hitting her…."

My aunt interrupted. "You don't know that," she said.

"Smart ones don't leave marks. People like that leave bruises where nobody will see them."

They sounded like the words of a person who had imagined a few too many episodes of *CSI—DesMoines*. My aunt tried to defuse it a bit.

"Maybe just anti-social," my aunt said, "but he isn't abusive. I just had a feeling about it."

My uncle conceded slightly. "Misfit," he said, his face reddening. "Waited in the car for Eveline to finish dinner, then when we were saying our goodbyes on the front stoop, he leaned on the horn."

"Thomas," my aunt said, "shall we get another bottle of wine…for you?"

That little jab settled things down, but not before I learned what had made that previous occasion so bitter: they never saw their niece again. Kasi helped us shift ourselves away from the topic with some general nondescript chatter, as a modicum of civility returned.

After a tableful of cannoli none of us was able to finish, Lucille invited Kasi to follow us home, and my uncle even volunteered to drive her back to her car later if she wanted to ride with us. She was certainly the girl for me, if my uncle was making the choices. In fact, as soon as we got back home, my uncle and aunt said they were too tired to be good company and were going to sleep. I told them it was still early and tried to sweeten the deal.

"I'll light a fire," I said.

"It was 80° today," Uncle Thomas said. "If you have any other ideas, run them past the young lady first."

"Then how about an igloo?"

"Let us know how it turns out," my aunt said. "And don't track snow on the carpeting."

They sauntered off to bed.

"Lovely people," Kasi said. "Now I know why your uncle was flirting—he was filling in for you."

"I don't…you know…."

"I know the deal, Daniel. I know about Bethany and I'd have been disappointed if you had flirted with me. Loyalty means something."

"How about lost causes?"

"That's for you to decide. But your relatives aren't too subtle—I'm surprised there's not a sign on that couch that says 'For making out'."

"And that's where they always sit," I said. "They couldn't have left the room any faster if it was burning. But since we do have the couch, let's see what we can dig up on this Hendricks dude," I said, "and maybe some coffee?"

I retrieved her packet of Eveline info, then went and found a coffee filter, filled the basket, and switched on the coffeemaker. With several mugs of very, very black coffee keeping us awake (I'd been unable to find the measuring scoop and more or less eyeballed everything), and my uncle's verbal assault on Hendricks fresh in our minds, we sought out references to him, buttressing what Eveline had left with more from the Internet. The accusation of abuse never materialized, but Martin Hendricks had actually served time. He had also worked several different jobs and been married twice, though he was unmarried when Eveline died. There were photos of him in a group of dour-looking men in khaki, the only black man in the group. There were symbols on the uniforms, but we couldn't make them out. They weren't swastikas, that much we could tell, but as Kasi said, that's setting a pretty low bar for normality.

There did not seem to be a racial component to my uncle's antipathy—he'd never had a problem with Bethany—so we assumed that Hendricks was genuinely a bad operator, color notwithstanding. We continued sifting through and found that line again, this time in Kasi's bundle: *I don't know how things got so out of control. If I could rein it back in, I would.*

"That's twice I've seen that," I said.

Kasi shook her head. "Remorse, regret, they're horrible emotions. How many things in our lives do we want to go back and undo, or redo? All that crap about seeing your life pass before you? Some of what passes must be…well, most people probably want to look away."

It was near midnight when we drained the dregs from the carafe—about a quarter cup each of a viscous solution one could presumably identify as coffee—and started packing up. It was in that process when Kasi showed me a somewhat crumpled flyer for a gun show. On it were photos of rifles and handguns, but also assault weapons and what appeared to be grenade launchers. I wasn't shocked—gun ownership is down in the Midwest, like the rest of the country, but collectors and traders are everywhere and people who do own guns own more of them.

"Yeah? So?"

"Look at the wild-eyed guy holding the grenade launcher, upper right."

It was late and my eyes were tired, but not so tired that I couldn't recognize Hendricks.

"My God," I said. "Why the hell would my sister hook up with someone like that?"

"We seek what we need," Kasi said. "How about we get together before you head home. Tomorrow at the airport? I want you to meet someone."

I reminded her I had driven here. "The airport works best."

"And meet someone? As a chaperone? I could ask my aunt and uncle to come along."

"They're enablers, Daniel. Good people but enablers. Or maybe they're afraid you're going to move back permanently and they'd rather marry you off. One way or another, we won't need your aunt and uncle, but I have a former colleague. He's very good."

"Retired like you?"

"Retired like a real retiree. Lives in Dallas now, writing a novel."

"On crash investigation?"

"About dishonesty."

"He's going to have to narrow down that topic a little." She gave me a sideways glance.

"Unbecoming?" I said. "Possibly."

"Self-evaluation probably returns some negative results. Plus I'm tired. This friend of yours…."

"He can be here before you wake up tomorrow."

Dallas to DesMoines—maybe a two hour flight. Certainly doable. But I doubted any airline was running that service as a shuttle—just hop on whenever. Boston to Philly? Yep. L.A. To Frisco? Yep. Dallas to DesMoines? No. Not without connections, or a private jet, or his own jet. Or, as I suggested to Kasi, Superman. Connections, she said.

"And Jake would just do that as a favor?"

Her eyes widened—no small feat at this time of the morning. "How'd you know his name?"

"I only know his first name. There's this photo," I told her, then dug through the pile to find it. "Three people: *Kasi, Jake, me.*"

"Good call," she said. "Yes, Jake Moss." She held the picture close to her eyes, examining the details. "That was kind of a good day. I remember thinking that your sister probably didn't have many of those. Makes me even sadder."

She laid it down gently, as though it might break. "Didn't mean to bum you out," I said.

"Someone died—we're supposed to be bummed out."

Yes, I was about to say, like this poem I know. But I held back. Sad as I was, I was glad too that Eveline's death had mattered to somebody, inconvenienced somebody besides me.

CHAPTER 7

A credit card receipt from a Hartford restaurant—$42.51

A parking violation from East Hartford—restricted zone—$30.00.

A flyer from a farmer's market in Windsor Locks.

Some photos of an old barn, a county fair, a crowded beach.

An article about Ken Mullins. And another. And another.

An obituary on someone named Mitchell Oakes from Collinsville, Oklahoma.

A story about me from the Tribune, *my name buried among twenty-five* simultaneous promotions.

Several travel brochures: Greece, Brazil, Mexico, more.

A photo of an Airstream trailer resting on three wheels and some cinder blocks.

A picture of Eveline at something called the Festival of Lights in Hartford.

Everything told a story, but even though we could piece together some of it—even though we knew the point of view, the motivation, even the denouement, the inherent arc of the narrative eluded us. I can't compare it to a jigsaw puzzle, because Eveline's pieces didn't have corners and ends where you could logically begin. Everything was nubs and openings, daring to be fit together. But I still thought it was possible if I had enough time, and that aspect I would have to work out with Gerald Crozier, my immediate superior.

Crozier tries like crazy to be a hardass, but he just doesn't have the temperament. As customary as it is to complain about one's boss, nobody complains about Crozier. Someday he'll take the next step up the corporate ladder and we'll all be screwed over by some lackey of a replacement, but until then, we'll continue to enjoy going to work. He's accessible too—maybe too accessible since I had his cell number and the temerity to call him on a Sunday morning.

None of that means he's a pushover. In fact, he let me get about ten words into my request for some vacation time before he read me a litany of reasons why I couldn't have it, all of them straight from the unofficial employee handbook. As he plodded through them, I could hear all sorts of metallic noises in the background.

"If you're busy," I said, "I can call back."

"The answer will be the same," he said. "I just hear a lot of clattering."

"It's a whisk. And a bowl. I have the kids this weekend and if I don't make them an omelet with bacon inside—not *on* the side, *in*side—I might as well relinquish custody altogether. How much vacation time?"

"I have 32 days coming."

"Well you sure as hell aren't taking a month off. Not during our busy season with the holidays just ahead."

"You mean Columbus Day and Halloween? 'Cause my calendar still says September."

"We have a number of new clients and merged companies. Goddammit!"

"Okay, I was just…."

"Not you. Goddam bacon splashing all over the place."

"Don't you have an apron? Or a microwave? Or some restraints on your language with the kids around."

"They're upstairs preparing to be piped down for their meal. Don't fuck with me, I'm not in the mood."

"Two weeks."

"Jesus, Daniel, I understand it's a family thing. But two weeks. I didn't even know you had a sister."

"I did. The fact that nobody knew—that's on me."

"And I'm sorry. I am. You want a long weekend? Take Monday and Tuesday off."

"I'm working with someone and trying to piece together some things."

"Things?"

"We have all this…this stuff from my sister. She wanted us to have it. Now we don't know what to do with it."

"Can't you put it in storage?"

"It's not that kind of stuff. It's papers. Documents."

"Hire a lawyer."

"It's not that kind either."

"So it's a mystery. Hire a novelist. Who's the someone you're working with?"

"Woman from DesMoines."

"Oh, a woman."

"It's not what you think."

"You know, it's never what anybody thinks, and then it is."

"This time it isn't."

"Hope not—we're not running a dating service, you know."

"Dude, really? W*e're not running a dating service*? Has there been confusion over that? If people think we're a dating service, PR has to work a little harder...." Even he knew how ridiculous it sounded. He was silent for a moment, though the number of cooking sounds increased. I offered to call him back when he was less harried, but instead he spit out an offer—a week and another long weekend. "That's like 10 days. Is that enough?"

"I may need the whole two weeks."

"Goddammit."

"Bacon?"

"No, this time it's you. Work with me on this, will you? I need you here."

"I can do a lot of things online, even contact clients from home. I won't be in Tahiti. Unfortunately I won't be in Chicago either."

"That would have made it easier."

"I know, but I can do everything else. I can do…whatever I can do."

"Brilliant."

I waited. I could hear children's voices. Zero hour for the food.

"Okay, okay. Your sister," he said, his tone softening. "Why didn't you tell me about her? We have personal days for that kind of thing, but you never said anything. So I never said anything. We've known each other way too long to let things go like that."

"Believe me, it's not a typical situation."

"No family situation is."

"And those arrangements had already been made without my input. But the time off I need, it may be related, it may be important, or it may be that you look up and see me at my desk on Tuesday."

Another silence. There may even have been a sigh thrown in. A loud one. But in the end he relented. Two weeks…with an option…for less.

"Different situation or not," he said. "I'm calling this a bereavement leave. You can still go to Tahiti if that chick from DesMoines is willing."

"How about you? Tahiti?"

"They eat omelets there? I'm asking for a friend."

"You're a good father, Mr. Crozier."

"Oh it's *Mr. Crozier* when you need time off. Look, I gotta run. The royal heirs are swarming. They must be fed."

I told him to enjoy breakfast, gave him a crash course on microwaving bacon, and left him to his hungry children. Every time I'm privy to Crozier's home life, I think of Bethany and where we'd be today had our marriage actually occurred, and more important, where our kids would be—who'd have weekend custody, or spend Christmas, or birthdays, or a Sunday splattering grease and probably (if I know Crozier) enjoying every minute of it.

But at least I had won some time. If all this turned out to be no more than a post-mortem that did little more than reflect Eveline's life of frustration, then I probably would be back in work shortly. But I remember thinking that even Eveline thought there was more, and that Martin Hendricks was part of it. And Mitchell Oakes, about whom a quick Google check turned up nothing special, at least in the Connecticut area.

No sooner had I hung up with Crozier than Kasi called.

"I'll pick you up in fifteen minutes," she said. "Jake's plane just landed."

"So he made it."

"Never a question," she said. "Be ready."

I didn't have much to do. I'd already showered and shaved and thrown on enough clothes to appear in public without being arrested. The morning was mild for mid-September—it can be that way in Iowa. Those are the days to savor. They don't last.

Kasi was in her coffeehouse outfit with a different hat—I-Cubs. They play on the outskirts of DesMoines and if there's any fixture in the area, it's them. I saw their games with my uncle and his friends in the eighties. I told Kasi, of course, I was a Sox fan. She said if I was, then where was my hat? Then she handed me a coffee. Point for her. Two, actually.

It turns out that she and Jake Moss had been partners only once, five years before, having been thrown together almost at random.

"We had a supervisor who liked to experiment. Of course Jake and I disliked each other from the opening, well, handshake," she told me. "I thought he'd look at me like a cute young kid that he could show the ropes. Instead he treated me like an infant that would need constant tending, something which he had no intention of providing to anybody. I was 33. That's still young enough to be cute to some old guy, isn't it?"

"Maybe calling him *some old guy* got things off on the wrong foot. As for your question, please forgive me for refusing to answer."

"Coward."

"Agreed. What were you working on?"

"Single-engine plane crash within the airport proper—a municipal field in Oklahoma. Collision with terrain—know the term?"

"Like I said before, I know too many terms."

"Anyway, significant damage to the aircraft, cuts and bruises for the pilot. That was it."

"Sounds cut-and-dried."

"Well we danced around each other for a day or two—it was like we were investigating two separate incidents. In his a single-engine plane seemed to have hit a piece of equipment on a closed runway and flipped over, injuring the pilot."

"And yours?"

"A single-engine plane seemed to have hit a piece of equipment on a closed runway and flipped over, injuring the pilot."

"And you managed to turn that into an argument?"

"I found something he'd missed, one that proved that the crash was no accident. Seems the pilot had a medical issue—had been asking about depression, how to treat it. I was certain he *aimed* for that payloader. Moss finally gave in. He was gracious about it, gave me the credit. After that he became a little more of a mentor. Said when I got to be as good as he was, he'd retire."

"How'd you find that out when he couldn't?"

"He knew. It was a test."

"We all have to prove ourselves."

"Oh sure," she said, with feigned disgust, "take the man's side."

"I have to stand up for my brothers."

"I think *brothers* is reserved for people of color or soldiers in combat."

"My former fiancé is a woman of color, does that count?"

"Only if she's your brother. What the hell were we talking about anyway?"

"Proving yourself."

"Oh yeah. I was an investigator, had already learned the ropes. Why did I have to prove myself all over again?"

I was with her on this one. Lately there'd been a lot of movement in the corporate environment to eliminate that kind of paternalism, but dinosaurs still roamed—if not freely—essentially unrestrained. And when people feel ownership for something—and maybe Jake did this with NTSB—they're reluctant to trust others to participate until they've shown they can. I'm not sure if gender is always the culprit, but it is often enough.

"This Moss sounds more paternalistic than sexist."

"Pretty much the same animal."

"But he retired, so you're as good as he is. Maybe better."

"He'd already given notice," she said, smiling. "Nowadays I like to bounce ideas off him, and it always works better in person."

"That doesn't explain your retirement."

"You're right," she said, pulling up to a gated fence." And we're here." The evasiveness was obvious. Kasi gave her name and Moss's to a guard who waved us through—past the terminal and onto a perimeter road.

"Over there," she said, pointing to a private plane with two engines on the fuselage. "The Learjet 45."

I'd heard the name Learjet without the number attached, always thought it to be synonymous with either wealthy plane-owners or with wealthy people who liked to fly in luxury and not be bothered by someone kicking their seat or offering them morning pretzels. And even though it was what I loosely called a small plane, it was impressive up close. I'd seen single engine jobs that seemed almost fragile, that looked as though they'd snap in two in a hard landing or flip over with a summer gust. This was nothing like that, and gleaming in the harshly angled early sun, it was almost majestic. Once inside, there was no *almost*.

Tan leather everywhere. The entire rear of the cabin comprised a small couch, a love seat, two swiveling armchairs, several folded-up tables on either side, and just behind the cockpit, two rear-facing arm chairs. Six people could ride comfortably, conduct a meeting, just enjoy life. I told Kasi I wasn't sure I could ever fly coach again. She told me to start saving my money.

We heard voices in the cockpit and found three people squeezed in, two in the crew seats and one leaning over the massive instrument panel. The only gauge, dial, or readout I could even come close to identifying was the one that read 10:13. "Ah ha," I said to Kasi. "A clock."

The man leaning over heard me and turned around..

"Central daylight," he said. "Did you think it would be GMT?"

"Jake," Kasi said. "Mr. Blaine here is not a pilot."

Her tone, her inflection, everything about that statement reflected one you might use if you were telling someone that I was an extraterrestrial, more lost than dangerous.

"Jake Moss," he said extending his hand anyway, "Pleasure to meet you Mr. Blaine."

"Daniel," I said.

He nodded. "Just talking with my millennial crew here. They're the best money can buy."

"And the money's good," the pilot said—at least she was in the left seat when I saw her. She was an Asian woman, younger than Kasi and much younger than Moss. She wore no uniform, no indication that she was a crew member other than the headphones draped around her neck.

"Donna likes to sound all business and profits, but she just loves to fly. Now Sean here, he enjoys the paycheck once in a while."

"Got two kids," he said. "I don't just *enjoy* the paycheck. What do you think of this crate?"

"Is it yours?"

Sean laughed. Everyone did except me. Moss asked what I thought that particular aircraft sold for. I just threw a number out there—two million.

"Used, maybe. Now these two make a good living, but there's a whole other level of people who can afford to actually *own* them. Probably people you work with in Chicago."

"Or work for. I'm not one of them."

"Few of us are."

He handed Donna a fifty.

"Why don't you two go grab some breakfast. Feel free to order the same thing. I don't want change, just give us 45 minutes."

They agreed, shut everything down that wasn't already shut down, and left. "What was that about ordering the same?" I asked him.

"If one of them gets gastroenteritis, the other can fly the sick person home. If they both do, and it's bad enough, well, imagine the possibilities."

"But you said…."

"Because in an emergency like that I can get a plane on the ground safely. Let's sit."

We moved back to the plushness of the cabin.

"Kasi told me about your sister," Moss said. "Sorry to hear that, man. No foul play, right?"

"No, why do you ask?"

"Almost forty years since it happened, but there are plenty of folks alive who'd rather we all forgot about it. I mean some asshole on the Titanic made the decision that they didn't need a lifeboat for every passenger, that they could steam ahead at full speed in a nighttime ice field, that they could use inferior steel for the hull. It's a terrible accident—I get that—but a lot of bad decisions went into making it. Same with A-191. Probably still some folks want to cover it up."

"Now you sound like Eveline. There's not much to cover any more."

"Lots of Evelines out there, children of the passengers, even brothers and sisters. There's an 85-year-old in Joliet who lost his wife on that flight. I still hear from him once in a while."

"Seriously? There's a group?"

"Think about it—almost 300 dead. Figure an immediate family of three or four. That's a thousand people. Then brothers, cousins, aunts, uncles, friends, co-workers, neighbors—maybe a hundred people affected by each death. Now you're up to 30,000. You know, every year there's a huge memorial service in New York at Ground Zero. There's a quieter one at O'Hare."

"You were there, weren't you?"

"At the memorial service?"

"You know what I mean, Mr. Moss. In '79." He didn't respond. He didn't have to.

CHAPTER 8

To Kasi, American 191 had been a chapter in a text, a worst-case scenario from which to learn about aircraft maintenance, about piloting, about crash investigation, and about corporate irresponsibility. But to Jake Moss, it had been a job—a phone call on a Friday afternoon as he and his wife were packing their car for a weekend at the Rhode Island shore.

"Believe it or not we were learning to surf," he said. "I was still married to Jeanette—man, that's a long time ago. We were living outside Boston, near the NTSB regional office."

"The organization was still new, wasn't it."

"It was. Twelve years old. We were feeling our way around."

"And you were called in."

"Yes. As summery as it was in Chicago that weekend, the forecast in New England was dismal—cloudy, cool, and damp all three days. We were going to go anyway—a hotel with room service would be a nice break—and maybe some dry weather would sneak in."

"You didn't stay in New England?"

"I always had my name in for other openings. I liked the east coast, but I was restless and Jeanette was the same. Two restless people," he said. "A recipe for disaster. We parted amicably enough. No children, no complications."

"And the weekend at the Rhode Island hotel?"

"Never happened. We were almost out the door when the phone rang. That was it. Can I get you two anything? We have a galley."

We declined. There were too many good questions I wanted to ask. "What was it like then, crash investigation?"

"Different. We weren't technically a federal unit. We were independent, still are. And we were busy. The day of the Chicago crash there were fatals in Arkansas and West Virginia…and I think out west, maybe Montana or Idaho. Smaller planes, but still, airline safety was not what it is today—a major crash was not unusual and investigations went on far beyond the initial incident. At times we were stretched pretty thin, and that weekend—remember, it was Memorial Day— some agents had already left on other assignments and others were owed downtime. So I was off and Jeanette got to spend her weekend relaxing."

"You didn't," I said.

His expression changed, seemed darker.

"Even in our job," he said, sweeping Kasi into the conversation, "you can avoid a lot of horrors. I mean, I wasn't a doctor or a nurse, faced with life and death daily. I was a detective looking for clues. But I'll tell you this: I wasn't ready for Chicago. I don't know if anybody can be. I know your dad was on that plane so…."

"I've imagined the worst all my life, seen pictures to match."

"Then you know. Investigators were poking around, found these piles of black ash. They were victims. You couldn't even tell."

"I have to ask you this," I said. "The findings said everyone died instantly. What do you think?"

He hesitated, and when he did I knew I didn't want to hear the rest. But when he asked me if I was sure I wanted the answer, I couldn't say no.

"I think—and this is just me talking—others feel differently."

"Honest, I understand. I'm not obsessing—I just want to know."

"Seven seconds, I think. That would have been the longest anyone lived. And I hate to say this but, the passengers in the back—I know your dad was in back— probably had the most time to…recognize what was happening."

"To suffer."

He nodded. "The cockpit crew died on impact, but the cockpit absorbed some impact. The plane hit nose first but not straight in—about a 45° angle. It crumbled for sure, but may also have compressed a little before it skidded. Maybe three, four seconds. The fuel tanks ruptured immediately, but it would have taken some time for the fuel to come in contact with the engines. Jet fuel is less volatile, so maybe two seconds more before ignition, then that was it. You know the picture, the fireball ten stories high. At that point no one would have survived another second or two."

"Catastrophic damage to the integrity of the aircraft. That's the term, right?"

"Right."

"Surviving family members," I said, "called it murder."

"And with justification. If not murder, at least negligent homicide."

"The pylons," I said.

He nodded. It was the part of the story everybody knew, the most damning part. And the most tragic. The DC-10 had three engines. I use the past tense, since so few are still flying, but they still have that distinctive appearance—an engine on each wing and one stuck in the middle of the tail. Servicing the wing-mounted engines was a bear. It required removing each from the attaching pylon and the pylon from the wing—some 200 man-hours worth of labor. Then someone devised a shortcut: why not remove the engine and pylon as one unit?

"It cut the time in half," Moss said. "Not only that, but shortcuts, which always seem to be dangerous, this time appeared to increase the safety. They reduced the number of disconnects in hydraulics, fuel lines, cables and wiring—less chance of reconnecting incorrectly. I hate to say it, but I even remember the numbers—from 79 steps to 27."

"I know the numbers," I said. "And letters—November-one-one-zero-alpha-alpha."

"The FAA designation, "Moss said. "You are a reluctant authority—that comes from your sister, right?"

"Of course."

"That plane was serviced in Tulsa—a top-notch crew that kept meticulous records."

"Top notch at doing the wrong thing," I said. Kasi disagreed.

"I'm sure you know this, but even though McDonnell-Douglas warned that the repeated removal of the two parts as one unit placed stress on the pylon, the company didn't forbid it, just advised against it. The maintenance crew had no leeway, not when the manufacturer says it's okay."

"And again, an outstanding crew in Tulsa, whose meticulous records damned them in the end."

I knew what he meant—one of the workers heard a cracking sound and the crew searched everywhere for damage. They were thorough but found nothing, because the crack in the pylon was hidden from visual inspection. It might have shown up on an x-ray, but nobody took one. So they finished up, tested all the systems and, when everything checked out, watched the plane take off perfectly and go back into service. Of course that first rotation, and everyone after it, made that hairline crack a little longer and a little wider."

"Until that day at O'Hare," I said.

"When everything went wrong. Remember that plane that landed on the

Hudson? Remember they gave all those pilots the same scenario and they either crashed in the river or crashed into buildings. Until they were told in advance what would happen. Same with 191. If the flight crew in Chicago had known that the engine actually fell off the plane and not just flamed out, they might have made a safe landing. It's debatable—a ruined wing would make flying difficult but not impossible. People would have died had they skidded across that field, but some would have lived."

"After it was all over and done," Kasi said, "American used a simulator to reenact the situation. Over the course of time, seventy pilots tried to get that plane down safely. In the first scenario—with no knowledge of what had happened to the wing—one of them made a crash landing which, by official estimates, would have destroyed the plane and killed half the passengers. That was the *best* outcome. No one else came even that close. But when pilots were told exactly what was going to happen, then put into the simulator, more than half of them made a basically uneventful landing—it became more a function of flight experience. And the ones who received in-flight feedback—ninety percent of them landed without incident."

"Then came the settlements," Moss said. "Your sister knew that those were the real tragedy. And there are stories of people not on the plane, not related, not anything."

"Like Mitchell Oakes?" Moss looked surprised.

"How do you know that name?"

"Saw it in the papers Eveline left behind. Who is he?"

"More or less a scapegoat. He was part of the Tulsa crew that tore down that DC-10."

"He lives in Collinsville, Oklahoma? Know where that is?"

"Outside Tulsa, but he doesn't live there anymore—he doesn't live anywhere. Forty years, Daniel. Lots of the principals involved in this are gone. He was an early casualty. It's in the book."

Before I could ask which book, he reached behind a compartment and pulled out a ragged paperback, beat-up and dogeared, then thumbed through it until he found the right page.

"Brought this with me," he said. "Eveline gave me a copy. Kasi's seen this."

I had too. *Murder at O'Hare: The True Story of Flight 191.* Years ago Eveline had sent me a copy, some self-published screed filled with misprints and poor grammar. Individual accounts from victims' relatives and friends, affecting but not substantiated. I read a chapter or two, got the gist, checked the index for my father's name in the victims list—it was there—then stuck it on a shelf.

"Oakes is in the index," Moss said, "not on the casualty list. You have time?"

"You're the one who flew up from Dallas," I said.

"Then bear with me."

He riffled through the pages until he found the passage.

Three months before the crash, he read, *Oakes had seen the forklift operator maneuver the engine/pylon assembly away from the wing, had been part of the service crew that inspected the GE engines and authorized their return back to service. Oakes had skill and expertise, even longevity, everything but authority. He had told his wife months before that cutting corners on DC-10 maintenance was dangerous, and stress on metal parts was cumulative, and that eventually there'd be a price to pay. It wasn't pleasant bedtime conversation, but many of his co-workers agreed, and even his supervisor attempted to change the protocol. No luck.*

"That's it?"

"If there's more, it's not here. You know what happened at the trial, don't you?"

"American and McDonnell-Douglas blamed each other, sued each other. Both corporations were shifting blame, trying to keep the case in litigation until surviving family members got too frustrated to continue."

"Right," Moss said. "Basic American business practice. No offense, Daniel. I'm sure your company is different. But workers like Oakes often became the face of negligence, the man who worked on the plane—the man who signed off on its safety—the man who could have prevented all this from happening. He was basically following a manual, no more."

"There were whistleblowers in other fields around then," Kasi said. "Karen Silkwood was active in the early seventies. It wasn't unheard of, but it did take courage."

"More than courage," Moss said. "Karen Silkwood was poisoned and then murdered. Not exactly motivational for others like her. Now maybe some goons protecting nuclear energy weren't the same as the federal government investigating a disaster, but the results might have been the same. Oakes was probably aware of that, never found the nerve to go to the papers or contact the FAA. Plus he had a wife and kids. He couldn't afford to be unemployed and blackballed."

He handed me the book.

"Hang on to it," he said. "Maybe it'll come in handy."

"I don't want it," I said. "No offense. Just tell me—what happenedto Oakes?"

"He started drinking, of course, like a character in some cautionary movie. He'd act okay during the day, go to work and all, play with the kids, whatever young fathers do. I was never one of them. Kinda late to start, I suppose. How about you, Daniel, kids?"

"No wife. No kids. No dogs or cats."

I thought he glanced at Kasi then, maybe to gauge her reaction, but without prompting he was back to Oakes.

"His normal days kind of mutated into abnormal nights. He'd start with the bourbon after the kids went to bed. His wife would have one with him—one or two were her limit, but I guess—and these are her words—they used liquor as a bit of an aphrodisiac like lots of people do. Release the inhibitions and all. Eventually she couldn't get him to come to bed—he just stayed up and drank. He was hungover every morning, finally got a verbal warning at work, then a written reprimand when they found him asleep on a toilet. His wife—eighteen years of marriage—she was patient, counseled him, got him to drink a little less, planned day trips for the whole family just to keep him from being alone. Always, mixed results."

"So he was fired?"

He shook his head. "One night she woke up at three and found him in the living room, passed out in his underwear, an empty bottle of bourbon next to him. No glass. She was furious, but backed away for a moment and gathered herself before coming close and putting a hand on his. She nudged him awake and asked him to come to bed. He mumbled something, then awakened fully and looked at her as if he had never seen her before."

"How do you know all this?"

"It came out," he said. "More trials—it just gets worse."

Moss was narrating from memory and apologized for not having all the details; but what he did have was grisly enough. Oakes hit his wife that night. Whether from anger or disorientation, he swung his arm around and caught her with the back of his hand just below the eye. Some ring he wore ripped open a gash, blood was everywhere. He'd never hit her before.

Three kids were sleeping upstairs so she didn't call the cops. She stanched the bleeding, eased him back onto the couch, and put the bottle away. She cleaned up the blood, even turned on the TV so that if the kids came down, they'd think their father was one of those guys who fall asleep each night watching the news—a funny anecdote to share with their friends with similarly goofy parents.

For her, band-aids, some aspirin, some make-up. She stayed awake the rest of the night listening to her husband's drunken breathing in the living room. She couldn't stop shaking.

"So many details," I said. "You interviewed her personally, didn't you?"

"Long afterwards. It's obvious, I guess. In the morning they talked. He was groggy, contrite, angry: a jumble of emotions and behaviors that was beyond his wife's ability—anyone's ability—to manage. He left for work and she called somebody, a counsellor, tried to get help for both of them."

"Did she leave him?"

"No. She didn't want to give up, be a quitter. Next morning Oakes called in sick and they found a counsellor. Two visits. A week later, after some reasonably calm days, he drove his car off an overpass on Route 11, crashed to the pavement below, and died instantly. It was a showery morning and the roads were slick: the police called it an accident—said he had lost control of his vehicle. Everyone knew better."

"Everyone?"

"Not everyone. There are those who believe the car was tampered with—that someone from the airline or McDonnell tampered with his car. But why would they? Why would they kill their fall guy? I say suicide."

"Jesus, just like that?"

"Just like that. A widow with three kids at 38. Now, Daniel, I knew your sister—that's your story too, isn't it, your mother? Like I said—multiply these little tragedies by all the people on board that day and the misery is almost endless. Some stories have legs—this crash has tentacles."

"Did you marry her?"

"The wife?" He laughed. "Funny you would say that. I thought of it. That crash—the aftermath—everything—that was the end for Jeanette and me. Tina Oakes was a great lady—strong, I even liked the kids. But a father of three—that wasn't anything I'd be good at. Why did you ask?"

"When you tell the story," I said, "it sounds like yours."

"It's not, but we kept in touch. It took us both a long time to find someone else. I often wondered if I had made a life with Tina Oakes, would my happiness have come at the cost of all those lives? Would I have always felt guilty? Maybe."

"So in a way," I said, "you're another victim." Moss nodded. "Like I said, tentacles."

CHAPTER 9

In the forty years that I had heard stories of that crash, Moss's was not the first that ended in suicide. Others were just as bleak, tales punctuated by divorce, addiction, even insanity. There never seemed to be a silver lining. On the contrary, some stories were almost too horrible to be believed.

One man watched his fiancée die in the crash, then—airport security less stringent than it is today—scaled a fence and ran down the runway toward the flames. A departing plane just missed him and the backwash knocked him over. He lay there on the runway bleeding until security reached him. He survived. Planes do lots of things, but they don't swerve very swell.

Relatives collapsed in the terminal. One man took a swing at an airline ticket agent and broke the man's jaw. Another agent who tried to intercede wound up with her arm broken. People stopped their cars on the expressway and began walking back to the airport. Miraculously, no one was killed. A woman pulled a gun from her purse and threatened to kill a flight attendant who had just exited her parked car and was walking to her assignment on a different airline.

Angry passengers waiting to board became impatient, even testy, started little skirmishes among themselves. It was not a good day to catalogue the strengths of humanity.

"But there were heroes, too," Kasi said.

Moss agreed.

"Absolutely," he said. "One man drove a distraught husband, whose wife had been aboard, back to Evanston *in the husband's car* just so the man could tend to his kids, then took a cab back to O'Hare to pick up his own car. But even on Sunday, when things had settled down, passengers began asking which runway their plane would be using, begging not to go anywhere near 32-R. It was the kind of request no passengers had ever made before. It took months for that request to fade.

"I suppose my sister knew all this," I said.

Kasi nodded. "I've skimmed the material she left. I don't think there's much she didn't know."

"And so," Moss said, "I have to ask. Why?"

"Why what?"

"Why are you here? Why am I here. I don't mean existentially," he said to me with a smile, "I mean what's the endgame, justifying your sister's obsession? We already know all there is to know. Or are you out to punish Ken Mullins—he may not be the culprit here. Are we going to pick up her flag and carry it into our own battle? Or is it guilt?"

I can't claim that Moss was badgering me, but he wanted an answer, not so much for himself, but because I think he still relished his role as either a guardian or a mentor for Kasi and didn't want her wasting her time on something frivolous. "There's some guilt here," I said, "I'll admit that, but I don't know if there's a flag to carry. I took a week off from work to settle this, so…."

"Good, good," Moss said. "I'm going to give you a name to start with, Mr. Blaine. Alex Carmichael."

"He's a victim's relative?"

"He's FBI."

"Seriously?"

"He's at Bradley right now, will be for a while. There was an incident with a drone and a business jet last week. The pilot got a little spooked. No contact and no harm, but now everyone has to deal with it."

"Did it shut down the airport?"

"Like Gatwick last year? No. Some kid said it was his, but then a man reported it missing. So the police figured the kid stole it, tried to cover it up, got caught, end of story. He was underage so he'll get his hand slapped—no video games for a week."

"And that requires the FBI?"

"Not usually," Kasi said, "but the man who reported the stolen drone was someone we know—Martin Hendricks. He's a…well, an acquaintance of the FBI."

"He's in the picture of my sister. With the grenade launcher."

"Then be sure to show that to Carmichael," he said.

"You think…?"

"Don't know what to think, but I know what you can do with your week off from work. I'll tell Carmichael to keep an eye out for you, although," he said, glancing at Kasi, "are you going too?"

"We haven't really discussed that," she said.

"Why wouldn't you? You knew the girl, you know the airport, you even know

Mullins."

"I also know Carmichael," she said, without enthusiasm. "Is that a deal-breaker?"

"I'd have no authority."

Moss smiled. "That's not really what I asked. You're a pretty girl. Alex Carmichael is in charge. You think he's going to create difficulties for you?"

"Really," I said. I was surprised. "With all the concerns about workplace behavior?"

"You can't legislate decorum," Moss said. "The guy is a bit of a dinosaur; on the other hand he would eviscerate anyone who was the least bit indiscreet with Kasi, with any woman."

"That doesn't absolve him," she said. "Like I said, dinosaur."

"And your friend," Kasi said to Moss with a hint of reprimand.

"Can't deny it…for many years," he said, "and a good agent. Don't let dumb politicians lead you into believing the FBI isn't competent. Or dedicated. And Carmichael is tops."

"But he's investigating a stolen drone," I said.

"It's more than that. Mullins is retiring a week from today or tomorrow—one of the two. It's a big deal. He transformed Bradley from a curiosity between New York and Boston into a viable airport—or so his promo material says."

"It's not true?"

"Yeah, it is. You have to winnow out the bullshit in any self-promotion, but next Sunday the first Triple 7 lands there, the culmination of major improvements. Carmichael is there to make sure everything goes all right."

"Does he think it won't?"

"Carmichael is pretty sure nothing will ever go all right—that's why he's a good agent. I'll let him know you'll be around, if that's okay?"

The proper answer was no. First off, my expertise in criminology did not extend much beyond a few games of Clue when I was younger, and I don't remember ever having won any of them. Second, someone as adept as Carmichael would have no use for excess baggage traipsing along behind him. But the proper answer did not allow for my guilt from having been absent when my sister died, of having been critical of her obsession forever. If I could induce some good from it—maybe salvage her good name if only in *my* mind—then I guess I had to seize the opportunity. I hadn't done much else for her.

"I'll tell him to expect you," Moss said, then turned to Kasi. "The two of you?"

Kasi shrugged. I took that to mean she was not interested and tried to bail her out.

"I think I have to do this alone," I said.

"I guess that's…commendable?" Moss said. "You know airplanes, or maybe one airplane. But consider the potential advantages of having an expert with you in all the fields you don't know…including your sister. Sorry. Had to say it."

"Had to?"

"To prevent you from making a mistake. Kasi here won't steer you wrong. Did she give you Moss's first law of aviation?"

"I don't think so."

"It never came up," Kasi said.

"Well maybe we should share it with our neophyte friend here. Here," he said, grabbed a pad and pencil, and wrote something down. "Read it later when you have time to ponder it. Wise words require reflection. Now tell me, do I let Carmichael know you're coming, or do you just show up?"

"Let's keep it professional, at least at our end. Tell him."

Soon afterwards the crew returned, we descended the steps, and Kasi and I watched the Learjet lift into the cloudless Iowa sky. By noon the two of us had booked a flight for Monday morning, O'Hare to Hartford. Meanwhile, Kasi and I were going to get to know each other better on the drive from DesMoines to Chicago. That meant no radio blasting music no one else could possibly like, and no singing along at the top of my lungs. Conversation instead. And podcasts where I learned about the impossibly powerful influence of social media and an interview with a South American leader I'd never heard of. She said a few times that we didn't have to listen, but I lied and listened, interrupting the talking heads with several stops for coffee and food and necessities.

Monday morning, two hours to Bradley, no luggage, just carry-ons and two briefcases converted to all-purpose carriers for my sister's collection of…collectibles. A quick, uneventful flight on a single-aisle Airbus. As we were checking the labyrinth of terminal signage, looking for the airport hotel, I heard Kasi mutter something under her breath. I couldn't pick out the words, but I could pick out the tone. Then I saw the reason: a large sign, maybe a yard square, with the word Kasi encased in a large heart that looked as if it had been drawn by a toddler, though it was held by a man whose toddling years had left him far behind. I didn't have to ask who it was.

She slipped behind me as he approached and lifted the sign a little higher. "I didn't want you to miss me," he said. "Are you Blaine?"

"Daniel, yes. You're Alex." It was hardly a lucky guess.

He nodded, rolled up the sign, then shoved it into some oversized leather coat. "Mr. Blaine. How long have you been a human shield? I mean isn't that…why I believe it's Kasi Brennan hiding behind you."

She moved out into the open. "From embarrassment." Everything was off to a fine start. And it only got better.

"Moss told me you'd be here and I found the flight," he said. "I also reserved two rooms for you—FBI courtesy, but you're paying."

"Already done," Kasi said.

"I checked. You don't want to stay there," Carmichael said. "It's the noisy side."

"We'll be fine."

"Of course you will—that's why I canceled them for you. You're on the fourth floor now, when you get off the elevator…"

"You don't understand," Kasi said. "I have reservations." Carmichael shook his head. He looked incredulous. "Really?"

"Really."

"Okay then, I'll take care of getting the inferior rooms back. You won't have any trouble—certainly nobody wants them."

"We want them."

Carmichael looked at me, grinned, asked me if I had anything to do with this. I think he knew the answer.

Kasi didn't give me a chance to respond. "It's not his call," she said. "The Board reserves our rooms."

"They do," he said, and I thought he winked. If he didn't, he had the right to.

Kasi Brennan—at that particular moment—was no more NTSB than I was.

There was a momentary silence before Carmichael adopted a more philosophical attitude.

"Don't matter. I'll make it good. And if I'm not being officious, how about eight tonight—over there—Three Down—pretty good food and lousy drinks. Just three of us. Maybe more. Dinner's on me. Kasi will explain."

He waited for blowback. When none came, he left for the front desk. Moments later we had our rooms—seventh floor and close to each other. My view of the taxiway was unobstructed, and right on cue as I opened the door, a plane roared away from the gate. Kasi was standing next to me, but neither of us commented on it.

"I told you about Carmichael," she said.

"Was he trying to be helpful, or was it just more paternalism? He seemed to know the better rooms."

"That's the definition of paternalism," she said.

It wasn't. It isn't. He was not her superior; in fact, I thought his effort to find us a decent place to stay was commendable. But her history with him went back a lot further than mine did, and I had a feeling that a woman's perspective on this was understandably different too.

"What are you supposed to explain to me?"

"I don't know, maybe the restaurant name," she said. "Three down?"

"Three down and locked—one of those items you check off when landing—all three sets of wheels are down and locked. TD&L."

"Clever name. Did you like his airport greeting sign?" She spat out some undecipherable reply.

"I suppose it's a pain to deal with stuff like that, but I thought it was funny."

"And I thought it looked like a sign to greet some little girl who'd just made her first flight alone. I'll bet everyone looked at it and said, 'aw, how cute,' then waited for me to appear…or am I being too sensitive?"

"That's going to be one of those questions…."

"That you won't answer. Are you so afraid of offending people?"

"Should I be more like Carmichael?"

She didn't like that answer. She didn't like my room either, and walked away. I told her I'd see her at eight and, since her room was down two from mine, I didn't bother escorting her the rest of the way. I'm never sure anymore what's officious, what's gallant, what's just common courtesy. After our discussion of paternalism, I just watched her get inside her room safely while I made believe I wasn't watching her get inside her room safely.

With some time to kill I spread some of the materials out on the bed. Like everyone else, I'd grown accustomed to shifting back and forth with a mouse click or two. The old-school approach without a mouse or a keyboard seemed alien, but an airport concessionaire at O'Hare had been willing to sell me a hundred Post-it notes at a 200% mark-up. I knew I'd need them to get things sorted.

Then I remembered Moss's hastily scribbled note—and couldn't find it. I'd put it in my pocket, but with all the harried travel and packing and checking-in and ticketing, I'd misplaced it. I called Kasi's room.

"Moss's words of wisdom to ponder? I lost them."

"Good thing you weren't one of Christ's apostles. The Bible would be a lot thinner."

"It could use some editing. Do you know what he wrote?"

"Of course."

"And you'll tell me?"

"Of course. An airplane is just a metal tube with people inside." I waited—there was no more.

"And that's it? Those are his words of wisdom?"

"Remember that and everything else makes sense."

I figured I'd have no trouble remembering it; making sense out of it might be a different matter.

CHAPTER 10

Despite where our lives ended up, as kids Eveline and I were a pretty normal pair of bickering siblings. Living without birth parents as we did, I think we both knew that we had to behave; that in itself wasn't difficult. I liked her well enough and she found me no less unbearable than any other little brother. We were always cognizant of the sequence of events that had brought us to that point, but we didn't dwell on it. We fought over toys and seats in the car and who was cheating at what card game—in short, we were two kids in a family of seven.

We were sensitive to plane crashes, and whenever one of them dominated a news cycle, we felt uncomfortable around each other. The Sioux City crash in 1989 was difficult—a mechanical failure, a DC-10, tremendous loss of life, and a nightmarish video of a stricken and burning plane careening in the background. Even though there were survivors, the image of a massive fireball and oily black smoke mimicked the Chicago crash much too closely.

Despite incidents like that, it was not until Eveline was in her twenties that she became obsessive, or maybe I became aware of the word. I was in my self-absorbed teens—had a girlfriend, played some soccer, smoked some weed, got decent grades. My life was as *special* as every other high school kid's, i.e., not so special, but too interesting to worry about my sister. Even in college, whenever people asked about Eveline, she was *fine*, or *doing well*, or *hanging in there*. And then Bethany became what some might call my obsession, and Eveline was pushed a little farther out on the perimeter.

There were times we could have reconciled, just done better, but we missed them. Once when I was just out of college, I drove her to Midway to catch a flight south. I'd been job hunting—successfully—I had offer; she seemed to be doing nothing and I chose that morning in the terminal to point that out. We quickly gained the attention of every passenger in the area and, soon after that, a few airport security people. Aside from her poking a finger into my chest, it wasn't physical—just Eveline pointing out my callous disregard for what had happened to our parents and my cowardice to make things right. I insisted that we don't make wrong things right; we simply go on and avoid the same mistakes. We learn lessons or we don't; beyond that, there isn't much.

We did not have to be pulled apart or restrained, but it was post-9/11 and altercations in airports were looked upon with some misgivings. Eventually I was allowed to walk away, she caught her flight, and we stopped all pretense of civility. The story is so pedestrian it's hardly worth retelling, but I guess I thought there would always be time for reconciliation—to have a beer and laugh about the time we almost got tossed out of the terminal at Midway. I hadn't anticipated that, still in her forties, she'd be reduced to a hodgepodge of paper scattered on a bed in a Hilton, eight-hundred miles from home. And I couldn't even tell myself that her life had come full circle. It had been linear, skidding ahead, getting nowhere.

I hauled that baggage and more into a quiet, subdued Three-Down.

Though restaurants in terminals do their greatest business on weekdays, evenings can be slow. I thought there'd be time for Kasi and me to have a drink first, but Carmichael was already there, and he wasn't alone.

"This is Lon Taggart," he said when I was barely in shouting distance, then with an arch smile added, "meet your brother-in-law, Danny."

More baggage.

I was determined not to be—or look—flustered. Nor was I going to slip into some banality like "sorry for your loss," which is so appropriate most times but seemed singularly out of place there.

"I prefer Daniel," I said to Taggart in my most non-confrontational voice, "but I'm sure Eveline told you that."

"That and more," he said, then stood and extended a hand. "Eveline has told me all about you," he said.

"I'm surprised you still want to shake my hand." He smiled without even a hint of insincerity.

"This is a bad time for both of us," he said. "Dredge up the past, all you get is mud. But I guess that's why we're here."

"Well thank God that turned out all right," Carmichael said. "I hate fights in restaurants."

Kasi glared at him. I should probably avoid saying that, since Kasi did little other than glare at him that first day or two. He knew exactly how to nettle her, often without saying a word, and maybe that had more to do with Kasi's distaste for him than his coming on to her. But I also think he had been nervous about putting my new brother-in-law and me at the same table, and that his relief was genuine.

"Whatever drink you're ordering," he said, "I warn you, make it a double. I checked out the place this afternoon and the bartender measured out the Scotch-rocks with a shot glass. That kind of OCD is never good in a bartender. They're supposed to pour drinks, not measure them. Anybody can measure things."

Despite the advice, when our server came around, nobody but Carmichael ordered a double anything.

"Don't say I didn't try," he said. "Different guy on tonight, but sometimes it's a restaurant policy and...."

He stopped mid-sentence as if even he knew he was babbling.

"And I completely forgot in all the excitement of this family reunion," he said, "Lon, this is Kasi Brennan. She used to work for the government."

"*With* the government," she said. Probably the exact response Carmichael wanted.

"I think we talked on the phone once," Taggart said. "Pleasure." Carmichael seemed pleased. "So now that we've all been reunited...."

"Not technically a reunion," I said.

Carmichael stopped. "What?"

"You can't get back together with people you've never been together with. You can't reunite if, you know, you've never united."

Carmichael nodded.

"English degree," he said. "I did some checking on you. For all your love of the language, you wound up with an investment firm."

"Still speak English—just make more money."

"We'll have to monitor our usage," he said.

He could have sounded snarky—even annoyed. It was, after all, his show and I had no lines to read. But he seemed fine with my intrusion, even happy with it. He enjoyed the battle, albeit a minor one, and didn't mind losing once in a while. It was the first time I thought maybe he was okay, that maybe I liked him. That thought vanished in the next seconds when he reached into his pants pocket.

"Lon," he said, "can I show these people the necklace?"

Taggart's eyes narrowed. "You didn't tell me you were going to...I thought...."

"I don't have to," Carmichael said. "Just trying to verify your story for these folks."

"I don't know any story yet," I said. I looked around and somewhere on the visual journey I made eye contact with my newfound brother-in-law. "How long were you and Eveline married?" I asked.

"Mr. Carmichael here was taking liberties when he said I was your brother-in-law: Eveline and I weren't actually married."

"Oh," I said. "That must have made it worse at the end."

"There are a lot of legalities to address when someone dies. Luckily your aunt and uncle were helpful. Can I tell you, I wanted to call you, and I think in a way Eveline wanted me to, but in another...."

"Not at all."

"You know how she could be."

"And that," Carmichael chimed in as the drinks arrived, "is where the necklace comes in. It's explanatory. It's visual. Good stories need that kind of thing."

When nobody responded, he picked up the old-fashioned glass pretty much filled with ice and a generous amount of a brown liquor, then took a prescription bottle out of his jacket pocket. "Allergies," he said. "Pills all the time."

Kasi pointed to his glass. "With alcohol?"

"A good single-malt provides a nice one-two punch" he said, then nodded toward me. "Vodka man, huh? Drink to get drunk—that's the spirit." He had no comment about Kasi's wine or Taggart's beer, but we all clinked glasses perfunctorily as if we were toasting something wonderful.

"It's your show," Taggart said to Carmichael. "Show it to them."

"You won't regret it," Carmichael said, then pulled out the chain with a tiny disk attached to the end. He held it up. "Can hardly see the E on it, but it's there. And real plutonium."

"Platinum," Taggart said.

"Didn't know there was a difference," he said.

"You'd know if you wore it long enough," Kasi said, "you'd start to glow."

"I always glow when you're around, Kasi."

I wanted to laugh—the joke was so lame; the attitude so tone-deaf. I even thought Kasi should have known better than to feed him such an easy line, but you can't go blaming the victim. Jake Moss had referred to Carmichael as a dinosaur, so any prehistoric attitudes should never have surprised me. Even so, I thought we'd established some boundaries over the past…oh…hundred years. As for confusing plutonium and platinum—he knew the difference—but the image of being radiated to death by a necklace still amuses me.

"I'm not going to embarrass anybody here," Carmichael said after the fact "so let's lay it all out. This here trinket came from Marty Hendricks. Apparently he was able to overlook the fact that the woman he liked was already spoken for."

I was already wishing I'd ordered a double, to start.

But Carmichael was at ease providing an extensive verbal dossier on Marty Hendricks, one filled with anti-government activity, open defiance of local, state, and sometimes federal law enforcement. Three arrests for unlawful assembly, one for threatening a councilman at a town meeting, another for letting a dog roam. As for traffic arrests, Carmichael said, the authorities had stopped tracking those years before.

In the mid-90s he had been linked to a slapdash plot to blow up the Statue of Liberty, but the so-called explosives experts he glommed onto were inexperienced and ineffectual. The bomb did not detonate and the perpetrators went to prison. Hendricks, who apparently was supposed to die in a blaze of martyrdom as the monument toppled over, slinked home and stayed out of sight.

"Of course that was after he sent his farewell letter to the president," Carmichael said. " 'I die with Liberty,' he said, along with other pseudo-patriotic bullshit. Nobody knew what it meant until they caught the ersatz bombers who gave him up. Hendricks denied it, said he knew them, said they were nuts, claimed he had tried to talk them out of it and never thought they'd go through with it. They were going to arrest him for a failure to report a plot against the government, but there'd been no crime committed and, eventually, they let him go."

I asked him about the letter to the president, but it had been traceable.

"No DNA," Carmichael said. "For someone who planned to die, Hendricks was pretty careful…if it was actually him. After that we beefed up security at some national parks and historic sites, but then came 9/11 and every ounce of subtlety vanished. Now we just overreact and apologize afterwards if we have to. Better that than another 3000 dead."

"And Hendricks," Kasi said, "is still dangerous, and we don't know where he is. Your sister," she said to me, "may have been the calming influence on him. Without her around, we don't know what he'll do."

Lon Taggart had been the quietest of the four while all this was going on, but it wasn't as if he were being frozen out. He more closely resembled an observer at a sport for which he did not know the rules. Still, he had made a joke before and I thought maybe....

"So Lon, is that name short for anything?"

"Leonard. I guess it's short for *I didn't like Leo.* Look, your sister understood."

"Your name?"

"No. You."

"Understood what?"

"That your life was centered on different things than hers. That your job did not involve carrying the ball for her. She was never mad at you. It's just that your paths were so divergent that she knew you could never get along."

"And that's why I got these things after...after?"

"She said if anything happened to her, make sure Daniel gets this stuff. She figured you'd toss it."

"So she sent bits of it to different people."

"I don't think it's a puzzle," Taggart said. "I think it's like an author with a manuscript that's so large and unwieldy that whatever story is in there can't get out until someone unlocks it."

"Or just a scrapbook."

"Maybe."

Carmichael liked the idea of a scrapbook. "So we're just here for funsies," he said. "Cool." He held up his glass. "Who's ready for another?"

When I said make mine a double, Carmichael smiled.

"You should listen to me," he said. "In matters of spirits, I know best."

"I thought the FBI didn't know anything anymore."

"Love to hear that shit," he said. "They keep saying it; we'll keep arresting them. Ever been arrested Taggart?"

"Once."

"Uh huh. Victim's name?"

"You know who it is, Agent."

"Cards on the table, Taggart. I'll tell you whatever you want to know about me.

Just ask. But now I'm asking. Who was the victim?"

By that point even I knew it was Hendricks and that it somehow involved platinum, plutonium, and the difference therein.

"We get it," I said. I think it was my first time actually talking back to a cop. It felt good, but had no effect on where the conversation was headed. Worse, Carmichael was a little miffed.

"I'm buying," the agent said, "and maybe when yours arrives and you loosen up a bit, you'll understand that sensitivities are not the issue. I'm sorry about what happened to your sister; hell, I'm sorry about a lot of things that happen, but if there's a bad guy involved here, I'm gonna catch the son of a bitch. It's our motto— we always get our man."

"I thought that was the Mounties."

"Is it? Canada's always stealing shit from us. Did you know there's Canadian football now?"

"Heard something to that effect," I said.

He tipped his glass far back, got nothing but ice, then put it back down a little too hard.

"Now the bad guy I'm gonna get—he ain't at this table. Lon here, he's the good guy, and he's put up with more bullshit than anybody in the universe. Sometimes there's a payoff for that and sometimes there isn't. And this is one of the bad times. So asking him the question that I asked needed to be done."

"Why?" Kasi asked.

"Because we need to know who we're working with, who we're trusting, who we're believing. Lon Taggart here I would trust with my life. Now you, Daniel, I'm not so sure."

"What about me?" Kasi said.

Carmichael laughed. " Absolutely. You don't like me and I know it. I like transparency."

"Wait a minute," I said. "You have no reason not to trust me."

"Maybe, but you wouldn't be here today if you hadn't received that package from your sister. Did you even know she died?"

"We didn't keep in touch."

"I guess that's an answer. A simple *no* would have worked also. And that's what bothers me. Family members who don't talk to each other. Family, for chrissake. How do you fucking do that?"

As a conversation stopper—everywhere in the restaurant—his little outburst at high volume was quite effective.

"Sorry," he said—to us, to everyone around us, punctuating the apology with a deferential wave. God, where were those second drinks?

"And never mind my question," he said. "Don't answer. I get it, I just don't like it. I figure Kasi here—if she doesn't like something I do, she's gonna tell me. Are you gonna tell me, Mr. Blaine, or are you gonna not speak to me?"

"I'm not like that."

"Wow," Carmichael said, his eyes wide in disbelief. "You're not like that? You're kidding, right?"

I knew better than to respond.

"Forget I asked. Over the next few days, we might be seeing a little bit of each other, at least up until the big retirement bash, and I'd like to know that we're on the same page, so to speak."

I asked what Mullins' retirement had to do with it, but I had a rough idea. Ken Mullins had accumulated his share of enemies over the years—my sister among them. A public retirement, a large crowd, resentment over the airport—I didn't know if it required FBI presence, but maybe there was more to it.

When the second round of drinks came, even my double vodka looked small. I suppose the size of a drink is inversely proportionate to the quality of the company. Or something equally mathematical.

The server took our food orders and left again, and while I wondered how far afield our next snippet of conversation would go, Carmichael asked me what I did and how safe his retirement fund was, and just like that we were off to traditional cocktail-hour conversations, as if my sister had never been born, as if Lon Taggart didn't exist, as if American-191 had been nothing but an uneventful flight to Los Angeles. Maybe Bethany and I were raising children somewhere.

Which only meant that Carmichael was in charge. Things quieted when Carmichael quieted them. The rest of us were the orchestra waiting for the downbeat.

We've all met people like Alex Carmichael. They're practiced at creating a comfort level, then—sometime between the entrée and the dessert—are likely to ask where we stashed the murder weapon or what we did with the money. I had so many antennae raised waiting for the next discomfiting question that I couldn't enjoy the entrée or the dessert.

CHAPTER 11

Carmichael left the table first. Allergies, he said—his eyes had been bothering him (or at least he'd been focusing and refocusing all evening) —then picked up the tab, refused our offers to leave a tip, even told us to get a receipt for anything else we ate or drank and he'd take care of it.

"That was generous," I said.

"He's got a girl," Kasi said. She did not sound conspiratorial; more like simply repeating common knowledge. But maybe the liquor had me feeling more expansive than accusatory, so I glossed over her comment.

"I don't think he was feeling great," I said. "His eyes were bothering him." Kasi wasn't making allowances.

"Maybe if he kept them in his sockets once in a while…."

The joke fell flat, but then I opened my mouth and set her off again.

"We should pay for any drinks we have from here on," I said. "I hate to take advantage of…."

"Did you hear me?" Kasi said. "About his eyes? I think so."

"No. He's married."

"And?"

"And you're okay with that?"

"Not in the slightest," I said, then, not wanting to enflame the situation, tried to make a joke, "but I'm not the one who's going to hell."

"It's more than the threat of hell…."

"I was kidding," I said, then glanced at Lon Taggart who had become a bystander in a conversation I didn't want to have. I know I was also a little buzzed, a fact that probably diminished my ability to be shocked or mortified. Taggart said nothing, but Kasi wasn't finished.

"He always has at least one on the side," she said. "Is that why you don't like him?"

"That's one reason. Did you say 'going to hell'? Are you serious?"

"That's how it works. Look at Bill Clinton—been in hell for twenty years. Doubtful he's getting out. He no longer has to go to the real one."

"Really," she said, leaning back a little. "How about his wife? What's her paradise look like?"

"Not much better," I said. "I did say I was kidding about hell…the real one."

"I met Carmichael's wife once," Kasi said, "and not that this gives me any insight or makes him any more evil, but when you know a person, everything becomes more…personal."

I could have argued that morality was even more universal, but the whole conversation was distracting. I wasn't interested in Carmichael, nor was I concerned with hell. I just thought that Lon Taggart had more to tell us than Kasi did, and that Carmichael's allergies or transgressions were not particularly relevant.

"The necklace," I said to him. "Can you just give us, you know, the details?"

"It's a necklace," he said. "What do you want to know?"

"Whatever you can tell me."

"It came in the mail one day," he said. "Eveline opened the box, then she showed it to me. There was no secretiveness, no stealth, no embarrassment, or for that matter, joy. Hendricks had sent other little gifts over the years—flowers, books, a scarf—and I had learned to accept them for what they were, gifts from an admirer whose only interest in Eveline was as a receiver of gifts."

I must have looked confused. I certainly felt that way and Taggart saw it.

"Let me clarify—there was no affair," he said, "no clandestine meetings, no sex. No gifts on her birthday either, or on Christmas. Just random acts of annoyance."

"Was Hendricks gay?"

"Eveline never gave any indication of that—I always assumed they'd had sex at one time or another— but who knows? It wasn't my place to ask."

"So it was platonic?"

"That lends it a certain intellectual motivation I don't think existed," Taggart said, spinning a gold band on his left ring finger. He saw me watching him.

"Marty didn't send me this," he said. "Your sister and I bought it together."

"She must have loved your sense of humor," I said. "But I have to ask—you lived together, you obviously loved each other, you had a house, you had a ring— why didn't you ever make it official."

"Tax purposes."

"Are you serious?"

"Of course not. Your sister knew two marriages. Your mom and dad we don't have to rehash, and then your uncle and aunt who were happy, content I suppose. Eveline didn't like the odds. Only 50-50. She didn't want a sure thing, but a surer thing. She had that—as long as there was nothing legally binding."

I could have contradicted him and said risk-taking was a part of life, but that never defined me. Instead he called the relationship amorphous but strong. It seemed like a contradiction, but if there's an opposite of a relationship specialist, I'm it.

Beyond that, Taggart was the wellspring of information that all those packages were not. Apparently my sister had met Marty Hendricks many years before. Eveline was just out of college, still fumbling from job to job, and Hendricks was settled with a wife and two kids, until he admitted to his wife that he loved my sister, left a generous settlement for her and the kids, never argued over visitation or anything else, and began a new life.

"Of nothing," I said. "He left his wife for…nothing."

"We all end up with nothing, Mr. Blaine. It just takes some of us longer to get there. I told your sister at one point she might find me boring. I think she'd had enough of the other life. Is that enough of an answer?"

"You said they'd both lost something? I know about Eveline, but…" He didn't let me finish.

"Hendricks had lost a relative in Viet Nam—an uncle, MIA. A man he never knew but whose memory permeated the family history. Hendricks blamed the government—not for the war itself, but for what came after—a seeming conspiracy not to divulge any information on the missing."

"Was there any? Information?"

"Let me ask you, Mr. Blaine. Is there any more information on flight 191? And if there isn't, aren't there people who think there is?"

"Always," I said. "With every conspiracy theorist…."

"Right. Who killed Kennedy? What happened to the Hindenburg? Shall I go on? Hendricks always said it was a conspiracy—that his uncle had been a spy and not just a soldier, that the CIA knew exactly where he was but wouldn't say. Or they had him killed.

"And the Statue of Liberty scheme?"

"Part of the same anger," Taggart said. "But after 9/11 a lot of these homegrown revolutionaries went underground. Of course then we had the anthrax mailings and the Maryland snipers, and the birthers. There's never a dearth of assholes around— they just change their focus."

"They're not all assholes."

"I didn't mean your sister. Her anger and frustration always made sense to me. But she never hurt others. That's where she was different, torn."

"And your arrest. My sister?"

"It was Hendricks. He came banging on the door around 1:00 a.m. I was awake—should have called the cops but I answered. He was drunk, stoned, who knows. He came in and I couldn't get him out. After a good fifteen minutes of trying to talk him down, Eveline picked up the phone, Hendricks tried to take it out of her hands, I backhanded him and he hit the floor. Unfortunately he got up, and he's a big guy. Some punches were thrown, a few landed. The cops took us both in."

"It was your house. You had a right to defend it."

"Not after I let him in. Carmichael was wrong—I was never charged. Hendricks dried out and paid a fine. Your sister never got hurt."

He seemed sincere, open, honest, but I thought he had told us as much as he had to tell. I was about to make a casual escape when Taggart said he'd love to see what Eveline sent us. I looked at Kasi. She nodded.

"Just don't tell Carmichael," she said.

I slipped Taggart my room key and gave him the number. "We'll be up in five," I said.

He hesitated.

"Just go, really. We'll be right up. Kasi and I need a private meeting." He shrugged a *whatever* and left.

"What's this about?" Kasi said. Her eyes were a little glassy but she was still in control.

"It gets old," I said. "What does?"

"You and Carmichael, the Hatfield and McCoys act."

"The what?"

"This feud you have, let it go. Sometimes you have to work with people you don't like, or don't respect. Sometimes you rub off on them and they become better."

"If you were a woman, you'd understand."

"You're probably right. I'm no role model; otherwise I wouldn't be here. But I think he likes you."

"Of course he does—I'm just his type: a woman."

"I don't see that. Look, he's a boor. I get it, everyone does. You can't be picking fights with him just to prove that. I don't know if his loopiness crosses the line from annoyance to sexual misconduct. But you're right, I'm not a woman. You tell me."

"Men should know. They're the ones who cross the line."

"Then tell me. Has he crossed the line with you? I mean, more than words."

"He never tried to rape me—does that pass for a compliment these days?"

"It shouldn't, but in some circles it does. Do you feel uncomfortable with him?"

"Yes."

"Threatened?"

"Look, we're not besties, not after a few days. So no confessions, okay? My feelings toward people like him are probably more complex than what I can hash out over drinks in some bar. This is no place for self-analysis—not for either of us. This is about him, not about you or me. And he…he just…takes over. Just comes in and barks orders and…takes over."

"If it's any consolation, I think he's gender-neutral when it comes to bossing people around. And at the risk of making you angry…angry-er…he's a cop! I'm not. Neither are you. Who better to help us sift through all this bullshit? To bark orders and take over."

"He shouldn't bark."

"Agreed. In the real world, Carmichael and I would never be friends. But for now…look, tell me if you don't want to be involved in this. I have a lot to atone for. You don't. You were kind of sucked into this mess when Jake Moss recommended that you be here. Maybe he has ulterior motives—wants you to get your hands dirty again, come back to work. I don't know what everyone is thinking. But watching you two—you and Carmichael—it's exhausting."

She sat back and roughly shifted a few items on the table. When she spoke again her tone had moderated.

"He brings out the worst in me," she said. "I'm not a victim. Not some delicate flower that needs kid gloves to…am I mixing metaphors?"

"Like a Waring blender. Listen, that bringing out the worst in people—that's Carmichael's gift to mankind. Let's forget him. Let's look at this from Taggart's point of view. He's as miserable as I probably should be. The sooner we sort through everything, the sooner he can move on."

"I don't think he's interested," she said. "Are we still talking about Carmichael?"

"Taggart. Moving on is meaningless without your sister. He won't recover from this. And Carmichael can stay, go, help, disappear—doesn't matter. I'm a professional—or was one—I work the job, not the people."

"So, do we go upstairs…I mean to, you know…? That sounded a bit suggestive."

"And you sound a bit drunk."

"Those doubles, they add up. You want to just let this go until morning? I can get rid of Taggart."

"No. Let's see what we can do. For his sake anyway."

We paid the bill and Kasi said no to a receipt. Probably didn't want to be any more beholden to her nemesis.

Moments later we found Taggart reading my extravagantly purchased Post-it notes.

"You two have done some work," he said. He didn't say thank you, but I think he meant it. Still, there wasn't much he considered new. Hendricks, Mullins, all in profusion. There was even *my* Bethany, of course, whom Eveline had liked and who had brought me into this. And the late Mitchell Oakes—even Taggart commented on that. But Mullins was omnipresent, abundantly represented in photos. References to our mother and father were less frequent, usually coinciding with a birthday or an anniversary—including of course May 25.

Then there was a name neither Kasi nor I recognized: Devin Walsh. "Know this guy?" I said to Taggart.

"We'll deal with him when the time comes."

It was the only cryptic comment I ever heard from the plainspoken Taggart. I let it pass.

Something else was bothering me—the only person more popular than Ken Mullins in Eveline's accumulation of data was me.

There's no comfort when you feel that someone has shut you out of her life, only to learn too late that you were always part of it. There was the newspaper article I'd seen before—my promotion—but there were all kinds of little PR pieces—fluff that corporations send out to assure the public their intentions are honorable. Somehow Eveline had found them, and I do mean *found*. In one of them, we had co-sponsored (along with a dozen other corporations) a 5K road race near the Field Museum with proceeds earmarked for the homeless in Chicago. My job: be at the start/finish line. Just…be.

It turned out I handed out water bottles at the end, and that earned me a color photo in the Living section of the *Tribune*—and a hand-drawn heart on the one Eveline had cut out. Of course no Facebook page is complete without a scattering of hearts, and an email from one friend to another must contain the requisite heart emoji to be valid. Hearts have certainly lost whatever significance they had years ago, but her hastily scribbled one—and not even in red!—was a dagger through mine.

"What?" Kasi said.

"What do you mean?"

"You stopped breathing."

"I'd be dead."

Taggart smiled. "Too much vodka. Gotta learn to hold your liquor, Blaine. Remain alert, do the job." But he knew.

For better or worse, I don't reach out to people, but I made an awkward attempt with Taggart, tried to rephrase the perfunctory expression of condolences I'd made earlier.

"I can't even imagine what it's like…."

"For both of us," he said. "I remember that photo. She was so happy for you." Another dagger. The room went uncomfortably quiet until Kasi saved us.

"As much a pain in the ass that Alex Carmichael is," she said, "now I know why he wanted us to drink more. Maybe we should knock off."

"Or empty the honor bar," I said.

I think we would have made a dent in it, right then and there in mid-mess, had it not been for Carmichael pounding on the door.

"Who's awake in there," he yelled. "And who's dressed?"

I jumped up and let him in before he disturbed every guest in the area and got us all tossed.

"We're all awake, like everybody else in this hall who woke up to answer your question."

"They'll live. Mr. Taggart, call Uber. You're headed home."

"What's going on?" I asked. "We're making progress here."

"Working hard, huh? Did you hear sirens before? You insisted on being on the noisy side and you ignore everything?"

"I heard them," I said. "I thought it was maybe an ambulance or something."

"And fire trucks, and some state and local, that's what's going on. If you'd like—and you're not too busy reminiscing—you can come with me. There's a broken Cessna tipped over about fifty yards from the terminal and apparently there's some interest in finding out why. Anybody willing? Any retirees with accident investigation experience—you know, before the real guys get here? Anybody? Don't be shy.

The question did little to ingratiate himself to Kasi, but her eyes betrayed no anger—just excitement.

CHAPTER 12

Gordon Krause, a colleague of mine who is slightly higher on the corporate food chain, looks up at the sky whenever a plane flies over. Occasionally we have lunch on the terrace, and depending on weather conditions and flight destinations, planes fly over at about 10,000 feet. He knows every plane by its silhouette. And if it's low enough for him to discern color, he'll tell you the airline. Krause is not alone—I've seen others do it too.

Where the fascination lies, I don't know. At any given time over the U.S. there are about 5000 scheduled airliners flying—from 50-passenger shuttles to coast-to-coast wide-bodies. And on any given day 5000 of them take off, fly, and land uneventfully. As for smaller aircraft, tens of thousands more. None of these facts matter to Krause and his ilk. I wonder if Eveline was like that…but I wonder also if when she did stare skyward at every passing airliner, she experienced apprehension or fear. Was this the next A-191? Maybe that's why I don't look up. Maybe I never wanted to be my sister.

That doesn't mean I didn't admire her. If she carried around a lifetime of anger, what kept her from becoming a suicide bomber, or a driver ramming a truck through a crowd. What prevented her from adding her name to that ever-increasing number of Americans forever linked to murder and horror: Thomas Paddock shooting from a Vegas hotel, Adam Lanza slaughtering children in a school building, Dylan Roof murdering worshippers in church, Patrick Wood Crusius turning a department store into a combat zone? She had never become a freak or a pariah—one of those monsters whose legacy comprises nothing but the misery of others. In her own way, and probably with great difficulty, she had held it together—something that I considered when Carmichael declared, with no proof, the plane crash a suicide. Despite the accord Kasi and I had reached about him, it seemed as if he made the statement just to annoy the only person there capable of investigating a crash: Kasi Brennan.

She said nothing, just allowed herself and me to be led to a cordoned-off area that only credentialed people could enter. Maybe a hundred feet out on the tarmac lay the wreckage of a Cessna—1980-vintage, Kasi thought—that had been stolen from a small airfield in eastern Connecticut. There'd been no flight plan, nor was one required, but someone on duty remembered seeing the plane taxi from north to south, then lift off and bank left. He assumed it was another flight to the Cape or the Islands and went about his responsibilities as a quasi-night watchman and security guard. According to radar, about a mile from the Rhode Island border the eastbound plane changed direction almost 180°, ending up at Bradley.

"What kind of pilot does that?" Carmichael said. "Who flies east just to turn around and fly west. No fog. No weather problems of any kind. Nothing to avoid. Obviously plenty of fuel. And where's Ken Mullins? This airport is his baby— why isn't he here changing its diaper?"

He didn't wait for an answer. "Probably on suicide watch," Carmichael added. "He doesn't like people messing up his toys."

The agent seemed unusually agitated, even more so when an airport worker said Mullins had been and gone, but was due back.

"You don't just walk away," he said, then muttered something about being here for the duration. I steered clear of responses. So did Kasi who, though we weren't allowed a close inspection of the wreckage, was inspecting anyway.

"You mentioned no fog," she said, "but night flying—he could have become disoriented."

"It's an old plane," Carmichael said, "but not so old not to be equipped with navigational equipment. A freakin' compass would have done it. I can't wait to see the tox screen on this asshole. And how in the good Christ do you hit this building from that angle? He may have taken off from a dark airport, but it sure as hell isn't dark here."

I asked him if that's why he thought it was suicide, but he didn't answer. He seemed distracted, walked away from us, then came back with another airport employee, a woman in some sort of olive-drab uniform and a smartphone with a link to an airport security. We saw a surveillance video showing the final seconds of the flight—saw the plane touch down, bounce a little, then flip over and skid toward the baggage area below the terminal. It never got there.

"Intentional or incompetent?" Carmichael asked.

Kasi wanted to know if any ID had been found, plane registration, that sort of thing.

"The Red Baron wannabe is…was a nice fellow named Wesley Barrett," Carmichael said, then looked at me. "Know him?"

"How could I know him?"

"Indiana driver's license. That's out your way, right?"

"Trust me, I don't know him."

"*Didn't* know him. He's dead," Carmichael said. "And the crash was not even particularly violent. He should have survived it, maybe. I don't know. They're still interviewing witnesses, waiting on the NTSB. Isn't that you, Kasi? Why don't you get out there and tell us what…oh wait, I forgot you're retired."

"Why does that bother you?"

He pointed to the wreckage. "That's why. You could be helping, but no, you and Moss, the two renegades of aviation. Unfortunately, jobless."

This was a different Carmichael from the one who had picked up the tab earlier, who had been sardonic but focused. Now he was pacing, even (it seemed) when he was standing still.

"What's going on?" Kasi said.

"There," Carmichael shouted, pointing to the crumpled fuselage. "That's what's going on."

"If we're in the way," Kasi said, "we can leave."

"Lucky," he said. "Must be nice to dabble. Everything is optional. "

I was about to do something really officious—maybe what Kasi would call paternalistic—I was about to lead her away, then thought better of it. I shouldn't have. I could have gotten her out before she asked him if we were taking him away from something. There weren't too many somethings in which a person could be involved at two in the morning that didn't include some form of intimacy. Kasi's implication was clear, and not lost on Carmichael.

"You know, fuck you. Fuck the both of you."

He headed toward another small group. I wasn't going to follow unless Kasi did. She started, then stopped.

"Better to let him be," I said. "He's all wired for some reason."

"Been drinking all night, probably."

"With someone."

"Same as us."

"You know what I mean, Daniel."

While we debated the cause, the same Carmichael who had angrily dismissed us waved us over. He seemed calmer, more professional.

"Looks like one of those photos you see after a hurricane; a plane upside down."

"Can we get any closer?"

"Not until *your* people get here. Until then…."

"The engine wasn't running when he hit," Kasi said before he could finish.

I was impressed. "You can tell that from here?"

"It's about all I can tell. If it had been turning, the propeller would have been mangled. From here it looks pretty good. Might have been at three and nine when the plane hit."

"Three and nine what?" Carmichael said.

"O'clock," Kasi said. "You know, like a clock face."

"Oh yeah, I forgot that's how clocks used to look back in the day. Why would the propeller not have been turning?"

"Nine times out of ten it's a fuel problem. Broken pump, clogged line, bad fuel—or the wrong fuel, or of course no fuel."

"Out of gas," he said.

"I don't smell a lot of gasoline," she said. "Even if there was a spill and the ground crew got it cleaned up, there'd be residual odor…unless the tanks held together. They're on the wing, just above the cockpit. The thing flips over, I'd be shocked if they didn't rupture."

"Could he have dumped fuel?" Carmichael said.

"A Cessna?" she said. "Why?"

"I don't know, why do planes dump fuel?"

"Sometimes in an emergency if you want to diminish the chances of fire or explosion, a plane will dump fuel. But usually it's because planes have landing weights, and they can't land safely if they're too far above them. You can't brake as efficiently, and even the reverse thrusters won't be as effective. You could reach the end of the runway pretty fast, and then when you skid off onto rough terrain and start bouncing around, that extra fuel becomes a real hazard."

"And the Cessna?"

"Fifty gallons of fuel? What's that, 400 pounds give or take. You'd never need more than three football fields feet to land a 172 and we've got an 11,000-foot runway here. Either this Barrett is the worst pilot in Connecticut or he had a target in mind and just missed it.

"For a disgraced investigator," Carmichael said, "you know a shitload of stuff. Jake was right about you. Said you were the best."

"No one was disgraced," she said. "What is *with* you?"

"Did I say disgraced? I meant…let's say *idle* instead. An idle investigator."

"People change jobs all the time," I said in her defense. "Maybe not in your generation."

Carmichael laughed. "I'm fifty, not ninety."

He turned back to Kasi. "Sorry about before, but you'll have to tell me sometime why you'd walk away from a profession you obviously know. Christ, I'd hire you in a second if you were interested."

She shook her head. "You gotta be kidding."

"Don't worry," he said. "I don't need an answer right this minute."

As he walked away, I began searching for something to say, but Kasi made it easy.

"I don't want to talk about this," she said. "But you can't just…."

"Look, it's not even 'me-too' stuff. It's just him being an asshole."

But it wasn't. The Carmichael at dinner ordering drinks and bitching about their size had morphed into something ornery and nasty. Liquor can do that—the mean drunk is hardly an unknown type—but that didn't seem to be it either. I let it go until the airport officials rousted us out of there and Kasi and I were on the hotel elevator. She was still fuming.

"I suppose you want to know why I'm not working."

"If you want to tell me."

"I don't."

"All righty then," I said as the doors slid open. We walked down the hall toward our rooms.

"I guess I do want to know," I said, "when you're ready."

"Google it."

"I need some key words, besides you."

"Try *airplane*."

"They say the more specific the search…."

"Now *this* is harassment." She wasn't serious, but she was still angry, agitated, maybe by what had happened, maybe by playing investigator again. Whatever it was, she wasn't ready to sleep. She swiped the card and the tiny green lights flashed, promising admittance, then told me to come in. I followed, parked myself on a chair near a desk, then wondered exactly what I was doing there. She sat on the edge of the bed and I turned a desk chair around to face her.

"It's a long sad saga," she said. "You're sure you want to hear it?"

"All sagas are long," I said.

She smiled. "Are you *trying* to be annoying, Blaine? Because I just came from one annoying person."

"Just lightening the mood."

"It's not working. Do you want to hear the *long* sad saga or not?"

"Only if you want to tell me."

She took off her shoes and tucked her legs under her.

"In 2014," she said, "Jake Moss and I were working together reconstructing a motor vehicle accident," she said. "A tanker had exploded on an Oklahoma Interstate, there'd been some casualties and hints of negligence. There may also have been a car that ran the driver into a ditch. Halfway through the job, Jake was called to D.C. Sometime before there'd been a crash in New Orleans. A 727. Know what they look like?"

"First plane I ever flew in."

"Airlines don't use them anymore, but they're still around hauling freight mostly."

"And the one in New Orleans?"

"A conversion—a cargo plane. There was this new outfit, Newsome Air Freight, and they had bought two of them from a boneyard in Arizona, had them modified, updated, checked out. The idea was to run a freight service from New Orleans to Dallas to Phoenix. A pretty modest operation, but the owner had done some market research and she thought there were possibilities."

"A woman owned it?'

"Divorced. On her own. No kids. And not that I'm looking in that direction, but beautiful."

"Was Jake looking in that direction?"

"If his head wasn't turned, I'd be surprised; but if it went any further than that, I'd be shocked. Of course others may have thought differently, you know, projected their own…whatever.…"

"Desires?"

"I was thinking lack of principles, but whatever, this Newsome owned the company and hired a pilot who, at times, drank too much."

"That's not usually good business practice."

"Yeah, huh? He'd flown in Vietnam, he'd flown charters, his reputation as a pilot was flawless. The drinking had never affected his performance."

"As far as anybody knew, right? Lots of drivers drive drunk and escape because others are careful."

"Different in a plane," she says. "Not many collisions. Run off the road and you make a course correction instead of calling the tow truck. I'd say he kept his piloting and his drinking separate."

"So what then?"

"That's still the question," she said. "The CVR from the crash…you know what that is?"

"I am my sister's brother, remember?"

"Fair enough," she said. "The CVR has him slurring words and sounding almost giddy at times, but the voice recorder itself was antiquated, then beat up in the crash; my investigation says that weather conditions deteriorated so rapidly that the pilot was, in a sense, misled by an air traffic controller—he's not drunk, but maybe astonished that his visuals didn't match their commands."

"Those ATC guys don't screw up runway operations very often, do they" I asked.

"No, but some pilots listen to the tower and hear something else. This controller had a spotless record, but the ceiling was tricky. If you don't know this stuff, stop me."

"Keep going."

"Then you know that ceiling can have a couple meanings in aviation, but let's just say it's the height of the lowest cloud deck. You know how on a rainy day the clouds seem to be almost touching the ground? That ceiling might be too low to land safely and maybe he should have gone around. Later he claimed the touchdown aim point came out of the fog too fast. He already had full flaps so he cut all power and just hit too hard. Blew out the starboard gear and started skidding."

"So he survived."

"So did the plane, more or less. One wing was severely damaged, but the engines on a 727 are up and out of harm's way. Newsome was able to recoup some of the losses by selling them for spare parts. Of course there aren't many of those 727s flying anymore. Anyway, once the wings are gone…"

"…a metal tube with people inside."

"You remembered. See?"

"But what do you think? Should he have gone around?"

"With passenger safety involved, no question. But this was just a flight crew in agreement. And remember, you're talking about a small company living on the edge. That plane goes around and you've just sucked down $1500 of profit on jet fuel, maybe more. And then there's the possibility that the clearance is withdrawn and you're looking for an alternate airport. And this was a 727, the most reliable aircraft ever built. Sturdy, dependable, and designed for what? To land on short runways. Hindsight says he should have gone around, but I'd have tried it too."

"So there was a trial?"

"A hearing. Pilot incompetence or negligence—or a hangover—and there'd be no chance of the company realizing any insurance settlement. But an act of God might keep them solvent for a while. Jake Moss led the investigation and skewed the results, they say."

"What do *you* say?"

"It wasn't my call."

I didn't ask you that."

"I hold with Jake. Still do. The problem was that Jake did the humanitarian thing, but he did it for a beautiful divorcée who everyone figured he was sleeping with."

"So he lied."

"It's never that simple."

"It is where I work. I liked the guy, but he can't lie. NTSB fired him?"

"Suspended him. He then told them more or less to go fuck themselves. Then they fired him."

"And you defended him and quit your job."

"Not in so many words."

"I read this short story once…."

"Please, no more literature lessons."

"…about a kid who quit his job to impress a girl in a bathing suit. She never knew he did it. Didn't care."

"I wasn't wearing a bathing suit."

"Nor was that the point of the story."

She knew the point. I'm not sure if she regretted her rashness, but she understood the immaturity, maybe the misplaced loyalty. And yet, this Jake Moss, summarily dismissed and *persona non grata*, was somehow able to commandeer a plane and fly to DesMoines, no questions asked.

"He knows people," Kasi said. "The agency knows his skills—he's more or less on continuous retainer. Worldwide. That Malaysian jet liner that went down about five years ago and nobody ever found. I hear the Aussies had Jake on speed dial."

"Nobody uses speed dial anymore."

"Just an expression. Stop channeling Carmichael."

"Nobody channels anymore either," I said. I wouldn't say she smiled, but she didn't scowl, so that was good. I asked her if she thought maybe Jake should be here off the books.

"You mean now that we have a crash to investigate? I don't think so. This seems cut and dried—it may turn out to be a crime scene, in which case it's FBI. Until then, our powers are limited."

She paused.

"Our powers," she repeated. "I talk as if I'm still on some go-team. Did you know that the NTSB did not investigate 9/11 even though it involved planes?"

"Because it was a crime scene?"

"Exactly. Considering what's going on here with Ken Mullins's retirement and the possibility of threats against him—I doubt if your sister was the only one—this may be a crime scene too."

"Carmichael will let us know. Maybe he should be the one between jobs. I'm no expert, but that blow-up and then so calm—with all the talk about opioid addiction, should we say something? Especially the pills."

"That's just him," Kasi said. "Give him more time. He'll grow on you. Then you'll really hate him."

CHAPTER 13

Wesley Barrett, the only fatality in the Cessna crash, possessed a history filled with the intriguing and the doubtful, much of which we learned the next morning after a few hours of sleep. Although Barrett was been born in Indiana, he was well known in northern Connecticut—he told stories of time spent with David Koresh at Waco, including his narrow escape a day or two before the inferno. He also claimed to have warned the government in the summer of 2001 that a major terrorist attack was looming. Barrett had been taking some pilot training in Florida, thus giving his story a bit more credibility. But there's no record of his report having been given, heard, handled, or addressed. From most accounts, Barrett—well known in the area—was a harmless oddball. No arrests, though he'd been escorted out of a few restaurants and stores for activities that landed somewhere under the category of *general nuisance*, and a few of his political lawn signs had transcended good taste; still he'd managed to make a living, using his job in the town assessor's office to support his wife and teenage daughter, at least until they moved to Maine. He made his mortgage payments, drove a late-model compact, and acquired all the technological trappings that made someone a twenty-first century American. There was even a cellphone in the cockpit, its battery dead.

His flying lessons had not panned out, and he quit before he earned a license. After 9/11 his support of sketchy political groups waned, the result of ever more radical ideas entering the mainstream and rendering very little shocking anymore; cabals that once huddled in darkness now carried torches through the streets. If he lamented the shift in mores, he was grateful that his wilder ideas had never reached fruition.

His secrecy and reticence changed when he met Marty Hendricks. Whatever strictures Barrett had imposed on his own restless radicalism let loose under his new mentor—the tranche of papers Eveline had accumulated seemed to prove that.

Hendricks, Barrett, someone named Ben Palmer, and a few others met on a somewhat informal schedule to voice complaints about the government and society in general. There'd be an occasional letter to the editor and some screed on social media, but they never seemed particularly radical, nor that terribly interested in the airport or in Ken Mullins. In fact, their whining was so pedestrian that, rather than a movement, they more closely resembled a gang of malcontents lamenting the world on the strength of a few too many beers in a bar. My sister may have been part of it, but I think they frustrated her too. Several times she spoke of trying to get them back on topic—the crash at O'Hare and the subsequent government failures—but it appeared that the others were generally too drunk or stoned to be interested. She blamed Palmer, whom she called the "weed-eater," for the group's disarray.

"If he weren't smoking dope all the time, he'd be at least partly useful." Her words.

Devoid of any long-range goals, the group might just as easily have been a poker group or a gathering of quilters. As a band of revolutionaries, they fell far short.

*****

And so Kasi and I learned new names but little more as we plodded along through our inherited collection while Post-it notes flew, stuck, came loose, were slammed back down. Eventually we started to put together a theory—a theory that there was no theory—that my sister had made friends and acquaintances who were sympathetic to her situation, but nowhere near as dedicated as she was. Another disappointment.

Kasi decided that Ben Palmer was worth talking to. I wasn't so sure. "To what end?" I said.

She sat on the edge of the bed so as not to further disrupt anything.

"Not sure," she said. "But we don't want to become lethargic and impatient. A good investigator cannot afford to be either."

"Maybe I'm not a good investigator."

"Well I am. And you're my partner. Let's go see Ben Palmer. I'll give him a call."

And Carmichael?"

"We're visiting an old friend of your sister's. It's not an interview. Has nothing to do with him. Besides, he's probably bullshitting with the other agents—FBI and NTSB—at the crash site."

"He won't like it."

"Then he'll fire us. Come on, we're visiting.

Visiting?"

"I'm calling it a visit. I feel confined here, don't you?"

"You used to work in the field," I said. "I work in confinement every day."

"All the more reason for you to want out. Half hour. Meet you in the lobby." We had found a satellite photo of Ludlow Road in Suffield, one town over, and

Palmer's at the end of it. Even from 500 miles up, you could almost pick out the ruts on the unpaved street. Of course the trip demanded a car, which we lacked until I rented one, then sprung for delivery. I was hoping that Carmichael, maybe in a better mood, could finagle the Bureau into picking up the tab. Kasi laughed when I told her. I took that as a positive sign—that I'd be paying.

I sought out Carmichael— found him on the tarmac. It was off limits to me, but I had my cell and his number. He came over to the fence and I asked about the rental.

"Ride sharing, Danny boy, welcome to the new millennium. Looks like you'll have to bill your hotshot financial department in Chicago."

"So that's a no?"

"You know we're under a microscope these days—we can't even afford double-sided scotch tape any more. It's single-sided or nothing. And staples we have to push in by hand."

"And your shredder is a pair of scissors?"

"Not even a pair—one scissor. So you're on your own with this rental—or cancel it and use mine. I can add you as a driver."

"Probably better my way," I said. "I'll pay."

"What do you need a car for?"

"Friend of my sister's. We thought we'd let her know what happened."

"Danny boy, don't mean to be harsh, but everyone knew what happened except you. You're not lying to the FBI are you? That's sometimes frowned upon."

"Not really lying, but we found a name and didn't want to bother you—someone connected in some way to Barrett and Hendricks. Name's Palmer."

"That would be ol' Ben," he said. "The weed-eater. Good luck with that. Beware of airborne residue. If you find yourself with the munchies, don't say I didn't warn you."

"So I've heard. How do you know him?"

"He's on a list of people who have had problems with the airport, with Mullins, with authority in general. Palmer is pretty mellow, but be careful. If you feel the least bit uncomfortable, call me. Taking Kasi with you?"

"Of course."

"Tell her…tell her to be careful. Palmer has accumulated several warnings for discharging firearms, though never at people. I don't think he has many remaining friends in the animal kingdom. Not living anyway. Avoid bunny suits. And don't pass yourselves off as government agents."

"What did you want me to tell Kasi?"

"I just told you."

"You're sure there isn't more? You were a little tough on her last night."

"She's wasting her time. You can't fucking do that." He pointed at the wreckage and the swarm of people in white jump suits. "Look at them—not even eight hours since that plane went down and already there's a team here. Kasi should be with them. They don't even know her."

"How do you know?"

"I asked them—do you guys know Kasi Brennan? One woman thought maybe she'd heard the name. She's supposed to be this great investigator and they don't even know her."

"Fame is fleeting."

"Thank you, oh wise one. Go get high with Ben." He began to walk away. I stopped him.

"It's her choice, isn't it? To give up that job?"

"Absolutely. Enjoy the day."

"Maybe she had a good reason."

"Am I arguing? You're right. She's right. She has every right to retire and sit on her ass all day."

"Everyone needs some time to think, to reconsider."

"God, you are hopeless. Don't call me again or I'll block your number."

I let him go. For that day, it appeared, Kasi and I were on our own. A short time later we rode off in search of god-knows-what in a cramped, but marvelously cheap, rental. Kasi called it frugal—a very kind assessment. It had all the comfort of a motorcycle sidecar.

I mentioned to Kasi my earlier conversation with Carmichael. She wasn't surprised that nobody on the go-team recognized her. A big organization and all that—hard to keep track of everyone. She was dismissive for whatever reason. I didn't bring it up again.

A few words about the town of Suffield: it's big. And it's old. I guess that's two words. Like a lot of big old towns that predate the American Revolution, there's a historic section showcasing Georgian and colonial mansions. Old money. Picturesque. Opulent. Beyond that, obscure country roads hide massive contemporary estates on five-hundred-acre lots, many of which were, at one time, working farms. Athletes, producers, financiers, actors, writers—a tourist with sufficient tenacity could find them all, along with the showplaces where they live—enclaves for those who make their fortunes in New York City and need a place to spend it in hiding. A tree-shaded Main Street punctuated by a renowned academy add definition and appeal, but like all towns everywhere, even the pretty New England villages, there's always that section beyond the visitor's milieu. Fifty yards on Ludlow Road was enough to tell us that Benjamin Palmer would not have been a destination on any celebrity tour.

There hardly seemed a need for the mile-long road at all. A house or two on the left near the turnoff, then nothing for at least half a mile, then what looked as though it might have once been a working farm on the left, then more emptiness until three structures, a farmhouse and barn on the left and then, a hundred yards beyond them on the other side, Palmer's place.

The bungalow, like several other single-story homes on the street, hinted of *1919* more than 2019. Constructed well before the heyday of developments, well before Levittown forever changed the face of the American suburb, the house had survived mainly through cosmetic repairs. It was vinyl-sided in an innocuous beige, but what had preceded that was probably a history of paint, more paint, aluminum siding, etc. Generations of owners had cared for it, but even so, something about it sagged like an old horse ridden too long and too often.

We pulled in behind a battered Chevrolet pick-up which, even with my limited knowledge of body styles and auto chronology, I figured was forty-odd years old. A large black and brown dog of a mixed and indeterminate breed lounged nearby, untethered. It stood up when we pulled in, barked once, but made no movements threatening or otherwise. As soon as I turned off the car we heard a voice from behind a closed, wood-frame screen door.

"It's a seventy-two short bed—almost two hundred thousand miles on the son of a bitch."

"I assume he doesn't mean the dog," Kasi said. She was more comfortable without Carmichael.

"I heard that," the man said. "Some watch dog, huh? As soon as I watch him, he barks."

And so we met Ben Palmer—barefoot and white-haired, wearing jeans and a stained, yellowing plain white t-shirt. He shielded his eyes from the sun, then took a step or two toward us as the dog, showing a tad more interest, barked again. Palmer ignored it.

"'Course that truck runs like shit now, but that's because I don't drive much and quit takin' care of it. I'm Ben Palmer. You're Kasi with a K, the one I talked to on the phone. I knew a Cassie with a C back in high school. Cute girl. Married some hot shot from Albany who came through here with his parents every summer and stayed at one of the lakes up in the hills. Only one of those lakes left now. Missed my chance with her."

He took a breath, then made another stride away from the house. "And you're Daniel, right? Good Biblical name. You Jewish?"

"Not much of any religion these days."

Palmer shook his head. "Welcome to the club. Wanna come in?"

He shifted his ponytail from one shoulder to the other, like a tassel on graduation day, then ushered us inside. By contrast to an exterior that seemed held together by spit, the inside was spotless; and it didn't look as though Palmer had gone around picking up just for company.

"We can sit in the living room," he said, "but it's more comfortable in the kitchen. How about some coffee?"

I begged off, but Kasi accepted the offer and Palmer went to work.

"People grind their own beans—think that's special. I *roast* my own. Bought a roaster at a tag sale up in Pittsfield a few years ago. Love the smell of coffee— it's like an air-freshener, isn't it?"

"What air are you trying to freshen?" she said.

"Oh, I get it. That 'former NTSB' story, the 'friend from Chicago.' You're both locals, looking to bust me for weed. Or shooting rabbits again? Well you're welcome to look."

"Whoa, wait," I said, and I managed to keep from laughing. "I don't care what you smoke. As for the rabbits, that's between you and them."

"Yeah, well, I've got a little reputation."

"That's your business," I said. I felt like an idiot—the house reeked of marijuana. Growing up I'd had friends whose parents smoked regular cigarettes. Eventually the odor permeated everything—even the walls. I had the feeling Palmer's place was suffering the same fate, but I repeated my assurance.

"Grind the beans—believe me, we're not here to give you a hard time."

"Good, good. Already brewed. Just tryin' to keep these old bones active."

He wasn't really much older than I was (an Internet site indicated he was 50-55) but he did look old, with that white hair and the roughened face of a cattle rancher or lumberjack, and even a little bend to his posture, though. He reached for some cups on an open shelf near the stove and filled each of them from a stainless steel percolator on the stove, then opened the refrigerator and extracted an armful of cartons.

"I got half-and-half, I got 1%, I got regular. You want to mix 'em and get some other fractions, you go on ahead."

He had ignored my turning down the coffee, but I didn't think pointing that out to him would have any major effect—no more than my drinking it.

We all know a Ben Palmer. Crusty, quirky, obnoxious, but weirdly appealing. A thousand people would harbor a thousand different opinions, but more than anything he was adaptable. Living alone like this practically off the grid, but still able to retain some social skills, he was a lot more gracious than he might have been with two strangers barging in.

"Mr. Palmer "

"Please, it's Ben, or Palmer, or Benjamin. I ain't a professor."

"OK, Ben, you know why we're here."

"That I do—heard about the crash. Poor Wes, never quite got things right, outside his head or in."

"So you're not surprised."

"Feel bad. I mean if anyone was going to steal a plane and crash it, I'd have figured that for someone else."

I asked him if he meant Marty Hendricks.

"Now you're talking," he said. "Crazy son of a bitch, all pissed off at everything. Always whining how people let him down, his country let him down, you name it. Everyone failed him."

"There was that MIA," Kasi said.

"You know, you gotta let things go. Jesus H, we're talking about something that happened fifty years ago. There are people who don't even make it to the age of fifty.

I agreed—it wasn't the time to mention my sister's crusade.

"Hated Clinton," he said, "tolerated Obama, don't have to tell you who the asshole voted for last time. Like I said, pissed off at everything."

He took a breath.

"Sorry for the tirade, but people don't change. Not really. He'll be fucked up forever."

He glanced at Kasi. "Sorry, little lady. Old habits..."

"I'm not that little."

"Uh oh," Palmer said. "Like I said, old habits."

"They can always be unlearned."

"Teachable moment, huh? Understood, Cassandra. You know who Cassandra was, don't you?"

Kasi nodded. "Told the future but no one listened."

"It was quite a curse. It all wound up bad because she wouldn't sleep with that Apollo guy. Never is any sense in being that choosy. I'd have done it—I mean if he was a woman. Wouldn't you?"

"I have no gift of prophecy," she said. "I don't think he'd be interested."

"Don't sell yourself short, hon...."

He stopped himself with "honey" almost off his tongue and suppressed a sheepish grin.

"Another teachable moment," he said, "Busy day for me."

He scattered some paper napkins on the table, and just when I had determined not to mention Hendricks again, he sat down and took another deliberate calming breath.

"Feel bad about Wes," he said, "but if you want to talk about Hendricks. I got plenty to say."

CHAPTER 14

Marty Hendricks, according to Palmer, was a loud, overbearing, basically ineffectual malcontent who, despite his obsessions, could always be distracted or dissuaded by Palmer's newest crop of weed.

"He'd lost an uncle in Vietnam," Palmer said, and when we told him we knew that, he asked us if we remembered the Unabomber.

"Kaczynski," I said.

"Ted. Marty thought of him as some kind of hero."

"And you?"

"I don't think he thought of me as a hero."

"Let me rephrase that," I said, but I didn't have to.

"Just trying to inject a little humor," Palmer said. "No, Kaczynski was a murderer, pure and simple. You can paint him anyway you want to; a sociopath is still a sociopath. Now Marty, he wasn't that bad. Talked a lot of anarchy but never went for the big kill."

Kasi took a notebook out of her handbag. Palmer noticed.

"I don't want to be quoted," he said. He seemed a little uncomfortable with the possibility. Kasi said she'd put it away if he insisted, but that she just liked to write down a word now and then, just to jog her memory later. He seemed amenable to that.

"I ain't so much afraid of Marty, but I'm never sure what he's going to do. A few years back, right around Thanksgiving, Marty came by with plans for bomb-making and said he wanted to blow up something. With Kaczynski in jail, I guess he thought it was too quiet out there. And Christmas was always a cause celebre."

"Too commercial?" I asked. "Put the Christ back in Christmas?"

"Now that would be a common attempt. Marty's not common. He was gonna blow up the crèche over by the Methodist church."

"So," Kasi said, "take the Christ *out* of Christmas?"

"More or less *blow* the Christ out of Christmas. I kind of talked him down, but someone stole one of the sheep one night. I'm sure he was the thief."

"Not a live...."

"Wood. Primitive. Logs and sticks."

"That Unabomber stuff," Kasi said, "did Hendricks actually build any bombs?"

Palmer took a deep breath. "Well, the short answer is no. The long one is...well...I mean he was my friend and he spouted off about lots of shit, but he wasn't real bright. Is that a good enough answer?"

"It'll do," I said.

"But I would be remiss," he said, and smiled, "he did get involved with the idiot twins. The Thoricks. Know them?"

We didn't. Palmer did.

They were Rudy and Rachel. Married. Not twins. And we did know them in a way, since they had been Hendricks' mentors or accomplices or whatever designation they deserve in the aborted Statue of Liberty plot when the bombers went to jail and Hendricks got off. The Thoricks were the bombers.

"I call them the idiot twins," Palmer said, "because Rudy was lurching around the ferry from Battery Park like an escaped convict. He couldn't have called more attention to himself. Of course, back before 9/11 things like that happened all the time."

"Where are the...twins now?" Jake asked.

"Served some time, moved out west somewhere. My wife used to say if she died before I did, I should make a play for Rachel. Beautiful woman."

"For an anarchist," Kasi said.

"Of course," Palmer admitted, "but I've always tried to overlook minor faults in attractive women. Still, surprising how little interest I have in looking her up. I'm digressing, right? I tend to do that."

"A little," Kasi said. "You live here alone?"

"That hurts," he said.

"I didn't mean..." she said, but he interrupted her. "Lives alone, talks to himself, I get it."

"I just mean you mentioned your wife. Are you still married?"

"Sandy's been dead eleven years—eleven last month. She was thirty-five. I was older than her by a few years. That's somethin', huh? Thirty-five? You figure you're halfway through your life at worst. Then it ends."

Cancer, I thought, Eveline's death foremost in my mind. I was wrong. "Accident," Palmer said. "Drunk driver slammed into her right at the end of this street. She was turning left across the lane, he came up behind her, tried to pass her on the right. Going way too fast, no room to get by, clipped Sandy's car, spun it into a tree. There was a fire that she could have escaped but they say she was stunned, knocked out. Smoke got her."

"My God," Kasi said, her voice tinged with anger as much as sympathy. I was sure that from a law enforcement point of view, this was no accident. It was murder.

"August," Palmer continued. "Hotter than hell that day. And where was I? Sitting right here with the A/C blasting. I heard the sirens—never gave it a thought until I started thinking where the hell is Sandy? Damnedest thing, I mean who gets killed on their own street in the middle of the day?"

"Tell me they got the guy," Kasi said.

"He, as they say, remained at the scene—until the rescue team cut him out of the vehicle. He'd been late for some appointment. It would have taken five seconds for him to wait until the car was out of his way. Five seconds. He wound up with a short jail sentence, a fine, and a license suspension. Not bad for killing somebody, huh? Most days I wish he'd a killed me 'stead of Sandy. She was a good lady."

"I know it happened a while ago," Kasi said, "but I'm—we're sorry for your loss."

"Tell ya', that time the cops were on my side, weed or no weed. They were so pissed off at the sentencing, they threatened to stop setting up check points, doing breath analysis, everything except what they were absolutely required to do until that bleeding heart of a judge was replaced."

"Was he?"

"Transferred. Small victory. The sentence stood. The driver lives in town. Got a wife and a couple of kids. Maybe he's reformed, volunteering in a soup kitchen or running clothes drives for the Salvation Army—whatever it is you do to atone for killing somebody. Or maybe he's forgotten. I've seen him. I look the other way. I used to read the obits, hoping he was dead. What would that prove? Sandy's not coming back so I just muddle along. Now, since we're confessing, what are you two doing?"

"I told you, we're just looking into some threats at Bradley."

"You're a civilian, Mr. Blaine. And Ms. Brennan here don't work for the NTSB anymore—funny the stuff you can find out with a phone call or a laptop or both.

Don't get all embarrassed—I got no problem with it, especially since cause I enjoy talking to people, but…what the fuck? And what the fuck happened at Bradley last night with that small plane?"

"That we don't know yet," Kasi said. "As for the rest, well," and she looked at me, "tell him why you're here."

And so I began…again…the story that began and ended with Eveline.

The story of my sister and me had been mine for so long—shared with no one but Bethany—that I probably never realized how offensive it all was, and that I was the chief offender. The more I verbalized how I'd cast aside my only sibling for twenty years, the less I looked like the hero of the piece, or even the justifiably estranged party. With Palmer I could sense the empathy gradually fading, but I pushed on and included everything except her death—I didn't want this to look like a murder investigation. As soon as I finished, though, he took some rolling papers from a kitchen drawer. I guess he was sure neither of us possessed any legal authority.

"Now I ain't offerin'," he said, "but you know, I want to be a good host."

"We're not here to entrap anyone, Ben, or to get high."

"Okay then, I knew your sister. I knew Eveline. Saw her not that long ago."

"Where?"

"Right here. Right where you're sitting. She was with Hendricks, chasing down some lead he'd discovered. In truth he was in the purchasing mood that day."

"And you were selling."

"I was."

He placed a small plastic bag on the table. "You two sure? I got plenty."

"We're good," Kasi said.

"Maybe you are," he said to her, then turned to me. "You and your sister—you ought to put an end to that whatever—feud—before it's too late."

There was no sense keeping the last bit of information from him. "She died," I said, "a few weeks back."

"Knew that," Palmer said, "figured you did but I wasn't going to be the one to tell you. High as I always am, I'm not unconscious or ignorant."

"Guess she'd been sick for a while."

"Off and on, remission and relapse. Chrissake, we have all these medical breakthroughs and then…I'm sorry, man, really. I gotta, you know…."

He pulled a lighter out of his pocket and, within seconds, I was at one of those concerts from my youth, trying to breathe. Palmer didn't notice my discomfort, though he made an effort to blow the smoke downwind…if there is such a thing indoors.

"Daniel, this is going to sound disrespectful, but…."

"You were smitten. Apparently everyone was. 'Cept me."

"Brothers and sisters—great when they get along," he said, holding the joint up to us. Again we declined.

"I know we're not official here," Kasi said, "so you can just tell us to get out."

"I could," Palmer said, "what's the question coming after that condition, 'cause I know there is one."

"Another name," Kasi said. "Devin Walsh. Know him?" He paused for a moment.

"Well, here's the thing," Palmer said. "I mean with Eveline being your sister and all."

"You can speak freely."

"I don't know, Daniel. You hear things, and these days when everything is bullshit. I don't know."

The weed had not reduced his discomfort level by very much, but Kasi apparently saw a way out.

"I'll try some of that homegrown," she said, "if you can stand an honest review."

"I always guarantee my product," he said, and passed the joint to Kasi. A few hits later she gave him a thumbs up.

"I can post a Yelp review."

"Be sure to mention it's organic" Palmer said. "I suppose you still want to hear about Walsh. All I know is there was some connection between him and Eveline. I don't know if it was romantic."

"Jesus," I said, "how many men…."

Kasi didn't let me finish. "That's not a question you need answered, is it? And if you did, even though it's none of your business, you might have asked *before* she died."

Palmer took a few hits in rapid succession, but it did a poor job of filling the silence. He offered the joint to Kasi, but she turned it down with a word. Walsh.

"He lives north of here," Palmer said, "over the state line in Massachusetts, not

far from Springfield. As for your sister, I don't know what kind of deal they had."

"Deal?" I said. "This Walsh guy wasn't a drug dealer, was he?"

"You mean like me?"

"I mean opioids, shit like that."

That didn't sit well with Kasi either. "Your sister? Really Daniel? That's what you think?"

"She wasn't good at keeping a job. She wasn't sitting in on any executive boards anywhere, that's for sure."

"Yeah," Kasi said, "and she had a life. She probably shopped and cooked meals, maybe read books, played some golf, had coffee with friends; maybe Lon worked his job all day and came home at night and they had dinner, or fought over money, or watched a movie. Maybe they had a normal life."

"A few miles from the airport," I said. "Not that normal."

Palmer shook his head. "You two want me to leave? You seem to be answering the questions just fine on your own."

"No, no. Sorry," I said.

"You have a difference of opinion. I wish I could help you. Daniel, I didn't know your sister very well. I liked her. Is that why you came here?"

"No."

"See, if you lived around here like she did," Palmer said, then without finishing the thought, stood up and took a somewhat beat-up pamphlet from a pile of mail and gave it to me.

"Don't have to read it all unless you really have nothing to do for the next two hours. It's a prospectus for a new road system, better access to the airport and an impact study of surrounding areas. What it says is there'll be nice new roads in Suffield. What it means is we'll pay more and have more traffic, and the nice areas in town will stay the same. That's what Mullins told us using different words. You know Ken Mullins?"

"What about Walsh?"

"Getting to that. Mullins. The Bradley CEO? Know him?"

"He's on our list."

"Not your shit list, I hope," Palmer said. "The Golden Boy of Bradley doesn't like to be on anyone's shit list."

"Is he on yours?" I asked.

"I know people who don't like him. Keep saying he's to blame for everything that goes wrong around here from too many mosquitos to bear attacks. I always thought he was a typical arrogant CEO, just trying to make a name for himself, build a legacy, get a jetport named after him, you know. Bradley or Mullins. National or Reagan. Change the name it's the same place."

"And you," I said again. "What do you think?"

"Not going to affect me much, but there's plenty of anger. This is all about getting more passengers here. No need to expand—airlines are using smaller planes so the runways are fine. But there's the matter of taxes. We needed a mid-term re-val to adjust property assessments and balance them off with surrounding towns. I like that word adjust—it means pay more and get less. Nobody got too pissed because towns usually drop the mill rate accordingly when they reevaluate your property."

"They didn't this time?" Kasi asked.

"Not so's you'd notice. We were gettin' screwed more ways than a double-jointed whore. So we wrote letters, not just to the local rag, to the Hartford papers too, even the *New York Times*—so many New Yorkers in the area. 'Course they were the rich ones—no planes buzzing their mansions or creating traffic problems for their limo drivers. As it got closer to the assessment, Marty and I and a few others called some informal town meetings, some of them right where you're sitting. Hell, we handed out pamphlets, made speeches, issued statements, threatened to get the Feds involved. Nothing came of it."

"I can sympathize," Kasi said. "I've seen the government at work up close. Better to have diminished expectations."

"We learned that fast," Palmer said. "At the formal town meeting, Mullins came dressed up in his New York suit and his Italian shoes, or maybe the other way around. The town voted yes; then we learned that increased air traffic meant increased vehicular traffic too."

"And road improvement."

"Damn right," Palmer said, his hands moving more rapidly. "There's a route you'd take if you were coming from Albany and you wanted to fly out of Bradley. It don't even go through town, but we got stuck paying for improving it."

"Not to point out the obvious, but why wouldn't someone just fly out of Albany?"

"Live halfway between, or want a bigger airport with more options, you'll choose the new Bradley. Want to fly direct to Dallas? Atlanta? Salt Lake? Frisco? You choose Bradley. Albany's limited; we're not. And if you had a choice of driving down I-87 and over the bridges to the New York airports, fighting the parking at Logan, or coming to friendly Bradley, well that's the selling job we got."

"We?"

"Love it or hate it, it's ours. It also occurs to me that, somewhere during that tirade, I said something off-color about a double-jointed whore. Like I said, I live alone now—don't have a template to follow anymore."

"No worries," Kasi said. "And I hate to keep harping, but Devin Walsh?"

"Oh yeah, Walsh. A bit of a celebrity in his own right. But different from Mullins. Mullins didn't murder his wife. At least I don't think he did. Haven't seen the news today so I can't be sure."

"You're serious," I said.

"You look shocked," Palmer said. "Men kill their wives all the time. If a woman is ever murdered, her husband did it. If you want to pass yourselves off as fake investigators, you need to learn the basics."

He laid the joint down on a makeshift ashtray, and stood up. "Hang on," he said. "I'll get the book."

CHAPTER 15

The book, a thin and dismal paperback, purported to tell—according to the cover—a tragic story of young love. I always thought Shakespeare had covered that pretty well by way of some judicious poisonings and a lot of really bad timing, but apparently the story of the Walshes would outdo even *Romeo and Juliet*.

"There was a buck to be made," Palmer said, laying the book on the table. "It's got love, loss, death, pathos, regret, even atonement. What it doesn't have is an indictment and an arrest warrant for Devin Walsh."

"So there's even a villain?" Kasi asked.

"Not officially" Palmer said, though he qualified the statement instantly. "The story is clean, it's Walsh who's dirty."

Benjamin Palmer was an odd combination; he pulled no punches in one instance, then he was all undercurrents and innuendo at another, especially with Devin Walsh. Living alone like this, not technically off the grid but isolated in other ways, had left him with an air of casualness that permitted him to say what he wanted, when he wanted. Declaring him a social misfit would have been unkind, but arguable. There remained, however, some consciousness of conventions—he proved that when he took another hit, then stared through the smoke.

"Not a good host," he said, waving an arm through the haze. "People these days have all kinds of allergies. If this all bothers you, we can sit on the porch. I don't have that many visitors who don't, you know…."

"Imbibe?" I said.

"Yeah. Imbibe."

"We're okay here," Kasi said. "Go on."

"Okay," he said. "So where was I?"

We waited. He knew exactly where he was.

Devin Walsh and his wife Mollie—Palmer needed no book for reference—had been a typical young married couple only inasmuch as they were young and married. They had no nest egg to amass, no golden days to strive for. They had already achieved both. Walsh had been a wiz in high school and even a better one at MIT where he zipped through the School of Engineering accumulating accolades and honors almost as quickly as job offers. He'd been pre-hired by an outfit in Georgia—Savannah River Technologies—at the end of his sophomore year, and though he always remained motivated, the obsession with academics waned toward the end and the highest honors at graduation eluded him. It hardly mattered: the promised and agreed upon compensation that awaited him far surpassed that of any of his classmates, and if he had to trade a valedictory speech for a seven-figure starting salary, he was happy to make the *sacrifice*.

"Dream job," Palmer said. "I'll show you."

He opened his laptop and Googled Savannah River Tech. Before us sprang a slick and visually appealing web site, exactly what one would expect from a self-proclaimed cutting edge Silicon Valley company transplanted to the burgeoning South. We lingered for a moment on the CEO page—not a tie or sports jacket in sight—then linked to some photos of buildings on Northeast Campus—SRT's name for the multi-acre complex of four four-story boxes sitting amid beautifully manicured grounds encircling a bench-filled, tree-lined quadrangle—red maples and hickories in fall splendor. A bike trail, some tennis courts, a scattering of picnic tables—if it had been a university, I'd have considered returning to school.

"Makes you want to vacation there, don't it?" Palmer asked, then clicked to another page that featured workers in white coveralls inside a massive clean room. On another a Learjet with company markings climbed skyward off the top of the page. Jake Moss had laughed when I asked if his crew owned their Learjet. No one in Savannah was laughing.

I skimmed the self-promotional blurb, one which basically said I owe my cellphone, my laptop, airport security, and most all my belongings to the whiz-bang phenoms at SRT. The claim would have been hard to dispute. The very first page informed me as to how indebted I really was.

Comprising the most brilliant minds in digital, cellular, wireless, and cloud technology since 1985, SRT remains at the forefront of the rapidly developing fields of communication and security. And government contracts extending decades into the future indicate even greater accomplishments ahead....

"Science and technology," Kasi said. "That's all that ever matters."

"What was your major?" I asked.

"Double. Philosophy and English."

"No, seriously."

"See that's what I mean," she said. "If you can't make money, it's not worth doing."

"Some things never change," Palmer said. "Want to see more?"

"I'd like to *hear* more," I said. "How did this dream job turn into a home in Connecticut?"

"Massachusetts actually, just over the state line. But here's where it all gets a little sticky," Palmer said. "You'll have to pick and choose the story you like."

"It's not on the website?" I said.

"No, the simple truth is they transferred him to Boston, then let him work offsite."

"Work from home."

"They were afraid if he took a job with someone else, he'd let every SRT cat out of the bag."

"That doesn't tell me why they let him go…or let him move."

"Nobody knows. There was rumor floating around that he was selling tech to the Russians, then the Chinese, then ISIS, then some far right locals. I think the bosses in Savannah were afraid he'd take his brain to another company, so they bought him out, got him to sign a non-disclosure agreement, and figured paying him a million or so a year was better than watching their best tech wind up with someone else.

"And his wife?"

"Mollie. She was some kind of designer," Palmer said, then Kasi interrupted. "Visual designer, worked from home, very much in demand—says so on the back cover. They had it made."

"Not according to Hendricks," Palmer said. "They were buddies, he and Devin, as you know…which takes me back to your sister. Are we okay going back there?"

"I told you," I said. "Tell me what you know."

Palmer looked like someone who had, in drunken bravado, signed up for skydiving and then realized it involved jumping out of a plane.

"I'm just not comfortable, you know, speaking ill of the dead, and she's your sister and all."

"Mr. Palmer…Ben…Kasi and I have traveled some distance. We're not going to make this our life's work so we need to learn fast. You're probably going to tell me things I didn't know, but since I really didn't know much of anything…start with Walsh being married. That's a good spot, right?"

"Sure," Palmer said.

"So Hendricks was infatuated with my sister and Walsh joined in."

"Yes, but it's more than that. Hendricks saw Walsh as a source."

"Of what?"

"If you look at that Savannah website, you'll see that the company is involved with weapons."

"That sounds like Hendricks. For that matter, we saw a picture of him at some gun show. But if he wants weapons, in this country can't he pretty much stroll into any gun shop and buy something?"

"Pardon the pun, but Marty aimed a little higher: grenade launchers, machine guns, mortars, missiles, items beyond the usual gun store inventory."

"Missiles? Seriously?"

"Goddam stealth bomber if he could get one," Palmer said, "but I think he understood his limits. Preparing for war requires certain compromises. Anyway deals were made."

"What kind of deals?"

"Deals. Devin Walsh got to meet your sister, and Marty Hendricks began plotting his next act of sabotage."

"Another manger?"

"We don't question Hendricks, not after all this time."

"But my sister—I know I keep saying she's a stranger to me—but she's my sister. Stubborn and focused and I guess obsessive, but not violent. Not someone who wants to blow things up. What could Walsh have offered her?"

"That I don't know," Palmer said. "The thing with Walsh, his genius covers a lot of ground. Coming up with some sophisticated explosive device and attaching it to a drone would be child's play. Now what Hendricks planned to do with it, well I don't know, maybe like you said, blow up another manger…."

"Can we just back up for a minute?" I said. "When Eveline and Walsh met, he was married?"

"You mean was his wife still alive? Yes. I think your sister knew him for a while before, you know, anything happened."

"What did happen, I mean with his wife. You said he murdered her."

"Opinion. Papers said different. Tragic story. Heartbreaking."

"Is the story online?"

"Everything is online, but I'll save you the trouble. Hang on."

He walked into an adjoining room and came out with a pile of newspapers. "Devin and Mollie—the late Mollie—were big for a week or two. Here," he said, handing a paper to Kasi.

She skimmed the page quickly. "No mention of foul play that I can see."

"Like I said, tragic story, heartbreaking. And of course," Ben added, "she was pregnant, so that made it all a little worse."

Kasi didn't like that; neither did I. Palmer, for whatever distance he had placed between himself and reality, was not so unaware that he didn't realize it.

"I'm skeptical," he said, "but I'm not cruel. It was bad. But listen, both of you, this is just me talking, right? I mean no one's been arrested or anything and I'm not accusing anyone. I probably shouldn't be saying anything."

"We're not reporters," Kasi said. "You're not going to read your comments in the paper."

"Yeah," Palmer said, "but things have a way of getting out."

His fear of Hendricks was palpable. Or maybe it was Walsh. Still, Palmer had talked about shooting rabbits, so we knew he had a gun to provide some protection. And there was the dog, though the somewhat lethargic animal seemed well past the age where it would be a deterrent.

"Tell you what," I said. "Just give us the party line on those two. If there's more to it, we'll dig it up on our own."

"I ain't gonna color anything," Palmer said. He held up the plastic bag. "Mind if I…?"

"We'll be gone in two minutes," Kasi said. "Can you wait?"

"For you my dear, yes. Where was I?"

"Mollie was pregnant."

"Right, so Devin was going to take her on a second honeymoon. South America. For her it was going back—she had been there before for some reason, college I guess."

"Where in South America?"

"Brazil, but not like Rio. You know, the woods."

"The jungles?"

"That's the word. Anyway, the story goes she got sick along the way somewhere out on some godforsaken river nobody ever heard of...."

"Paraná," Kasi said. "It's in the article."

"Oh yeah. I always wondered if there were piranha in the Paraná. I should Google that, huh?"

We waited.

"Maybe another time. So anyway, very sick. By the time they got her to a doctor it was too late. The rest of it is mostly human interest. I don't mean to sound...."

Kasi suggested *callous* as a possibility. She was growing weary of Palmer's constant straying from the story, his asides, his general aloofness. Palmer may have been high, but he was aware of Kasi's criticism.

"You think I'm callous," he said. "Maybe. Maybe I still see everything through the same lens. Maybe it's distorted. Maybe my sad story is sadder than his—maybe waiting for your wife to come home and finding her dead at the end of your street because some drunk couldn't wait five seconds to get wherever the fuck he was going—maybe that's just as sad. I ain't selling my story to the papers or waiting for a novel just to show the world I'm some kind of victim. It takes a special kind of creep...."

He took a deep breath, exhaled loudly, pointed to the residue in the ashtray. "You're supposed to smoke this shit to feel better," he said. "My bad." Kasi leaned over and put a hand on his arm.

"I didn't mean that you were insensitive. I can't imagine what you must have gone through," she said. "And the last thing we want to do is make it worse."

"Pretty good at doing that without your help," he said, and gently pulled his arm away.

He told us to keep the newspaper—he said he had a few more copies. I wanted to tell him to throw them out, that they were not helping. But he'd have to arrive at that conclusion himself.

Devin Walsh was everything that Ben Palmer despised in a husband—in a man—full of the same carelessness and recklessness—the same egoism that causes a driver to risk someone's life to save a few seconds. Devin Walsh had not killed Ben's wife, but the same attitude was at play. And Walsh had not even endured a trial for what he may have done; instead he came away from it all as a sympathetic victim with his life intact, not even encumbered by the child to whom he would have been the father. If that's mean-spirited on my part, I'll own up to it; but people like Walsh, even from Palmer's incomplete description, can't abide the idea of their lives being interrupted by children.

I remembered a past conversation with Bethany. Self-awareness, she said, kept us all from becoming monsters. I told her that was a little harsh, but she insisted there were times in our lives—in everybody's life—when we make a crucial choice, and we can make the right one only if we know ourselves. Conscience, I said, but she thought that was simplistic. I wondered what she would she say about Devin Walsh. Did he look in the mirror and see a victimized widower, or did he see the same amoral bastard that Palmer did?

When I was a child my aunt the wordsmith once told me that truly good people see their own peccadillos—one of many pieces of advice that sent me straight to the dictionary. I like to think I know mine…which I don't feel I have to share with the world. But I think I was better able, maybe more willing, to recognize Eveline's faults than my own; and maybe that *was* my peccadillo. Maybe my worst. Usually my self-motivational speeches involve Bethany and how I should move on. I wonder what Devin Walsh's are like, or if he thinks he needs them.

CHAPTER 16

No sooner had we pulled back onto the rutted street when Kasi repeated Palmer's reference to Walsh—just over the state line. I'd been thinking the same thing—while we were out visiting anyway. We grabbed some lunch at a diner off I-91, performed a few basic Internet searches, and wound up with his street and a picture of his house, a large colonial with an attached two-car garage. I was new to Connecticut, didn't realize that Suffield abuts Massachusetts and that Palmer's statement that Walsh lived "over the line" wasn't nearly so far away as we thought.

We were within a block or two when Kasi reiterated what we already knew, that this was the kind of thing that Carmichael should handle.

"It's really within his bailiwick," she said

"Bailiwick? There's an English/philosophy major word."

"Don't change the subject. Visiting this guy won't be easy for you either."

"I'm counting on you to run interference."

"You keep forgetting, I knew your sister too. Maybe not that well, but if this guy is as big a jerk as Palmer says, it won't be easy for me either"

"Maybe we can try the good cop-bad cop approach."

"Good one, if we were cops. If Palmer saw through us…maybe we shouldn't…."

"No," I insisted. "We can do this."

"Not if it's atonement," she said.

"Of course not," I said, but it was, or at least it was part of a hopeless jumble of other emotions. There was guilt, of course—siblings should treat each other better than we had…than I had. And nothing goes with guilt better than regret. Except maybe self-loathing. That fact—that I was disgusted with myself—assured me that I could handle a conversation with Walsh. At the very least I could be the big brother standing up for his little sister, who this time was seven years his senior. I think Kasi got all that, but she was sensitive to my ambivalence.

"Here's the thing," she said. "I don't want to be waiting for the EMTs to arrive after you lose control and wind up with your shoe on his throat."

"That's not me. We can do this."

"I'd feel better if we were, you know, people with credentials."

"We're credentialed," I said. "I'm the brother of a woman who knew a man who knew a man who failed to crash his plane into a terminal. And you *used to be* NTSB. We're like high-rollers in Vegas with Monopoly money—eventually the nice security guard is going to ask us to get our asses out the door, but until then…"

"We can keep placing bets."

"I guess."

The always unflappable GPS lady ignored our crisis of conscience and guided us to Vance Drive and told us we had arrived at our destination, a statement that always rang of foreboding.

"Pull into the driveway," Kasi said. "I'll park in the street."

"Driveway. It's more officious. More annoying."

"Is this from the NTSB playbook?"

"The Kasi Brennan addendum, especially when the person you want to annoy is right there."

And he was, not far from the low-slung black sports car that contradicted the middle class ambience that he seemed to have carefully nurtured—beautiful landscaping, modest and tasteful statuary, even an autumn-hued floral design on the front door, all corn stalks and berries in orange, brown, and maize. At first I thought—he must have a new girlfriend—and in the same instant I thought Eveline picked that out, and he didn't have enough consideration to take it down. Kasi had been right—I was already angry.

Walsh himself, in maroon running shorts and a long-sleeved navy t-shirt, was raking a flowerbed—probably one of those change-of-seasons jobs a homeowner squeezes in before the leaves cover everything.

He stopped when we pulled into the driveway, leaning on the rake and wiping his forehead with his sleeve.

"He thinks we're selling something," Kasi said as she unbuckled her seatbelt.

"No he doesn't," I said. There was something about his expression. "He knows who I am."

I never knew my father of course, and any memories of my mother are so vague and thin as to be totally unreliable, but there were plenty of pictures of me…of Eveline, of our parents. Eveline favored our mother—light complexioned, almost blonde, with features that some would call striking but less polite observers would consider stark, rawboned, harsh. Not exactly *American Gothic*, but leaning toward

Wyeth. I, on the other hand, had all my father's classic good looks. I say that ironically because I heard it uttered a few too many times to take it seriously. I have not engendered a lot of swooning, not in my awkward teenage years and certainly not in my equally awkward adult ones. When I think of classic good looks, I think of George Clooney. It's unlikely he'd use me as his example.

But though Eveline and I didn't look much alike, we had both acquired a few common features—the angular nose (*pointy* would also work), and eyes that seemed less deep-set than they should have been, as if the slightest movement might jar them out of their sockets. As children we were asked several times by people first meeting us, if we were brother and sister.

Devin Walsh made the connection even from a distance, ruining my plan to spring it on him, gauge his reaction, let him wonder if I'd come for revenge like some mafia consigliere tasked with the job of reclaiming his sister's honor.

"You talk," I whispered to Kasi. But before we could get close enough for polite conversation, Walsh shouted at us across the lawn, his voice not antagonistic but far from cordial.

"Is there something I can do for you?"

"If you're Devin Walsh, yes." Kasi's voice was calm and even. I was impressed. "And who are you?"

"I'm Kasi Brennan. National Transportation Safety Board. We're tying up some loose ends on the Bradley incident."

"What Bradley incident was that?"

"A small plane crashed, flipped. The pilot died."

"Oh yeah, I heard that on the news," he said, then looked at me. "You said we. Is this your partner?"

"Yes," Kasi said. It wasn't exactly a lie, but it didn't brush up against much truth either. I couldn't let it go.

"I'm not NTSB," I said.

"I know that. You're Daniel Blaine if I'm not mistaken. My sympathies."

"So you know Eveline died."

"Of course I know. I visited her in the hospital."

"Even when her husband was there?"

Kasi nudged me, but it was too late.

"First off," Walsh said, "she wasn't married. Second, who else was at her bedside is not important, and if you had been there, you wouldn't have to ask the question."

That was enough to silence me, but Kasi maintained some credibility. "To be honest," she said, "Mr. Blaine is helping me out with…."

"*To be honest?* Listen, I don't want to be a prick, but neither one of you has any authority to be here, not even to be standing on my property once I tell you to leave. Out of respect for Eveline, I'm willing to cut you some slack. But Mr. Blaine, if you've come to reminisce about your sister, we probably don't have much to say. Eveline and I had a passing relationship. I'm not trying to make anybody uncomfortable here, but you above all know how it is. Sometimes things work and sometimes they don't."

Kasi tried again.

"I know you're dealing with your own grief," she said. "We were sorry to hear about your wife."

"Oh you're good, Ms. Brennan. A little deflection, a bit of diversion, where in the NTSB training did you acquire that?"

"Mr. Walsh," she said, "I thought you *didn't* want to be a prick."

"Okay," he said. "Yes, my wife died and life sucks. Either we move forward or we die ourselves, but I appreciate the sympathy."

The brief silence that followed seemed to mollify him a bit.

"Look," he said, "I understand. We treat someone badly while they're alive, then they die and we feel that instant remorse. Eveline was an interesting woman and I liked her—but beyond that I don't have much to say. Now, if you don't mind, I really have to get this yard in order."

"Why the leaf blower?" Kasi asked. "You have this small maple and that's it."

"I must enjoy the sound," he said. "You're not NTSB, Ms. Brennan."

"I'm kind of working off the books here, just doing a favor for a friend."

"See, I may not *want* to be a prick, but you're making it easy. You're lying. Or misrepresenting. Or half-way impersonating a government official. Try telling the truth. Sometimes that works."

"Here's the truth," Kasi said. "You're not under any obligation to answer anything; we're just trying to tie some names together to figure out what happened to Eveline."

He shook his head.

"You know what happened—she got sick and died. That information is on file somewhere. As next of kin, it would be available to you. If you came here in mourning trying to learn about your sister, I guess I'd have no reason not to speak with you. But dragging a fake government agent with you sours things for me."

"That's my fault," I said. "Kasi got sucked into this because she used to be NTSB. My sister and I...."

"I get that. I get family stuff. I still don't know what you expect from me."

"My sister kept notes, a journal, I don't know what you'd call the medley of papers and scraps, and news articles. Your name was in it and we wondered why."

"I told you—we had a relationship. That's really all I'm going to say. I'm not going to turn you two in for impersonating whoever you're impersonating, but if this is about Marty Hendricks throwing my name around, you can leave right now.

I know there's no statute of limitations on insanity, but in his case there goddam well should be."

"It wasn't Hendricks—we don't even know where he is."

"That narrows it down I suppose. Look whatever you know now is probably all there is. She was for all intents and purposes married. I was married. Neither of us was happy. We gave it a shot. End of story."

"She wasn't happy?"

"Mr. Blaine, if you get some prurient thrill out of hearing details...."

"Don't be an asshole, Walsh."

Kasi grabbed my arm, grabbed it hard enough so I could feel individual fingers digging in. When I think of it now, I'm surprised at how fast I let everything deteriorate, at how quickly I lost patience. I had admonished Kasi about the need to work with people we didn't like, but I had developed an almost instant, almost overwhelming antipathy for Walsh. I didn't want to work with him, talk with him, be on the same planet with him.

"Let's go," she said, not releasing her grip. If she thought a fistfight lay ahead, Walsh corroborated her fear and let the rake fall to the ground.

"We can settle this any way you want to, Blaine. But you don't want to fight—you prefer a quieter, more enduring path to revenge, isn't that right?"

"We're leaving," Kasi said, not to him but to me. Walsh wasn't done.

"I'll make a deal with you," he said. "I'll try not to be an asshole. I'll try even harder if you two promise not to come here high anymore. You think I can't smell it? You think I don't know where you've been? And you, missy, take your story about tying up loose ends and try it on someone else. NTSB investigations take months, years. You're not tying up anything a day or two after an incident."

Kasi had not released her grip, now she pulled at me. I wasn't about to hit the guy. I don't think I've ever hit anybody, though this was one of those times I understood the motivation. But *Missy* had raised Kasi's ire too.

"Lon found out about you two, right, and gave his sister an ultimatum? Or was it your wife who found out?"

He ignored her. "You know, Blaine, I'm glad I finally met you. You're even shallower and more ignorant than I thought. Eveline always defended you—I don't know why—I doubt if you ever once stood up for her. And now you've found a new friend to share your…your misery."

Kasi repeated the question, but Walsh wasn't giving an inch.

"I'm not discussing Mollie with either of you. Eveline found me useful, then she didn't. Men always take the blame for being exploitive, but women can play the same game. We both played. It ended in a draw."

Kasi held fast. "It wasn't a draw. You won. Your wife didn't. Some say you played the game with your own rules, or someplace where they weren't any."

"Well put, Ms. Brennan. Maybe you're brighter than your friend here. Still, don't let your drug dealer become your private investigator, It's not a good combination. Now before I call the real police, I think it's time we went our separate ways. If things go well from here on out, I'll never see either one of you again. You'll forget about me, and I'll forget that you were pretending to be what you weren't."

He picked up the rake and turned his back to us. I guess he was able to read me enough to know I wouldn't attack him from behind, as much pleasure as that would have given me. No goodbyes. No thank-yous.

We drove off, took the corner, then stopped and sat in the car for a moment while we both calmed down a little.

"Want me to drive?" Kasi said. "I got this."

I made a U-turn just past a No U-Turn sign, then drove back down Vance, past Walsh still working in his yard, and headed back toward the state line. I was just regaining some equilibrium when Kasi told me to slow down.

"You're going 45 in a 35 zone," she said, " and there's a cop behind us." I looked. It was a blue Camry.

"I don't think so."

"He's definitely following us," she said. "You didn't notice—he flashed his lights. You should pull over."

"Is it Walsh?"

"No," she said, then took out her phone, punched something in, and told me to pull into a convenience store parking lot just ahead.

"I just texted Jake Moss the license plate," she said. "If anything happens, he'll know who did it."

"And that helps you and me how?"

"Leverage," she said. "Pull over."

It turned out we didn't need leverage. Our pursuer was a Springfield cop named Seidel. Unlike us he had actual credentials. I dug for my license and the rental registration.

"Was I speeding?"

"Of course you were. Everyone is. This is not official," he said. "I don't need your paperwork. I need a minute."

"First time a cop has ever asked me that," I said. "You got it. And may I compliment you on the most unmarked of unmarked cars. A blue Camry?"

"My wife's. Right now she's waiting for me to bring it home. Come on, get out and stretch your legs."

We walked over near Seidel's. In the rear seat was a little girl, maybe two years old, snugly strapped in. Seidel leaned into the car and lifted her out.

"This is Olive," he said. "Olive likes to run so I'm going to hold her for a minute. Is that okay, Olive?"

She said no, of course, an answer that had no effect on her father.

"If I asked her to say hello to my friends," he said, "that'll just make things worse. Olive is a little upset because I drove by a Dairy Queen before and didn't stop."

"I'd be angry too," Kasi said, already captivated, mugging for the child. He shifted the child to the other arm. Kasi moved accordingly.

"Getting heavy," the cop said. "Drove by and saw you talking with Walsh. You two had that 'Look at us, we're Feds' thing going for you, and he appeared to be silently telling you to get the hell off his property. Nice ride though, that Jag of his. Santorini black metallic. Somewhere in the area of 120k, depending on the power train."

"We never talked about it. Were we that obvious?"

"You were, miss. Then again, I do a little detective work, how about you?" When I told him I worked in finance, he laughed.

"Then you caught it from your partner," he said, then looked at Kasi. "You do not work in finance. You texted someone my plate, right?"

"I used to be NTSB. Why were you cruising Walsh's?"

"Don't like him. Don't like his story. I'm not alone, but the department has no open case so, you know, I drive by once in a while. It's practically on my way home—just five miles out of my way."

"Just five. That's convenient," I said.

He smiled. But Kasi had another concern.

"Could that be considered harassment?" she asked.

"I never stop, hardly slow down. If I see a different car in the driveway I might run a plate."

"Casual surveillance," I said.

"Yeah, that. Olive likes to ride, just in case there's ice cream involved. You talked to him, right? Didn't you want to kick him in the…" he glanced at his daughter, "eviscerate him?"

Seidel was a big man, easily six-three. Even in a car he would be noticeable to anyone paying attention, but then Walsh was pretty secure and maybe couldn't be bothered.

"Here's the thing," the cop said. "I never knew the guy's wife, Mollie. Her maiden name was Lynch. I went to school with some Lynches. Nice people. Never had a crush on Mollie, but I don't know many who didn't. I do know that her folks think there's something wrong here, so I thought I'd quietly check around. Now you don't have to share anything with me…."

"Nothing to share," Kasi said. "Walsh is smug and confident. He knew his rights and knew we were outside ours."

Seidel nodded.

"And not giving anything away. You two be careful," he said. "Walsh is a SOB. If he killed his wife, he wouldn't be above harming two trespassers."

"You think he did? Kill his wife?"

He didn't answer, just strapped Olive back into place, reached into his shirt pocket, and gave us each a card. "If you hear anything, be in touch. And listen, stay away from him when you have no authority. You have nothing to gain."

Kasi leaned in and said goodbye to the girl who basically ignored her, then we headed toward the car. Seidel stopped us.

"If you have weed in the car, legal or not, be careful."

We gave him a sketchy but believable account of why we smelled like stoners and thanked him for not busting us, but all I felt afterwards was more apprehension. Even the cops thought Walsh was dangerous…and they were armed.

CHAPTER 17

"He didn't need a leaf blower," Kasi said. "Why did he have one?"

"Stole it?"

"I'm serious. He's got all kinds of money and doesn't have to worry about a couple hundred bucks—I get that—but why? Why do that work at all? Hire somebody."

"It gets him outside?"

"It does more than that, I'll bet. Pull over somewhere," she said. "Another cop?"

"No, I have an idea."

"About a leaf blower?"

She said no, so I found another convenience store/gas station combo and stopped the car. I didn't realize she had dialed anyone until I heard her speaking.

"My name is Kasi Brennan," she said, and from then on I picked up only half of the conversation. "...just visiting...Iowa...freelancing...the Mollie Walsh incident...wondered if I might talk to somebody who worked on that story...ten minutes tops."

A few moments went by, then she said, "Terrific—we'll be there inside of a half hour. Kasi Brennan...and friend."

She clicked off.

"I always wanted to be someone's friend," I said. "Who was that?"

"Wait here," she said, went into the store and came back with a container of moist towelettes.

"We're showering together," she said. "Hope you're not prudish."

"The cop was right. We stink. But our clothes will still stink," I said. "Face, hands, exposed skin—it'll help. Car windows open."

A few moments later we each smelled like a hospital hallway, but we deemed it an improvement.

"Back the other way," she said. "Find the Interstate."

"You haven't told me where. "

"Got an appointment at the *Republican*," she said. "We're only ten minutes away."

"The what?"

"It's a newspaper. The reporter who did the Mollie Lynch feature is on assignment, but there's an intern there we can talk to."

"Is she credible?"

"She sounded almost manic on the phone, but if she can hold it together, I think so. Anyway, she's expecting us. We ask for Rachel."

The GPS cut in and eleven windblown minutes later, we arrived. Of course it took another eleven minutes to find the parking garage, but the young lady had left Kasi's name with security and we were spared further delay.

Rachel was Rachel Mendez—born in Puerto Rico, came to Springfield as an infant, graduated from Springfield College, had been at the paper through the summer and was hoping to latch on. Even though her degree was in history, she was seeking a Masters in journalism like her boyfriend who already worked at the paper. She'd had very few opportunities to play reporter, but she was happy to do it for us, even though as Kasi had implied before and Rachel verified, "I get a little emotional—such a sad story."

But she claimed to have plenty of Kleenex, which I had learned the hard way were superior to paper towels. One more gaffe in my life with Bethany, I thought, as Rachel plopped the box on her desk.

"Now, what do you want to know?"

"Kasi's reply of "everything" sat well with Rachel who, though she was interrupted a few times by phone calls, took us through the whole event in less than ten minutes with only a hint of tears and occasional references to her laptop.

The South America trip had been Mollie and Devin's fifth anniversary gift to each other. Devin did the planning, but Mollie had been to Brazil as part of a college program, and had always wanted to return.

"Devin went out and learned Spanish," Rachel said. "Imagine that."

I imagined it, but I also knew that Portuguese was the language of Brazil. When I mentioned that, Rachel didn't skip a beat.

"You would think someone that smart…" she said, and shook her head. "To some people that's what makes it so romantic."

"How about you?"

"Dumb," she said, "but I'm not a romantic. So they headed off for Brazil. It was supposed to be four weeks total. An expedition on the Paraná River—not piranha like the fish…."

I smiled, but refrained from asking Palmer's question about piranha in the Paraná. She even spelled it for us—didn't have to consult anything. She knew her stuff.

"And it was just like they said, amazing."

"How do you know?" Kasi said.

"Devin knows a local writer who contributes an article now and then, wanted to know if the guy could use the photos to do an environmental story, you know, the destruction of rain forests or something like that."

"By tourists like Devin Walsh?" I said.

Rachel laughed. "I thought the same thing," she said. I thought she was going to high-five me, but she contained herself. "I shouldn't editorialize," she said. "You want a story, not an exposé."

"We want whatever you can tell us," Kasi said.

She had more to tell. Mollie Walsh the photographer was also a decent artist with a sketchbook filled that first week, along with a couple hundred pictures accessible on the cloud. She sent no text to speak of, but several selfies were evidence of the wonderful time they were having. She promised to turn over her trip journal when she got back, maybe even parlay it into a book someday.

I almost had to catch my breath, remembering that forty years earlier a woman wandered about Chicago with a Minolta and some film, her intentions similar. Another plan that went awry. I saw no point in sharing that comparison, but I immediately felt some kinship for the two of them, one of whom I'd just learned about; the other I'd never known.

"Daniel," Kasi said. "You with us?"

"Off somewhere," I said. "Just…go on."

She did, but it was a different Rachel—her voice ominously lower.

"Towards the end of the second week, Mollie got sick—woke up in the night with a blinding headache and terrible muscle pain. They had had all the shots and they had practically bathed in insect repellent, especially in the morning and the evening, so they weren't too concerned. I guess she used to get migraines once in a while anyway and she had a prescription for them. This was different though. The symptoms didn't go away."

"That's her husband's account?" Kasi asked.

Rachel nodded. It was difficult to tell where her sympathies lay, but I thought I saw, or maybe heard, some skepticism when she pointed out that he was the only credible witness.

"How long did that last?" Kasi said, "the headaches."

"According to Devin, she slept most of that first day and then in the evening—and this is the bad part—she was better and everyone thought 'well, that's it. No big deal.' They were near a hospital when she first took ill, but her *recovery* removed the need for one. Of course the next day, after they'd moved on, she was worse."

From there her story traced the inexorable decline. There was no doctor aboard, but on the second night they took her to a small medical facility and had her examined. The staff diagnosed some mosquito-borne illness—probably Dengue Fever—gave her some antibiotics, and told her to drink fluids. Mollie told her husband not to worry, that she had had the same disease in Brazil and so had all her friends. She said she'd be better in a day or two and kept apologizing for ruining the trip.

"Dengue is unpleasant but doesn't kill people," Rachel said, "but if you've had it before, it can return as some kind of mutation, a hemorrhagic fever. Had the doctors known of the previous illness, maybe they would have treated her differently. I don't know. Nobody knows. By the time they got her to a real hospital in Paraguay, her organs had begun to fail…that was it."

"That fast?" Kasi said. "A young woman like that?"

"Surprising, I know. Unprecedented, some would say."

She was good—letting us draw our own conclusions while feeding us just enough to make sure we didn't miss anything.

"Then came the rest," she said. "The interviews, the articles, the hastily published book, TV, all that."

"And the regret?" I asked.

Rachel didn't exactly answer, and her face lost most of its expression.

"If this newspaper gig doesn't work out," I said, "try poker. You give away nothing."

"I don't want to…I think the news should be the provable truth."

"I agree," I said. "From your observation of what appears to be the truth—even if your sources are questionable—was there regret?"

"Yes," she said.

"Genuine?"

"People grieve differently."

Or not at all—I knew she wanted to say that, but it would not have been objective enough.

"Ms. Mendez," Kasi said to her, "you seem to want to tell us more, but you're going to wait for us to ask the right questions first. We don't know the questions. Can you help us out?"

"I'm just filling in," she said.

"Then off the record," I said. "Was there regret? Remorse? Exploitation?" She leaned forward a little, symbolically, at least, drew us into her confidence.

"There was something off about it," she said. "He seemed too eager to tell the story, and not like some cautionary tale to prevent others from making the same mistake. It was different—it was his suffering over the loss of his wife, and not so much hers. That's just my feeling. Like I said, I'm just filling in."

"And theoretically, in your role as a fill-in, if you had had a disease before and it came back, wouldn't you have told the doctor who was treating you?"

"Damn right I would."

"But she didn't," I said. "Did anyone ask why? I mean obviously they couldn't ask her afterwards, but was there an inquiry?"

"That I don't know. Maybe when she relapsed she was too ill—maybe too delirious to tell anyone anything? We have only her husband's account."

"Some say he killed her."

"Some say."

Her expression didn't change.

A phone call interrupted the conversation, but she had told us everything she knew and some things she didn't. We waited for her to hang up, then I asked her what the next step was. She looked puzzled.

"I don't understand."

"For you, I mean. You're too good to be handling phone calls or filling in," I said. "At the paper here, what's your next step?"

"Wait for a retirement. Post résumés. Hope for a nibble."

"Wait, post, and hope? Sounds like a law firm—a failing one. Where are you posting?"

"Wherever."

I took out my business card and had Kasi write her email address on the back. Rachel seemed grateful.

"Is this one of those big money places?" she said.

"Yes, but no one's gone to jail. If you ever need a recommendation, let us know."

"In finance? No offense, Mr. Blaine, but I've always wanted to be a reporter."

"So be a reporter in Chicago."

"I don't think big-city newspapers are looking for small college history majors."

"No, but they're looking for good reporters. Could be you."

She turned the card over a few times she seemed pensive. "There was something else," she said. "A rumor."

"A woman?"

"Yes, Mr. Blaine. How did you know?"

"Even original stories are sometimes built on clichés," I said. "Nothing more banal than a love triangle, and nothing more predictable."

Rachel shrugged. "I guess. It is only a rumor. I can't speak to it."

"Wouldn't want you to," Kasi said, adding, "you've been great." I think Kasi was trying to end the conversation, save me the embarrassment of yet another Eveline story. I appreciated the effort, but it was already too late for that.

"Tell you what," I said to Rachel. "Build up your résumé here. Ever hear of American 191—a plane crash in Chicago a few years back?"

"What my friend here means by 'a few years back'," Kasi said, smiling, "is about twenty years before you were born."

"That might be true," I said, "but a good story is always a good story. We have, well, *stuff* that we can turn over to you when we're done. It'll be like research done for you."

"Sure," she said, though she really didn't know what we were talking about. "If you're interested. I mean it's old news and all, but there are other stories involved in it. Other people. You put it together, add your perspective, the worst they can do is reject it. And the material—if we do this—we'll send it to your home, not here."

"Cloak and dagger," she said.

"Cloak, I suppose. Probably no dagger."

Rachel seemed pleased that we'd taken an interest, but I was pretty sure we hadn't convinced her to risk a move. She liked Springfield, she had a boyfriend, she wanted to get ahead, but she was comfortable. We left her alone.

On the way to the car, Kasi took my arm. "You were that close to telling her about your sister, weren't you?'

"I was."

"Why didn't you?"

"I didn't want to play the victim just for sympathy," I said. "It's ugly and repulsive. But if she follows through on the story and we get her what she needs, she can decide where the sympathy comes to rest."

"And someone will tell your sister's story. What if it's not positive? For all those years you weren't sympathetic."

"A fresh perspective," I said. "Sometimes we need one."

We found our way back to the Interstate and crossed the state line.

"Death in the jungle," Kasi said. "Can you imagine the news coverage on that incident, especially these days with Washington such an embarrassment. A little hometown tragedy can bring people around. Renew some empathy."

"And stigmatize them—can you ever hear Sandy Hook without thinking of murdered children? Sometimes the price we pay for that empathy is too damn high."

"I suppose. What were you getting at with all those 'unconscious' questions about Mollie? Why was that important?"

"I think he let her die, or helped her die."

"Or killed her?"

"Yeah, but maybe I'm reading too much into this…."

"…because you didn't like Walsh."

"Oh he's a creep, no doubt about that, but is he a big enough creep to lure his wife into a South American jungle in order to kill her, then hope to live happily ever after with his new…with my sister?"

"Now you're stretching. I mean did he also hire the mosquito that bit her?"

"Yes, let's say he hired a mosquito, or diluted the repellant, or provided her with a repellant that wasn't a repellant?"

"Now you're flailing."

"Or injected her with something. A brilliant chemist like him? She was prescribed medicine—what if he gave her the wrong meds? Sugar pills. What's he *not* capable of?"

"Men act like assholes all the time, but they don't all murder their wives in the process."

Her response was dismissive, but her tone wasn't. One encounter with Devin Walsh was enough to give credence to my hare-brained theories, the collusive mosquito aside.

We drove back toward Bradley without discussing Walsh, his dead wife, or the Paraná River any further, but none of it strayed far from my thoughts. Or Kasi's either, I'd bet.

CHAPTER 18

The sanitized version of the Walsh story also omitted the fact that Mollie's folks lived in Northampton—we could have been there in under a half hour—but their only concrete knowledge would have come from their son-in-law—hardly a credible witness. And we'd have looked like sordid curiosity seekers, uncredentialed as we were.

Since all of this was new to me, I had no idea if we had wasted the day or if we were making real progress in understanding why that single-engine plane had strewn itself and its pilot all over the tarmac at Bradley or why my sister was somehow associated with it. Kasi, more studied in the process, assured me that not knowing was, in fact, the process.

"Walsh was right about one thing. NTSB investigations proceed slowly," Kasi said. "It's not unusual for a crash site itself to be active for a month or more."

"I have a week off from work," I said. "Give me your assessment of today."

"A good day," she said. "No dead ends, nothing startling, some leads, you know, a decent day."

"Good or decent? You said both."

"Because I don't use those terms, not as the investigation proceeds. You piece things together; then, when it's over, you figure out if you did a good job. That's the only good day."

"We know some facts we didn't know yesterday."

"In a way," Kasi said, "but Palmer's *facts* may be somewhat hazy, and Walsh's only *fact* is that he better not see us anymore. The intern though, Rachel, she was good. After that, all we have is your theory that Walsh hired mosquitos to murder his wife."

"And we don't even have a description of the little buggers. Without that, they all kinda look the same."

She smiled. "It is good to have a sense of humor. You know, we kind ofduped that intern. I think she thought we were more official than we were."

"Which is not official at all."

"I don't like lying to people. I'll have some flowers delivered to her when I get back."

"They'll think she has a boyfriend."

"Which she already has. Maybe they'll think somebody likes her and they'll worry about losing her and maybe give her a real position."

"Oh yeah, that's possible too."

"It's not?"

"It's not."

Kasi and I—oil and water.

We were within two or three exits of Bradley when Kasi suggested we shoot by Palmer's again. Since we'd met with Walsh and got more firsthand information from the intern, she thought maybe Palmer could fill in some holes in the story—how he might react to the prospect of further investigations ahead, especially when they concerned Devin Walsh.

"We'll need more towelettes," I said. "We'll lure him outside."

It was 2:45. The time wasn't significant, except it was early on a fairly mild, fairly nondescript autumn afternoon—too early for rush hour traffic, even for a Friday, let alone a Tuesday. When we got to Ludlow Road, we were greeted by flashing blue lights and a police officer directing traffic, one lane open at a time. Palmer's wife had been killed right there and I wondered how many others had met a similar fate at this little turnoff.

But there was no ambulance. If it was, in fact, an accident site, the victims and the vehicles had already been removed and only the reconstruction crew remained. But Ludlow Road itself was barricaded, and as soon as I switched on the turn signal indicating my intent to proceed there, a trooper straddling the solid line in the middle of the street immediately flagged me over. I rolled down the window.

"Can I get down Ludlow?"

"Do you live down there?"

"Visiting."

"Uh huh, well the street is temporarily closed sir."

"Accident?"

"No, sir," the trooper said. "You'll have to come back later—unless you live down there."

He was a young guy—certainly not out of his twenties—and I thought his youth might make him more accessible. I leaned out the window and tried to sound conspiratorial. "What if I told you I did?"

"I'd have to see some identification and see if it matched up."

"And if I didn't have any?"

"And you already said you were visiting? Then I'd arrest you for impeding a police investigation and interfering with a law enforcement officer. Do you live down there sir?"

"Not when you put it that way," I said. "Listen, I have no legal rights to cross a police line. We're—my partner and I—we're conducting an informal investigation of the incident at Bradley."

I heard Kasi swear, then lean across the front seat.

"No we're not, officer. We're dealing with a family matter and trying to get some closure on a death."

The cop looked at me. "Your partner says she's not your partner. Care to explain?"

"We're not partners in the relationship sense."

"Uh huh. Sir, please step out of the car."

"We'll leave. We just wanted to…we visited someone this morning and we wanted to get back there."

"Sir?" the cop repeated. I surmised the rest of the question—I got out of the car. "Have some ID?" I showed him enough to establish I was Daniel Blaine. "Chicago, huh? And your *partner*?"

"DesMoines. Honest, we don't want to be in the way. We can come back later."

"Who'd you want to see down there. Not many people live on Ludlow."

"Yes sir, Benjamin Palmer—he's the last house on the right."

"Uh huh," the trooper said. His nonchalant response didn't jibe with the instantaneous radio call he made or the fact that, moments later, we were bouncing along the sand and gravel of Ludlow Street, trying to keep up with a gunmetal gray state police SUV, with another one behind us.

When we arrived Palmer's truck was still in the driveway, but nothing else was the same. The previously quiet yard had been overrun. Everywhere small groups, seemingly having nothing to do with each other, purposefully and silently meandered about. Had it not been for the loosely strung ribbon of yellow tape surrounding it all, they'd have resembled swarming guests at a country picnic. On the street, parked at various angles, were other state police vehicles, several Suffield PD sedans, and an ambulance improvising a colorful but disconcerting light show. The only vehicle parked within the tape, the only one close to the house itself, was a large but basically nondescript black panel truck that bore no flashing lights, an unremarkable vehicle made ugly by white lettering stenciled on the driver's side rear: **Coroner**.

Kasi grabbed my arm as we sat in the car. Neither one of us wanted to ask the obvious question or assume the obvious outcome. Another trooper opened Kasi's door to let her out. I followed.

"Wait here," the man said. "Let me tell Lieutenant Weber you're here. He's going to want to see ID, and also, ma'am could I just have a quick look at the contents of that bag."

"Like going to a concert," I said. The trooper smiled politely but wasn't amused.

I knew my pat down was next. It was mercifully brief.

"It's a crime scene," he said by way of explanation, "and we don't know who committed the crime."

"Can I ask what the crime was."

A voice from behind us answered. "Not sure. I'm Lieutenant Weber. Can I see some identification?"

He wore a sports jacket, no tie, and a photo ID on a red lanyard that kept swaying so that I couldn't read his first name. When he finally stood motionless and stared at our drivers' licenses, I was finally able to see the letters: Franklin.

"Chicago? DesMoines? If you're here for the foliage, it's too early. Peak would be maybe two weeks."

"We're not," I said, though I knew that he knew. "Kind of far from home, aren't you?"

"We are."

"Sergeant Dale says—did you meet Sergeant Dale? He was directing traffic when you tried to convince him you lived here and lied about being investigators and partners. That's Sergeant Dale, but I digress."

"I didn't really," I said. "We were…."

"We? You shouldn't throw the young lady under the bus. Of course Sergeant Dale is new and I don't think he always gets the story straight—but he says you're conducting an *informal investigation*. Now I, and I'm embarrassed to admit this, I never did one of those—how does that work?"

We explained to him as best we could, and sounded even more pathetic doing so. I watched his expression vacillate between skepticism and amusement, neither of which ameliorated the situation. I don't think he considered us suspects, but he didn't consider us colleagues or peers, that much was certain. We weren't bargaining from a position of strength, but I had to ask if something happened to Ben.

"Something, yes, he's dead. Two rounds in the chest, Dale says you were here earlier. When?"

"How could he be dead?" Kasi asked. "He was fine a few hours ago."

"Two rounds in the chest. Listen, was he high?"

"I don't want to incriminate…."

"He's dead, Mr. Blaine. Drug violations can't really hurt him anymore. And we all knew Ben. Was he high?"

"I think so."

"You think so? Was he smoking while you were there?"

"You mean marijuana."

"No I mean pork shoulder. Seriously, can you just answer?"

"He smoked a little while we were there."

"Did you?"

"No."

"Wait here."

He walked away, leaving Kasi and me stranded. I asked her if she thought we would be arrested. She took a step or two away from me, waited for Weber to get out of hearing, then asked what the hell I meant by conducting an investigation.

"It's like getting a diagnosis from a specialist, then saying, 'well here's what I was able to find out in Wikipedia.' Jesus, Daniel, these are professionals—they do this for a living. Bending a phrase or two for that intern at the newspaper was one thing—this is different."

We waited in silence. Maybe five minutes went by before we saw Weber on the porch, coming our way.

"You feel up to coming inside?" he said.

I hesitated. "Are you sure you want us in there? I mean, it's a crime scene and all."

"Sir, your 'partner' claims to have been NTSB. *You* may faint, but she'll be...." Kasi didn't let him finish. "How do you know that?"

"We ran your IDs."

"That fast?"

"Yeah, also that FBI guy told us."

He pointed to the porch where we'd been standing hours earlier. It was Alex Carmichael, arms folded, staring at us, shaking his head.

Kasi muttered something under her breath, but I saw him as someone who could at least vouch for us.

"I was worried," Carmichael shouted, walking toward us. "When I heard the police call, I figured it was you."

"The victim or the culprit?" Kasi said.

"I've been doing this too long to assume anything. What the hell happened?"

"I thought answering questions like that was your job, Agent," Kasi said. "Good one. And you're right, ma'am, you're absolutely right." He turned to Weber and said, "They're yours. I'd hold them both on suspicion."

"All right wait," I said. "This is all new to me."

"Of course it is," Carmichael said, his smugness exasperating; nevertheless, my admission was the opening he needed. "That's because you're not a cop, not an agent, not NTSB. You do spreadsheets. And you," he pointed to Kasi, "you do nothing. Now let me ask you two again, what the hell happened?"

"We told you we were coming here."

"Still waiting," Carmichael said. "Miss Brennan, before you dropped out of the work force, you wrote summaries. Give me one—what happened here?"

"Nothing," she said. "We fucked up. But we didn't do...this. Ben Palmer was alive and well when we left."

"You knew we were coming," I said. "I told you."

"And I told you to keep it casual. You're doing follow-ups? Did you gather some DNA evidence while you were here? If you conducted a paraffin test on yourselves, well, we can all go home."

Even Weber cracked a smile at that one. I might have too, but though I knew what paraffin was and was even familiar with the word *test*, together I had nothing. I did wonder how concrete our alibi would have to be, whether that creep Walsh would vouch for our being at his house. There was that cop too we'd spoken with, but I didn't want to involve him while he worked off the books. In the end it didn't matter. Neither Weber nor Carmichael considered us suspects, but that didn't mean we were home free.

"Chicago and DesMoines," Weber said. "Don't plan on seeing those towns for a while. We may have more questions. Are we clear?"

"Yes." I almost added *sir*, but it would have made me sound too much like Oliver Twist.

"Now, can one or both of you come in the house with me?"

I was afraid to say no, but more afraid of what the interior looked like. Weber probably saw the panic.

I asked about the coroner's vehicle, but Carmichael, calm again, said it was the forensics team poking around. The body was already in the morgue.

"It's all right," the cop said. "Palmer died outside. He isn't in there."

"And was it, I mean how did he, you know…"

"Die?" Weber said. "It wasn't a heart attack."

Weber and Carmichael led us into the house, still smelling of marijuana.

Nothing had changed—just a normal residence outside and in.

"Look around," Weber said to us, "Everything look all right to you?"

"All yours," I said to Kasi. She'd done this sort of thing before and I thought she had probably been observing even when I wasn't aware of it. I was right.

"His laptop," she said, pointing to a small table near the kitchen door. "It was there. It isn't there now."

Weber immediately pegged a couple of his officers to find it. Kasi said everything else looked about the same and, aside from cups that were dirty when we left and now lay clean on a drying rack, I thought so too.

"Did he say anything about being in fear of…anyone, anything?" Weber asked. "I doubt if it would have come up in casual conversation," I said "but maybe there's something in that pile of papers."

I thought at the time, if I were stealing his laptop, I'd take those papers too. But there they were, lying on the counter where we'd left them hours before. It was the first time I felt a little queasy, not because Ben Palmer and I were such great friends, but that he could have been alive and blustering in the middle of the day and cold and dead a few hours later.

"I want to get some air," I said, and went outside again where the coroner's panel truck was the first thing to catch my eye, before the vegetable garden with a profusion of ripened tomatoes, peppers and yellow squash…and the garden behind

the garden where he undoubtedly grew his marijuana. I wondered if the cops would burn it. He seemed to have a decent relationship with them, both caught in the throes of a stupid law—he was flouting it; they were enforcing it.

While I tried to regain some equilibrium, Kasi walked over. "You all right, Daniel?"

"I just needed some air."

"At a time like this…."

I didn't let her finish.

"He was harmless. Palmer. He was harmless. I mean maybe he was selling drugs to little kids, but I doubt it. He just wanted to be left alone."

"I guess a religious person would say he's been reunited with his wife."

"If that were true, murderers wouldn't be imprisoned—they'd get a commendation for reuniting families. And why find a cure for cancer if…."

"Okay," she said, and she smiled. "You're not a religious man. Me neither. Let's get that asshole Carmichael to get us out of here."

"In which case…."

"Yeah, he'd be less of an asshole. That's as far as I'll go."

"It gets old."

"You already told me that."

"It's gotten older since. Look, I shouldn't have told that cop up the road I was conducting an investigation, but I didn't know Palmer was…dead…murdered. But Carmichael had our backs just now. I mean we could have been two murderers returning to the scene of the crime."

"A paraffin test would have cleared us."

"And what the hell is that anyway?"

"A test for gun residue. We wouldn't have any on us."

"We still shouldn't have come back."

"And that was my idea. But either way, Ben Palmer would still be dead." That would have been hard to argue. Then I remembered the dog.

"Lieutenant Weber," I yelled. He was maybe thirty feet away near some plants. "Was there a dog?"

"What? What do you mean?"

"Before, when we were here. There was a dog tied up near the pickup. Name's Tracker. "

Weber shook his head slowly enough so that I understood it wasn't merely a no.

"We took it away," he said, paused a moment, then went back to the others.

Maybe there was a merciful aspect to it. If the dog had survived, could it have adjusted to a life without its best—maybe only—companion? Would it have been miserable, forlorn, maybe even abandoned. Still, ascribing mercy to Palmer's murderer was absurd. The expanding crime scene was proof.

CHAPTER 19

Before we left we incurred another mild dressing down from Weber, one that ended with his request—well, his demand—that we stay the hell away from the crime scene, but not stray too far for a couple of days anyway. If there are arrangements you have to make…he said.

There weren't, not for me. But that evening, with Kasi and I still sparring with each other but trying to cooperate, she called her old mentor Jake Moss and put him on speaker. He was not pleased with the way things were going, and Kasi had to convince him that it wasn't our fault. He wasn't so sure; neither were we.

"Your statements should have been sufficient, but if you have to stay around for formal depositions," he said, "keep a low profile until then. This Palmer, if he was tied up with drugs, he could have had enemies, or just people who wanted the weed and didn't want to pay for it. People get killed over bad drug deals."

"Over pot? No disrespect," Kasi said, "but he wasn't cooking meth or dealing opioids. It was just marijuana."

"You don't have to be an addict to be an idiot. Just be careful. This Weber, the cop, do you like him?"

I said he seemed okay—an old-fashioned detective dressed like an ivy-leaguer. "He could have treated us with more disdain than he did," I said. "For that matter, he probably could have found something to charge us with."

"Did you tell him about Hendricks?"

"He was in with Carmichael for quite a while," Kasi said. "He must know."

"Make sure. I know Carmichael—he's good at what he does, but he can be possessive with evidence, with leads. And sometimes he keeps secrets because it's dangerous for amateurs to know things."

"Like us?" I said.

"Exactly like you, Mr. Blaine. And Kasi, you know I love you, but there's no such credential as "formerly with the NTSB," and making believe there is might get you in serious trouble. I know your field experience is unquestionable, and there's nothing wrong with consulting with an old-timer like me, but letting on that you're doing it—then using it in a shooting death? That's another plateau. Got that?"

She did. And I did.

We spent a quiet evening that began in the hotel restaurant, continued in the hotel bar, then moved inexorably to my room where we continued poring over the materials that Jake Moss had more or less warned us to let go of. Neither one of us was ready to do that, so we dug up some more stories on Mollie and Devin Walsh. Their tragic tale had been, as the young reporter intimated, quite an event. National news even, though I'd missed it.

Well before midnight Kasi was gone. I watched some of the market reports before shutting down also.

I was just on the edge of sleep when I heard the annoying hum of a cellphone on a table. It was Weber.

"Hope I didn't wake you," he said, "meet me downstairs in the bar. Both of you."

"It's still open?"

"Maybe."

In my normal life—which I'd lived until a few days earlier—I'd have said something to the effect that it was after midnight and I was going to bed. But that sort of normality was on the decline, and I probably owed Weber. I called Kasi— she was awake—told her to be in my room in ten for a meeting with Weber, then called him back.

"Kasi's on her way over—you come up."

He already knew the room number. He was there in minutes, wearing the same sports jacket he'd been wearing at the crime scene. He'd added a grey knit tie.

"Still crime-solving, I see."

I hadn't tried to hide the mess of papers and notes—he certainly knew we hadn't given up—but I reminded him that we weren't looking at any crimes, other than the one that may have happened forty years ago. He halfway bought that, but before I was forced to explain further, Kasi arrived in jeans and a sweatshirt, and the flowered hat.

"You don't see this hair when it needs washing," she said. "What's up?"

"Honestly," Weber said, "I thought you two would be together. Jeez, you put two single people in a hotel room, and they're supposed to…well…."

"Things are different from when you were young," Kasi said. I thought she winked. I hope she did.

"Touché," he said. "But you are both single. I conducted one of your *informal investigations.* I was pretty good at it."

"You sound like Carmichael," I said. "That's not a good thing. Surprised he isn't with you."

"Don't know where he is, but I didn't come here to bust your chops. Shook you up a bit, didn't it? Palmer?"

"It did," Kasi said. "Accidental deaths are one thing, but a murder? I never even asked—who found the body."

"Jogger. At the end of the street there's a trail that goes for miles through the woods. People run it all the time. Guy came by and saw Palmer lying there. Thought he had a heart attack and called 9-1-1."

"I wonder how long he'd been there."

"Still waiting for forensics, but at first glance, maybe an hour. The reason we moved the body was that he was still breathing when the paramedics found him. Two in the chest and still alive, but he died before he got to the hospital. Never regained consciousness. Of course moving him impedes the investigation, but you have to save the life first if you can. We do know the window between your leaving and his being found. We're interviewing others on the street, but he was so isolated, it's not going to help."

"How about surveillance cameras?"

"Nothing on Ludlow, but there are cameras in the area. We may get a hit.

Reason I came by though, did you see a gun at Palmer's place?"

I told him no, which was the truth, but Palmer had talked about shooting rabbits and it seemed likely that he owned one.

"More than rabbits," Weber said. "Anything he considered a pest—including at least one wandering chicken. Palmer made restitution so I doubt the chicken owner would have killed him. Anyway, we couldn't find a weapon. Maybe it was a robbery. Did you notice anything valuable like paintings? Sculpture?"

I laughed.

"Not to be insensitive, detective, but seriously? As immaculate as that interior was, his prized possessions all leaned toward coffee and dope. I suppose he could have been some kind of eccentric with millions he never spent, but I don't think so."

"Yeah," Weber said, "that's what I thought. The only reason to rob someone like that is it's easy. He's out of the way, no security or traffic cams, few patrols, no close neighbors. You guys didn't do it, did you? I mean you were returning to the scene of the crime just like you're supposed to."

"Maybe we did it," I said, "out of reverse psychology, trying to look so guilty that you wouldn't consider us."

"I consider everybody. Except you two. And when you get a chance, look up *reverse psychology*."

"Are you using it now, lieutenant?"

"Not even a little bit." He looked toward Kasi. "Carmichael says you used to be a star. What happened?"

"Alex Carmichael isn't always the best judge of things."

"Of course he is. Is that true you're retired?"

"In a way."

"I hope I look like that when I'm 65."

"You can let your hair grow and shave your legs. That'll be a start."

"I'll take it under advisement. Look, if you have a few good years left," he said, "this is a nice area. We're always looking."

I laughed. "A new job offer every day, Kasi. First the FBI, now the local PD."

"You'd like it here. My wife knows everybody. You'd begin with a circle of friends."

"The commute from DesMoines might bother me. And the gun."

"Deal breaker, huh? Well," Weber said, looking only slightly disappointed, "I gave it a shot. Tell me what you did between the time you left Palmer's and the time you came back."

We offered a fairly extensive account of our visit with Devin Walsh and the intern in Springfield. We didn't mention the cop working off the books.

"Ah yes, the Walsh affair," Weber said. The tears, the publicity, the outpouring of grief. I thought I sensed a little cynicism in his voice, a little more than usual.

"Too much grief?" I said.

"Oh I'm sure it was tragic, but enough is enough. This Walsh seemed ready to move on even before the reporters and hangers-on. This intern, did you tell anyone about her? I mean Walsh doesn't know about it, right?"

"I don't see how he could."

"Okay, just don't want any innocent bystanders getting hurt."

I don't think he intended to scare us, but he did. The thought that we had somehow imperiled the young lady at the *Republican* was frightening. "Can you, you know, protect her?"

"I know some cops in Springfield," Weber said, and wrote down the young lady's name. "They can't *guard* her, but they can keep half an eye on things, at least until the weekend when this Mullins thing blows over."

"Did you investigate Mollie Walsh's death?"

"Me personally? Not my jurisdiction."

"Did you want to?" Kasi asked.

"You know, really, I did. I talked to some people who—well I can't say they worked on the case, because there was no case—let's say they were privy to information."

"Did they think his wife's death was suspicious?"

"I wouldn't go that far."

"How far would you go?"

"Unofficially? I didn't like the husband."

"You met him?"

"Didn't have to. Did you like him, Mr. Blaine?"

"No."

"See? All that Will Rogers stuff about never meeting a man he didn't like? Sometimes you do. Rumors were he had something on the side, but that would have ruined the story so that kinda got squelched."

"So you don't think he killed his wife?"

"Wow, Blaine" Weber said, "you sure do skip the intermediate steps. You know something I don't?"

"His something on the side was probably my sister." Weber went limp. "Jesus. I never meant…."

"Sure you did—you just didn't think I'd be that open about it. Eveline is dead. I'm just trying to figure out what her life was like before she died."

"For what it's worth, Mr. Blaine, we know the community, hear the rumors. I never heard a bad word about your sister. But Walsh…there are some Massachusetts cops aiming to lock him up yesterday."

"We met one today. Didn't get his name."

"Sure you did but don't want to say. No worries, let him work. Can I just ask, what led you to Palmer's in the first place?"

"His name showed up among our…papers," I said.

The cop pulled a folded up piece of paper out of his inside jacket pocket. "I guess I won't be needing this."

"Subpoena?" Kasi asked.

"Search warrant, but you two already know more than I could figure out by going through everything. And I doubt if anything would provide an insight into Palmer's death. But listen, you have to call me if you do find something. And remember," he said, waving the paper, "I still have this. You two take care, get some sleep, stay safe, I dunno, whatever."

He was about to leave when Kasi stopped him. "Did you come here to offer me a job?"

"Partly, why?"

"You're not embarrassed to admit that?"

"Why? Should I be? Carmichael said you were the best. Shouldn't you be doing what you're best at?"

"Wouldn't I have to go through the academy and all, then do traffic duty, handle a few domestic disturbances?"

"You could go that route, or you could get yourself licensed as a PI and work with us."

"Is that legal?"

He smiled. "You two are conducting an off-the-books investigation without even having a book to be off of. And you want to know if *my* offer is legal?"

"Good point," she said

"Carmichael is your recommendation. You couldn't bribe a better testimonial than one from him."

"Oh I know he likes me," Kasi said. Weber frowned.

"If you think he…believe me…he *likes* you as a professional. Do you even know him, know what's going on in his life?"

"I know enough," she said.

"Well, that's too bad. I like a little more curiosity in a PI." He looked disappointed as he walked toward the door.

"Anyway, I was just checking on you. People see a murder or become involved in one, they get a little skittish—just wanted to make sure you were all right."

After he left, and Kasi did too, I felt more tension rather than less. Carmichael had been a convenient whipping boy for Kasi—presumably justified until Weber implied she was wrong. Weber's impromptu visit had been enlightening, but not therapeutic in the slightest. Sleep was elusive—I kept wondering if we'd somehow been responsible for Ben Palmer's death. I know that not everything that happens *after* happens *because,* but here was a guy leading a quiet peaceful life on an all-but-forgotten country road—a guy still grieving over his wife who had been killed less than a mile away. His life was certainly not perfect, but he was settled, getting by, surviving…until we dropped by.

First thing I did the following morning when I woke up—my only real proof that I eventually slept—was to call Lon Taggart.

"Thought I'd catch you before you went to work," I said. I didn't even know where, or if he had a job.

"Store opens at nine," he said. "I have a few minutes. I heard about the murder, if that's why you're calling."

"Partly."

"I didn't do it," he said. He was joking, but there was an element of apprehension that he couldn't quite conceal. "Have they caught anybody?"

"I don't think so. You knew Ben Palmer, right?"

"Slightly. Seemed decent."

"Do you know anyone who might have wanted to kill him?"

"You're a little late to the party on that one," he said. "Mr. FBI called on me last night, late, and some locals came by this morning, early. Told them what I'll tell you. Palmer minded his own business—there'd be no reason for anyone to do him harm. For the record I was at work yesterday afternoon."

"Think it might have been a bad drug deal?"

"This isn't Juarez, Mr. Blaine. Crazy teenagers may shoot each other over an ounce, but Palmer was past all that. I never heard him argue with anybody."

"How about Hendricks?"

"He is the exception to every answer. Even so, I can't imagine him shooting somebody. Maybe a death beam from outer space, or some kind of deadly laser, but something as…as pedestrian as a gun wouldn't sit well with Marty."

Taggart was in a rush so I let him go. Turns out he worked in a small hardware store in Suffield—a three-man operation whose main business was being the last holdout against Home Depot and Lowes. Where I work we don't handle the portfolios of too many three-man operations, but I still feel good about their being around. It's like running out to buy something from the ice cream man, or squeezing into a photo booth at an amusement park—utterly unnecessary, but nostalgic anyway.

By the time I got off the phone with Taggart, it was suitably late enough to call Kasi without fear of waking her out of a sound sleep. She answered right away—from the restaurant downstairs—where she had just ordered breakfast. She sounded a little less edgy than earlier that morning, but I thought we remained more associates than friends. Still, associates can eat together.

"Order for me, too," I said. "I'll be down there in ten."

CHAPTER 20

Breakfast came with a price, not just a check.

"I have to ask," Kasi said. "What was the tipping point?"

"What?"

"You and your sister. What was it?"

"I told you—she wouldn't let anything go...."

"...and eventually it wore you down. I'm sure there's some truth in that, but the hostility—where did that come from? It wasn't that skirmish in the airport. Was it money?"

"Of course not."

"I've seen marriages," she said. "They're a mess and both parties want out, but they hang on until there's a blow-up somewhere. It's usually over money, though adultery works pretty well too. Don't forget withdrawal of affection, abuse, drugs, some family faux pas, drinking, weight gain...."

"You seem pretty familiar with all this. Were you ever married?"

"Once."

"And?"

"I asked you first. What happened?"

"Eveline and I didn't owe each other any money."

"How about the other items?"

"It wasn't weight gain either."

"Okay fine," she said, and shrugged. "I'm in no hurry. I intend to go through the whole list if I have to."

"It's not important."

"It is. When Jake and I worked together, we were partners. We didn't tell each other everything, just enough to be...partners. Two individuals pursuing a single goal. It wasn't just a courtesy or some foolish bonding exercise. It was something that allowed us to predict the other's movements, approaches. Cops do that because it can save a life when one knows how the other will act. Jake and I weren't ever in a life-or-death situation, but we understood. Now you, you work alone, right?"

"In that respect, yes. But you and I are not partners. And we're certainly not responsible for each other's safety. And unless I'm way off base, I don't expect any life-and-death situations."

"Ben Palmer is dead. Mollie Walsh is dead. Are you sure?"

"I'm sure."

"All I'm saying is that you may have colleagues in work, Daniel, but we're partners, if only temporarily. Is it that you don't like partners?"

"Can we stop talking about partners? It sounds like we're at a square dance." She allowed a slight smile, but she persisted.

"Come on, Daniel. What was it? What was the coup de grâce for you and Eveline? Tell your partner."

I wasn't about to answer, and when the pancakes arrived, I could be silent with a mouthful.

"Did I order this?"

"I did. All you do is eat eggs. It's not healthy."

"And this syrup satisfies what dietary requirement?"

"Sugar. What happened between you and your sister?"

I fiddled with the pancakes, unstacked them by fanning them out across the plate, then turned my juice glass slightly clockwise. I was sure I wouldn't enjoy the pancakes I didn't order unless I came clean.

One of her guesses, it turned out, was right.

"Family faux pas," I said, "but a horrible one." And I told her about my other sister, half-sister, step-sister, cousin—we never knew what to call each other. Younger sister always worked for me in school.

My aunt and uncle spent a lot of time listening to counselors and school psychologists dealing with her—Summer—their middle child. She needed goals, objectives, strategies, and procedures to become, apparently, a normal teenager. She wasn't one—not at all. She wore vintage clothing, her mother's dresses and her father's hats. She listened to the Church and Jane's Addiction while the rest of us were happy with Aerosmith and Billy Idol. For a while she was a vegetarian, then went to no sugar, then ate only fallen fruit. She was a threat to her own hair every time she was near a pair of scissors or in a drug store beauty aisle and later, any tattoo parlor or piercing salon. She was good to Eveline and me, asked her parents several times if I could be her brother instead of her real brother who was my age but her nemesis—straitlaced and studious. One time I actually let Summer cut my hair—she didn't do a bad job. It was hard to dislike her, but hard not to worry about her either.

She made it through high school somehow and went to a community college, wound up working in a clothing store at a mall and, against all odds, kept getting promotions. I saw her a few times over the years. She had a roommate named Barbara whom I met a few times and even took out to dinner once. Whether my cousin's living arrangement was an economic expediency or a sexual relationship, I never asked. I do know there were never any sparks between Barbara and me, or for that matter, between Summer and me, but I've never been known to set off many. The point is, for all the concern she'd drawn from parents and counsellors and teachers in high school hell-bent on normalizing her, she'd turned out fine.

One afternoon there was one of those shootings, right outside the store where she had become an assistant manager. The shooter wasn't a sniper or terrorist mowing down shoppers. It was just a woman with a gun and another woman without one and some guy they were both, to be euphemistic, interested in. The woman with the gun had stolen it from her father and had little idea how to use it or what kind of weapon it was. She knew it was loaded because her father had always warned her of the fact. Afterwards he claimed to have locked it up at all times. Nobody believed him.

So the girl had the gun, and she knew where to find her adversary. They argued, the gun went off, and, off, and off, surprising even the shooter who eventually dropped it and ran for an exit.

"And your cousin was hit?"

"The stupid shit never hit the girl she wanted to kill, but got Summer in the throat. She bled out before the EMTs even got the call."

"Your poor aunt and uncle. Such nice people."

"They probably figured if she gets past 16, 18, if she makes it to 21. You set up all these artificial indicators and with every one that goes by, things look better. Then it all falls apart with one asshole and a gun."

"Did they get the shooter?"

"Yeah. She got manslaughter for what was truly a first degree murder. She fucking planned to kill and did it—it was just the wrong person. Her lawyer insisted the gun was just a threat, but everyone knew she left the house to kill the other girl."

"Then it's not...you know...first-degree murder."

"I know that, in my rational brain. If you kill the wrong person, the premeditation becomes sketchy."

"You don't have to tell me the rest. I didn't mean to upset you."

"Too late."

I pushed the dish toward the center of the table and leaned back.

"Eveline was here…there…somewhere. I had a number and I called to say what had happened. The five of us kids had always got along, I mean there were squabbles and disagreements, but never anything serious—never anything that would lead to a feud. And those cousins—I mean the plane crash completely altered their lives but they plowed ahead as my sister and I barged in. So when Eveline said she wasn't coming back for the funeral, I was dumbstruck. *If it's the money*, I said to her, *I'll get you a plane ticket, or transfer funds, whatever you need.*

It wasn't money, she said, but she couldn't miss work.

Death in the family, I told her. That trumps everything. I probably said some unkind things about the importance of her job in whatever office she was changing toner cartridges.

"You said that?" Kasi asked.

"Or something like it. I was furious and I kept at her. Even now with all the guilt I feel, I don't regret a single syllable. I knew she was lying about work—it was something related to the crash and this idiot she'd been seeing. Finally she came clean—she was going to Vermont to interview someone who had worked on the design of the DC-10. Someone whose testimony was already a matter of public record, who had given his deposition twenty-five years before. She could have read it online, but instead she had to talk to the guy."

"She was desperate."

"Really? That's your explanation? That's how you rationalize a complete lack of any social graces? Of loyalty? Gratitude?"

By that point some other patrons were following along, and I thought I was maybe a decibel or two from being asked to eat my pancakes elsewhere, or not at all. I felt the same fury I'd felt at my cousin's funeral, and some of the ill will I'd felt toward Eveline for all those years—the ill will I'd been regretting since I heard of her passing, came rushing back.

Kasi was silent. I think she thought saying nothing would calm me a little. She was right. When my face returned to its normal pasty color, she pushed the dish closer to me again.

"You should eat something," she said.

I grunted some agreement and picked up my fork, then laid it down again. "How could she do that?"

"Can I say something? I'm not defending anyone…her. But maybe after a while we lose perspective and every lead looks like *the big one*."

"No, no offense, Kasi, but don't equate what you do—or did—with my sister's obsession. A day or two would not have mattered, not after years and years."

"You don't know. Maybe this Hendricks was hounding her."

"That is not a good enough reason. Don't make it out to be one."

"Like I said, I'm not defending her. So after that?"

"She sent a card and, maybe, flowers. There were so many there…."

"*Did* she send flowers?"

"I told you, the place was full of them."

"Your sister—did she send flowers?"

"Yeah. Big fucking deal. You make a phone call to a florist or press a key on your laptop. Done."

"Don't kill me on this, Daniel. I'm on your side. She should have been there. Period. I'm just saying that we don't always recognize…I don't know…conditions in others."

"You can use the word *crazy*. God knows I did. I feel like shit now that she's gone, and that's something I'll have to live with, but that doesn't excuse what she did to the family."

"To you?"

"No. Not me. I was embarrassed, but my uncle and aunt were hurt."

"They apparently forgave her."

"I didn't."

"Look, we don't know each other very well—I'm a little uncomfortable coming off like some sort of expert, but can I just say…it's common to paint someone's whole life with a broad brush."

"She painted it herself with a roller," I said. "My sister spent forty years chasing down a story that was dead for thirty-nine."

"See? That's why I'm a little uncomfortable. You're stuck in the middle—defending yourself while you're suddenly trying to defend her. And you probably feel she wasted her life, but you still want her life to have meant something…anything. The broad brush doesn't allow that, but the little brushes detail a lot of disturbing issues."

"Like the many men in her life."

"Yes. You're not okay with that, but maybe that's not so important. How many great writers and poets led questionable, even dissolute personal lives? We still honor their work."

"Robert Frost beat his sister."

"Bullshit!"

I laughed. "You brought up questionable lives, not me. Anyway, that's what people say."

"Well thanks for ruining some of my favorite poems for me."

"No more 'miles to go before I sleep'?"

"Maybe I'll keep that one," she said. "Can I just say something else while we're talking about painting and poetry?"

"The floor is yours."

"What would you say to a doctor—let's say she's a GP, internal medicine, whatever…. Let's say her mother dies of brain cancer and this doctor leaves her practice and devotes the rest of her life to research to finding a cure?"

"Does she find one?"

"Does it matter? The greater question concerns her motivation. Is it altruism or revenge?"

"Revenge against a disease?"

"We do personify diseases. We battle the flu. We fight cancer. We march against AIDS. The disease your sister was battling took almost 300 lives, and her father, and her mother, and, to be truthful, her brother. Maybe the revenge was warranted. One thing for sure—if I were writing your sister's biography, like a certain reporter up in Springfield, I'd want to know that story. It won't show up in our notes—call her sometime when you get back home."

"I'll do that." I must have sounded dismissive. "I'm serious. Do you remember her name?"

"It began with an *R*."

"Close enough," she said, then pointed to the dish in front of me. "You haven't touched your pancakes."

She was right. There they were, still neatly stacked. And getting cold.

*****

Bethany and I had once had words over…well over words. She had introduced me to some female friends, one of whom I later referred to as *attractive*. She pounced on the word and asked me if I was actually attracted to the woman. I said no, and she countered by saying I should not have used that word. She suggested *good-looking, pretty*, even *beautiful*; but I said I'd often seen good-looking sandwiches and pretty sunrises on Lake Michigan. As for beautiful, maybe someone whose moral stature superseded everything else. I didn't know this woman's moral stature, I said. I think I may have added something about her being a murderer for all I knew. Predictably, the conversation deteriorated from there and led to another time period when Bethany and I did not marry.

I mention this because that little breakfast squabble with Kasi made her more interesting.

And attractive.

But as was always the case, a few moments passed and the image faded, my thoughts returned to Bethany and what sheer pleasure it would be to lounge about a hotel room with *her* all day in various stages of undress. Supplanting those chapters of my fantasies would not happen over a stack of pancakes—no matter how, well, good-looking.

CHAPTER 21

At the end of the hotel corridor was a room marked Business Lounge, a pre-laptop, pre-smartphone windowless chamber housing a small printer and a 1990s fax machine which presumably authenticated the term Business Lounge. It looked more like a business museum, but once we found it, spreading out some of my sister's scrapbook collection became easier.

That's where Carmichael found us later, poring over this disordered array.

"Well isn't this cozy," he said, then spotted the fax. "And nostalgic."

"Needed some room to spread out," Kasi said, her tone neither argumentative nor dismissive. I was surprised, and I think Carmichael was too, though he didn't have time to address it.

"You got the fax machine. All you need now is the CD player." He held up a CD jewel case from Eveline's belongings. "The Eagles," he said. "Was your sister a fan?"

Of course I had no answer. We'd grown up with music and I still had my favorites, but any intricacies of her life had long ago escaped me. Who knew what she listened to, or if she listened at all?

"This is a later one too, maybe ten, twelve years ago," he said. "What's the 10 mean?"

"What do you mean?"

"She scribbled the number 10 on the case, or you did. Was it you?"

I picked it up. He was right—*10* in permanent black marker scribbled on the paper insert—a photo of what looked like a desert dune.

"*Long Road out of Eden*," Carmichael said. Maybe it's the tenth Eagles album? Where are the other nine?"

He didn't wait for an answer, not that I had one.

"Or maybe she liked it and gave it a 10. Double CD—mind if I take it with me?" Carmichael asked. "I'll give it back."

"I'm sure I won't need it."

"Never know."

He slid it into a Manila folder, already stuffed to overflowing.

"I'm going to pay Ken Mullins a little visit," he said. "For an airport manager, he's been pretty scarce lately. You guys want to come with?"

I asked him why, though I wanted to say yes just to escape our newfound dungeon.

"Well for one thing," he said, "you might want to meet the object of your sister's scorn. For another, we may have a problem."

"We?" I said.

"Me. Him. But you're welcome to join."

He meant Kasi, of course. She had the skills and experience. I had a week off from work.

Kasi asked if there was anything new to report on the Palmer killing. "Ballistics identified the gun which, of course, belonged to Palmer. No prints.

Not wiped but the shooter appears to have worn gloves. Some fibers here and there. A few people on the street saw some cars; of course one of them was yours, and we're almost ready to eliminate you two as suspects."

"That's reassuring," I said. "So what's the newer problem?"

"Put this shit back in your room and come with me."

I cringed at the description. He noticed. "No offense, Blaine. Come on."

"Haven't seen you lately," I said.

"Been around," he said in a tone which was intended to, and actually did, close the discussion.

We followed him, and moments later I finally got to meet Ken Mullins, or, as Carmichael had called him—the object of my sister's scorn. He hardly looked scornworthy. In Eveline's stash I'd seen pictures of the man, never without a suit and tie, never less than exquisitely dressed or perfectly coiffed. Eveline had wasted few opportunities to berate his cold aloofness which she believed was evidenced by his fanatical grooming habits. She wasn't aware (and I never told her) that the building where I worked housed hundreds of Ken Mullins lookalikes in the same suits with the same modest ties and perfectly starched spread collars…or that one of them was me.

But on this day he looked freakishly aberrant in wrinkled, somewhat dirty khakis and an oversized black sweatshirt. Even his office reflected the disorder, resembling a rented and neglected storage cubicle more than an executive suite. He was packing and sorting and labeling, and his appearance—appearances in general—had apparently become unimportant. Only the color-coding of the neatly stacked cartons offered any proof that the real Ken Mullins was still in charge.

The real Kenneth Mullins—he may have been retiring, but he wasn't out of things—not at *his* airport.

"Alex," he said, "what's the story on that murder up in Suffield?"

"No story," Carmichael said, "not yet anyway. Let me introduce you." He didn't pay much attention to me, but he stared at Kasi.

"We've met, I think," he said, squinting, as if she were a hundred yards away and he couldn't quite make her out. "Where're you from?"

"DesMoines."

"No help. Did you ever investigate anything here at Bradley?"

"Sorry."

"Then it's the name. Ever been in on any big investigations? I read every one, obviously."

"Worked a few major accidents with Jake Moss."

"Then that's it," he nearly shouted. "Jake's partner."

"On occasion. Formerly. You know him?"

Mullins laughed out loud. "He's pretty much a legend, isn't he? Are you as good as he is?"

"I'm as far removed from the NTSB as he is."

"You too, huh? That's too bad. You tell Jake that Kenny says hey."

She agreed, but I doubted she would follow through. She didn't seem like the "hey!" type. Then he turned to me.

"Blaine, huh? Do I need to ask if you're related to Eveline?"

"My sister," I said. I tried not to sound apologetic, but apparently failed.

"No reason to hide it," he said. "I understand where she's coming from. Losing everything like that, both of you I guess. You…how do I put this?…you've come to terms with it differently?"

"I wasn't even born when that plane went down," I said.

"Doesn't make it any easier," he said. "Other pregnant women lost husbands on 9/11. The regret, the anger, the myriad of emotions—all the same, probably passed on to their children. Anyway, I'm glad to make your acquaintance, but I understand you may not feel the same."

"My sister and I," I said, "we weren't close."

The instant betrayal—Judas could not have done better. I immediately walked it back by explaining we had grown apart, but even that was a half-truth. And my final attempt—"of course we loved each other" must have embarrassed even Mullins. But he seemed more puzzled than anything else.

"*Weren't? Loved?* Is she…okay?"

He didn't even know she was dead. This then would be my chance at redemption. Yes I'd betrayed her, but at least I could express some sorrow at her passing.

I never got the chance.

"She died a little while back," Carmichael said with the same emotion as a newscaster might announce a traffic delay.

Mullins was stunned. "I didn't know. Was it in the papers?"

"There was an obit locally," I said. "You could have missed it."

"I've been so out of things these past few weeks. Leaving. Then that accident the other night. Your sister and I…I often wished she would leave me alone, let it go, whatever. She never threatened me or anything, just a note once in a while whenever there was some negligence in the industry. But I never wished her any harm. What happened to her?"

"She was sick," I said, "but she left us a lot of material to sift through. A kind of autobiographical journey"

"I'm afraid my name figures prominently," he said. "Still, I'm sorry for your loss, Mr. Blaine."

He seemed sincere, partly because his current problem far exceeded the possibility of an adversary writing angry letters. But also, other problems loomed.

"We came about the letter," Carmichael said to Mullins, "can I see it?" Mullins unfolded a piece of paper from a back pocket and handed it to

Carmichael. We waited while he read it—it could not have been more than five seconds.

"Triple-7," Carmichael said. "That's the plane landing here, the 777?" Mullins nodded.

"And then what's a Tenerife?" Carmichael asked. "It says 'Tenerife will be a walk in the park.' What does that mean?"

"Jesus," Kasi said. She looked stunned. I was too, reluctantly well versed as I was in air tragedies.

Carmichael was the only one in the dark. "Someone want to tell me?"

I knew enough details to acquaint him with a bulletpoint outline.

•Two 747s had been rerouted to the same airport in the Canary Islands. Tenerife.

•There was fog, there was poor communication with the tower, there were misunderstandings, there was recklessness, and there was impatience.

•One of the planes tried to take off while the other was taxiing down the runway directly at it.

The fog was so thick that neither could see the other and the tower couldn't see either one.

Almost 600 people died.

I looked at Mullins. "Is that about right?"

"Five-hundred eighty-three souls." he said. "Every crash comprises a lot of little mistakes, but usually we see only the big one. Mr. Blaine, your sister would not have written that letter."

"I wouldn't think so," I said. "Who did?"

"Whew," Mullins said, "how much time do you have? I mean do you want to know the names of the people who complained about the new landing pattern? Or the ones whose quiet streets now empty onto a major thoroughfare? Or the ones whose taxes shot up because their houses are now, and I quote, 'proximate to a major airport'? The list is long, my friend. Some of the anonymous ones are threatening—this one falls into that category. These get reported; your sister's got read. For someone that traumatized, she did acceptably well."

"I get the difference," Carmichael said, "but I also get the difference between some angry homeowner scribbling a letter-to-the-editor and a person intent on killing 583 people. Does a 777 hold that many people?"

"It can hold 500, but this model holds in the threes, and I'm not sure even a terrorist can engineer a collision. But anything that interferes with the flight of a passenger plane can cost hundreds of lives. That's why I called you."

We all dutifully looked at the note, as if there was something cryptic that one of us would notice. There wasn't. We didn't.

It was then that I noticed the photo: the grainy monochrome in a thin grey frame—the slightly blurred picture of a DC-10, rolling impossibly to port, the wings slightly past vertical like the hands of an analog clock face reading 12:25— the left wing, devoid of its engine, trailing some harmless looking white smoke.

It was American 191, O'Hare to LA, the plane that took my father—and nearly 300 others—to their deaths. Mullins saw me staring.

"That picture comes down last," Mullins said when he noted that I was staring at it.

"Of all the aviation photos you could have here," I said, "why this?"

"It's famous, of course. And that plane should have been rolling right with the left engine gone. You probably know that."

"Eveline studied it more than I did."

"It's two tragedies, and each multiplied hundreds of times by individual loss."

"Why two tragedies?" Kasi said.

"You already know the answer," he said. "It wasn't just that so many were killed; it was that everyone could have been saved if the pilot had only known what he was dealing with, if he knew he'd lost an engine, if the first officer had known about the stall, if repairs had been sufficient. So many factors. Textbook for you NTSB people, Ms. Brennan. Also one of the first crashes to be photographed— someone in the parking lot with a camera."

"It was an unlucky number," Kasi added. "The Delta crash in Dallas was also Flight 191."

"Six years later, yes, I know that too, but this one here—this one was mine. I didn't want it, but I got it. I'm sure you know the story, Mr. Blaine."

"I know a side of it."

"Maybe mine won't match up," he said, but I told him I wanted to hear it. "Sure," he said. "I'd tell you to make yourselves comfortable, but with this mess....

"We'll lean," Carmichael said. "Go ahead." He laid the letter on one of the cartons.

"I'd been at O'Hare for a short time," he began, "and had just been named a supervisor. I thought I was pretty cool. Of course in time I found out there were over two-hundred supervisors there in one capacity or another. But look, you know what happened that day—it's what came after that was worse."

"The court cases," I said.

"Yes. You sit and read the transcripts and listen to the arguments and you can't believe it. I understand that corporate attorneys don't possess the most savory of reputations, but this was beyond the pale. And American and McDonnell-Douglas kept running end-arounds to blame each other and fix it so nobody could blame anyone. It was as if the number of deaths was so high as to be unimaginable; then *unimaginable* became *unbelievable,* and that became *questionable.*"

"That's nuts," I said. "Everyone knew the numbers."

"It's the psyche of the people," Mullins said. "It's like that idiotic conspiracy theory that Sandy Hook never happened. Only a fool would claim it and only other fools would believe it, but sometimes the act is so heinous that we need to pretend it didn't happen. Someone dies in an accident and earns a million-dollar settlement and we say okay, that seems fair. But 300 people die, well do they all get a million? Does your father—a breadwinner and successful businessman—get as much as a little girl in elementary school with no earning power?"

"It was all horrific," Kasi said.

"But heard daily in those courtrooms all through the early eighties. The man is flying west to consummate a million-dollar deal and maybe provide jobs for hundreds—the little girl is flying to San Diego to visit her grandmother. Who gets the million?"

We were silent.

"Just quoting," Mullins said. "Those questions came up over and over. After a while as the cases dragged on, victims' families were willing to accept less just to end the ordeal and, in some cases, the humiliation."

"And where did you fit in?"

"I was the airport guy in the suit. Some days I was the face of O'Hare. I had nothing to do with the airline or the manufacturer or the maintenance, didn't know a pylon from a python, but I was there in my *supervisory* capacity.

For a moment nobody said anything. He may not have been responsible for the event or the aftermath, but he wasn't a sympathetic character. I think he knew it.

"One more thing," he said, and he glanced at Kasi. "I'm sure you know—why didn't you say it?"

"It's not my confession," she said. He nodded, flashed a rueful grin.

"No, it's mine." He paused to gather himself. "During the early days of the hearings a reporter approached me. It was the end of a long session and everyone was tired and frustrated and probably angry too. I know I was—all three. So this young guy from the *Sun-Times* stuck a microphone in my face and asked what my early take was on the accident."

Mullins paused, shook his head. "I was young and...not stupid but inexperienced," he said.

"Glib?" Kasi asked.

"Maybe that too. I made a mistake—I told the reporter that the victims had all been in the wrong place at the wrong time. It was true, but it sounded dismissive and, yes, glib. The next day the headline read "Airport Exec on Crash: Wrong Place; Wrong Time.""

"You survived it," Kasi said.

"But for that day I exonerated the aircraft manufacturer, the airline, the maintenance crew, everyone involved in that accident...reduced it all to fate. I should have been fired. I should have apologized to each surviving family member personally. Of course I withdrew the statement. If I were a current-day politician, I'd say I misspoke. But that wasn't a 1980s word, so I just said I hadn't meant it the way it sounded. But yes, I survived. I came here and I've had a good run."

He walked to the window overlooking a taxiway.

"Planes keep taking off and landing and nothing goes wrong," he said, "day after day and year after year. But you can't take it for granted. I see that photo every day and so does everyone else who comes into this office. It's a reminder. And I think of that headline just as often."

"Especially when things are going acceptably well," I said. He nodded, unaware that the little phrase of his had annoyed me. He'd used it in reference to Eveline for whom nothing had ever gone acceptably well.

The photo may have been a poignant reminder, and the headline an unpleasant memory, but on his desk was the letter that threatened to end that "good run," and much more. There would be no going back—no establishing of a second career—if an unimaginable tragedy befell Bradley.

I wasn't sure why Carmichael had asked Kasi and me to come along. This letter—this threat—this was FBI work, not the province of two "informal investigators."

CHAPTER 22

The plan for Mullins's Sunday retirement ceremony involved a C-5 low pass from Westover—only about twenty miles to the north, the arrival of the Triple-7 with the requisite fire brigade and high-arcing hoses, a tastefully small balloon release, a high school band, and a few short speeches by some state and local dignitaries. Some protests were scheduled too, but far from the epicenter of activity—well monitored and probably peaceful.

"If the low pass doesn't scare everyone to death," Kasi said, "it should be a nice ceremony."

"It's a noisy mother," Mullins said, "but an amazing sight. "The passengers on the 777," she said, "do they disembark?"

"No. It's Boston to LA. We're calling it the Champagne Flight—hors d'oeuvres and free drinks for their agreement to spend an extra forty-five minutes of flight time. It's all approved, as long as most of it is completed while the plane is parked."

"But eventually it leaves," Carmichael said. "Then you have 300 drunks in an aluminum tube at 35,000 feet."

"More likely 34,000," Kasi said. "Westbound flights use even-numbered altitudes."

"And I didn't know that?" Carmichael said, feigning astonishment. The room went silent as the old tension between them returned, only to be quickly suppressed by Carmichael himself. "If I'd known it was only 34,000 feet, I wouldn't have even brought it up. And yet...."

"The booze is free," Mullins said, "but not unlimited. Drink tickets by seat, checked off as they're delivered. And there's food too, and two extra sky marshals. And every passenger was alerted beforehand, given the chance to exchange tickets. We had a dozen or so do that; the rest trust us to handle it, and we will."

"Maybe so, but all I want to do when I get on a plane is get off the plane. Adding an extra hour to the flight does me no favors."

"The passengers understand."

"I get that, but this," he said, waving the hand-written note, "we need to know if this is legit."

The response, loud and raucous, came from the doorway.

"I think that's my job."

We were all startled. We'd been huddled around the itinerary trying to assess the threat, and hadn't heard someone enter the room—a large man, probably my age (though the drooping grey mustache made him look older) in black jeans and a black t-shirt with a red pack of cigarettes protruding from the chest pocket. Dirty white hi-tops, one of which was untied, completed a look of casual insouciance, or better yet, inappropriate sloppiness. Just behind him stood Mullins's administrative assistant, a smallish woman who (and I say this despite the discomfort we felt at having a stranger eavesdrop on us) looked downright silly. She was a foot shorter and half his weight, or less—and trying to impede his entry. "I'm sorry," she said, as if she could have tackled him before he made it through the door.

"Don't you worry about it, ma'am," the stranger said to her. "No harm, no foul." Then he turned to us.

"You," he said, and looked directly at me. "Daniel Blaine. Why weren't you nicer to your sister?"

And that's how I met Marty Hendricks.

*****

I had seen him in a photograph, most memorably the one where he held a grenade launcher, but he'd either been seated or slouched over. His size was daunting, but aside from that he looked pretty much like any of my co-workers who had taken the concept of "casual Friday" too far. His voice too, even when he accused me of mistreating Eveline, was calm and steady, not the least bit strident—not that of a wild-eyed radical, or maybe that of an actual wild-eyed radical who had learned a measure of self-control. And though he must have known he was the odd man out in that room, his demeanor remained mild and non-confrontational.

"First thing," he said, "before Daniel here comes up with a reasonable answer for my question, who's the cop here?"

"Who wants to know?" Carmichael said.

Hendricks shook his head. "That sounds like a line from a Cagney movie? Isn't Cagney dead? I mean seriously, what kind of question is that—*who wants to know*? *I* want to know. I'm the one whose lips were moving when you heard the sound. It came from me."

Nobody spoke. I was sure Carmichael was going to kill him.

"Well never mind," Hendricks said, smiling at him. "You answered my question. Now before you tell me not to *crack wise* or some other phrase from your youth, I just wanted to alert you to the fact that I own guns but I'm not carrying one right now. You're welcome to pat me down if that kind of thing appeals to you."

He held both arms above his head. Carmichael accepted the offer. Hendricks smiled. "If I were a white man you wouldn't...."

"In a heartbeat," Carmichael said. "You wouldn't have made it this far with a gun anyway. And how *did* you make it this far?"

"I made it this far with some spurious IDs and a knowledge of magnetic devices. Don't underestimate me. Now, Daniel, about your sister. What exactly was your problem?"

I suppose there are times in every person's reclamation when you have to stop apologizing and move on—when you know you've been wrong, and you admit you've been wrong, and you make the recompense you can, then just grow weary of the self-flagellation. I wasn't there yet—maybe didn't deserve to be there yet—but there was no room for someone like Hendricks in the queue waiting for me to beseech forgiveness.

"My problem?" I said to him. "Because I didn't give her a necklace?" Hendricks was not intimidated.

"Seems you didn't give her much of anything, but I guess that answers my question. You're not going to answer my question. Rather than waste my breath, let me talk to the people who matter—the ones who might keep me alive for another day or two. And I don't mean a doctor."

Carmichael reached for his pill bottle.

"See?" he said, tossing a few into his mouth, "this is why I can keep my stomach settled. Now tell me big guy, who outside this room wants you gone?"

"For starters, whoever murdered Ben Palmer. If someone thinks even *he* was dangerous, then I'd have to be next. I mean really, with my past, you really think I'd be here talking to cops if I didn't have to."

"We're not cops," Carmichael said.

"FBI? You're the best cops. And these two are the civilians who talked to Palmer. Don't go thinking I'm psychic—he called me after you left."

"No he didn't," I said. "Benjamin Palmer thought you were nuts."

"I'll bet he never said that. I'll bet he said I was unpredictable and obsessive. Did he say he hated me? Don't answer—I know Ben, or knew him. He told me about your little visit between the time you left and the time Devin Walsh shot him. You knew that, right?"

"You're a witness?" Carmichael asked.

"Don't have to be a witness, just have to pay attention. You go and question Palmer about the threat, then go and tell Walsh that Palmer sent you."

"We didn't do that," I said. "Never mentioned his name."

"Two and two," Hendricks said. "Walsh is a genius—he can add two and two. Seems you people can't, seeing as Walsh hasn't been arrested. I figure you need more proof."

"Which you have none of," Carmichael said.

"Here's what happened: Walsh figures, uh-oh, that fucking pothead is going to spill everything, so he gets in his car, drives, what, ten minutes, shoots Palmer, and drives home. Back roads. Easy-peasy. Problem solved. What took you so long to get back there, Blaine?"

"Made a stop," I said.

"Probably saved yourselves the trouble of getting shot along with him. Can I sit down? This is fatiguing, writing your own death warrant."

Carmichael slid a carton next to him.

"We're a little pressed for furniture," Mullins said.

"What a mess," Hendricks said. "Nice to retire, throw everything away, start over."

"Palmer," Carmichael said. "The murder. Do you actually know anything?"

"I'm no Boy Scout," Hendricks said, "promise me you won't arrest me when I'm done."

"If you broke the law, I can't make that kind of deal," Carmichael said. "You probably know that."

"I suppose." He turned to Kasi. "How about you ma'am, immunity from prosecution?"

"Ma'am? You don't remember me?"

"Didn't want to embarrass you in front of your friends, Kasi. Nobody wants to admit knowing Marty Hendricks. Eveline liked you."

"You didn't"

"You're okay, just another bureaucrat with a roll of red tape. How about that immunity?"

"How about a free coffee next time you're in DesMoines? Would that help?"

"You people are worthless," he said in mock disgust. "Let's get serious here.

There's a plan to take down that big-ass jet you got flying in here on Sunday, which, I might add as a local, doesn't make any sense anyway. Too big for this area. Now the 787, smaller, quieter, that at least has possibilities. Environmentally it's a much better choice."

Carmichael let him finish the sentence, before trying to wrangle him back on track. "You mentioned a plan?"

"Of course not even the 787 will save Mollie Walsh's life, will it? You know her husband killed her, right?"

"He's a busy guy," I said, "running around killing people."

"Cracking wise, huh? Good for you. Just let me say that Devin Walsh is smarter than anyone in this room, 'cept me. There's Taggart of course, smarter than all of us combined."

"And he's not in the room," I said, "So aside from who's smart and who's not, you claim Walsh killed his wife. Did he tell you he was going to do that?"

"I said he was smart," Hendricks answered. "Does that sound smart? Now listen, how did that woman die? Some tropical fruit fever right? You know what the death rate is for those illnesses when there's medical care present? Don't answer. There isn't one. So here's a healthy young woman—and not that it matters but pretty and very nice...."

"You met her?" Carmichael asked.

"Sure would have liked to—she'd be alive and, if I know me, collecting a nice alimony check every few months. Unless she opted for a lump sum—I don't have that kind of liquidity, of course."

Carmichael cleared his throat loudly. "You're drifting, Mr. Hendricks. You were talking about medical care?"

"Yeah, that illness—it can lay you up for a day or two but it killed her? Ding! Ding! Ding! Alarm bells, anyone?"

We waited. I'd have to say he had our attention, if not our confidence.

"Ricin. You know that poison from *Breaking Bad*. Did you know there really is a poison like that?"

When there was no response, he seemed more agitated.

"You people ever watch TV?"

I'd never seen the show, though it was one of those that people talked about before streaming made such conversations fruitless. I'd heard of ricin as it related to some incident where it was sent through the mail and inhaled, or caught in time. I knew it existed. I was going to ask where Walsh would get it, but then I remembered—the science whiz paid to stay out of the lab. Hell, the average high-school chem student could probably make a batch.

"I've heard of it," Kasi said, "but how do you get someone to inhale a white powder."

"Mix it with Talc, put a little on a face towel. You brush your hair? Maybe I sprinkle a little on your hairbrush to get it airborne. Maybe a little dot in your toothpaste. And the two of them alone together? Simple. Once you produce a few symptoms, then you go in for the kill, so to speak."

He winked. Carmichael reminded him this was serious. Hendricks offered a few vulgarities to assure us he understood before continuing.

"Powder is good; ingestion is better. One day she's under the weather, you remind her that some tea with honey always makes a person feel better, and she's like *oh yeah, tea with honey, thanks sweetie*, and if you can get enough in that tea, the second dose will kill her in days. No antidote—you treat the symptoms but— OMG—they keep getting worse. And of course, you're in the jungle, so logically it's some tropical disease or you were bitten by a Komodo dragon or something and didn't notice with all the monkeys and giant spiders swinging in front of you. And then you die. And then," and Hendricks turned to me, "he can live happily ever after with your sister. Except she must have figured out he'd murdered his wife. She was pretty smart, that girl. Fucked up, yes, by things beyond her control and left to fend for herself by…well by you, little brother, but brilliant, sharp. Did you at least know that?"

"A Komodo dragon?" Carmichael said, before I could try to defend myself. "Wouldn't you know if some six-foot lizard bit you?"

"My luck," Hendricks said, "I wind up in the only room where some geek knows what a Komodo dragon is. Mullins, do you have any liquor? Don't CEOs keep a bottle in their desks?"

"I don't," he said.

"You should. Eveline always blamed you, but she knew you were the symbol. That's why she was so conflicted. She told me once she wanted you to pay with your life, but it would add to the death toll and it would be on her. Plus I don't think she could have done it."

"Done it?" Mullins asked. "You mean kill…someone."

"You. You can say it—it's not going to happen."

"How about you," Mullins said. "Could you kill someone?"

"Well you got me there. I'd say no, but it's hard to tell. See, people like me, Palmer, other 'social critics,' we make a lot of noise, but we don't want to hurt anybody. Walsh, though, he has no social conscience—he has no conscience of any kind. Most psychopaths don't. He played us, made us think we shared concerns."

"Like getting high?" Carmichael said.

"Yeah, while he was getting away with murder. He didn't kill your sister, Blaine, so don't go looking for trouble where there ain't none. Plenty of trouble where there is."

"Done?" Carmichael asked.

Hendricks shook his head. "Still don't know what kind of CEO don't keep no bottle in his desk."

"And I don't know what kind of college-educated person talks like that," Carmichael, "so we're even."

CHAPTER 23

I reminded Hendricks that my sister had cancer, that she wasn't one of Walsh's victims.

"In some ways she was," Hendricks said. "We all were, and we're not through." Carmichael interrupted our dialogue.

"Mr. Hendricks," he said, "how do we know you don't want Walsh arrested because you're afraid of him?"

"You don't. And I am. But I'm just helping you build a case."

"Even if that's true," I said, "why such a ham-handed method of killing Ben Palmer. A gun in broad daylight?"

"Because Devin Walsh may be a lot of things, but he isn't a serial killer," he said. "And if he's a murderer, he's not a criminal mastermind."

"Just a regular mastermind," I said.

"Right. There's no protocol or ritual involved. If he has to make an adjustment, he does it on the fly. Not the best technique. If it was Walsh in Palmer's yard yesterday, I would think Ben was probably looking for his own gun. There was no element of surprise there. Plus there was no time for a sinister plot involving a toxin. Your conversation with Ben Palmer sealed the deal."

That got Carmichael's attention. "Nobody in this room is responsible for a murder."

Hendricks became defensive. "It's not like anyone did it on purpose. You just didn't know what Walsh was capable of."

"We could have known if you had told us."

"Really? Why do you think I'm here today? Think I got a call from the FBI saying 'we need your help, Marty'? I don't get calls like that. I knew you people were sniffing around because of that Cessna that Barrett brought down, but I had no information about that other than to verify that the *pilot* was a nutcase who wanted to impress me, or maybe Eveline, or who knows? But—and I don't mean to sound crass—when the bodies kept piling up, I started looking at Walsh, just like you."

I didn't tell him that we weren't "looking at him" for that reason because, for a moment I thought Hendricks was offering some sort of expertise, some sort of knowledge of what *had happened* and what *was* happening, but Carmichael disabused me of that idea.

"So you want protection," he said to Hendricks. "You figure you're next."

"I think that's a possibility. If it's loose ends the guy is trying to tie up, I'm as loose as they come in his opinion."

"And in your opinion?" Carmichael asked. Hendricks shook his head.

"I've led a weird life," he said, "a bit outré I suppose."

"A bit what?" Carmichael asked.

"Weird."

"Did you *say* weird?"

"No."

"Next time say *weird*."

Hendricks smiled, I think for the first time. I hadn't thought he was capable of that sort of expression.

"Okay, weird, but I've been pretty honorable. Sort of. A few times."

I asked him about the manger, and what element of blowing up a fake animal fell under the category of honorable acts.

"Oh, that."

"Well?"

"Nobody got hurt except a make-believe sheep. I wouldn't have killed a real one."

"Of course," I said. "And your personal hero is Lincoln? Roosevelt? Gandhi? Oh no, sorry, it's Ted Kaczynski." He paused, took a breath.

"Okay. I'm not proud of that, but I never did anything to hurt anybody. I just understood the guy's frustration."

"He was nuts. He terrorized people for twenty years."

"Seventeen, but not to quibble. How long has the government been terrorizing people? You get a letter from the IRS, what do you feel? Some ICE agent walks into your house, how do you feel? The president says a nuclear war is winnable, what's your reaction? The government has been terrorizing us for two-hundred years. What's seventeen by comparison?"

Carmichael offered a few hand claps.

"You know, of course, I am employed by that government."

"Then you live with it. Look, Kaczynski is not my hero anymore. The position is open. Maybe it'll be you, Blaine. Maybe you'll do something heroic. Or you, Kasi Brennan, coming all this way for someone you hardly knew. Or maybe it'll be nobody and Walsh will win. He's a coward but plenty of cowards are doing well today."

"Then why do you think you're on Walsh's victims list?"

"He probably thinks I'm a wild-eyed obsessive compulsive. Surprising, isn't it? He also probably thinks I blame him for Eveline's death. Which I do in my own way. He'd probably like to eliminate the accuser, even one like me. Blaine, let me tell you something about your sister. She had mellowed quite a bit in recent years. I think she knew that anger and vengeance had cost her everything, made her life a shambles. She really wanted to look past it, but every time she took a step forward, something new happened—a plane crash, Mullins's name in the paper, a reference to Chicago, even a TV ad of a family together. Every day was filled with traps and Lon accepted the job of trying to avoid them. Of course the thing about traps—with good ones anyway—is you don't see them until it's too late."

He pointed to the photo on Mullin's wall.

"Like that," he said. "That would set her back a week."

"It's more than that," Kasi said. "Speaking of traps, how did her affair with you stabilize her life?"

"Golly-gee-willikers you people ask the best questions. I hope the answer clarifies that quest you have for the meaning of life, but it really isn't much of an answer. We had something going once, then we didn't. The gifts? I was in love with her and sometimes I saw something and thought, Evie would like this. I never followed through. I never expected anything in return. She was in love with Lon— he was good for her. No necklace was going to wreck that relationship."

I had stopped paying attention a few sentences before. "You called her Evie?"

"You didn't?"

"Only my uncle called her that."

"Is that a problem for you?"

He stood up, more agitated now but in no way threatening. "Can I continue?" He didn't wait for an answer.

"Walsh was a setback, but there was a reason. That plane crash in San Francisco a few years back—it had nothing to do with anything, but it occurred right at the airport, appeared to have been pilot error, and was certainly avoidable. The confluence of events reminded Evie too much of 191; then Walsh came along and she slipped."

"And my retirement?" Mullins said.

"She wanted to ruin it, ruin your legacy, whatever; and Walsh probably offered her an opportunity. Difference is, she wanted to make a statement—maybe phone in a bomb scare, everyone would scatter, there'd be no triple-7 landing, the event would be a fiasco. Walsh was never into that sort of thing. He had bigger plans and they did not include Lon Taggart or anyone else in her sphere. Loss of life during the retirement ceremony? Not even worth mentioning."

Mullins was shaken. "I've never even met the man."

Hendricks waved a finger at us. "No problemo, amigo. He doesn't require personal contact—you don't have to meet him; he doesn't have to meet you."

I couldn't believe that my sister could be involved with someone like that, but Hendricks was convinced she didn't really know him—that he had sugarcoated whatever plans he had and convinced Eveline for a good long time that he was a decent guy in a lousy marriage and wanted understanding and empathy more than sex.

"Old story," Hendricks said. "Old bullshit. She figured it out. Now he's on his own continuing with whatever plans they made for Sunday. And he has no guardrails now with Evie gone. Whatever catastrophe he's planning, it's all him."

"This catastrophe," Mullins said. "How?"

"I'm not a fortune-teller," Hendricks answered, "but my guess? He's gotta get that plane down. Missile?"

Mullins almost catapulted himself out of the chair. "Are you serious? A missile. Like a military….?"

"Surface to air. It's the only way to go if you don't have a plane to launch it from."

"Who the hell gets access to weaponry like that," Mullins said. "Go to a gun show."

Carmichael scoffed. "Nobody sells missiles at a gun show."

"That's true, but while you're there, just talk to people. Drop hints, you know, you're looking for something to defend your remodeled bunker, that sort of thing.

You'll find people as nutty as you are, and they all know a guy who knows a guy. Presto! All due respect, folks, this *is* the United States."

"And someone would kill all those people to make a point?"

Hendricks looked at Kasi. "Help me out here, honey. Would someone do that? Russians maybe? In 2014?"

She nodded. "He means MH-17, the Malaysian Airlines flight shot down over Ukraine, summer of that year."

"Right, July 2014. But there are more, right?"

"If you mean Korean Air 007, that was probably air to air missiles."

"Yes. Missiles. It's not unprecedented. Russians twice. We've made it difficult to sneak explosives onto flights. Hitting from the outside is the only option."

"That's horrific," Mullins said. "What kind of revenge is that, killing hundreds of innocent people to make up for killing hundreds of innocent people?"

"I hate to keep saying this, folks," Hendricks said, "because time is not on our side. But let's separate Blaine's sister from Devin Walsh. Evie was a good person; Walsh is an amoral and disturbed son of a bitch. I don't know how many other ways I can say that before you believe me."

"Even so," Carmichael said, "it's a little difficult to hide a missile launcher. You can't exactly park it at the curb."

"Check a satellite map—plenty of woods around here," Hendricks said. "Find an old fire trail, haul it in with a jeep, find a clearing, camouflage the launcher, then just wait. For that matter, a fenced in backyard would do the trick. We're not talking about a Saturn rocket and a ten-story launch pad."

"We can find it with satellite imagery," Carmichael said.

"Which Walsh knows. Look," Hendricks said, "I know you think you're one step ahead because you have the Bureau behind you. I hope you're right, but you're not dealing with an ordinary criminal. And for what it's worth, I wouldn't look for a missile launcher, Officer Carmichael."

"It's *Agent Carmichael,* for the record. You know, for when you sell your story to the papers."

"You obviously don't know me very well, *Agent* Carmichael, but I'll keep that in mind. As far as looking for a missile launcher, you're talking about a multi-person operation. Psychos work better alone."

"Shoulder-mounted," Carmichael said.

"Right. That's how you got to be an agent. They call 'em MPADS. It stands for…I don't know, mounted something."

"Man Portable Air Defense System," Kasi said. "Every country has them. Every country makes them. Seen the advisories. They're about six feet long, weigh thirty or forty pounds. Their effective range is maybe four miles at the outside."

"Any plane flying above 20,000 feet is safe," Hendricks said, "but of course landing requires flying lower."

"*Airplane,*" Carmichael said, "I saw the movie."

"I may have stolen that line," Hendricks said, "but it's true. For a plane at cruising altitude a missile like that is useless. It's only on take-offs and landings that there's vulnerability. Not only that, but—and I don't want to sound overconfident here—that missile could not knock a 777 out of the sky, isn't that right Agent Brennan? Are you an agent too, 'cause I'm losing track."

"It could do damage," Kasi said, "if it took out the lowered gear, then you've got a rough landing or maybe a spinout."

While she was going over possibilities, I tried to remember if any planes had flown over Walsh's house when we were there. He was not far from the airport as the crow flies, but I couldn't remember seeing any. As brazen as Walsh may have been, or may have felt, firing a missile in a residential area would not go unnoticed. I mentioned it to Hendricks, but Mullins answered instead.

"A plane landing from the north would be somewhere around 4,000 feet at that point. Less, maybe. It's within range, but if he wants something to happen here at Bradley, in front of an audience, that won't do it. Seems to me," he said, "we have all these experts on the various aspects of flying, of human behavior, of running airports. And we have one law enforcement guy who's the only one who can arrest this asshole."

"Without evidence?" Hendricks said. "The local hero—the local *tragic* hero—the widower extraordinaire? Is the FBI gonna swoop in and put him in jail because his wife died? I doubt that."

"How about on suspicion?" I said.

Carmichael knew better. "Of what, exactly? What Mr. Hendricks has provided would never get me a warrant. And suspicion that Walsh was involved in other deaths is just that. Suspicion. We'd need someone to place him at Palmer's when

Palmer was killed, and at that end of the street there's nobody. We can surveil him, and short of harassment we can question him again, but without facts or evidence, our hands are tied."

Carmichael waited, and when nobody offered a response, he continued. "There is, of course, a solution of sorts."

"I'm not calling this off," Mullins said. "If there's a legitimate threat…."

"Conjecture is not a legitimate threat," Mullins said. "That's why we have security, and the FBI."

"And morgues," Hendricks said. "They'll be busy." Mullins responded immediately.

"You don't make that call, Mr. Hendricks. You're a man with a story—and a compelling one. But you aren't law enforcement or security. And aside from your reputation as—I don't know what—you shouldn't be here at all. I can see why you need protection."

It was the angriest I'd seen Mullins; even Carmichael seemed surprised. "This is credible," he said.

"Not if you can't arrest him. Beef up security, do whatever you have to. I'm not giving in to…to terrorists."

It was then that I began seeing Mullins in a different light, maybe the way Eveline saw him. He wasn't just a guy who made a careless statement to the papers; there was a tinge of myopia in him, one that he suppressed nearly all the time. This was not one of those times.

Hendricks realized it too.

"Well that's all straightened out. Don't anyone worry—I don't require an apology."

Carmichael glared at him. "I got an idea. How's about we lock you up on general principles, not bother with immunity."

Hendricks shrugged. It wasn't the response the FBI agent wanted, but the fact that the man had not said anything else stupid worked in our favor. Carmichael was pacing; we waited, still waiting for a solution.

"I'm send two agents up to interview Walsh," he said. "Officially. Evidence of drug activity in the neighborhood or some bullshit."

"He won't buy it," Hendricks said. "It'll have to be Excedrin in that neighborhood. It's the middle of middle America, East Coast version. Not even opioids dented that area."

Carmichael disagreed. "No one is free from opioids these days. A little too much Oxy in the neighborhood—these places no one suspects are the places everyone is starting to suspect. Kasi, why don't you and Daniel go through the papers and see if there's anything that relates directly to Devin Walsh, or missiles, or terrorism. Wanna help, Hendricks?"

"I was hoping for protective custody."

"For how long?"

"Until you put me in witness protection. I've got the rest of my life mapped out—it involves a lot of Caribbean beaches and rum drinks, at least until Devin Walsh goes to jail."

"Or dies?" I asked. "Works for me."

"I'll get you a cheap hotel room and a bottle of Bacardi. Will that do?"

"In Jamaica?"

"In East Hartford."

"I have to pay for my room?"

"No, just the Bacardi."

To me it seemed like too much caution. Despite the death of Ben Palmer, Hendricks was not some isolated pothead living in the sticks. He was right here with us, had an apartment in town. What kind of danger could he be facing? As for Walsh, he may have been an amoral louse, but Hendricks's claim that the man was a psychopath seemed like an exaggeration. We'd spoken with him: we didn't like him much, but he was lucid and articulate. Certainly a psychopath could fake that, but it seemed like a stretch.

It was later in the afternoon when all my notions and conclusions changed.

That's when we couldn't find Kasi Brennan.

CHAPTER 24

Kasi and I were supposed to meet downstairs at around 6:00. I was early and, out of curiosity, walked over to where the Cessna had crashed. The plane had apparently been moved, though whether to a scrapyard or a repair facility, I wasn't sure. The area looked clean, devoid of yellow tape and any hints of an accident only days before. I wondered if there were still some NTSB agents around, but only Kasi would have known that. I called to say I'd meet her in the bar. She didn't answer. Probably sleeping, I thought. She'd been tired. It was only 5:15.

I could have hung out in Three Down of course, but killing forty-five minutes alone in a bar would have left me a little loopy by the time Kasi arrived, so, back to my room. When I turned the corner to my corridor, I saw a woman standing outside the room next to mine. She was not wearing the typical housekeeping garb, but I thought, maybe hotel management? Had someone left the shower running, not turned something off or on? Were all the adjacent rooms—including mine—flooded? I'm not a pessimist, but I can also imagine a lot of things going awry.

The woman did not seem harried at all—I said hello the way you would greet a passing stranger.

"Are you Daniel Blaine? The desk wouldn't give me a room number and I've been knocking and making a fool of myself."

She looked to be my aunt's age, maybe early seventies, with almost-white curly hair that hung just above her shoulders. A critical person might call it frizzy but it actually looked pretty cool. Too cool. For a moment I thought, so this was the woman Devin Walsh had dispatched to kill me. I quickly chalked that up to Hendricks paranoia and hoped for the best.

"Did you start on the lower floors and work up."

"No, thank God. Went the other route. Are you Daniel?"

"I am. Have we met?"

She let out a long sigh, then slumped noticeably. I thought she might faint, but rallied a bit leaning against the wall.

"After all this," she said. "I'm Christine Oakes."

I shrugged, held my hands out. "I'm sorry, I don't…."

"Mitch was my husband. Mitchell Oakes. He worked on the plane? The one that went down."

For a moment all I could think of was Wesley Barrett and the Cessna, and then I remembered: Tulsa, the mechanic, the suicide. Mitchell Oakes was one of the names among so many my sister's search had accumulated, but one that stood out. A tragedy attached to a tragedy. Another suicide and another family left behind.

"I know the story," I said, "or at least the telling of it. I'm so sorry for what happened to your…to your life."

"And yours," she said. "And Eveline's. She tried to reach me so many times. I never returned her calls."

"We have that in common, I guess, Mrs. Oakes. She and I were…distant."

"As good a word as any," she said. "And it's just Tina, please, and no longer Oakes either. I remarried after the…accident. Can we talk? I saw a lounge on one of my passes."

I followed her around a corner and into a small sitting area where two kids were playing a video game on their phones.

"This was empty a few minutes ago," she said. She looked tired and frustrated. "My room," I said, "if that's okay."

"Yes, please. I'm not staying that long."

I slid another chair to the window and got her a bottle of water from the honor bar. We sat facing each other on the opposite sides of a small wood table. She draped her grey jacket across her lap.

"I just wanted you to know something about Ken Mullins," she said. "I understand he's retiring Sunday."

"The ceremony, yes. I'm not sure when the official…"

"People should know," she said. "His hands are far from clean. My husband's weren't either. Did you know—did your sister know—Mitch was having an affair at the time?"

"Like I said, my sister and I…."

"I know, and I know it's forty years—I don't hold any kind of grudge against Mitch. I'm not angry. Like I said, I remarried, the kids grew up in a stable environment—this isn't about Mitch's infidelity."

"Your husband worked maintenance in Tulsa, right? Worked on the DC-10 that went down?"

"But called in sick and missed most of that day because he was shacked up with a woman. But apparently she had a job and had to leave early, so Mitch figured, what the hell, he'd go in and log a few hours, say he was feeling better."

"He'd been drinking?"

"Good guess. Yes, of course, though the alcohol problem came later. He wasn't at his best when he showed up, but he was alert enough to watch the process finish. He heard the telltale sound—the crack in the pylon."

"He didn't say anything?"

"He knew there was liquor on his breath. He knew that one thing inebriated people have in common is this idea that others don't notice they're inebriated. So no, he didn't want to call attention to himself—become involved in anything, even told himself he'd heard something totally unrelated—a piece of machinery somewhere else on the floor.

"He told you this?"

"He told me everything. At the time I was less interested in some factory fuck-up than my husband with another woman. It wasn't the first time for him either—there'd been others—and please, don't ask me why I stayed with him."

"I wouldn't presume. Did he go to the authorities?"

"He'd have been fired. There were other workers there who knew about his little dalliance. Under oath they'd have talked, he'd be gone. So no, he told only me. But when he died, somebody from the airline came to see me. I guess there were rumblings about Mitch, about shoddy workmanship, carelessness."

She took out a cigarette.

"You can't smoke in this room."

"I know," she said. "I need to hold it. Where was I."

I told her while I stole a glance at my watch. I didn't want to be late to meet Kasi, and I was curious as to why she hadn't called, or even knocked on her way by. Tina noticed.

"I'm taking up too much of your time," she said, and made as if to stand. I stopped her.

"I'm meeting someone at six. She has a cellphone and so do I. Please finish. You've come all this way. Tulsa is not exactly around the corner."

"Albuquerque," she said. "Moved."

"Even farther. Go on."

"I was saying, a man from the airline came—wanted to know what I knew. I was cautious, but he wasn't buying it. He said if I told my story, Mitch might be held accountable. At the very least his good name would be ruined, but beyond that there might be lawsuits that would erode his life insurance settlement and leave us penniless."

"And so he offered you a…settlement?"

"You can call it a bribe," she said, "or a payoff. $100,000 to squelch the investigation into my husband's role in the accident, lay it off to untraceable error. Then came the vow to be better in the future. That last part was to mollify me for the deaths of 273 people."

"You took the money."

"A widow with two kids and an insurance company willing to fight over whether the death was accidental. I took it."

"Nobody would ever blame you. Did you have a sense that your husband was suicidal?"

"Officially he died in a motor vehicle accident, but I know what everyone says. Suicidal? No. He was angry. He was conflicted. He loved me—he loved the kids— he loved his job. But there were the women, and there was this crash, and there was this investigation. I think he combined everything in his head—if he hadn't been screwing around, he'd have been in work, he'd have caught the error, there'd have been no plane crash. Guilt is a powerful force."

"It brought me here," I said.

"It's too late," she said. "It gives me no pleasure to say that, but if you don't realize that immediately, you end up the way Mitch did."

I wasn't ready to accept her pronouncement, but I wasn't able or willing to contest it either.

"What happened the day he died? I mean was it something that set him off?"

"He left for work, hungover as usual, ready to spend another morning with the woman and told her he had information for her. I think the plan was to kill himself and her. But then—who knows why?—he dropped her off at a 7-Eleven, sent her in for some beer, and drove off. A short time later, he was dead."

"How do you know all this?"

"The woman, his girlfriend. We met and talked. She insisted."

"Was that a…good thing?"

"I'm not going to tell you I liked her—she ruined my life. But he did worse—he left me alone. So this woman—she has a name but it doesn't matter— told me that he'd been manic that morning, that when he dropped her off to go into the store, she had no intention of getting back in the car with him anyway."

"So the money?"

"In 1980, $100,000 bought two college educations. I couldn't turn it down."

"And the guy who made the offer—did you ever hear from him again."

"He wrote out the check, I deposited it, he called the next day to make sure everything had gone acceptably well."

I caught my breath. "Those were his words? Acceptably well?"

"Yes," she said. "Are you okay?"

I wasn't.

"That's why you're here. Ken Mullins brought that check."

"Not for blackmail," she said, "or extortion. I don't want to see him, but someone has to know what he did."

I know I looked awful. I wasn't shaking. I wasn't sweating. I wasn't doing any of those things people do when they find that most of their life has been spent worshipping the wrong gods. But Eveline had been right in laying blame where it belonged. How many others had Mullins bribed, or I should say acted as a go-between, making his offers to other family members, survivors, mechanics? It wasn't Ken Mullins's money, and it may not even have been Ken Mullins's idea, but he effected it, executed it, and became the face of the powerful. Eveline knew. I wondered, not only how many had been bribed, but how many more like my sister were out there living with it.

She didn't ask what I planned to do with the information—in fact there was even some light conversation about her kids all grown and doing well. I asked her if she wanted to join Kasi and me for dinner, but she said no, her husband was waiting and they were going to Boston to visit his college friends. We hugged. I think we might even have said something about keeping in touch. I have blurred recollections but little if anything definite, except my utter scorn for Kenneth Mullins, hero of the airport.

I don't think I'm capable of murder, but for a while I was more than capable of thinking about it.

It was well after six, when I finally made it to the restaurant. I was eager to tell Kasi what I'd learned, though I wasn't sure how it would inform anything else we did. She wasn't there.

I described her to a waitress, asked if she'd been waiting. Nobody had seen her. I called her room—nothing. With the irrationality reserved for such occasions, I began to redirect some of my anger her way. Where the hell was she, especially now when I learned that everything my sister believed was right. I called her room a few more times, tried her cellphone, slammed mine on the table, picked it up again, and called Carmichael.

He was on the road somewhere—he wasn't divulging his whereabouts but I assumed, with the conversations we'd had earlier, that it had something to do with Walsh and the threats concerning Sunday. I didn't want to talk to him on the phone. My conversation with Tina deserved face-to-face reactions and decisions.

"Trying to reach Kasi," I said.

"She's not with me," he said. I thought I heard a woman's laughter in the background. Music too.

"Having fun?"

"Is there a problem?"

"There's…no…like I said…"

"She's a big girl," he said above the music playing softer in the background. "Maybe she found someone."

"In an hour?"

"You don't believe in love at first sight?" More laughter.

"I'm serious."

"So am I. You know, just because she doesn't like me doesn't make her a lesbian."

He himself laughed this time, maybe a bit too hard, at his own observation. He sounded drunk.

"That kind of observation is probably why she doesn't like you."

"I'm kidding, Blaine, Jeez. When did you last see her?"

"Two hours ago, give or take"

"Did she leave the hotel?"

"How would I know?"

"Check the security cameras."

"I don't think there's an app for that. You may have that kind of authority; I sure don't."

"You sound stressed, Blaine. That shit will kill you. Who was the cop from Palmer's crime scene, Weber? Call him. Call him personally. Don't go the 9-1-1 route and get some swat team over there. Emptying the hotel will make you look bad."

He laughed again.

"Are you…have you been drinking?"

"All my life, pal."

"I mean today.

"I may have had a few belts. Why? Feeling left out?"

"And you're driving?"

"Someone's driving…I hope…I'm in a moving vehicle. Hey thanks for that Eagles CD. Not my favorite, but it's okay. You realize how lucky we were to find a car with a CD player. They're phasing them out, you know."

"We? *We* found a car?"

"Uh oh, my bad."

More laughter, but not from me. Kasi's ongoing contention that he had a woman was true after all. This time I was the one who was furious, and not about the morality of it. No, he had chosen that particular hour when I was stressed to leave me on my own with no authority and access to nothing.

"Will he do it?" I said. "Will who do what?"

"Weber. Will he look at the tapes?"

"He can access them. So can the hotel, but Weber has authority. You don't. Of course the cops might also say that an adult missing for two hours is not a missing person. If it doesn't work out, call me again. Don't wait too long…even if it's wrong you've got to do something."

"What? What are you talking about?"

"Just singing along. Hey, gotta go."

"When are you coming back?"

"A while," he said. "You can do this. Have Weber call me tomorrow if he needs to."

Tomorrow?

I'd been working with two competent people. Unfortunately, one was now missing and the other was, it appeared, drunk. I was on my own with, apparently, song lyrics as a guide. I couldn't wait to tell Kasi how right she'd been about Carmichael, but I needed to find her first.

CHAPTER 25

I sat and waited a while longer, then worked through a series of minor communication roadblocks and actually reached Weber at his desk. At first he asked some questions I didn't feel comfortable answering—implied accusations that all my faith was in the FBI until right now when I had to make do with the locals. But I made up a story about wanting to keep it as low key as possible so as not to embarrass Kasi—or Carmichael—and gave it credibility by implying a relationship with Kasi. Since I'm not a good liar, the hints were pretty oblique. I wasn't sure he believed me, but pretending made finding her more crucial and personal to me. I needed Weber to bend a rule or two.

"You and the lady—I thought so," he said. "Give me a half hour and meet me in the lobby."

"Yours or...."

"We don't have a lobby," he said and hung up.

He was prompt. He came alone, sports jacket and tie as usual. It was kind of a cool look—almost throwback. It might not pass muster in the conservative-suit corridors where I work, but I resolved to find a Harris tweed jacket when I got back to Chicago and try it.

"We gotta get into her room," he said, and I instantly stopped thinking about clothes. The peremptory tone made me consider the possibility that something really bad might have happened right there, that maybe she'd been assaulted and left for dead a few rooms down from me. The idea of it seemed so vivid that I didn't even ask Weber what he thought he'd find for fear he'd verify my thoughts. The manager called one of the housekeeping staff still on duty and she met us at the door.

"You have a badge?" she said to me.

"He does," and Weber showed her. She slid the card and we were in.

The room looked fine. There was no sign of a struggle, as they say in the cop shows, especially the ones with lots of struggles. Neither was there anything amiss, and though I was hesitant about checking the bathroom, Weber said it looked okay. (I could then erase the image of her dead body in a tub of cold water. Again, too much television.)

"How about fingerprints?" I said. "Can we get them?"

"We? No. This is not a crime scene; in fact it looks less like a crime scene than I imagined it when you called. We can't toss the room for no reason."

"But she's missing."

"No, she's not in her room. There's a difference."

"You think she was kidnapped?"

"Honestly, Mr. Blaine, I think she took a cab into Hartford, found a mall, did some shopping, maybe saw a movie, stopped for a drink—in peace—and lost track of the time. Now look, don't panic, but…" he pulled a pair of thin white cloth gloves from his jacket pocket and slid them on "…just protocol." Then he moved about the room, touching objects here and there. I did my best to pretend this was perfectly normal behavior when a woman went to the movies, but I'm sure the concern was in my voice.

"She would have called," I said.

He ignored me, poked around a bit more, then removed the gloves.

"Let's go. She probably won't be happy finding us poking around in her room when she gets back."

"You did most of the poking."

"So?"

"No, I just…everyone says Kasi Brennan is one of the best," I said. "You don't get to be called that by losing track of time."

"When it's personal," he said—and I couldn't deny it "everything is magnified. We'll do what we can within reason, but we don't have a crime here. Not even a hint of one."

"Can we take a look at surveillance?"

He agreed in his most placating voice and, back at the main desk we met Todd, a young man whose nameplate read assistant manager. He was also, it appears, the head of security and able to set up the system so that we could watch the video. No discredit to Todd, but I don't think anybody can understand how abysmally boring a security tape is unless he's seen one, especially one where nothing happens. Nothing.

We had maybe watched fifteen minutes of it, with plenty of fast-forwarding—when Carmichael arrived with another agent, a younger man. Either he had called for backup or he hadn't been working alone after all. I didn't smell any liquor on his breath, but his eyes looked a little foggier than usual. Weber filled him in on what we had accomplished thus far. It didn't take long. "And the tape?" Carmichael asked.

"Nothing."

"Watch it again," Carmichael said, then turned to the other agent.

"You can go, I got this," he said, then made Weber the same offer, but he declined.

"I want to be here when Kasi comes back and reads Blaine here the riot act for embarrassing her."

"I like that," Carmichael said. "And that kid I just sent home—I don't need to be instructing at a time like this. He'll be a good agent someday, whatever his name is."

I could have argued the value of apprenticeship, but Carmichael did not appear to be in the mood for debate. He turned to the hotel assistant again. "Play it again, Sam."

"It's Todd," the young man said, aware that there was a joke there somewhere that he wasn't privy to. But he played it again, and we watched again, and there was nothing again. Normal activity. No Kasi. Until Carmichael leaned in closer to the screen.

"Back it up a few frames," he told the assistant.

We watched the same actionless frame again, and again. The third time through he said "stop it there" and marked the time from the time stamp. I still saw nothing. He looked at us and smiled.

"Watch this segment," he said, "and watch for anything unusual. Anything." We did. Weber saw it. Then to my complete shame, Todd did.

"Okay," I said, the odd man out, "fill me in." Carmichael turned to the young assistant manager. "Go ahead, tell him."

"I'm not sure if this is what you mean," Todd said, "but right around then we had a notification sound—the door to the parking garage. It's not an alarm and it's a legal exit, but someone left it ajar once and a squirrel got in." He looked at Weber. "Maybe you remember."

"Surprisingly," Weber said, trying to be polite, "I don't remember the squirrel affair. Is there a camera near the alarm?"

"Pretty sure they're right next to each other."

"Probably on the same circuit."

"Probably."

"So," Carmichael said, "when the alarm sounded, you all assumed that someone had left the door ajar. Nobody thought a person had messed with the circuit, bypassed it for maybe ten seconds. Is there another camera?"

"Some distance away. And the lighting is poor. It a long story, but…."

"Cutting corners," Weber said. "I get it. I'm not a safety inspector, but if this case really is a case, everything is going to wind up in my report—including faulty cameras and burned out bulbs. Cue up the other camera."

In seconds **Garage 3—Security** appeared on the screen with a moving time-stamp. Weber was right. The video was dark and the camera mounted on an angle that provided only a short glimpse of anyone using the door, but a much better view of people entering. We fast-forwarded to the time in and waited for a miracle. The one we got was not the one we wanted. At 4:52 a man in a baseball cap entered the garage from the hotel, supporting a woman who seemed drunk. Her face was obscured by the man's shoulder, and the distance and graininess clouded everything else. But I could at least discern her height and her hair.

"It's her," I said. "Positive?"

"No, of course not, It's so fucking dark in there…."

"Relax," Carmichael said. "I'll handle the editorial work. Give me a percentage.

Fifty per cent sure? Eighty? Ten?"

"I'm 100% sure," I said, "but I couldn't swear to it in a court of law."

"Then you're not…."

"Ninety then. Jesus, that's her hat he's wearing to cover his face. If we check her room again, her hat will be gone."

Todd called the manager who, fearing an investigation and a fine, was only too happy to let us back into Kasi's room. We couldn't find her hat: proof of almost nothing, but it made me a more credible observer.

"Call her again," Carmichael said.

"You think I didn't try that a million times?"

"Make it a million and one," he said. Seconds later we heard the muffled sound of her phone from under a pillow on the bed.

"That I don't like," Carmichael said. "Who turned down the bed? And this is not a time to be delicate."

"We're not sleeping together."

"That's on me," Weber said. "I should have lifted the pillow."

The cop stood silently for a moment or two before making his own call.

"I need a…a guy here," he said. "Don't send a team. Minimal. Prints. Not much more. Send Bernie if he's around this late and, you know, don't broadcast it. And listen, you need to have him check for any trace residue of a gas. Make sure he brings everything. It's maybe less minimal than I said."

"What kind of gas?" I said when he hung up.

"There are a few. If he found a way to pump it into her room, by the time she noticed she was too sleepy to stand, he'd have been able to haul her away and she'd be just conscious enough to assist him by not falling to the ground. Someone with a scientific background, chemistry and such, it wouldn't be much of a stretch for him to come up with something clever."

"But why?"

"Don't know that part," Carmichael said. He didn't look as carefree as I wanted him too. Even Weber had to know that, with every passing minute, his easy explanations became less credible.

We waited for Bernie—Bernard Dawes his badge read. I don't know a lot of forensics people so I can't say whether a Megadeth t-shirt, and a small briefcase chained to their wrists are the standard uniform. He looked even younger than Todd the security maven, if that's legally possible. But I remembered the t-shirt— he had been at Ben Palmer's the day before, though at the time I had thought he was a customer lamenting the break in the marijuana supply chain. This time he laid out his panoply of sprays and powders and brushes and went to work.

"My nose tells me no on the gas," he said, "though it could be some odorless shit the guy picked up. If she was drugged, I'd go with an injection…and the guy better have known what he was doing. People die," he said, a little too clinically for my taste, then went back to work. He found nothing glaring, though he agreed that there might be DNA evidence useful at a trial.

Weber told him we didn't have that kind of time to wait, but left with me as Bernie continued his poking.

"Why does he chain the briefcase to his wrist?" I said.

"He thinks it's cool," Weber said. "He's good. We adjust."

Carmichael came with us, still seething. I wasn't the object of his disdain, but I was filling in for whoever was. I knew that when he asked how I could *let* Kasi disappear. I hung close to my new friend Weber who probably carried a gun.

Kasi had been missing less than three hours, but it seemed like days. And there was still Tina Oakes's story which, mere hours before, had changed everything, and which, seemingly in seconds, became a sidebar at best.

CHAPTER 26

Bernie the forensics guy came down a short time later.

"Gas," he said. "Don't know what kind, but the oxygen levels aren't what they should be. I can get a team in here and narrow it down. Where's the lieutenant?"

"Weber left," I said.

"Then why am I talking to you? Nothing personal." He started for the door. "The gas," I said. "Is it harmful?"

"It ain't healthy," Bernie said, "but I'd bet it was used to disable someone temporarily. There'd be no lasting effects other than a strong desire to throw up. One thing you can tell Weber," he said, "or I will. You got yourself a crime scene. Nobody in or out of that room."

Carmichael relayed the order to the desk clerk who altered the room combination: if Kasi were to wander back, she'd need to check in.

"Now what?" I said to Carmichael. "We go back to Walsh's?"

"He's not there, neither is she. I sent someone over after your frenzied phone call. Walsh isn't that stupid."

Carmichael took out his cellphone, then shoved it back into his pocket.

"We have company," he said. I turned around—it was Lon Taggart. Carmichael was not pleased to see him.

"What are you doing here?"

He looked nervous, kept glancing around. "I knew it," he said.

"You knew what?"

"Where's the girl?"

He didn't allow for a response.

"He said if the law got involved, it would not go well."

"Hold on," I said. "Who?"

"Marty Hendricks," he said. "He never trusted you people."

"Then he must be in real agony now," Carmichael answered. "He's in protective custody with us people. Next question?"

"Who does *he* want to be protected from, himself?"

"Don't try my patience," Carmichael said. "You're the one who came crashing in here asking about *the girl*. Why don't *you* tell me why?"

"Hendricks is afraid of everybody," Taggart said. "Usually with good cause.

What did he tell you?"

Carmichael shook his head. "Let me give you the condensed version of how law enforcement operates, Mr. Taggart. We question you. Now if you have nothing for us, we're kind of busy."

"Just tell me this," Taggart said. "Is she safe?"

"You're still asking questions."

The stalemate was getting us nowhere.

"We don't know where she is." I said. "We can't find her."

Carmichael didn't care much for my attempt at mediation. "Goddam it, Blaine, stop talking to this guy."

"*This guy* has been helpful."

"Then why are we still standing here with our thumbs up our asses."

"Not my thumb, Agent."

"Please stop," Taggart said. "I need to ask another question. Am I going to get another lecture on law enforcement?"

"Not if your question has any relevance. Any chance that might happen?"

"You're quite a hardass, aren't you? That working out well for you, Agent?"

"Well enough. What's your question?"

"Can we get a drink?" Carmichael laughed. "Go home."

"I'm serious," Taggart said. "I'm staring at a bar, almost empty, and I'm buying.

Conversations are friendlier in bars. People like me are more talkative."

I told him we were pressed for time. Being cryptic was futile—he knew something was wrong and that it somehow involved Kasi Brennan, but there was an air of calmness about him too, and it appeared that—as precarious as the situation might have been—he could make it better.

"Fifteen minutes," he said. "What do you have to lose?"

I looked at Carmichael, then followed him into the bar. We found a table near the entrance, and moments later we were sitting with three bourbons in front of us, neat.

"Thought you were a beer man," Carmichael said, "and Blaine here…"

"Vodka. I remember. But bourbon is my preference. The thing I like about it, over and above the taste, is that there are rules for making it. Gotta be in the United

States, gotta be more than half corn, gotta be aged in certain containers."

"Charred barrels," Carmichael said.

Taggart smiled. "That's the thing with people like you," he said. "So freakin' smart, so much knowledge, and yet you have to put up this wall. And you, vodka boy" he said, nodding toward me. "We sip this stuff. We don't toss it back."

"Will that lower me in your estimation?"

"Quite a bit."

I eschewed the ice. I sipped.

"Now about Hendricks," Carmichael said. Taggart laid the glass down.

"Eveline's choice," he said. "She wanted an open relationship and I accepted. There was nothing physical with others, but she made it clear that as much as she loved me, her goal was always the same."

"Vengeance," I said.

"*Reparation*, she called it. It always sounded more humane. Now Hendricks could be violent—or I should say had a history of violence. Before we met, Eveline had called the cops on him once, but when they arrived, Hendricks was passed out drunk. She agreed to press charges if they'd get him out of the house. They did. He spent the night in jail. Any intimacy in their relationship ended. I met her a little after that."

"You'll have to fast forward a little," Carmichael said.

"Yes. So Hendricks eventually became almost a satellite, floating around her periphery, all in with her plans but never capable of grasping her motives. Still, when Mullins announced his retirement the clock began ticking louder. She knew I wouldn't buy into anything where people got hurt. Then, and I'm guessing here, Hendricks hatched this plot to disrupt—ruin—Mullins's retirement ceremony."

"But he's in protective custody."

"Which leaves Walsh. Hendricks isn't afraid of me."

"Explain," Carmichael said, "what do you mean that leaves Walsh."

"The only one who would want to disrupt everything you're doing."

"And Kasi?"

"Walsh prides himself on being able to get whatever woman he wants. Any chance they're together?"

"If you mean dating," I said, "then no. Kasi had no use for him as a human being, let alone a boyfriend."

"Did he abduct her?"

That got Carmichael's attention. "Why would you say that?"

"Things are winding down," Taggart said. "Years and years of false starts and dead ends and misspent energy—all of that—and it goes on at whatever pace because there's no last page. And then there is. Sunday. Mullins will be gone, and even though he'll still be alive, he won't be the symbol of anything anymore. Just another retiree."

He meant Eveline. All that time and energy—forty-odd years of it—all for naught on one Sunday in the fall. It would be easy for even the most circumspect person to panic, to lose that caution, to become impulsive, imprudent, even reckless. I still didn't know what role Kasi played in this seeming endgame, but it seemed even more crucial that we find her fast.

I didn't have to point out any of that to Carmichael. "Help us out," he said to Taggart. "Where is she?"

"If she's with Walsh…"

"Let's assume that—and they're not at his home."

"There's another place," Taggart said. "I'm not proud to admit this, Blaine, but I followed your sister one afternoon. It wasn't to catch her, though. It was to protect her. Does that make sense?"

Carmichael wasn't interested in motivation. "And this other place?"

"Walsh had apparently inherited some land from his folks or his grandparents, an undeveloped parcel in Suffield only a few miles from Ben Palmer's place. Got a map?"

We called up a satellite surveillance photo on my phone. The area was heavily wooded, connected to the state route only by a dirt road. And there was something on the property that looked like a skinny cabin.

"It's an old Airstream," Taggart said. "The previous property owner had moved it there with the anticipation of building someday. I checked. There had to be a variance—it was granted maybe five years ago. Walsh didn't bother getting rid of it because it was a place to be, you know, to watch his property. Now there's no reason to drag a woman there, not if he lives alone and has already murdered his wife…."

"Hold on," Carmichael said, his voice approaching earlier levels. "Are you saying that's where Kasi is?"

"If Walsh has her."

"But you're guessing. You're more than guessing. You're just throwing out bullshit possibilities about some kind of abduction. Look, I feel bad for you, Taggart. For you and Blaine both. But you can't expect law enforcement...on a whim...without anything tangible...."

"I'm giving you my word, Agent. I don't do that lightly. Kasi may not be there, but Walsh owns that property."

Carmichael thought for a moment—he wasn't much of a ponderer and the delay heightened the tension for me.

"Okay, order another round. Or two. I have to go make a phone call." He left but we passed on ordering another.

"Five minutes," Carmichael said when he came back. "I talked to Weber—I don't want any problems with jurisdiction. He'll be here in five minutes—we'll all go."

"A caravan," Taggart said. "Sounds like fun."

"You'll be watching it pull away," Carmichael said. "Weber said no civilians."

"I'm out?" I said. "And Lon here who gave you the...whatever...intelligence?"

"The locals are in charge."

"Of a kidnapping? That's FBI. That's why there's an FBI. I don't have to tell you."

"This is not the Lindbergh baby. This is someone who may be missing...."

"The surveillance tape," I said.

"Then let me rephrase that—someone who may be in a surveillance tape that appears to show someone dragging a drunk person through a garage. And beyond all that, we may still have a woman who went shopping, met someone, had dinner, is on her way back right now."

"Without her phone," I said. "People do forget things."

"The gas in her room?"

"None of that specifically identifies her or an illegal act."

"Look," I said, "I work in a field where caution is always advised but the winners take risks. It may not be life or death in those offices, but for some people it's damn close. Their investments are their lives."

"We take necessary risks all the time," Carmichael said.

"Then take one now. Taggart here knows the area and I know Kasi. And she's a federal agent."

"Retired," Carmichael shot back. "She's a civilian."

"Like us. Call it a suspected abduction then and let's go. We're going to argue here for nothing. Eventually we'll be riding along."

Carmichael assured us that it didn't always work that way in real life, but when Weber arrived hell-bent on keeping all civilians out of the procedure, it was Carmichael who defended us. I thanked him, though in truth, all I wanted in those moments before we left for some dark woods somewhere was for Kasi to stroll through the door and ask if she'd missed anything.

It didn't happen.

Two hours had elapsed since my conversation with Tina Oakes, since her revelation about her husband and his role in the flight that had irrevocably altered so many lives. Two hours since I couldn't wait to share the information with Kasi, with everyone, to put an end to Mullins's misbegotten adulation and to expose him for what he was.

And yet, in those two hours that entire conversation had become more of a distant dream than an exposé, and I'd even begun to distrust its significance. Nothing she had said was going to help us find Kasi, but drawing a straight line from Mitchell Oakes to Ken Mullins to Taggart and Walsh was easier than I'd have ever thought—and more depressing.

CHAPTER 27

Even with the high beams blazing, we drove right past the turnoff that Taggart had been continuously warning us to "look out for." So did the vehicle behind us. Even a GPS is useless when the road more closely resembles a hiking trail. Carmichael swore a few times; then one y-turn later we were rumbling over what could optimistically be called a dirt road.

"It's a quarter mile down," Taggart said, his voice strained but more animated than we were used to. Carmichael was aware of it also.

"We're not going to have a problem with you, are we?"

"I'm fine," Taggart said.

He wasn't, but with an FBI agent and an SUV full of locals behind us, Carmichael probably felt he could contain one loose cannon. It was, nevertheless, unnerving—the darkness, the silence. But as apprehensive as I felt, it had to be worse for Taggart. I could hardly imagine what it had been like trailing after my sister like some hapless detective, never knowing what lay ahead but certain beyond doubt it wasn't good. And then to arrive at a place like this and find her with someone like Walsh, regardless of what her ulterior motives may have been, and now to return to the same place—with an audience, no less—if the loose cannon was going to discharge, this would be the time. Or maybe he wanted something to go wrong—that an agent or a cop would put Walsh down for good. I figured he wanted vengeance—that was a desire I understood—but there was something sphinxlike about Taggart that made him difficult to read. I quietly hoped for the best.

Carmichael, the car headlights off, pushed his nose against the windshield and moved us along at a crawl. I expected at any moment to be stopped dead by a fallen tree or some other blockage, but as the woods thinned a little and more moonlight slipped through, we could even discern some seasonal cabins and outbuildings. Little else.

"At one time," Taggart said, "this was supposed to be a development. There's a lake nearby and the plans were set. Then the crash in 2008 came along and that ended it."

"How near is the lake?" Carmichael asked. "Not so near as you'll drive into it."

"You're reading my mind, pal."

"You're more likely to come across a mountain lion or a coyote."

"Thanks for that," Carmichael said. "I have a gun."

"Then Weber will have to arrest you. They're endangered." Carmichael took a deep breath.

"Taggart…don't talk anymore."

"Got it."

Even in the darkness we did see some evidence of land preparation, some areas that had been cleared. In one of them Carmichael stopped the car, the spot offering a clear view of the Airstream and a small sedan parked next to it. Apparently Walsh didn't like taking the black sports car down here.

"Close enough," Carmichael said. "Time to see what's going on."

"I wouldn't, you know, underestimate him," Taggart said.

"I didn't live this long underestimating people," he said, and opened the door. From the back seat Taggart put a hand on Carmichael's shoulder.

"Can we do this my way?"

To Carmichael's credit, he didn't laugh too hard.

"You don't have a *way*, Taggart. You're only here because you know the territory."

"I understand all that. I still think. "

Carmichael remained calm. "Look, I understand. I really do. But, what do you think we should do while you're doing it your way?"

"What do you mean?"

"I mean should we be hiding behind the trailer? Stooping behind some bushes? Pressing up against a big tree trunk? Pick him off when we get a clean shot? Because none of that's gonna happen. It would be dangerous and downright irresponsible to let you handle what is really a police matter."

He slapped the steering wheel. "Jesus, if I don't lose my job for letting you two tag along, I'll be fired for turning you loose to negotiate a hostage release."

"So you do think there's a hostage?" I said.

"I think we'll figure it out soon enough. But I don't want an M.E. out here poring over a corpse because you pissed somebody off."

"I don't want to negotiate anything," Taggart said. "I just want to talk to him."

"And I appreciate your sense of civic responsibility, but you didn't hear me.

Now sit quietly so that we don't have to cuff you."

"I just…."

"Or gag you. Now wait here."

Carmichael left, said something to the crew behind us, then stood outside the car to make a call. In my mind's eye I saw the woods filling with FBI agents, all with high-powered weapons, all aimed at a trailer in a clearing—just a hazy October night, dimly moonlit, with the faintest shiver of a breeze through the dying foliage…and a battalion ready for war. Or maybe it was just a couple of cars on a rutted road. Things are seldom what they appear, though to be honest, I've thought the opposite just as often.

Carmichael returned. "The scanners say there's only one person in that trailer. If it's Kasi, we get her and go home."

We all knew it wasn't Kasi, a fact verified a moment later when the door opened and a man peered out. Backlit by the trailer, he was difficult to identify, but with one hand behind his back, I had no reason to doubt he was armed.

"Who's out there?" he yelled. "This is private property."

"Public access." It was Weber—maybe this was a local matter. "Devin Walsh?"

"Who's asking?"

"Suffield Police," he said. "Are you alone?"

"Why should that matter?"

"Are you alone?"

"Are you?"

"No. We want to talk to you," Weber said, "and we don't want anybody getting hurt."

"Why would anybody get hurt? Unless you were to be shot for trespassing, which is within my rights."

His reply was calm and steady. He sounded bored, maybe tired, but in no way angry or intimidated. Then again, he was alone there, on his own property, in a trailer that belonged to him. I was beginning to wonder why—if Kasi wasn't there—we still were. Six hours had elapsed since she failed to show in the restaurant, and these woods seemed like little more than another place she wasn't.

Weber, however, showed the same equanimity.

"If you shoot somebody from thirty yards, you'd have trouble proving you were defending yourself. And I do have a witness or two, many of them unimpeachable.

Are you ready for jail time or do you want to have a civil conversation?"

"Thirty yards? Too bad I don't have a tape measure."

"Shoot a cop and I doubt you'll have one in prison either, nor will you have thirty yards of anything. Now I've identified myself as police and I'm happy to show you my badge."

"Never mind," the voice said. "Only you locals would be desperate enough to be poking through these woods at midnight."

"Later than that," Weber said. "We just get going at midnight. Are you Devin Walsh?"

"Men in blue, protecting and serving as always. Yes I'm Walsh. What's that you said about unimpeachable witnesses? Got an army out there?"

"We have some personnel. How about your weapons on the ground and we'll talk."

"You have an army. Who's the general?"

"I'm Lieutenant Weber."

"Is this a local operation or is it federal. I know you've got Bureau people with you. I don't want you arguing over whose gonna shoot me. That's how accidents happen. Who else is out there?"

Weber nodded toward Carmichael.

"Alex Carmichael, FBI. I won't insult your intelligence by explaining the abbreviation. Now could you put down your weapon and step away from the door, please?"

"First off, Agent Carmichael, the gun is registered and I'm licensed to carry it. Second, you haven't shown me any ID—how do I know you're not a bunch of teenagers on my property in the middle of the night. Maybe you've come to rob me. Or do something for Halloween. Come back in the morning if you want to talk."

"We need to talk now. We think you might have information on a missing person, woman named Kasi Brennan."

"Met her yesterday, "Walsh said. "Very attractive. Would have asked her out but she was with her boyfriend. I suppose he's with you. Are you out there, Blaine?"

Carmichael grabbed my wrist, his way of telling me not to say anything stupid, or anything *else* stupid.

"He's here," Carmichael said. "We just want to know if Ms. Brennan has tried to get in touch with you."

"With me? I'd be thrilled, but I don't think I'm her type. I didn't see any sparks."

"We have intel that she's with you," Carmichael said. "Mind if we take a look around inside?"

"Intel? Got a drone overhead for a shitty old Airstream? And a beat up one at that? You people must have some budget."

"Can we come in?"

"It's a bit of a mess but, ah what the hell, one of you can come in. The FBI guy."

"Then put the gun down," Carmichael said, but I could tell by his voice that he was disappointed. If Kasi had been in there, the last thing Walsh would allow was entry by anyone involved in law enforcement. Devin Walsh was going to play it out. He went inside, ostensibly to relinquish his weapon, and returned with his hands raised.

"No gun," he sneered. "Don't shoot."

"You know what?" Carmichael said before Walsh could get too close, "I think we went to the wrong slum. No way Kasi Brennan would allow herself to step foot in that piece of shit."

"No need to insult my vacation home," Walsh said.

"Good luck with that," Carmichael said, turning to walk away, then looking back. "You have a good night now."

"We can't be leaving," I whispered. "What did we even come here for?"

"We were looking for Kasi Brennan. Remember her?"

"But Walsh...."

"Hasn't broken any laws. There's no one here."

"Is this some kind of hunch?" I said, "because if it is, it's ridiculous."

"No one is in there," Carmichael repeated, "and we're not going to beat a confession out of Devin Walsh. He's not going anywhere without our knowing about it."

"Should we search his house? I mean his real house?"

Carmichael didn't answer, but Taggart who had been silent throughout the previous exchange, answered instead.

"Already done," he said. "They know what they're doing."

"Maybe, but this Walsh…"

"He's smart, and he has her—I'd bet my life on it. But I don't know what the game is. No one does. Be patient."

We piled back into the cars, swung around without grazing too many trees, then drove away. As we reached the state road Carmichael looked back at us.

"Not one of your better predictions, Taggart. But at least you kept your mouth shut."

"It's one less place he can't disappear to," Taggart said. "You're welcome."

"Yeah yeah yeah," Carmichael said. "Invaluable information. Now both of you kids sit quietly until we get home."

I obeyed, at least for a few moments, but somebody had to ask the question, and I figured, what the hell.

"Now what?"

At my real job, where I assumed I still had a parking spot with my name on it, silences were not an option; and though we were encouraged to think on our own, all that reflection paid off only when we shared, modified, and perfected it. We weren't perfecting anything in that car, especially with Carmichael giving me the silent treatment. It was Taggart who spoke up.

"We need Hendricks," he said. "We need him to go through all that shit and see if we've missed something. I know he's nuts, but he wouldn't do anything to hurt Kasi."

"He's terrified of Walsh," Carmichael said.

"All the more reason to work with us," Taggart said, trying to make the case. "Otherwise, what's going to happen? We check Walsh's house again? She's not there. We go back into the woods, he's there alone. It's whack-a-mole."

"Sort of," Carmichael said, "while everything moves forward except us."

"No disrespect," Taggart said, "but the mole doesn't move forward in that game. He just, you know, pops up."

I thought Carmichael was going to shoot him. But instead, he laughed.

"Well that's helpful. Nothing better than having a mole expert around. Look, if you think someone like Hendricks can help us, and if he's not too frightened to be exposed to the outside world, I'll get him over to the hotel."

*****

Back in my crowded room, Carmichael kept dozing off, Hendricks kept avoiding the windows, and I—I was operating on fumes.

It was 1:00 a.m. and we were past bleary-eyed when there was a knock on the door. I looked at Carmichael—I guess I thought he was going to pull a gun and fire through the peephole at Devin Walsh, but instead he just looked through it and opened up. Ken Mullins stood in the doorway alongside a strikingly beautiful woman in dark-washed jeans, a silky tan top, and an olive green jacket. She was tall, taller than Mullins, but she was wearing heels too, so I won't even guess at her height. I thought she may have been Jamaican. I also thought I was the only one who didn't know her, but I was wrong.

"This is Mallory," Mullins said. "She's here to straighten out this mess."

"At whose request?" Carmichael said.

"Jake Moss."

I didn't know how a discredited NTSB investigator was going to help, but even Carmichael knew the name.

"Is he here?"

"Out of the country with his wife," the woman said, her voice full of modulated nuance, a striking contrast to her expressionless face. "He tried to reach Kasi to find out how things were going. He got nervous. He called me. Here I am. Wanna fill me in?"

"Not really," Carmichael said. "You're kind of late to an ongoing investigation.

Coming in like that...."

"Moss said you'd be a pain in the ass," Mallory said. "Look, I don't want to make this a jurisdictional thing, and you're right: you don't even have to let me into the room. But Jake thinks I can help, and if this all goes south and you didn't let me at least try, you're going to hate yourself. Though not as much as Jake Moss will. Got an honor bar in this room?"

"What?"

"Honor bar. You know, one of those...."

"I know what an honor bar is," Carmichael said. "I'm not used to raiding it pre-dawn."

"Desperate times," Mallory said. "I've been on the road for two hours—let's open 'er up. Last one standing gets to work on this case; the other goes right to the ER."

She was hard not to like, but just as hard to bank on. "And picks up the tab," she added.

Hendricks had been quiet for the entire exchange, then he stood in the middle of the room. "Do I have to be the sane one here? Me? The only certifiable nut job? What the fuck, Alex, let her help."

"It's *Agent* Carmichael, Hendricks."

"Yes, let's stand on ceremony," he said, "while someone shoots me through this window."

He drew the blackout curtains as if to underscore the possibility. I didn't find the act as outlandish as I might have the day before.

"Those won't stop a bullet," Carmichael said. "Why don't you introduce yourself."

"Martin Hendricks," he said to Mallory. "Nice to meet a sistah. I'm in witness protection. Someone wants to kill me. If he doesn't I'm going to get some help. And how's your day going?"

"First off, it's good that you have a plan," she said without skipping a beat. "Now what part of Gabon were you born in?"

"What part of what?"

"If I were really your 'sistah,' you'd know. Call me Mallory—I'm comfortable with that."

"Gabon. Is that one of those African countries?"

She smiled. "Are you sure only one person wants to kill you?"

"Well, is it?"

"West coast, yes. Learn some geography, *brother*."

"Point taken. Come on, I'll show you the good stuff we're sifting through. It's like the Pentagon Papers and the Dead Sea Scrolls all rolled into one. Hey, scrolls are already rolled right? That's pretty good."

The Alex Carmichael I'd grown to know over the past days would never have tolerated such a meaningless conversation, but he seemed out of it, vacillating between moments of energy and those where his head lolled noticeably.

"Just tired," he said, and teetered toward the door. "Be right back."

It occurred to me after Carmichael left that this was the first time I'd seen Mullins since Tina Oakes had explained the man's role in my life, in Eveline's, in thousands of others'.

"I spoke with an old acquaintance of yours this afternoon," I said to him. "Christine Oakes.

"Uh huh," he said, opening the door. "I'll leave you folks to your work."

Weber frowned. "Christine who?"

"Mutual friend," I said, and let the subject drop.

CHAPTER 28

Mallory's forte was negotiating hostage releases.

It was a fact I'd rather not have known at the time, because it left little doubt as to the consensus on Kasi Brennan. Still, there had been no demands, no phone calls, nothing to indicate that there had been an abduction, let alone a ransom. There was even some tacit sense of relief that she was alive, but if Walsh was involved, then the traditional idea of a kidnapping was probably out the window.

We were too bleary-eyed to empty the honor bar—I think Mallory found something to her liking—but we did work on the material my sister had left us. It was like reading the same page of the same book over and over—you always get something out of it, but you're never sure if it means anything. Mallory offered the best chance: new eyes, but I kept interrupting her.

"How many kidnapping victims are recovered alive?"

I could not have been the only one considering that, though I wasn't sure I wanted to hear the answer. I think she was reluctant to talk to me, not out of any protocol or confidentiality, but because she was used to working with law enforcement and speaking their language. My financial résumé would probably not have impressed her.

"Don't get ahead of yourself, Mr. Blaine," she said. "There's no request for money. There's no quid pro quo."

"Do we get her back?"

"And you mean in good shape, and the answer is, usually, yes; but it all depends on the victim and on us."

"Why the victim?"

"Because when the victim does something stupid, the outcome is usually less than favorable. I don't know Kasi Brennan personally, but she comes highly recommended. I know I asked before, but seriously, is there something going on between you two?"

"No. Seriously."

"I'm surprised. Your body language, your phrasing…."

I felt as if I was in middle school being badgered by friends to admit I *liked* somebody.

"Just kind of thrown together by my sister," I said, pointing to the accumulated piles of material. "Would that matter?"

"People in love make unwise decisions."

Hendricks, still hiding from possible assassins, looked up. "You get paid to make observations like that? Hell, I'm your poster boy."

"You have to stop skulking around," Mallory replied quickly. "You're making me nervous."

"Sister, we're black. We should be used to being nervous."

"Thank you, *brother*," she said, her tone icy enough to ensure the fact that Hendricks would never again confuse her with a sister, or any other family relation. Mallory turned back to me.

"As I was saying, unwise decisions," she said. "Or let's say the victim hears the kidnapper toss around some ransom figure, let's say ten million dollars. So the victim makes a logical assumption that no one will pay that kind of money, expresses that belief to her abductor. It's perfectly reasonable. And in a short time the kidnapper believes it too and, seeing no advantage in keeping the person, may decide to eliminate her entirely. That's what I mean by unwise."

"So it's good for the victim to keep his mouth shut."

"Up to a point. He can't be silent or give the appearance of arrogance or condescension either. There has to be a balance of humanity. I mean unless you're dealing with a true psychopath, every bit of kindness or consideration the abductors remove, the victim has to replenish. You maintain a balance and everyone is treated better."

"My apologies," Hendricks said. "May I speak?" We were silent.

"Reason I ask," he said, "is I don't want to be the cause of…."

"Speak, Mr. Hendricks, and get it over with."

"Okay. Okay. You said unless the kidnapper is a psychopath. Walsh *is* a psychopath. Okay, that's all."

"Diagnosed by whom?" Mallory said.

Hendricks looked insulted. "By me. Trust my judgment, sis…um, ma'am. I know one when I see one. Okay, I'll shut up now."

"I doubt it," Mallory said, "but thanks. If he's unbalanced, we have to be even more cautious. We can trust the victim to remain calm?"

"She's a pro," Carmichael said. "She'll handle it."

"She'll be angry," Mallory said, "but as long as she can direct the anger at the situation itself, not the person, she'll be okay."

Hendricks perked up. "Something else."

I thought Mallory was going to have him removed, but she waited.

"Don't want to make you mad," he said, "but when I called Walsh a psychopath before, I was speaking loosely. I'm not really a psychiatrist."

"Noted and recorded," Carmichael said.

"And no one mentioned this, but you've gotta be thinking it, I don't think he would do anything sexually."

Mallory moved a few steps closer to him. "More guesswork?"

"He's too convinced of his own charm. Forcing himself on someone would be humiliating."

"Is that it?"

Hendricks was pacing, all nervous energy and unsorted facts.

"No. When you speak with Kasi, when the kidnapper calls, don't ask if she's all right. It's stupid, right Mallory?"

He didn't wait for a response.

"If she were all right, she wouldn't be a kidnapping victim. We have to work with the abductors. They want something and we want something. They don't *want* the victim—that's just the means to an end. If they do want *her*, then we have some kind of personal motive at hand and that's never good."

I waited for Mallory to contradict him. She didn't. Quite the opposite.

"The man is right," she said, "although how he knows all this leads me to think he has either a law enforcement background, or a criminal one. Which is it, Hendricks? Was it you who kidnapped the Lindbergh baby?"

"Bruno Hauptmann they say, although...."

"We know."

"I kidnapped a fake sheep one time. There was no ransom." Mallory smiled, momentarily. It's all she would allow.

"Mr. Hendricks," she said, "if, when this is over, you're still not in jail or institutionalized, we should talk. But not until then. Who else here knows Walsh?"

I told her that Kasi and I had dropped in, how we had fabricated our roles in the investigation.

"You provided him with motivation," she said, "and you helped him identify his victim."

She rubbed her forehead as if fatigue had suddenly overwhelmed her.

"It doesn't necessarily change things," she said. "There's still a reason behind this and we still don't know it. So we wait and work. If this is all about the Mullins retirement, then we have a pretty strict timeline here. Today at 2:00. That gives us less than twelve hours. Let's push on."

We obeyed. We tried, but by 4:00 a.m. we were all pretty well cooked. No call ever came. No demands. We had gone over Eveline's notes so many times that everything began to blend in, and I couldn't tell the difference between one visit to Walsh's and another, one tirade against Mullins and another, one lament over a lost life and another. We called it quits, agreed on three hours of sleep, split up.

I lay awake for a while, the results of too much coffee and liquor, of course, but also regret and second-guessing. Mallory had made it clear that Kasi and I had made a mistake confronting Walsh at home as we had, and that particular gaffe, though it didn't set any wheels in motion, may have spun them faster. At one point I gave up staring at the smoke detector and turned on the television where I found a World Series game from 1979—ironically, an event that occurred only four months after Flight 191 went down. I wondered if it was a sign, but fell asleep before I came up with an answer.

I woke with a start at 5:17. I wasn't really dreaming, but I seemed to be in some nether state where I could see all the words my sister had written, all the newspaper clippings, Post-it notes, envelopes, photos, that CD, everything. I could even imagine, maybe envision her putting them all together, deciding who should get which one, wondering if anything good would come of them. Somewhere in that hodgepodge of indecipherable puzzles I had seen mention of a Monroe Street.

I'd grown up near one, and remembered as a child visiting my uncle's family out near Nebraska and seeing another one. It turns out that there are about 2000 streets with that name in the United States, probably dozens in Connecticut, more in Massachusetts. I knew the street where Palmer lived, and the Taggarts. Hendricks I wasn't sure of—it could have been a homeless shelter for all I knew— but I found his cell number and called it. He was apparently enjoying a restful sleep in protective custody and was less than enthusiastic when he heard my voice. He assured me that he didn't live on "any fucking Monroe Street," nor had he ever heard of one.

"Monroe Street of all things," I said. "Those were Eveline's words somewhere in that tranche of papers."

Hendricks repeated his lack of knowledge, punctuated it with some harsher language, and hung up.

My phone, which I'd forgotten to charge, registered 13%, but regardless, I used it to zero in on Vance Street where Walsh lived. None of the cross streets was named Monroe, though there were a few other presidents represented. I was about to quit when I found it. It ran parallel with Vance, just to the north and about the same length.

It was still dark when I threw on some clothes, got the car, and drove to Walsh's house. I'm not impetuous or reckless, and I really had nothing in mind except driving the street and looking for anything suspicious. I also had no real thoughts about what that would comprise. I found, predictably, a lot of suspiciously unsuspicious cars near Walsh's place. Cops? FBI? I went past them at the speed limit so as not to arouse suspicion, though anyone driving at the speed limit that time of day is suspicious to begin with. When another car passed me going the opposite way. I felt more normal.

I took my next right and came to Monroe. I turned onto it—another residential neighborhood with adequately spaced homes and the requisite sidewalks and streetlights. I drove slowly past all of it, then turned around and drove back, this time with a car behind me so that I couldn't drive at my leisurely pace. Then the high beams started flashing in my rearview mirror and a uniformed officer stepped off the curb and waved a flashlight at my car.

I didn't recognize the cop, but I recognized the woman in the car behind me. "Kind of a lone wolf, are you?" she said. Mallory looked a lot more put together than I was.

"I was going to call someone," I said, getting out of the car. "When?"

"When I figured out what was going on. Is that one of those Lexus coupes?"

"Hybrid, yes. I like it."

"What's not to like? Isn't that ninety-grand?"

"Actually more. I went for the illuminated door sills."

"Of course," I said. "You don't want to miss a door sill at night. They must pay you well."

She said she *got by*—in a different sphere from the rest of us. Maybe she was that good—good enough so she had extra time to drive to accident sites while others flew coach—good enough to arrive at odd hours depending on highway traffic.

"So you followed me?" I said.

"That's what I do. You don't strike as the hero type, Blaine, but you like to go it alone. Then of course you met Kasi and you liked her and being alone wasn't as much fun. Shall I go on?"

"I thought Hendricks was the psychiatrist."

"Amateur. I'm the real thing. Follow me."

I did, then parked across the street from Walsh's, and not too close to the Lexus, though I wondered if maybe she had sprung for a protective force field to go with her illuminated door sills.

"Now what?" I said to her.

"Hang on," she said, then wandered through the small group of law-enforcement that had gathered.

"Well, we'll probably start with B&E, then move on to other matters."

"B&E?"

"I thought you were a make-believe cop. Gotta learn the lingo."

I told her I was more of a fake Fed. B&E. Breaking and entering. Should have known.

"Now why would a house be clammy in early October?" she asked. "What do you mean?"

"*I hate that clammy house on Monroe Street.* Isn't that why you're here?"

"No."

"There were a couple of references. That was one. Why would a house be clammy this time of year? Not much humidity. Not much dampness. Why?"

"Water?"

"Water?" she said. "How?"

"If it's near a river or stream, the water level rises, the basement gets flooded, there's no sump pump."

"There might be a few streams in the area," she said, "but they don't show on a map. I don't know what the water table is. When the town offices open…."

"It's Sunday," I reminded her.

"Then we'll open them," she said. "What else?"

"Maybe a house without air-conditioning, without a dehumidifier?"

She shook her head. She didn't like my answers. Was she looking for one out of ignorance, or was she waiting for some aha moment from me?

She looked at the brightening sky. "What time is sunrise?"

"You're asking me?"

"No, I wasn't really," she said, looking at her phone. I heard her phone rasp *seven a.m.*

"If we tell Walsh we know about another house, he may be less willing to stonewall us."

"Or he'll shoot us on sight. We're going back into the woods?"

"Nope. He's home. Those cars you saw parked on the street? Feds. Carmichael kept a few people around here to monitor activity. Walsh left the trailer about an hour after you did. Drove home."

"So Carmichael knows too. We should have called him and let him know."

"I did. He doesn't pick up."

"Shacked up," I said. That caught Mallory's attention.

"Where? With whom? We'll go get him. Not gonna let that happen, are we?" For a moment I thought she was serious, then I heard the accusation in her voice.

Maybe the anger. "No idea."

"No idea where? Or no idea if?"

"Both I guess."

"It always amazes me how people can make rash statements without an ounce of proof, and pass them off as facts. Don't do that again. Now come on, we'll work together a bit. It'll be like a date. You obviously don't have a girlfriend."

"Why do you say that?"

"A lifetime of observation. Come on, back door, we'll knock."

I had grown comfortable with Carmichael, but I felt some excitement—some fear of the unknown—being with Mallory. I had wondered how the other half lived. She was that other half, right down to her Lexus coupe.

"Back door," she said. "We'll knock. Sounds more urgent, less friendly."

I followed along to the back of the house and waited while she pounded on an aluminum screen door. I was pretty sure it was going to fall off the hinges, but somehow it held, even when she kicked it. The noise and urgency elicited nothing from within the house—no sounds, no lights, nothing. She repeated the assault. Again, nothing. We walked around front to check the attached garage, to see if his car was inside. The doors were windowless, and the only window on the side of the garage was blocked by a curtain.

"Who puts a curtain in a garage?" she said.

"Mollie Walsh," I said. "The wife Walsh allegedly murdered."

"So they say. You're wearing long sleeves, Blaine. Break the window."

"Do what now?"

"Break the window," she said. "I don't want to go digging around for a big rock."

"I'll help you dig. There must be one around...."

"Keep your back to the wall, quick jab with an elbow. Come on."

"Just like that?"

"Back to the wall...."

"Yes. I heard you the first time."

I got into what Mallory demonstrated as a starting position and gave the pane a jab. Nothing. She was silent. I assumed that was my signal to try it again. I did...and the pain radiated from my elbow in directions I didn't know existed. Nor did I even hear the glass shatter, but Mallory's faint smile of approval told me it had.

"There you go," she said. "If at first you don't...whatever...next time, use the flat surface above the elbow, avoid the funny bone."

That would have been good to know before, not after. Maybe there was more advice, but I'd stopped listening. I wasn't sure if I wanted to live in Mallory's half of the world after all, $100K coupe or not.

CHAPTER 29

Mallory seemed quite proud of herself.

"See?" she said. "Just like you're playing hockey."

"I don't play hockey."

"I can tell," she said, with less disdain than I'd have expected. "Do you hear an alarm?"

I didn't, but I saw what looked like the same car we'd seen parked near the Airstream in the woods. Next to that was his black coupe.

"Nice ride," she said. "Maserati. Now that's lovely. I wouldn't let that out of the garage."

"We saw it outside the other day."

"Idiot, she said. "If we climb through this window and break into the house through some interior door, what do you want to bet the place is empty?"

She didn't wait for an answer, but pulled out her phone. "Gonna try Alex again."

She did, and I heard the unmistakable words of a voice mail.

"Alex, we're at Walsh's, Blaine and I" she said. "It's around 6:30 getting light, we're all in a kind of holding pattern waiting on you. Call me."

She looked at me and shrugged. "Nothing. He'll find us."

I might have argued that with her, but then more police arrived and Mallory was occupied explaining our presence to a few more uniformed officers who showed up at the request of a neighbor who, peering out his window at 5:00 a.m., had seen *something suspicious at the Walsh place*. Mallory's ID carried some weight, but she had to attempt some serious tap-dancing to prevent my being hauled in for simple trespass—simple inasmuch as they hadn't seen the broken window. I wasn't sure she could pull it off, negotiator nonpareil she was supposed to be; but then Carmichael appeared. On the positive side he assured the locals of the integrity of the operation, but then he promised to repair the broken window the locals didn't know existed. I saw cops taking notes. I was pretty sure my name appeared in them. And unlike the inaccuracy in Eveline's obituary, I was pretty sure that this time I was Daniel.

Carmichael also promised that, as soon as things calmed down, the Bureau would deal with any agents who had overstepped their authority. He was good—a little bit of self-deprecation and a little bit of us-against-them. He and the locals were the "us." I didn't care for my new role, but Mallory was more solicitous, even requesting that the cops stay and provide assistance. There may have been some territorial antagonism here, but the overriding sense of duty trumped it, especially when Carmichael started directing the operation.

"We have to get into this house," he said. "We have reason to believe that the owner is holding a woman hostage."

One of the cops—a tall, burly older man named Dobbs—seemed to be in charge.

"How good a reason?" he asked.

Mallory answered. "A hunch, circumstantial evidence. This is Devin Walsh's house—the guy with the South America story, the dead wife?"

"I know that," the cop said, his tone revealing a familiar skepticism. I wondered just how many cops, besides the one Kasi and I had met, were working off the books to nail Walsh.

"Believe it?" she asked.

"I believe the woman is dead. Been on the job a long time—anything's possible—even things that sound a little sketchy."

"Well this is the guy," Mallory said, "but our being here has nothing directly to do with that. It's a different matter, but one that may involve an act of terrorism."

Dobbs laughed. "Terrorist? Seriously? I thought he was just a creep." He looked at Mallory, then at Carmichael. "The Bureau believes this?"

"We don't know, but not knowing where he is makes it more likely. Can you make a reasonable attempt to enter the home?"

"If it's a kidnapping, that's federal. Same with terrorism. Isn't that your domain?"

"Your town, your neighborhood, your jurisdiction," Carmichael said, "but your danger too. I'm happy to lead the charge. Say the word."

Dobbs thought for a moment, looked at the house again.

"Tell you what," the big cop said. "If there's a kidnapping involved, this is already too much conversation." He walked to the front stoop as we followed, leaned on the doorbell with one hand and pounded the door with the other. Nothing.

Mallory stood near him. "He may be armed. We think he may have shot somebody yesterday."

"The old guy in Suffield?"

"We can't prove it."

The increasing daylight revealed the concern on Dobbs's face, and maybe some doubt. He turned to Carmichael.

"The guy who lives in this house in this neighborhood—two murders and a kidnapping? Can I see those IDs again?"

Carmichael started to oblige.

"No, no," Dobbs said. "I believe you."

He sent another officer to the car for a vest and a shield.

Carmichael put an arm around him. "You look like a family man, Dobbs," he said. "I don't want to be the one explaining to that family why you don't come home anymore. If someone gets hurt here, it's not going to be you. Vest or no vest, theory or no theory. We all right on that?"

Dobbs appeared grateful, but undeterred.

"Break the door, hit the floor. Works every time."

"You've done this before?"

"No," Dobbs said, and smiled. "Should I have?"

And without any further discussion, he kicked it in. If he hit the floor, I didn't notice. There was no response from inside.

Mallory touched my arm.

"That's the way you do it," she whispered. "Try to remember." I made a mental note not to.

She was about to enter when Dobbs stopped her.

"No," he said. "I have an odd feeling. Sniffy goes in first."

Even I could figure out who Sniffy was, though I'd have thought they could come up with a more original name—one that a dog could be proud of.

"We have some time constraints," Carmichael said. "How long before Sniffy gets here?"

"Ten minutes," Dobbs said, "but only if the handler is around."

He wasn't. After 25 minutes of watching daylight overtake the neighborhood, watching the curious gather, and watching Dobbs fume and make threatening phone calls, Sniffy arrived—a large dog of no discernible breed but apparently one extraordinary talent. She had worked in airports for a while, but when it was time to taper back, the locals were able to purchase her. Like every animal, she stole the show when she arrived, and again when she gave the all clear with a few flicks of her tail. Nobody home. No bombs. No noxious atmosphere. The place was empty. "She's invaluable," Dobbs said while the dog was brought back to the vehicle. "I'm going in first—find the main breaker and pull it. You never know what's rigged to a light switch."

He was in and out in under a minute.

"Your show now, Agent Carmichael," Dobbs said. "Happy to watch from a distance."

"You're good," Carmichael said. "You know, I never broke down a door."

"Damn thing was harder than I thought," Dobbs said, holding the back of his leg. "I may have tweaked a hamstring. Probably need some bedrest this afternoon, you know, when the games are on."

"I'll write you a note if you need an eyewitness to the injury," Carmichael said, and shook his hand. Dobbs wasn't leaving, though—his street, his town.

I wasn't sure what was accomplished by breaking into an empty house, not with a deadline looming, but Carmichael said we'd narrowed Walsh's world by a lot.

"He can't come here. He can't go to the Airstream. Hendricks is under protection."

"But we're running out of time. Where the hell were you?"

Mallory shook her head—late advice that I should not have asked—then she nudged her way into the confrontation.

"I think we were concerned that…"

Carmichael wasn't listening: he was focused on me.

"That's not your business," he said. "And what the hell were you doing breaking into a private residence? Whose idea was this? And try to answer without throwing Mallory under the bus."

"I was looking for Kasi," I said.

"Oh, really. Did you ask me? I know where she is. Mallory obviously knows where she is now. The only one who doesn't is you, and yet you broke into Walsh's home—where she isn't. What the hell were you doing breaking into a private residence? Did I ask you that before, because I'll bet the cops would like to know too."

"Okay, I get it."

"And where I was or what I was doing is none of your business. I had something to attend to, I'm here now, fill me in." Mallory made another attempt to save me.

"The problem," she said, using her best mediation skills, "is that we can't stay ahead of Walsh so we have to react instantaneously. Maybe this wasn't the best idea, but under the circumstances, I was okay with it."

Carmichael was still angry. "Let's check with our investment advisor here and find out how to proceed."

Mallory paused for a moment to let the words die, then repeated "instantaneously."

"Okay," Carmichael said, "I get it. So he's over there?"

He pointed across the backyard to another house on the next street, Monroe. "Has to be," Mallory said. "The street is mentioned in Blaine's sister's notes. I checked with the locals before I made a move—the family that lives there notifies the police every year that they'll be gone for six months, that a neighbor is housesitting."

"Walsh," he said

"The leaf blower," I said. They waited.

"When we were here, he had all these tools outside, including a leaf blower. He has no trees, but maybe the other house does."

"And you picked up on that?" Carmichael said. "No," I mumbled. "Kasi did."

"Oooh, I was almost impressed. Maybe next time."

He looked up and down the street. Most lights were off—daylight had taken over.

"Okay," Mallory said. "Time to make the call."

I asked what she meant, but Carmichael answered for her.

"The one that turns this neighborhood into a war zone, Mr. Blaine. That'll be me."

For a while longer I was shunted aside. That's not a complaint: I actually felt more comfortable watching things unfold than trying to make believe I knew what I was doing.

Of course the locals thought I did—I kept waiting for one of them to ask who the hell I was, but I gained some credibility by seeming to be *with* Carmichael and being on a first name basis *with* Mallory. I think—I never did learn if that was her first or last name.

I lost sight of them both. Moments later the sirens began, and a peaceful suburban Sunday morning in southern New England exploded into a tsunami drill with Walsh's house serving as the epicenter. Mallory reappeared.

"Kasi Brennan. She's really not your girlfriend, right? That's what you said before?"

"Yes. We're just…you know…"

"Have you seen her naked yet?"

"What? no!"

"Just stay close."

Mallory seemed disappointed, as though she had misjudged. She was the kind who didn't abide that sort of error.

"Wait a minute," I said. "Yes?"

"Why did you ask me that?"

"Trying to gauge your relationship."

"We don't have one. I mean we get along and everything." Only after the words were out did I realize how stupid they sounded.

"I guess that'll have to do. Like I said, don't go anywhere." As if I would.

I did like Kasi. I had even gone a reasonable amount of time excluding Bethany from my conscious thoughts, at least until I realized I wasn't thinking about Bethany, which meant I was. Maybe just the guns and cops and the threat of a missile had distracted me. And Dobbs—there was a story I could tell if I ever survived this. I took Mallory's advice and stayed close—and out of the way—and quiet.

Full daylight more clearly detailed the simple white Cape on Monroe Street— a yard with a swing set and some fencing that indicated an in-ground pool, a strand of trees, some of which had already begun shedding their leaves. Only one maple retained any real color.

Determined as I was to steer clear of the action, I couldn't help hearing Carmichael in conversation with another agent. It sounded grim, but when he finished I got his attention and he came over.

"I don't want to bother you," I said, "but can you tell by radar or whatever how many people are in that house."

"It's not radar."

"And?"

"We're reluctant. We don't know what's in there, what kind of electronic equipment. Walsh is not your typical criminal. He may not be the smartest guy in the world, but he'd hold his own."

"So what do we do?"

"Hang tight."

"That's it? That's your plan?"

"No. That's my plan for you. You'll be busy enough soon, especially if you want to help your…whatever she is."

"Mallory asked me if I'd seen her naked. Why would she ask that?"

"Why don't you ask her?"

"I did. Look, Agent, I'm sorry about before."

"Good. As for Mallory, she's probably wondering how you're each going to respond to the other. Is she going to trust you, you know, that sort of thing."

"But I'm just…here."

"You'll be busy soon enough," he said again. This time it seemed more like a threat. Before I could ask for an explanation, though, the weapons arrived on the shoulders of four men in military uniforms who wordlessly marched through the broken doorway and ascended the steps to the second floor. Then, just as the sun had reached high enough to delineate every long shadow, Lon Taggart arrived.

After that, remaining blasé, or even hopeful, became more challenging.

CHAPTER 30

Taggart, huddled in the driveway with Carmichael and Mallory, looked like a man plotting a revolution. I kept out of the way, waiting until it was my turn to elbow another pane of glass.

I'm not complaining about my supposed role. These were jobs for law enforcement, investigators…that sort. Still, there was something almost seductive in being caught up in it, being a part of it. The feelings were sporadic and always transient—always tempered by the fact that Kasi remained in danger…and I didn't.

Then Carmichael waved me over and in one terse comment, that changed too. "We're going over there," he said, looking at me. "Just the two of us."

"You and Mallory?"

"Am I talking to Mallory? The two of us. *Us.*"

"But I…" I looked at Mallory for support. Her face exuded that artificial confidence—like the smiling parent taking his kid on the roller coaster, certain that neither of them was ever coming back.

"Why me?" I asked.

"We're not storming the place," Carmichael said. "If he's in there—and we think he is, or someone is—at least we're two people he knows. And if Kasi is in there with him, he'll know we're not going to do anything crazy and endanger her."

"Is Kasi in there?"

"Yes," Mallory said.

"So you did use radar then," I said, "or some kind of scan?"

"Not really," Mallory said. "I peeked in the window. Sometimes that works too.

So what do you say?"

"This is going to sound like an excuse, but Walsh doesn't like me."

Carmichael laughed. "Not sure if I do either, but Kasi does. She'll feel more comfortable knowing that you're not the law but you're still there—so that maybe it isn't so serious. The thing is, if he hasn't tried to run with all that's going on nearby, then he has other cards to play. Even if we can't see them, we'll at least know how many he has."

"Not to ruin your analogy, Agent Carmichael, but if you see five cards in my hand and they're garbage, how do you know they're not aces over jacks?"

"Because I'd see it in your face," he said, his tone rising. "Do you really want to debate this? I'll get a timer and some judges and a trophy for the winner. Or just say no—that's your right. But decide now."

"I don't want to be in the way or do something wrong."

"That will not be an issue. I'm the professional here and I don't fuck up. Now Lon over there, he wants to go but he might be too emotionally involved. Maybe too volatile. Walsh may see him as a rival. But understand, it's entirely up to you."

"If I don't?"

"I'll take another agent. But we're moving now. Time is on our side until he can attach faces and actions to what's happening."

Without pondering this any further, I said okay. I don't think I felt afraid. And even though I'm not a risk taker in the sense of skydiving or mountain climbing, I've taken some chances and felt the exhilaration involved in barreling down a ski slope or riding a zip line or once, even, parasailing with Bethany sitting next to me. Of course in none of those events did I expect someone to shoot me, and the unknown quantity—what lay behind the door we were expected to approach—made this a lot dicier.

Carmichael knew I'd agree, probably knew I had feelings for Kasi, even if they weren't romantic, knew that I wouldn't back away from a chance to help her.

It was Mallory, though, who made me wish I hadn't agreed.

"Just a word of caution," she said. "When you see Kasi—if she's in there—she's not going to look like the woman you saw the other day; don't point that out to her."

"Of course not."

"I don't think you're hearing me."

"I heard you. Don't overreact to…whatever."

"That's easy to say now. And don't lie, like you just did with me. Women know."

"Don't men know?"

"They're not lied to as much. Do you want to debate that too?"

"Yes, but not now. And don't worry I'll be able to handle it." My assurance had no effect on Mallory.

"She's a crime victim," the agent reminded me. "I've known women whose homes were burglarized who then burned their clothes—one lady torched them right in the fireplace and wound up with the fire department saving the place—from which a month later she moved anyway. Victims don't always brush things off or behave rationally."

"I'll do my best."

"I know you will, Mr. Blaine. But let me say one more thing. You might be angry when you see Kasi."

"Why would I be angry?"

"She's been victimized and she's your friend. Anger is normal. Just keep that out of the equation. She's there to be rescued—not judged or pitied."

"Comforted?"

"If you can speak with her, don't ask her how she feels. Ask her if she's thirsty, or hungry, or needs to pee. You can't make her feel good, but you can make things more bearable. Tell her you're there to help, don't say 'we're gonna get you out of here' even though everyone knows that's why you're there. We don't want Walsh to become defensive."

"You think they're both there?"

"My gut says yes," Mallory said. "But I saw only her."

"But you're the negotiator. Shouldn't you be doing this?"

"Walsh knows you. Kasi knows you. Introducing another stranger is ordinarily a good thing, but your relationship with the victim might help her. Another thing, I don't see this as a long-term negotiation. Whatever Walsh is planning, getting away from here is part of it."

"With Kasi?"

"As a hostage? Maybe. That's another unknown. Alex here will know when it's time to cut and run. Then I would take over."

"And pick up the pieces?"

That probably wasn't my wisest statement of the morning, and occurring so early left me lots of time to make even stupider ones.

"Just tell us if you're up to this," she said. She sounded impatient for the first time, and I was undoubtedly the cause. "If not we can...I don't know...."

"No, I am."

"Let's go," Carmichael yelled. "Car's out front. Or," and he pointed at me, "do you think we should cut across the back yard?"

"I don't want to fall into the pool," I said. Nobody laughed.

"Car, then," he said, then yelled at no one in particular. "Stand down on the other order until you hear from us."

We got into a blue, late model Honda Accord. I doubted it was FBI-issue. I got to ride shotgun with a dour-looking woman in dark jeans and black windbreaker and knot cap. She looked like a bank robber. My "partner" sat in back and tapped out a text message.

"Arranging for our wake? "I said.

He looked up. "Open or closed casket? They need to know."

"Open, "I said. "I don't like being confined."

"Done," he said, then finished texting.

"A few minutes ago," I said to him, "back at the house, what order did you rescind?"

"Shoot to kill. Try not to think about it."

"Try not to tell me next time."

"Try not to ask."

Our driver parked in front of the cape we'd seen only from the other side. An S-shaped sidewalk led to the front door through small patches of yellowing, summer-burnt grass. As ragged and exhausted as the lawn appeared, it had been recently mowed. Walsh may have been a homicidal maniac, but when he house-sat, he did it right.

Carmichael was more analytical. "No sense mowing if you don't fertilize," he said. "Can't just let the lawn go like that."

"I guess we can add your comment to Walsh's rap sheet," I said. "Incompetent house sitter."

"Rap sheet? Are you on the job?"

"No, it's you know, one of those terms…."

"…that cops use on television. You're not a cop. Not here or on television. Don't act like one or Walsh will think you are one. He already doesn't like you."

"Got it."

"Now, nice and easy," Carmichael said, "let's go in."

I didn't even have a chance to challenge his reprimand, to tell him this was no time to argue about a breach of protocol. Besides, once we exited the car and I kept hearing the term "dead man walking" rattling around my skull, I became less concerned with defending my right to use police jargon.

"Now listen, Blaine, just walk like you're…I don't know…walking?"

"Like visiting a friend?"

"Like that."

I tried to seem natural but felt I was lurching in every conceivable direction, as if the soles of my shoes were angled and the walkway was crooked. Then, when I saw the interior door was ajar and only a flimsy screen door stood between us and whatever, my legs felt even wobblier.

Carmichael knocked. After maybe ten seconds and no response, he knocked again. He was armed of course, but even that provided little comfort. Cops answering domestic violence reports had been senselessly ambushed and killed. Walsh's history seemed to deny that sort of thing, but someone so seemingly unprincipled was hard to predict. If a business exec from Chicago were to become collateral damage for him? No problem.

"Gonna go in," Carmichael said. "Stay close…as opposed to running down the street."

He pushed open the door and we looked into a modestly appointed but unoccupied living room.

"FBI," he shouted. "Anybody home?" His voice, despite the volume, showed no urgency other than demanding a response. Seconds later we heard, "in here."

After our previous encounters, I recognized the voice—the same arrogant tone I'd heard at his house and in the woods. It was Walsh.

Here was a kitchen with the curtains drawn, shutting out the brightest of the sunlight but allowing a filtered version to seep through. Near a small table Walsh sat with a cup of something, a cell phone in front of him, and a half-opened newspaper on the table.

"One of your functions," Carmichael said. "Take care of the paper."

"Actually the family stops the paper. Just doing an old crossword. Ever do those?"

"Can't be bothered," Carmichael said.

"Really? Someone like you? Good mental exercise, especially as you get older."

"I'm sure it comes in handy in everyday use."

"Helps me concentrate," Walsh said. "Especially *this* morning—all that craziness out in the street and over at my house. I got a broken glass warning on my phone. Any idea what that's all about."

"Could be a bird strike," Carmichael said. "Autumn. Migrations. Lots of those big ones around."

"I guess. What *is* happening over there?"

"Some son of a bitch is getting arrested."

"I'll bet it's the Dunnes next door. They smoke marijuana all the time. I can smell it. Thank goodness for law enforcement. What would we do without them?"

"What indeed," Carmichael said, pulled another chair over and sat. I remained standing.

"So, what can I do for you gentlemen that we didn't tend to last night? And I'm sorry—he pointed at me—I've forgotten your name."

"No you haven't," I said.

He frowned. I don't think he enjoyed my contradicting him, but he knew my sister and he was damned well going to know me. He leaned back, settled himself.

"Blaine, I remember now. So? What's up?" Carmichael leaned toward Walsh.

"We're looking for somebody," Carmichael said. "A young woman."

"Kasi Brennan," Walsh said, then looked at me. "She's your girlfriend right? The two of you were up here recently nosing around. I didn't realize then you were a real Fed. Or are you just tagging along as a nobody again?"

"He's with me," Carmichael said.

"You know, I meant to tell you the other day. You're a good-looking man, but never could quite finish the deal with your old girlfriend, right? Your sister used to worry about you, told me she wished you'd been able to settle down. But that's water over the dam at this point."

"Under the bridge," Carmichael said, before I could respond. I don't think he wanted me engaging. "Any idea where we might find her?"

"I know exactly where you *will* find her," he said cheerily. "Come on."

Walsh stood up and Carmichael shoved him back down so hard that he slammed into the chair and tipped backwards slightly before steadying himself. Walsh glared at us, but some of the edge was gone from his voice.

"What was that all about?"

"Just wondered if you were packing."

"There's a verbal method, you know. It's called asking."

"I guess that might have worked too. I'm going to remember for next time."

"It's true what they say about the FBI—the Neanderthals of law enforcement."

"I like that," Carmichael said. "That would look great on our seal, the one that says fidelity, bravery, integrity. Tell you, some days I feel most of those myself. Today I'm not feeling that third one."

"I don't think you're in a position to threaten me."

Walsh was still in control and, at some level, we all knew that. But Carmichael had overpowered him physically; and Walsh, most of whose abuses seemed to have involved people weaker than he, had lost a little swagger.

"Like I said before you went all caveman on me, come on."

He slid his coffee cup to the center of the table and tried standing again. This time Carmichael allowed it. We followed Walsh through the kitchen and into the attached garage where an old sedan was parked—a small Pontiac.

"The owners don't want a new car—they're never here. It's the last year GM made the Pontiac. Nice, huh?"

"Open the trunk," Carmichael said. "Why?"

"Because it'll save me the trouble of finding a crowbar in this garage and opening it that way. I don't want to ruin this classic of yours."

"I don't know what you think you'll find there, or what you think I am, but have at it."

Walsh opened the trunk with a great flourish—it was filled with junk—rags, empty water bottles, bound newspapers, probably a spare under it all

"Happy?"

"You were supposed to bring us to Kasi."

"I said I knew where she was. In a minute so will you. Now I'm going for a ride," he said. "But you're not coming with me. And between now and this afternoon, you won't follow me, you won't triangulate me, you won't do anything that interferes with my life. And Kasi—who is fine—will remain that way as long as you behave."

He took his cell phone from his pocket. "In return, when the time comes, I'll dial a certain number and disarm the device. Do we have a deal?"

I thought Carmichael was going to knock him down again. "What device?"

"There has to be a device, Agent Carmichael. You can't have an explosion without a device."

"What about Kasi?" Carmichael said.

"This is about Kasi, goddammit," Walsh said, the barbed words belying the placid expression. It was the first time I'd seen him angry or frustrated. I didn't like the look.

"She's inside," he said, forcing himself to be calm. "She'll be fine, and all you have to do is nothing. How hard is that?"

"And if we don't."

"I'll dial a different number. Or maybe no number. After a while, each will have the same effect."

"And blow up a plane."

Walsh laughed. "You two—are you really the best they have? I told you, this is about Kasi. Do we have a deal or not? What do you say, Agent Carmichael?"

"Go," he said. "I'll make sure you're not followed."

"Or traced. I'm pretty smart—I'll be able to tell. Of course the deal will be off."

"You're pretty smart. We got that."

"Are you sure?"

"Enjoy the day, Walsh. We never know which one will be our last, or our final day of real freedom. So yes, take your phone and enjoy."

"How very kind of you. Now about Kasi—first floor, dining room. You walked right past her. She's a little drowsy. She wasn't, of course, until you started setting up for war across the way. In a half hour or so she'll be fine, and there's no reason she can't stay that way. Now give the order or whatever—the one that lets me drive out of here."

He didn't wait for an answer, just pushed back the seat and backed slowly toward the street.

I heard Carmichael bark orders into his phone—*don't follow him. Let him go.*

Then after a brief silence, a louder command. *There's a hostage. Let him go.*

He clicked off.

"I'm going to kill that son of a bitch myself," he said, then rushed back into the house. I could barely keep up.

CHAPTER 31

She's there to be rescued—not judged, not pitied, not comforted, Mallory had said, advice I'd forgotten until I rushed into that den and saw Kasi sitting upright in a straight back chair, naked from the waist up. Mallory's earlier seemingly impertinent question made the agent seem suddenly prescient. In truth, most of Kasi's upper body was adventitiously but discreetly shrouded by a mass of wires and cylindrical objects that, even to my untrained eye, could be nothing other than incendiaries, detonators, whatever components make up a bomb. *You can't have an explosion without a device*—Walsh's taunt from moments before. I wanted to kill the son of a bitch too.

She looked woozy, but she was awake and, at least to some degree, aware.

Carmichael, awkwardly looking away, motioned for her to be still. "We don't want any undue motion," he said.

"You can look at me when you're talking," she said.

"I just don't want to…you know…"

"Embarrass me? Believe me, you seeing me like this is not the most important thing on my mind right now."

"Then let me just," he began, still hesitating but moving closer, "let me take a look at this…this mess."

I watched him lean in close, pull back, walk once around the chair, lean in once more, then back away. He stood next to me and took a deep breath.

"Blaine, go on back to Walsh's house."

"And do what?"

"And don't come back—you can't stay here."

"He's right," Kasi said. "This is a crime scene."

"If anyone should be here, it's me."

"Because of your sister," Kasi said." That's guilt, not logic. We need technical people."

"She's right," Carmichael said. "One way or another, someone was going to end up here, or somewhere like here. It's not fate; it's a logical sequence of events that took forty years to play out. I understand guilt, but you probably had less to do with this than you think. Now leave before you're forcibly removed."

"By you? I'm bigger than you are."

"I have a gun."

"Seriously, you're going to shoot me and take a chance on this…thing…going off?"

"Daniel," Kasi said. "This is not the place to make a stand. This is not your environment."

She spoke with authority and even, I guess, the confidence born of her earlier experiences. But she didn't look the same. Her streaked blond hair that had looked so cute in that coffee house in DesMoines, now appeared darker, matted, the brightness and luster gone. Her eyes were a dingy gray, their color having been diluted, erased. And all this after one day—what became of innocent people locked up for months? Years?

The dissonance of tension and fear, maybe even the deprivation of hunger, had altered her. And as if to underscore her helplessness, some of her clothes lay carefully folded on a chair nearby as if she'd been a young child and her mother had cleaned up after her.

Her head lolled slightly and her eyes shuttered half-closed. "What did he give you," Carmichael asked.

"Don't know. Something to keep me calm. It's not working anymore."

"Better than you think," Carmichael said. "Don't fight it. He said it would wear off, but if you think you can't stay still while we work on this, I can have a nurse come in…."

"I want to be awake for…whatever," she said. "Can this be disarmed? I can't see what's behind me."

"I'm no expert," he said, "but it's standard fare—everything can be disarmed." It was a non-answer, or an evasive one at best. Sidestepping the question had made the danger seem even more immediate. I asked him if he planned to call it in, to get some bomb disposal people on the scene.

He seemed deep in thought, at least at first. Then I wondered if he was there at all.

"Agent," I said.

He took some pills from his pocket and chewed them. I had heard that people having a heart attack were supposed to chew aspirin immediately.

"Agent, are we okay here?"

He grimaced, swallowed hard two or three times.

"No," he said. "We aren't because you're supposed to be gone."

"Then throw me out. You have a gun."

"Really? This is you being the hero now?"

"I told you, I belong here."

He shook his head. "The time I spend arguing with you is time I'm wasting trying to get this kid out of here. So stay, sit down, make yourself a sandwich, raid the liquor cabinet…do whatever, just try not to detonate anything."

I was about to thank him when the landline in the kitchen rang. "Mallory," I said.

"No. It's not."

He answered on the third ring.

"What did you do to her?" Carmichael said. It wasn't Mallory.

A few seconds went by, then Carmichael pushed a button and laid the phone on the kitchen counter.

"We're all here listening. Go ahead."

"You should both pay attention," the voice said. It was Walsh, still confident and smarmy. "The girl will be fine unless you fuck up. Now listen to me. Be careful where you walk. Stay out of the area immediately surrounding her. I don't want you tripping a switch or catching your finger on some wire while you're trying to slip a sweater over her head. If you haven't seen a naked woman by this point in your lives, then you're too pathetic to worry about. And if she hasn't been seen naked, then she's already missed out on too much. Are we clear so far?"

"You're an asshole," Carmichael said, "and I'm going to enjoy watching a bullet enter your brain."

"It's a good brain. What a waste that would be. And bullets travel faster than your old eyes could see. Speaking of old age, why aren't you spending time with your wife? Years pass, agent. People die. You're wasting a weekend on me?"

Carmichael went silent. He may not have been my favorite person, but seeing him silenced was disconcerting, even though he wasn't quiet for long.

"What about the drug?" he said. "What did you give her?"

"Don't want to talk about the family, huh? I understand. We all have secrets."

"The drug," Carmichael repeated, "what is it?"

"It's my own proprietary blend. Chemists can do all sorts of shit you people can't. And listen—no aftereffects or psychosis. So stay focused. Kasi will be fully awake and alert in a few minutes. Be there when it happens so she doesn't freak. I told her what was going on and told her she'd be safe as long as she didn't struggle. But if the stuff wears off and she's hyper, my warning won't be any good. Are you two getting this?"

"She's already awake. Your timing is off. Wonder what else you fucked up."

"Sowing the seeds of doubt. Good for you, agent. Now listen to me." Against my better judgment, I interrupted.

"You had to undress her?"

"That you, Blaine? I don't deal with you. You're not part of this."

"What about Eveline? Should I ask for an autopsy?"

"She got sick and died. What do you want from me?"

"Maybe I'll ask for an autopsy."

"Be sure to let me know how that works out. Look, Blaine, if you feel remorse, that's not on me."

"What kind of chemical concoction did you use on your wife?"

"Is that the Daniel Blaine shotgun method of crime-solving. Fire away and hope you hit someone? You do whatever you want—you aren't part of any equation. And as for Kasi, she's wearing underwear. I needed the workspace. I wasn't going to worry about some underwire bra or metal buttons or anything else. It wasn't personal or deviant. I never touched her. You can ask her."

"Oh sure," Carmichael said, rebounding, "we'll ask the woman you drugged if you raped her."

"Time is wasting," Walsh said. "Whatever you think happened, didn't. Whatever you're afraid is going to happen, will. Are we clear? Now Agent, go back in the room and stand behind her. Carefully."

He did. I hung back a few feet.

"There's a digital timer? It's dark. Don't touch it."

"I don't see it," Carmichael said.

"Look again."

Then even I saw it—numbers filling a small readout.

"Pretty cool, huh?" Walsh said. Now we're armed. Four hours and thirteen minutes takes us right to 2:00 p.m."

"Then what?"

"Then you can do whatever you want. The device will neutralize all by itself.

You can cut wires, jiggle the detonators, hit it with a golf club…it'll be harmless. You know how people have to fight against the clock to disarm a bomb? The tension? The sweat? All the delicate maneuvering? It's the opposite for you two— once the time is up, everything will be okay. Until then, not so much. Are we clear?"

"Did you actually build this?"

"I copied the plans from an expert, made a few adjustments, added a few complexities. Yeah, I built it. Impressed?"

"I am," Carmichael said. "Would a Google search show me a way to disarm it?"

"That's amateur hour, Agent. And Blaine, if you're still there, your sister spent forty years trying to get even and I'm giving her the chance. Why are you interfering?"

"She would not have wanted this."

"You didn't know her. You chose not to know her. You're not honoring her life; you're just being a hypocrite."

"I know that in forty years she never murdered anyone."

"I tend to think you're right. Of course we never know everything about anybody, but I'll give you that one. Can I say one more thing? I know human nature—the curiosity, the desire to help. Understand something please—a bomb kills in several ways."

"We don't need your science," Carmichael said.

"Maybe you do. When a bomb goes off, the force of the blast can take your head off, or your arms or legs. You saw what happened at the marathon that time. Grisly. But you know what else? The blast can bruise your lungs—they bleed, you die. Just as grisly. It can sever veins, rupture the liver, and that's just the blast. The shrapnel can rip you open, the impact can destroy the brain, and we haven't even talked about burns, fire, a devastated structure falling on the victim and suffocating him. You don't want to mess with any of that. You don't want Kasi to be the victim of some misplaced courage or benevolence. Are we clear?"

"Yes," Carmichael said. "Can I add to your list of effects?"

"It's pretty complete."

"Humor me."

"You don't really have time for…."

"A continual hunched over position, a tendency to walk in circles, the disappearance of all social skills, the inability to reason or calculate. Then there's hallucinations, paranoia, memory loss—I heard of a man who became obsessed with incontinence that he spent every hour of every day in front of the toilet trying to pee."

"What are you talking about?"

"I'm talking about your future, Walsh—a lifetime of solitary confinement. Kiss your brain goodbye. Say hello to a lot of blubbering and drooling."

"You seem a bit overwrought, Agent. Calm yourself."

"What drug did you use on her?"

"I told you, it's my own concoction. It's all I had. She'll be fine when she wakes up."

"GHB?"

"A bit, and don't read into that. I never needed any seduction assistance. I ask you again, are we clear?"

"We're clear."

"And you're thinking you'll evacuate the airport, cancel the event, divert the 777, everyone lives happily after. You can do that of course...."

"But then you detonate."

"Absolutely. And I can just take down another plane or another building or maybe a neighborhood like mine right where you are. No, your best bet is to let things take their course. The girl lives and the Bureau has something to do—search for a mass murderer. When the Russians shot down that plane and nobody paid? This time you'll have a culprit. You just won't be able to find him. And I won't be like the Vegas guy with the arsenal in his room. I plan to live."

He hung up. Instantly Carmichael was on his cellphone. He wanted a medic, someone who knows drugs, anesthesia, pain killers, anything.

"And I want a bomb disposal unit ASAP."

He was breathing heavily, his anger boiling over.

"I need a minute," he said, took some deep breaths, and leaned on a table. I waited quietly.

"Okay," he said. "I'm okay."

"All those things about solitary confinement," I said, "are they true?"

"I fucking hope so," he said, and he was on the cellphone again.

CHAPTER 32

"GHB," Carmichael whispered in the kitchen, but I'd heard of it. The date-rape drug. It would surprise some people what kinds of meetings take place in the corporate world—like what amounted to a drug seminar a few years back when the opioid crisis began to take hold. The facilitator mentioned a whole host of acronyms and initials I'd heard of in passing, GHB among them. "It can put you out," the speaker had said, "and leave you manic." Kasi seemed to be coming out of it all right, but I asked Carmichael if I could stay close so that she could see a friendly face.

"For a minute or two," he said. He had rallied from whatever little episode he'd suffered and seemed manic himself.

I thought of Mallory's question—if I'd seen Kasi naked. I don't think this is what she had in mind, although maybe when she peeked through the window she had seen enough to know. At any rate she probably anticipated a tense situation of some kind where I would present a safe space, where if nothing else I wouldn't stare. Looking her in the eye was not only gracious but damn preferable to staring at whatever Walsh had constructed and strapped to her torso. It would be idiotic to say that things were normalizing, but at least we knew where we stood, though only for a moment. That's when Kasi told me she was going to throw up.

I was about to tell her she couldn't when Carmichael rushed in with a small canister and held it close to her mouth. She heaved once—nothing. The second one though pretty much ensured the fact that said canister would not be holding sugar or flour ever again. Moments later she exhaled loudly.

"I want to get dressed."

"You can't," I said. "I mean not right now. You can't move. There's a bomb…."

"I know what a bomb is," she said, "and Walsh told me what he was going to do. He didn't tell me he was undressing me, or that men would be gawking at me. Now I want my clothes. And where *is* Walsh? Did you arrest him?"

Carmichael had gone to discard the piece of crockery, then came racing back in.

"You throw up a lot, Kasi?"

"What kind of question is that? No. Never."

"That's a drug reaction," he said. "Not necessarily dangerous, but the drugs are still working. You can't control your stomach, but you have to control your brain. You aren't going anywhere and you're not getting any clothes, not yet. I don't care if you're okay with that—I'm not either—but that's how it goes for now."

"Always in charge," she said.

"You have a problem with me. I get that. But let me do my job. Your friend, boyfriend, whatever this guy is, he feels some duty to you. Or to his sister. But he's standing here a few feet away from enough explosives to blow all our appendages into the next county. Try to tolerate me for a while and you'll never see me again. Deal?"

I was about to criticize his "bedside manner," but Kasi beat me to it. "The tough love approach," Kasi said. "It's quite transparent, you know."

"Is it?" Carmichael said, smiling. "We're all going to be transparent soon if you don't stop making asinine requests. You too Blaine—who shouldn't be hanging about a crime scene. I'd be happy to cover this woman with a blanket, but someone is going to have to work on that thing and a blanket will make the work area appreciably darker. But hey, it's your call."

He waited. No one responded.

"Good. Nobody's gonna die here today if we can manage to keep our heads. I'm not going to ask you if you understand, Ms. Brennan, because I know you do. Now let's begin again with that little bout of nausea, is your stomach better?"

"I don't feel like I have to throw up, if that's what you mean."

"That's what I mean. I have questions. Are you able to answer?"

He didn't wait for a response, but slid a chair in front of her, turned it sideways, and took out his phone. "I'm recording. Did you see the bomb before he strapped it on you?"

"I was already tied up."

"With your clothes still on."

"Yes."

"How did he drug you?"

"I don't know. He could have dissolved something in the water."

"You don't remember an injection or anything."

"No."

"And the clothes—you were out when he removed them."

"You think I'd *let* him do that?"

"Ms. Brennan, with a gun to your head or a knife to your throat, yes, you'd readily remove them yourself."

"I was…out."

"All right. Now I'm trying to be delicate here, do you want a nurse to come in?"

"I wasn't raped."

"But if you were out…."

"You think I wouldn't know?"

"Good. Good," Carmichael said, and he looked relieved. It was the first release of any kind since Walsh had sped away. He moved the chair away and walked toward the door, then stopped.

"There's nothing I can do for you right now, Ms. Brennan. I mean, it's cool in here, but I'm hesitant to turn the heat on—to turn anything on until we see what's going on with this device. Do you understand?"

She nodded.

"And from now on," he said. "Make believe I'm blind. First off, it'll make you feel better; second, a blind person couldn't see you nodding. I don't want you nodding. Just sit still, talk when you have to, and we'll get this sorted."

"I just threw up—that didn't detonate it."

"Maybe a coughing fit would be all right too, but I'd prefer to avoid it."

I got her a glass of water, and immediately Carmichael reminded her not to choke. She took a few sips. As she started to level off, if not exactly calm down, she told us more: Walsh had the device ready, claimed to have built it himself, and said it was guaranteed—as if someone else had built it.

"Someone even smarter," Carmichael said. "Only one of those around. I wonder what your brother-in-law is doing on an early Sunday morning. Was your sister a churchgoer?"

"I don't have a brother-in-law."

"You sort of do. Let's get him over here."

"You're bringing in more people?"

"There'll be a bomb disposal unit here in no time, except I have the feeling this is beyond them."

"Then call them off," Kasi said.

"Not my call. If they don't at least look at it and something goes wrong, we're all dead. Twice."

Kasi shook her head; Carmichael reminded her not to, and not to scream either. "You can do it after," he said. "We all will. I'm going to get Mallory over here. She's a…woman."

"I could tell the pronoun," Kasi said.

"Yeah, I figure if you don't have to pee right now, you will."

"I have to pee right now."

Carmichael's reaction was absurdly fast—a jaunt to the kitchen and his voice on a cellphone: "Mallory, the victim has to pee. I need you right now!"

Moments later Mallory arrived with a plastic bag full of accoutrements I didn't care to see, though the bedpan itself was difficult to hide. We waited in the kitchen, Taggart included. Nobody asked for details—if there was a catheter involved, I didn't need to know.

It was after Mallory emptied the bedpan that Carmichael looked almost relieved.

"Thanks, Mallory, if you weren't gay, I'd kiss you."

"You know, Alex," Mallory responded. "You can kiss a lesbian. It's not catchy.

It just wouldn't make my day the way it would make yours."

"Get Taggart first, then I'll think about it."

"He's right outside," she said. "I figured you needed him."

"Really, if you weren't…."

"Yeah, I know, if I weren't a lesbian…do I get to stay?"

"I don't outrank you, and having a woman for the kid would be good. But putting more people in danger is wrong."

"My choice," Mallory said. She went outside and retrieved Taggart, who carried a thin case that looked like a laptop—which it was—along with a myriad of screwdrivers and other small tools. Even before he got to Kasi, he was on high alert.

"Anyone scan this place?" he asked.

When we told him no, he took out what looked like a small remote and stood in the doorway of the room where Kasi sat.

"I'm coming in," he said. "Sorry. Just going to walk around."

"It's fine," she said. "As long as you can fix this."

"Gonna try like hell to get you free of it, then we'll worry about the rest."

He made a walkthrough similar to what ours had been, then told Kasi he'd be right back.

He led all of us outside.

"Walsh can see us," he said. "But I'm 99% sure he can't hear us. Above Kasi is what looks like a smoke alarm but isn't."

"A camera?" Carmichael asked.

"Worse. Let's go back in so Kasi hears this too, so we're all on the same page."

It turned out to be a page nobody wanted to read, but Taggart explained it anyway.

"It's a repurposed smoke detector. Actual smoke detectors blink green maybe once a minute. This one goes every…well wait."

It blinked, he counted to seven, it blinked again.

"There's your trigger," he said, "or at least one of them. It's either sending or receiving a signal and the bomb completes the circuit. Move either one and it detonates in seven seconds. Not sure what the radius is down here at floor level—maybe three feet? Maybe less. And the detector is hardwired, no battery, so cutting power is the same as removing the battery, breaking the beam. Seven seconds later, it blows. You know, if the power company is thinking about…anything…."

"That's been taken care of," Carmichael said.

"So I figure this," Taggart said. "If I cut this loose, and I stay here and hold it, Kasi's free."

Carmichael laughed. "There is a minor flaw in your reasoning," he said. "Won't the bomb eventually blow up in your hands?"

"We could slide a table under it."

I was beginning to envision this precision operation when Taggart interrupted the moment of optimism.

"Not that simple," he said. "There's more than one trigger. One is in the straps—the other is more conventional—a cut wire or broken circuit somewhere."

"And you know this how?" Kasi said. "Because I do."

He asked me for a pencil and paper, then wrote down some words next to a drawing that a kindergartner would have been ashamed of.

"Your sister was the artist," he said to me. "A talent she got from my mother."

"I know."

He tossed me the pencil. "Did Carmichael say the bomb squad was coming?"

"Pretty sure."

"Call them off," Taggart said. "This is beyond them—probably beyond me."

"Then…what?"

"I'll do it. I know it."

"Because you designed it," Carmichael said. "Am I right?." Taggart nodded.

"It was a theoretical discussion with a person I detested," Taggart said, "a pissing contest—who was smarter? You get into one of those things and you figure, "I'll pick his brain." And you do that, but meanwhile he picks yours. The smoke alarm, though, that's brilliant. I don't know what other little Easter Eggs he's engineered into it. I need to work alone, though. Can you make that happen, Blaine? Convince the FBI? No bomb experts interfering?"

"Me?"

"Make it happen."

He had hardly made the request when the apparatus arrived: huge pieces of machinery on a flatbed truck, one of them a tank that could have held a whale. I brought Taggart to the front door. Carmichael was already there talking with one of the crew.

"Can you do better than they can?" I asked Taggart.

"Kasi will be alive when I'm done. Does that sound better?"

"Only if I can stay too," I whispered. "Moral support."

He winked. "Moral support," he said. "You're quite the humanitarian."

We waited while Carmichael continued his conversation, one that became more animated with time. When it ended, he returned, shaking his head.

"They won't leave," he said, "but they won't interfere. One of them wants to see it."

"But Kasi," I said, "she's…."

"Naked. You can say the word. I told him that she was in a fragile state and another stranger would set her off again. Their supervisor—he's top notch and a decent guy—but he has to see the device—or someone he delegates can take a look."

"You?"

"Nope, Candace something or other."

"A woman."

"I told you, he gets it."

And so Candace arrived. I guess she was a woman, though her protective white jumpsuit could have been covering an ape for all we knew. Only her voice gave her away, though she didn't talk much until after she'd inspected the area.

"Whose your bomb-disposal guy," she said when she left the room. Taggart stepped forward.

What followed was a brief—let's call it technical—discussion which comprised words and phrases of which I could recognize ten percent, at best. I did pick up *timing mechanism* and *blast radius* and, I thought, *pies*? Whatever they were discussing made perfect sense to them and they agreed to stay out of each other's way. The bomb disposal unit would remain on site just in case, and Taggart could work without the threat of interference. I felt a little more confident until Candace, on her way back to the truck turned and said to anyone within earshot, "never seen a device like that. I'd love to have a go at it, but your man—he's the one. Not sure if I would have picked up on the smoke detector. Anyway, we'll be on site until he's done."

Carmichael thanked her, but it was an empty acknowledgment. If Taggart failed, the bomb squad would have little to do other than assign causes of death and determine the explosive used.

"Pies," I said to Taggart once we were back in the house.

"A simple mnemonic: power, initiator, explosive, switch. Every bomb is different but every one needs those four components. When you can determine all four, you can dismantle it."

"This one?"

"We have two hours."

"And you know everything else?"

"I know it's a low-explosive device."

"So that's good?"

"No," Taggart said, "The Boston Marathon bombs back in '13—they were low-explosive devices. It has to do with the chemistry of it, the detonation."

The image of people dying and losing limbs at the end of that race was not one I wanted in my head. I think I said something inane like, "well, let's get to work then," as if I had anything to do with it—as if Taggart needed prompting.

"Kasi," he said, "I'm going to be jiggling around behind you. If you feel something cold, it's just a tool."

"I'm already freezing," she said.

"Someone turn on the heat," Taggart said, but Carmichael demurred. "I don't know what a spark might do."

"I do. Unless it's right here, it'll do nothing."

Carmichael wasn't convinced. "What about a blown fuse? Power goes off to that smoke detector and you've got seven seconds to save everyone. Can you do that? Because if you can't, then we'll all freeze together. Everyone, remove your shirts."

He started to unbutton his.

Taggart smiled. "Please don't make me laugh."

"Seriously," Carmichael said, "I work out. I look good shirtless."

"Please, put your shirt back on," Taggart said, rubbing his hands to warm them. "I know that you know that in every house the furnace has its own circuit. I'm impressed by the thought process, though. I hadn't thought of that. But you can raise the thermostat. Better to get her some heat before she shakes this thing into detonating."

I heard the click and, in minutes, felt the change in air. In this constant vacillation between gloom and hope, I was feeling a little better. We had good people and we had two hours."

"We got this," I said to Kasi.

Then I heard Taggart curse—we waited.

"Square one," he said after a brief silence. then tapped Kasi on the shoulder. "But we got this."

Maybe. It didn't seem that way.

CHAPTER 33

The same low-lying fog that enveloped the home on Monroe Street hung thinly over Bradley, ten or so miles to the south. No take-offs had been delayed, and only one commuter plane had been forced to go around—a situation that had nothing to do with the weather and everything to do with another plane not being able to clear air space on time. At Bradley it was a typical Sunday morning. Slow.

At one end of the terminal, though, the far end to keep it from interfering with airport operations, a different procedure was taking shape. Tables and chairs were being hauled down a freight elevator and onto the tarmac, not far from the area where Wesley Barrett made his rather abrupt and deadly landing a few days earlier. Ken Mullins had wanted 200 seats, but some safety regulations had interfered and he settled for half that, placated by the fact that the view from the terminal would be just as good.

The retirement of an airport manager is equal in excitement to that of any CEO most people had never heard of. It may mean something in the immediate surroundings, but has very little cachet beyond that limited circle. The arrival of a Triple-7, though, at an airport like Bradley, was sure to draw a crowd. Curiosity seekers might be satisfied to park on the perimeter road and watch it fly overhead, but the true enthusiasts would want to be right there, to see it up close. Where Mullins fit in, most people didn't care.

Maybe after all he'd done for the place, the crowds should have been larger; but then there was the local unrest over the expansion, and the incident with the Cessna, and now the missing woman. If the FBI did its job correctly, of course, there'd be no harm done, but not even Mullins would deny that the shine had dulled.

Carmichael had promised that, if the event needed to be cancelled, he would call it by noon. He'd conferred several times with Washington while Mallory had spoken with her colleagues in the Boston office. The consensus was that the threat to the young lady far outweighed the threat to the aircraft and the ceremony, and further that acceding to Walsh's demands insured nothing in the way of safety.

Noon came and went. Kenneth Mullins picked out a burgundy tie with small bi-planes adorning it—his only concession to whimsy on this formal, gray suit-white shirt Sunday. Although he knew very few of the particulars of what was transpiring a few miles away, he had made it clear to anyone who would listen that he was counting on the authorities to come through. There wasn't a more reliable agent than Alex Carmichael, and with Mallory and the locals at work, and with all that ground fog having burned off to show an azure sky above it, he could not be blamed for exuding some confidence.

Carmichael's outlook was nowhere near so rosy. Walsh still on the loose and the threat to Kasi remained. And even if Walsh were to be located, then what? He still held all the cards. The only difference would be his proximity to make an eventual arrest easier. But with a two hour head start, he could have been in any of seven states, and not far from Canada.

Taggart soldiered on, the silence punctuated by the occasional curse, the occasional sigh, the occasional sound of satisfaction when something went right.

I had begun to pace. Carmichael seemed oblivious to it, but I guess my path was so wide that Mallory came out of the adjoining room and asked me to sit down—I was making everyone —her—nervous. I slowed down, but kept sneaking peaks into the den. I don't think I was waiting to die, but there had to be part of me eminently aware that the explosives in the next room were powerful enough to level the house we were in and maybe a few others nearby. I kept remembering Walsh's explanation of how an explosion kills, then realized that if the bomb were to go off, the last people to have any recollection of it would be the five of us.

Situations like that engender foolish questions, like when I asked Taggart if there was anything I could do to help.

"There's a circuit here that has me confused," he deadpanned. "Want to poke around a little and see what happens?"

He didn't have to wait for an answer. I decided to stop volunteering my assistance.

When the news arrived that Walsh's "borrowed" car had been found abandoned on the side of the road about five miles from the airport, nobody seemed surprised. Middle of nowhere," Mallory said. "I wonder if he has an accomplice. A partner."

None of us really thought so—that particular kind of sick amorality lends itself to lone-wolf activities. He wasn't even much of a social media user—not much interested in acceptance or adulation. No need for an accomplice.

Carmichael wanted to know exactly where they'd found Walsh's car. Taggart heard the request.

"If you're going to check a map on your phone," Taggart yelled, "pull it up from outside. I don't want any signals crossed in here—then show me."

A moment later he brought the phone in to Taggart. I waited out in the kitchen, but I could hear Carmichael clearly.

"We figure he had another car waiting or he…." Taggart stopped him.

"He's on foot. Look at the map, then find Ben Palmer's house."

"It's gotta be more than five miles away," Carmichael said, and traced the road that bore east in a circuitous route.

Taggart nodded. "Driving, yes, but not as the crow flies." He pointed to Palmer's road. "Look again. These woods are crisscrossed with old fire trails. Even if they're overgrown, they're easy to follow. Walsh is in good shape. Two miles, tops. He could run that in ten, fifteen minutes."

"Not carrying some shoulder-mounted missile," Carmichael said.

"But if it's waiting for him somewhere. Palmer's? How thoroughly did you check that place?"

"It was a murder scene," Carmichael said. "The locals were thorough. The house had no basement, but they covered everything right down to the crawl space."

"Then you missed something. A garage? An outbuilding?"

Taggart sounded testier than he had been before, and Carmichael who ordinarily would have given like for like, backed off.

"We'll check some more. You keep working," Carmichael said. "Thanks for the reminder, agent—I was losing interest."

Carmichael looked at me. I shrugged. I still wasn't sure if Carmichael was going to explode before the bomb did, but then Kasi spoke up.

"I can hear all this you know."

"We're all a little on edge," Carmichael said.

Taggart didn't respond, but instead got up from his kneeling position behind Kasi, took a chair, sat, then rubbed his eyes with both hands. Ninety minutes to go.

"Blaine," he said, "do you believe in an afterlife?"

"Not the time for this," Kasi said, "but I vote no. This is it."

"Blaine? How about you?"

"No."

"All that immortal soul stuff, no significance?"

"I don't know. Do I have to decide now? I'll go along with what you say."

"Some commitment, Blaine. Your sister was committed. Why aren't you?"

"We're different."

"Think she's watching us? Looking down, rooting for us? Or does she want this thing to go off so we can be reunited."

"My sister would never want that."

"Yeah, I know. But sometimes I wonder. All this spiritual stuff…the soul. If we can't see it, how do we know it doesn't survive? She could be watching, could be right here. I'll bet she knows the sequence, the code, whatever disarms this."

"This is uber-interesting," Kasi said, "but let's not figure it out today. There's no two-way passage from this world to that one. It's your expertise against Walsh's."

"Afraid of that," he said just as Carmichael returned.

"On Palmer's street. A barn," the agent said. I peered over his shoulder. "Couple barns. Looks like maybe a shed back there."

"Nothing's certain," Taggart said, "but a barn with Palmer to keep an eye on it? Isn't that a perfect storage facility? And then if Palmer got skittish about it, wouldn't that put him in harm's way?"

"Because of our visit," I said.

"Bad time for self-pity," Carmichael said, motioning toward Kasi. He dispatched some agents, then called Weber and had some nearby cops check it out. "With extreme caution," he said. "We don't know what's in there."

"Got a pretty good idea," Taggart said. "A storage area. Maybe more. Maybe a lab. If he does have a missile. What better place to store it than an abandoned barn on a non-working farm at the end of a dead-end street? But if he also uses it for bomb-making, with his expertise…tell your men to be careful."

"He still has us over a barrel," Mallory said. "We're a phone call away from a really bad mess here. If he has the slightest inkling that we're on to him…." She stopped, mid-sentence and put her finger to her lips, whispered "he could be listening."

"He can't hear us," Taggart said. "He can see us—he can see me right now. Kasi and I are ignoring the camera and you people stay out of here if you can't do the same. There's no audio, so you can say what you want. He'd never put a mic in that and take a chance on some extraneous vibration upsetting the mechanism.

He's watching; he's not listening. He sees a woman tied up and a guy struggling and sweating and getting nowhere. Besides, he's busy."

We were still forty-five minutes from the boarding of the Triple-7 at Logan, and forty-five past that until the landing at Bradley. I was tempted—we all were I'm sure—to ask Taggart for an estimate, but we knew better. He wasn't going to delay this for drama. And rushing it was out of the question. And even if he disarmed it, Walsh was still the loose cannon with the means of taking down an airliner.

While Mallory and Carmichael discussed strategy and manpower, I found a bottle of water in the refrigerator, uncapped it, and brought it into the den. The room, which had been chilly, was comfortably warm, and so my asking if anyone wanted water was not completely off base.

"Put it down next to me," Taggart said. "When I get a free hand, maybe."

Kasi declined. I got the impression she didn't want to talk to anyone, Taggart maybe the exception. She had rallied from the state she was in when we first found her, but had regressed again with every minute that device remained strapped to her. I remembered Mallory's advice—never ask the victim if she's all right.

"Everyone's working hard," I said. "Just hang in there."

"My mother," she said. "I'm just thinking, the season is over."

"What season?"

"Up at Saylorville, the lake, she works as a volunteer there, but the season is almost over."

"I've been there. My uncle and aunt used to take us. Eveline and me. There's a picture in…."

"I saw it—the pail of water. I was sad when I saw that picture. So much promise.

You have to do me a favor. If this doesn't go well…."

"No last wills," Taggart said. "It shakes my confidence."

"Just one," she said. "If this doesn't go well, tell my mother. Jake Moss knows the address."

"I won't need it," Taggart said. "I'm on this. I have a plan, and a backup plan. Just…chill."

"Chill?" she said. "Do people still say that?"

"In this room they do. Don't worry about your mom."

"I know, but winters are tough for her—not much to do but wait until spring when the area opens again. She'll have all those months to sit and brood. Daniel, maybe you could keep in touch."

"She won't want to hear from me."

"Say you'll try."

"I will," I said and I squeezed her hand, "but I trust this guy. We're going to get you out of here and that's final."

That was perfect—right from the Mallory list of forbidden statements, and she was in the other room. I awaited my reprimand, but it never came. Sometimes you need to say what needs to be said. Mallory probably knew that too.

Carmichael had other thoughts.

"Palmer grew pot," Carmichael said. "Kids know he's dead, they may decide to execute a few raids. I don't want someone wandering across the street and wondering how easy it might be getting into that barn to scorch a few."

He called Weber who dispatched two of the locals to Palmer's bungalow. We appeared to be covering all the bases, with one notable exception: several pounds of explosives strapped to Kasi Brennan.

Then I actually thought of something helpful, born of my unwanted but unavoidable knowledge of aviation.

"Which approach is the plane using?"

"Don't know," Carmichael said. "Should we? There's only one runway that plane can land on."

"Every runway is two runways," I said. Six is also 24, 13 is 31. Add 180° to each runway number up to 360° and you get both numbers. If he's landing on six, he's coming in from the northeast, but 24 is a southwest approach. ATC should know. There has to be a flight plan."

"Okay, Boston is northeast of here," Carmichael said, "so they'll come in on six."

"Except," Kasi said, "a lot of flights from Logan take off to the south, fly almost as far as the Cape before turning west. That would leave them south of here."

"Okay," Carmichael said, "tell me why we're having this conversation. I'm not interested in watching this plane."

I was about to answer—I actually knew—but Kasi beat me to it.

"Coming in on six," she said, "puts it nearly over Palmer's place. Easy target, and just far enough from the airport to make a normal landing difficult if there's damage to a wing or a stabilizer, flaps, landing gear, anything like that. It's not a depressurization problem, but people could die from an explosion and a direct hit could conceivably take it down, though the much greater likelihood would be a hard landing and structural damage to the plane. Tens of millions of dollars. From the other direction, though, that plane is never closer than ten miles from Palmer's—still within missile range but with less margin for error."

"So," Carmichael said, "we tell them to land on 24."

"Why?" Kasi said.

"You just said…"

"That's not what I mean. Walsh is probably monitoring airport chatter. A last minute change has to be warranted, not some whim because maybe there's a guy with a missile."

Carmichael was getting frustrated. "But there really is a guy with a missile."

"Then you divert the plane," she said, "but do it right. A warranted change."

"Name one." I said.

"Wind, sun angle, other traffic…none of those pertain here. There is something, though," she said.

Kasi was becoming animated and involved. Taggart reminded her to sit still. "Here's what you need to do," she said. "Find a commercial flight within a hundred-mile radius, even two hundred, locate the crew list and call one of the flight attendants."

"You mean the pilot."

"I mean an attendant," she said. "If Walsh is monitoring chatter, he'll hear communication from the cockpit. We need someone on the plane with a cell phone to have the captain report a problem to Bradley. Nothing serious. Not a Mayday, maybe a faulty warning light—even a sick passenger—anything short of a declared emergency which would bring up a whole new set of issues not so easily resolved."

"And he'll want to land."

"And if you time it right, then the Triple-7 that's lined up for whatever approach will have to go around. ATC might logically give them a new approach without arousing suspicion."

"On 24," I said.

"Right. But listen," Kasi said. "This is no small matter. It's not like getting off the Interstate an exit early."

I could tell Carmichael wanted to get things moving. "Tell us the procedure."

"You're going to have to indemnify the captain and the first officer, notify their airline, expect all kinds of blowback for the deception—you're never home free with the FAA. And you have to have that flight attendant's back too. That's you, Carmichael. If the FBI authorizes it...."

"Consider it authorized," he said. "Don't you want to know the cost?"

"No," he said. His reply went unheeded.

"Tens of thousands of dollars," she said. "Sorry. And scheduling snafus all the way down the line."

"Not my problem," Carmichael said. "You're my problem, and that...plane. I'll call Mullins."

"No." Kasi yelled.

"Jesus Christ!" Taggart said, even louder. "Will you fucking sit still?" Then we all sat still, even those of who were standing.

In silence. And waited.

If there had been an explosion, hearing it would have been the last thing we did.

There wasn't one. "Sorry," Kasi said.

"Me too," Taggart said, but I just...go on. Don't mind me."

"What I meant," Kasi said, "was Mullins wants his ceremony. He's not going to want it messed up by some diverted flight. If we luck out, that other plane won't have to land and the money won't be an issue. But don't call Mullins. Call Jake Moss."

Carmichael never hesitated. He picked up the cell phone and pointed it at me. "All that runway crap, the numbers and all. How do you know shit like that?"

"I'm still Eveline's brother," I said, then repeated it to myself. It was one of the few times in my life I'd said it without an apology.

CHAPTER 34

Tim Kenner was the captain.

His first officer was Marvin Hayes.

Coincidentally they both lived in Minneapolis but had never combined as a flight crew. Together they had more than 35 years' experience flying the MD-88 and other various permutations of the old DC-9. Today it was the MD-90 on a flight from Boston to Detroit; they were approaching cruising altitude when the odd request came through.

At first both Kenner and Hayes thought it was a joke, but knew that air traffic controllers aren't usually hired for their witticisms—don't come to work in the morning with punchlines or little jabs to practice on unsuspecting flight crews. Controllers can be friendly and even appear casual, but the tension is too high for levity, and controllers who have "lost" planes even through no fault of their own, seldom recover fully—often leave the job. To be frivolous or facetious and have it somehow go wrong and result in a tragedy would be too much to overcome.

The fact that the request came secondhand from a cell phone rendered it even less believable. And as if that weren't enough, the flight attendant who broke the news to them, a red-haired Australian named Gwen, was considered a bit of an extrovert—some would say a bit too uninhibited. Passengers actually paid attention to the pre-flight safety notifications when she offered them—or maybe *performed* them. She did voices, pantomimed foolishness, had a clever comment for every instruction. Yet she was calm and organized as she relayed the message to Kenner. He demurred immediately, certain that the FAA would have his ass, his license, his job, and his pension in short order. Gwen handed him her cellphone: at the other end was Jake Moss.

Kasi had chosen him wisely. He was someone whom pilots and others in aviation knew and trusted, someone who had connections at the FAA, who could promote this craziness with credibility. It still took some doing to convince Kenner, but he committed when Moss told him he didn't have to follow through, didn't have to alarm the passengers, simply needed to take a new heading and gradually drop about 6,000 feet, just in case someone with a phone app was watching. They were still under Boston control, but about to be handed off to ZNY, so there were people to notify. Within minutes of the initial cell phone call, thousands of people with phone apps must have known there was an MD-90 about to temporarily change course.

"I know it's weird," Moss said, "and please don't respond verbally—just in case. But the space is clear. There's a threat to another aircraft—the Feds aren't going to balk at this. We'll speed you through after that, even give you landing priority."

Kenner handed the controls off to Hayes and left the cockpit. In the forward lavatory with Gwen's cellphone, he told Moss he'd follow through, but insisted on talking to his airline.

"I can make it an order," Moss said, "if that's how you want to play it. There are hundreds of lives at risk, and the one thing we don't have is time for you to reach the airline. They're a business. They're going to see dollars and cents. I'm looking at lives saved by a ten minute course correction that may cost you a hundred pounds of fuel, maybe two. Nevertheless, Captain, you're in command."

"Without authorization," Kenner said, "I can't just…"

"ATC will be on the horn with a new vector and altitude. That's your authorization. And Captain Kenner, I'm looking at your record. I know about Phoenix, the jackscrew malfunction, the perfect landing. I'd want you in the left seat of my plane anytime. And ignoring your good sense is wrong. Period. But we have a situation that's spiraling out of control and you can slow it down. I'll leave you to your aircraft."

"I'll wait for ATC."

"That's all I ask," Moss said.

If Devin Walsh had been monitoring airport communications a few moments later, all he would have heard was an indication of an aircraft with a minor electrical problem and a pilot with a concern for his landing gear and a desire to get the plane on the ground. Bradley was the only logical choice, and delaying the Champagne flight's landing the only logical alternative.

Carmichael informed Taggart of the ploy.

"That's good," Taggart said, still focused on the components, "but does it change anything?"

"Control," Carmichael said. "It gives a few minutes of it, and maybe even a few minutes more for you."

"Then use this extra time. I'm gonna get this off her—that's a given—but if we have to detonate it or things go sideways, and I'm using the word literally, let's not have any collateral damage. Start evacuating nearby homes."

"So you can't disarm it?"

"That's still the plan, but the backup plan is detonating it away from people."

"You said you had two backups. What's the second?"

"Still working on it. Start moving folks away."

"Already being done," Carmichael said, but phoned the operation center across the way just to get an update. To everyone involved, Taggart's warning bore an ominous sound, the first genuine indication that he couldn't simply render the device harmless.

"I know what you're thinking," he said. "We should get the bomb disposal people in here. Trust me, it would not make a difference. What I'm doing here— why it's taking so long—is I'm running little programs, trying to go a step further each time. So far, nothing. I'm going to do three more—at 1:45, if I still can't get at it, we start. Blaine, can you get a blanket."

"To contain the blast?"

Taggart stared at me and the corners of his mouth curled up slightly

"Do you think a blanket is going to contain this thing? What would you use for a nuclear device, a sleeping bag?"

It had made a momentary modicum of sense, then just as quickly, no sense at all. But before I could retract it, Taggart would have his fun.

"If you're right, then you've advanced the cause of bomb disposal by decades. 'Hey there's a bomb here, someone get a blanket.' "

"Okay," I said. "You can stop now."

He wasn't finished. "It would have to be wool, I suppose. Maybe steel wool." Even Kasi was smiling.

"Thanks," she said. "I needed that. Now, about the blanket." Carmichael let me off the hook.

"Before he asks where to find one, let me just say that we learned all about linen closets in Quantico."

Moments later he was back and laid the folded blanket on Kasi's legs. Taggart was surprised. "How'd you know that's why I wanted it?"

"Why else?" he said, then turned to Kasi. No reason she should have to get out of this mess only to have people gawking at her."

Kasi said nothing. She may have been grateful, but the overriding danger remained.

"But there's another reason, too, right Taggart?"

"Yes, circulation, because…."

Carmichael was ahead of him, or with him. They both knew she had been stationary for so long that her legs were weak. I understood, but I also began to realize that the end of this was going to be a lot more chaotic than I'd hoped—than we'd all hoped."

And Taggart was still laboring away.

I suppose everyone begins projects with high expectations, anticipating their completion and a sense of accomplishment, whether it's rewiring a lamp or trying a new recipe. And we've all encountered frustrating little annoyances along the way that have turned us from sanguine to surly. Taggart was at that point, or likely past it. Those are the moments I like to be left alone. I gave some room.

In the kitchen I found Mallory poring over a local map which did in fact show a web of fire trails in the woods behind the barn not far from Palmer's bungalow. Some of them led directly to the abandoned car. It wasn't proof that Walsh was in there, but it was our only viable option, at least until Mallory presented another possibility.

"This Triple-7 has a laser operated missile defense system. They don't call it missile defense—it's missile deterrent. Instead of filling the air with shrapnel to confuse the missile's guidance system, it locks on to the attacking missile, hacks into its guidance system, and sends it someplace suitable according to its built in GPS, or straight up, then detonates it."

"And it works?"

"It's never been tested in real life situations. But yes, in mock-ups. It's just another option. This particular plane has it."

"It won't work," Kasi yelled from the other room. Taggart swore again. "Sorry," she said, "I'm keeping very still, but that system won't work. The airspeed will be about 160 knots at that point, too slow to redirect the missile."

"We'll just do it the old-fashioned way," Carmichael said. "Make up some lies and hope they work." So we waited.

At 1:30 Taggart called us in again, well short of his 1:45 estimate.

"Here's the deal," he said. "It's the best I can do. There's a five-second delay in the bomb itself from when the circuit is broken, and seven from the so-called smoke alarm. It doesn't give us twelve, though; they overlap. We get seven, no matter what, or less if we mistime it. Trip this by accident and you have five-seconds to punch in a code on this little keypad. Just two numbers."

"What are they?"

"I don't know, and since it's unlikely I can hit all 99 possibilities in five seconds, I did the next best thing. I added two seconds."

"How?" Carmichael asked.

"It's all electronic," he said. "Quartz technology like a watch. But there's an actual mechanical counter that goes from 1-10. It's the delay mechanism and it's not directly related to the trigger. I pushed it to seven so it aligns with the other trigger. I think pushing it higher would indicate tampering because I think it aligns with the smoke alarm."

I made believe I understood. I think Carmichael did the same. "You did that already?" he asked.

"Yes, I know what I'm doing."

"Okay, just, you know…."

"I know what I'm doing."

Carmichael was probably unnerved by Taggart's attempt to mess with the bomb. But I wasn't sure what difference two seconds made.

"Plenty," Taggart said when I asked. "We remove the bomb and we have seven seconds to get it out of the house and into that swimming pool back there."

"What?" Carmichael said, and I thought if the bomb didn't explode, his head would. "That…that's a plan?"

"It's absolutely a plan."

"All right, wait," Carmichael said, catching his breath. "First of all, no. Second of all, there is no second of all."

"Okay," Taggart said. "I'm willing to listen to the Bureau's counterproposal. Go ahead."

"We stay the course and you get that thing neutralized, or we get a bomb disposal unit in here."

"I don't claim to know everything," Taggart said, "but I know enough. Your team won't disarm it and this young lady will die, or there'll be significant loss of life somewhere else. Redirect the Triple-7 and he'll shoot down another plane, something smaller and even more vulnerable, or hit the terminal. I don't want any of those things to happen. I'm sure you don't either."

"I can't let a civilian do this," Carmichael said.

"I'm not in the military, Agent, but I've been poring over this device since around noon. Kind of late to complain about my credentials."

No one offered an answer. Except Taggart.

"Let me explain this to you, Agent Carmichael. You're an intelligent guy—take a look at this and tell me how you would extricate Kasi here (and he tapped her on the shoulder very lightly like a proud father) from this device. Which straps would you cut, which wires would you snip, and would you cut them at all or would that break a connection and start the countdown? Or would you just snip a blue wire because blue is a nice calming color—who would ever associate blue with danger? Or maybe...."

"All right, I get it," Carmichael said.

"I don't think you do. Adding that two seconds—that's a risk. That's hacking into the timing mechanism which is not some stopwatch from Walmart. It's a programmable chip that I think I reprogrammed, but I can't see a dial or a second hand so I have to go by what I know of the product. It's like adjusting a TV picture blindfolded. See the problem?"

"Of course I do," Carmichael said. "We all do."

"Then listen, I built this bomb. Not physically, but the design is mine. There's a website that deals with bomb-making and disarming—*can you build a bomb that nobody can neutralize*—that sort of thing. I used to go on there once in a while, and even though real names were at a premium, I recognized Walsh. He's too brilliant to miss. And too fucking arrogant. In one two-minute video he took my so-called foolproof bomb, defused it in front of me, then added some malignant enhancements to remove any backdoor, any bypass. I watched him do it. I still can't disarm this one. So the two seconds I stole—that's the best I can do."

"Okay," Carmichael said. "I'm going to have to run this by my superiors."

Taggart smiled. "Let me tell you something. I love the FBI. You guys are legends. Al Capone. Alger Hiss, the Rosenbergs, Lindbergh, all that. You know who solved those crimes? You. Agents. Not the suits in D.C. You. Here's your next case, Carmichael. *Your* case, not your superiors'."

"That's pretty shameless ass-kissing, you know," Carmichael said, "especially since we're not too popular in Washington these days."

"Assholes will always be politicians, and vice-versa. You know it and I know it."

"You're shameless."

"Actually I'm not. Just desperate. What do you say?"

"Let's say I agree to do this and you get your seven seconds. Then what."

"Then you leave the area, get someplace safe, done."

"What about Kasi?"

"That's why we're starting early. There are things to do. Someone has to check out the basement, tell me if there's a window down there that faces the back yard."

Mallory went immediately, returned in seconds. "A small one," she said, "facing the backyard."

"That's where we'll be," Taggart said, "away from that window but on that side of the cellar. When the glass shatters I don't want it flying through the air with all the other detritus and hitting us."

"Detritus?" Carmichael asked. "Scraps."

"Next time, help me out and say *scraps*. Detritus sounds like a freaking disease."

Taggart shook his head. "You're too smart to play dumb. One more thing, I'm going to need a volunteer…to get things moving. There are two circuits that need to be broken simultaneously. I can do that myself, but I need to time it with the flashing light in the smoke alarm to get all seven seconds. It would be easier with an assistant. Now Kasi here is the ideal choice, since she's already here, but since she's not a contortionist, I need someone else."

"I'm tempted to ask if you're serious," Carmichael said. "But I know better. I'll do it."

"I was thinking maybe one of the bomb-disposal guys."

"No," Carmichael said. "They aren't good at being subordinates."

"You have a wife, maybe kids? You can't endanger yourself now."

"No personal situation interferes with my work," Carmichael said.

"Noted." Taggart turned to me. "I'd rather have Blaine here. No offense, but he's younger and faster, less likely to fall down the stairs and take Kasi with him."

"You just undid all your ass-kissing," Carmichael said. "And he's still a civilian."

"Then deputize him."

"This isn't *Gunsmoke*," Carmichael said. "I can't just...."

"What's *Gunsmoke*?"

"Stop, please." It was Mallory. "Suggestion, gentlemen, before you continue your pissing contest. Daniel's here of his own volition—been here since dawn. He's invested in this for obvious reasons and some maybe more subtle. This is about Eveline. Now I never met the woman, Carmichael here never met the woman, but there seems to be a lot of interest in preserving her good name…from her brother. Now my way of thinking, Daniel, you've done your share—that elbow through the pain of glass was perfect. Well, almost perfect—so I'm fine with you getting out of harm's way; but you're not. You're in it and you want to stay in it." She turned to Carmichael. "Alex, I outrank you. This is my call—if things go wrong, you're off the hook. You wanted to dismiss him but I said, no let him stay. It'll be on me."

Carmichael was silent for a moment, then nodded.

"It's up to Blaine," he said, "but if he says yes, it's *my* call. It doesn't matter who outranks who. It's my operation."

Then he turned to me. "You in?"

I didn't give it a second thought, not because I was eager, but because the longer I waited, the less likely I was to accept. Though all that really influenced me was Taggart himself. I still believed he could get it done.

"I'm in," I said.

"Then we're settled," Mallory said, "but I'm not leaving. I'll be in the basement with you."

"Not without me," Carmichael said. "Looks like a party shaping up down there.

And listen, Taggart."

"What?"

"You better fucking be there, understand? Since you're so young and strong and fast like our investment counselor here, you better make sure you use that seven seconds wisely. I'm not hobbling upstairs to drag your ass down."

"Not a problem, officer."

"I'm going to let that *officer* go. So we're clear. That means you, too, Kasi. No delays. You'll have seven seconds, and your legs are wobbly from lack of use. I'm sure you don't want any of us yokels massaging the blood back into them."

"I'll do it now," Mallory said. "Get the flow back into the calves, everything else will work."

I looked at Kasi. "Are you sure you…um…"

"Mallory here is gay," Kasi said. "Now you won't have to get the message to me in sign language or…or smoke signals."

That pretty much silenced that conversation.

"Wow," Carmichael said. "I hope I don't die in this mess. I need some new stories to tell and this will be a good one. You Taggart, don't screw up. I don't want to die, understand? Mallory, get to work on her legs. And when it's time, Blaine, you make sure she doesn't fall."

"I won't fall," Kasi said.

"Goddam right you won't, because your boyfriend here is going to do his job because your legs might not work the way you want them to. Your first step out of this chair may not be an easy one."

He was, as he claimed, in charge.

We had accounted for the safety of Carmichael and Kasi, even Mallory and me.

It was Mallory who recognized we were one short.

"What about you," she said to Taggart. "Can you get rid of the bomb and make it to safety in seven seconds?"

"Never, but I can toss it into the pool, get back into the house, and hit the floor. There'll be glass flying, and my ears will be ringing for days, but I'll survive. And then, you get Walsh right away. He's going to know that this went off and he may not wait to launch something somewhere."

He looked at Carmichael. "Make whatever calls you have to make now."

He did, apprising the others at the house of what was going to happen, then turned back to Taggart.

"Should we evacuate more homes?"

"Two down on either side," Taggart said. "Beyond that tell people to stay indoors in at least a…I don't know…200-yard radius? Maybe more."

"We'll do it by cellphone," he said. "Pets, too."

I thought he was joking. "What?"

"Tell people to take in their pets."

I laughed. I didn't want to, but I couldn't help it and then I couldn't stop. "Sorry," I said, "but…pets?"

Mallory was laughing too, and even if it was merely another momentary release, Kasi smiled a little. Only Taggart remained serious.

"I like dogs," he said, "better than I like most people." Then he too smiled briefly before reminding us that maybe 300 yards would be better.

"And I wasn't kidding about the pets," he said. "Understand?"

"Pets," I said. "Done."

CHAPTER 35

Carmichael started clearing the path from the room where Kasi was imprisoned to the cellar door. There wasn't much in the way, a table near the doorway, but he didn't like the way the cellar door opened, found some tools, and removed it. I stayed with Kasi and learned about Ember, the yellow lab.

"Your sister," Taggart said, "rescued two dogs last year," then added, "one was sick and died shortly after, but we still have the other—Ember—a yellow Lab."

"Cool name for dog that color," Kasi said, her voice barely more than a whisper. I didn't know how she was able to get any words out at that point. She looked tiny, disappearing into the chair—held in place by the wires and devices that threatened to kill her. I wanted to get started, but Taggart wanted an all-clear from Carmichael.

"It is a cool name," Taggart said. "Even cooler for a black Lab, but Eveline wanted an E. My suggestion of Elvis didn't quite cut it."

He was trying to keep the conversation alive, and when Kasi didn't respond, he took a different tack.

"I think seven seconds is going to be it. I can't figure out another way."

"Seven will be enough," I said.

"I think so."

Another silence. We waited. My turn.

"We never had a dog when we were growing up," I said.

"Eveline said you never really had a home. I mean she loved your aunt and uncle, but it wasn't the same as having parents. Well, I guess you both turned out all right."

"Did my sister…did she ever talk about me? I mean without cursing?"

"Her successful brother? Of course."

"Then…why…?"

"You can tell yourself you have to let something go, but sometimes you just can't."

"Even if it ruins everything."

"Even if," he said. "I mean her story of the crash and the aftermath—even I wanted revenge. After a while we locked onto the incident, did research, looked for names, other victims, victims of other crashes. We were like conspiracy theorists with no conspiracy, just an event we couldn't escape. We had a life outside of that, but that quest was exhausting, and it exhausted us. Then Walsh came along and offered a new vantage point, maybe filled in the other aspects of her life."

"And you waited."

"I knew your sister—she could never fall for a creep like that, but she wouldn't be above using him. After a while she became not only disenchanted, but frightened. She was afraid he'd do something horrible."

"To her?"

"I don't think so, but something like today. Ruthless, sadistic."

"But if he thought Eveline would flip on him, then what?"

"I thought of that too. If he murdered his own wife, he'd have no qualms about doing the same to an…acquaintance. Maybe when we get this behind us and arrest him, we can pursue that a little more. Right now, though…."

"You think they'll catch him?"

"I like to be optimistic," he said. "That's not an answer."

"It'll do for now."

He peered in at the timer. "Carmichael, are we ready?"

"In a minute," he said. "One minute."

We heard tools and banging—Carmichael was taking no chances, except the big one of course.

I came a little closer to Taggart. "Just so you know—as if you didn't already—I never trusted her judgment much. Maybe I was wrong about everything."

"Nobody's wrong about everything," he said. "Not even you."

"I'm serious. You looked after her, were good to her."

He frowned a little. "That's an odd notion—*looking after*. I never thought I was looking after her. I loved her. Whatever followed from that was just…I don't know…the joy of loving someone. It's hard to get that back now."

"You will," Kasi whispered. "It takes time. You're still young. Once this is over, you'll see things differently."

Taggart smiled. "Ms. Brennan, I don't know what you're doing in this room with all these gloomy people. You belong someplace brighter. Let me get that taken care of before I plan for any future."

"Make sure there is one," she said. "And I'm not talking about me."

"I'm not the suicidal type," Taggart said. "Too cowardly. Some nights though, I look in the mirror and say, 'Okay, Lon, had enough?' But I always find something that needs to be done—mow the lawn, fix a leak, feed the dog. Without Eveline it's excuses to carry on, not reasons, but everyone who loses someone fights that battle. I'm not special."

"You have to keep passing the open windows."

"Never heard that one before," Taggart said. "You made that up?"

"I wish. It was John Irving, the author."

"The Garp guy. I like that," he said. "But I'll just keep my windows closed and avoid the temptation."

Carmichael still wasn't back and I wasn't sure how many more silences we could fill. Fortunately, Taggart had become talkative.

"You know," he said, "Eveline wanted to get pregnant. We knew with her age the odds were slim but she wanted a baby, maybe thought motherhood would save her. Maybe she was right, not that it matters anymore, "

Kasi's shoulders heaved slightly; Taggart grabbed them.

"Don't get emotional and short something out," he said. "I got a dog relying on me for her next meal."

"And," Kasi reminded him, "you like dogs better than people."

"Mostly. You guys are all right. Blaine, you still with us?"

"Yes, just surprised."

"You saw her one way; I saw her another. Then there's how she saw herself. Hard to reconcile all these viewpoints I suppose."

"Tell me about the end," I said.

"The real end—the anger, all that?"

"All that. Everything I missed."

"It wasn't pretty," he said. "She threw things, broke things, hit me once—right here," he said with a smile, and pointed to his left ear."

"I remember she was righthanded."

"Gotta protect the left side with people like that. But it was just that once, early on. As the treatments began and we started to see improvements, she became more philosophical I guess."

"Did she get good care?"

"The best I could find. I have money—that was never an issue. But the cancer itself just snuck up on us. She had a cold that wouldn't go away, then they called it bronchitis, then they thought, pleurisy, maybe pneumonia. I don't even remember the sequence anymore, but the longer the doctors have no idea, the worse it's going to be. Finally she got the diagnosis—it was in her lungs."

"If they had diagnosed it earlier?"

"Would have helped, at least a little. See when you get that diagnosis you start learning all the shit you don't want to learn—small cell, non-small cell, white blood count...."

"Was it small cell?"

"Yeah. You know what that means."

"I have an associate whose mother died from it not long ago. She wasn't sick very long."

"Neither was Eveline if you count everything up, less than a year. Look I know what you're going to say."

"I won't say you should have told me. It never should have come to that. At the end, though, was she...comfortable?"

"She was. I was there, we had a nurse, we had some friends and they were always around."

"Did Walsh ever come by?"

"He tried. Eveline wouldn't see him. I know what you're thinking—Walsh somehow hastened her death with some magic potion. Like he apparently murdered his wife. I doubt it. If he'd had a magic potion to keep her alive, he'd have used it. Sometimes I think all this is another overreaction to her death. It's Walsh lashing out at Mullins, at the world. Anyway, she wouldn't allow him in."

"My aunt and uncle?"

"No. Only for the funeral. Eveline was tough, made rules. I kept them." He looked up and smiled. "You know how it is."

He was hurting. I was too, but I deserved it. With only myself to blame, I found another object of scorn.

"That bastard Walsh can't die soon enough," I said. In context it meant nothing, but Taggart didn't question it.

"Then let's actually live to see it, huh?" he said, and called Carmichael. "Since you seem to be Mr. Fix-it, get the back screen door and fix it so it stays open. Should be a stop on the cylinder."

"Screw that," Carmichael said. "I remove doors.

He was gone. Mallory shrugged. "Man on a mission," she said. "Anything I can do."

"I need two pair of scissors. And some cotton."

She was gone only a few minutes before returning with three pair of scissors and a handful of cotton balls at the same time Carmichael informed us that the screen door now lay on the back lawn.

"I guess we're ready," Taggart said. There was a nonchalance in his voice—not unwelcome amid the increasing dread, but far from genuine. "Ms. Brennan, I'm going to undo the straps across your shoulders. You're going to place your hands under the mechanism and support it. Just so you aren't surprised, it weighs about three pounds—less than a half-gallon of milk."

"I don't think I've ever bought a half gallon of milk," Kasi said. "Orange juice?"

Carmichael exhaled loudly. "Can we move on?"

"Killjoy," Taggart said. "Three pounds, Kasi. You steady it while Blaine here—with his nice steady Chicago businessman hands—and I will cut two straps behind you simultaneously. They enclose the wiring. They need to be cut within a half-second of each other, maybe less, otherwise the delay mechanism fails. I could probably do it myself, but I want a free hand to hang onto anything that moves unexpectedly and I need to watch the smoke alarm. Still, Blaine, if you don't want to do it…"

"In for a penny, in for a pound," I said.

"The only way to be. Once the straps are cut, I take the device out the back door—that's three seconds; toss it into the pool; two more; and two seconds back to the house. Give or take."

"Give or take?" I yelled. "There's no room for…."

"I'm kidding, Blaine. You know Eveline had a minimal sense of humor, but she got my jokes. I guess the two of you really aren't that much alike."

"No, I knew you were joking."

"No you didn't. Also, the pool is covered. I need that cover off."

"Done," Mallory said on her way out of the room, "Let me tell the others it's time."

Kasi turned her head slightly toward Taggart.

"I want to thank you now," she said. "There'll be all sorts of confusion afterwards and I may not get the chance. Eveline made a good choice, didn't she Daniel?"

"I already said that."

"You should say it again," Kasi said. "We're so good at regretting things we didn't say, but we keep giving ourselves opportunities."

For some reason I looked at Carmichael but he looked away. Avoiding eye contact was unlike him. Maybe I was the last to know, but then I knew: there was no seven seconds, no tossing the bomb, no two seconds to return to safety, *give or take*. There was a survival plan, true, but no place in it for Taggart.

"There has to be another way," I said, my voice sounding an octave higher. "The bomb disposal unit."

"Now? At this point? They'll blow themselves up for sure," Taggart said. "And Kasi with them. Don't get cold feet now. This is going to work."

"I don't have cold feet. Not for me."

"Then for who, me?"

"You won't have time."

"I'm not jumping out any open window today, understand? Now just relax. You're making *me* nervous. Which scissors do you want?"

"Listen, about my sister. Thanks for…you know…taking care of her."

"I told you, I didn't…."

"For loving her then. For giving her someone to love."

"Got it, pal. Feel better? Which scissors? The red or the blue?"

"I meant what I said."

"And I appreciate it. Tell you what. Buy me a beer when it's over—we'll be even, you and I. Now let's do this so it actually *is* over. Kasi, you still with us?"

"I'm ready."

"Thank you for not nodding. When we cut the straps, you'll feel the weight. Support it for an instant, then get out of here. I'm staying because I want to keep that beam in place to get the full seven seconds. Don't watch me. You won't have time. Six or seven steps to the cellar door and down. Don't count—you don't want a distraction. Time is going to pass whether you count or not, and when this sucker goes off, you'll know anyway. The noise won't kill you and running while blocking your ears will slow you down. Mallory, cotton balls?"

Minimal directions, but she put some cotton in Kasi's ears. The rest of us declined until she insisted.

Mallory knew what I knew, what we all knew I guess. But still, the math rolling about in Taggart's head might very well have been superior to ours.

"Good to go," he said, handed me the scissors, got Carmichael out of the room, loosened the two leather straps that held the device to Kasi's chest, then pointed out the two straps that had to be cut.

"I'll count down from five," he said, "cut on one. *Cut. On. One.* If you wait for zero it will never come, nor will anything else. And Ms. Brennan…"

"Kasi."

"Kasi then. Focus on the destination, nothing else. Your legs feel okay?"

"The blanket helped—kept them warm."

"Gotta lose that now. Sorry."

"It's okay," she said, as Mallory took it, "but I'd rather not die naked."

"Then you won't die. Blaine, ready?"

I wasn't. How could I be? I was supposed to be in a corner office with an unobstructed view of the Navy Pier and Lake Michigan, maybe meeting someone for drinks or dinner, then watching a little TV, maybe reading some dumb novel, then climbing into a comfortable bed…without a package of plastic explosives impeding my view. Of course it was Sunday, so maybe I'd be riding my bike, or getting a deep-dish somewhere with friends, maybe check out the Bears game. Lots to do in Chicago on an autumn afternoon. I wondered if I'd ever do any of them again.

"Five," Taggart said, then stopped and yelled, "it's time, Blaine. Come back to us."

"I'm here," I said, then admitted, "I'm back."

I heard steps going into the cellar, and I heard Carmichael yell "we're good."

"Okay," Taggart said to me. "Trial run is over, here we go. Five…"

…and my thoughts of bicycling and pizza and football vanished. The four numbers went by in what seemed like a millisecond, closing out extraneous thoughts entirely. I almost felt as if I couldn't keep up. When I heard *one*, I cut.

The device came loose, and in one blindingly fast swipe Taggart lifted the pack from Kasi's shoulders and bolted out of the room, his long legs making huge strides. Kasi half-stumbled out of the chair but found her legs immediately and was gone with me right behind. A few steps from the bottom of the cellar stairs, I caught the back of her ankle and we both tumbled onto the concrete floor just in time to feel the house shake.

"Head down!" I said as a concussion of air swept past us and we heard the clatter of glass and dirt and whatever else lay between the pool and the house. Objects fell on the floor above us, then…nothing. Kasi was silent, and I thought she'd been hurt. But no, she'd been counting, like me.

We hadn't gotten close to the wall so we hadn't avoided the flying glass. Her knees were scraped from the fall, one worse than the other but both bleeding. On her forehead trickled a small stream of blood, apparently from a cut above her hairline. It didn't seem serious, though I was guessing, hoping. I seemed okay. My wrist hurt from catching myself as I hit the floor. A sprain at worst. The two of us—hobbled but alive.

Kasi limped for the stairs and Mallory practically tackled her.

"No," she said, holding her loosely. Mallory knew what awaited. We all did.

Kasi pulled away. "Let me go," she yelled. "I've been tied up for hours. He could be injured."

Mallory's voice was low and measured as she blocked the stairs. "Let the EMTs do their work."

"But Taggart."

"We'll just be in the way."

"Do you think he, you know, made it back in?"

"Let's just sit tight, okay?" Mallory said, her composure a stark contrast to the chaos we could hear above us. "Everyone knows where we are. "

Mallory sounded less like a negotiator and more like a bereavement counsellor—I held out less and less hope for Lon Taggart.

But we waited. It wasn't long before two paramedics descended the stairs and went to work. I actually had a cut on my forehead and another on my neck. Glass probably, but who knows? Some antiseptic and Band-aids were all I required. Mallory had a few marks on her face—she waved off any help. Kasi wasn't so lucky: both scraped and bleeding knees were wrapped and her forehead cleaned and bandaged. Throughout she held the blanket like a present-day Linus until Mallory put it around her.

There was no real silence after the explosion, not for me anyway. The sound had done its damage. I hoped the muffled ringing was temporary.

We waited, heard more voices upstairs as sounds returned. Carmichael. Weber. Everyone who had played a role in this little disaster except one. Nobody had to tell me what had happened, but in the little space between the explosion and the rescuers' arrival, Kasi had managed to compose herself a little. Carmichael was somber when he came back down the steps but seemed relieved.

"You did good," Carmichael said to Kasi, then asked if I felt capable of running upstairs and getting her clothes. He himself had stumbled coming back down and was limping slightly. Even for me running was out of the question, but I hobbled up and got them. They had survived the blast.

"If I'd known how this was going to end," Carmichael said, "I'd have installed one of those stair lifts. Might be time for a desk job."

I brought Kasi's clothes downstairs—they were covered with dust and what looked to be pieces of ceiling. Sometime later we got the all-clear and climbed the stairs. The kitchen was a shambles. The refrigerator remained upright and the range seemed to have moved very little. But everything else had been violently adjusted—even the faucet was leaking a thin but steady stream.

Taggart had overestimated the explosive power of the device, but not by much. A picket fence on a neighbor's property was flattened, a flowerbox was ripped from a window next door, and several pieces of backyard furniture were moved impressive distances and deposited in unlikely destinations at almost humorous angles. Broken glass was everywhere, on both sides of the street, and for an hour afterwards thick gray smoke hung motionless like sea fog on a sandbar, further muting the fading autumn hues. And the house itself—the half facing the blast seemed pushed in, bent, weirdly out of plumb. The other half, unscathed.

Taggart's plan had been sound. He knew that the empty swimming pool in the backyard, not ten feet from the back patio, would absorb much of the fury from the blast. And because he was a genius and a realist and a man who understood the laws of physics, he must also have known that he would absorb the rest.

CHAPTER 36

Walsh became a mere parenthesis.

After controlling my actions and dominating my thoughts for all those hours, I forgot him entirely, and forgot also that hundreds of lives remained in danger until Carmichael reminded me. We were standing amid EMTs and local cops on the relatively unscathed street side of the house—where we had followed that s-curved sidewalk what seemed like forever ago but was only a few hours. We were waiting for…for something. I didn't think the authorities were through with us, not until we told our stories.

Carmichael had been on his cellphone, then he told me.

"We shot down the missile. It landed somewhere in a field not far from Palmer's and never even detonated."

"What about Walsh himself?"

"We're closing in," Carmichael said. "Not many places to run."

"If he gets away…." I said.

"He doesn't. He won't."

"What happens when you catch him?"

"Fuck him," Carmichael said. "Don't even think about him. Not now. Not ever.

We think about this—right here."

Carmichael's little tirade was all the verification I needed. I never again asked about Taggart.

"And not that it matters," the agent said, "but Mullins' little ceremony will go on…is going on."

"Fuck Mullins, too," I said. "If it weren't for him forty years ago…."

"That's your sister talking," Kasi said. "That story has to end now. You have to make it end." She looked at Carmichael who suddenly seemed unsteady. "Are you sure you're all right? Let me see if your ankle swelled up."

"It's fine," he said, but Kasi got one of the paramedics anyway. The young man spoke with Carmichael for a moment, then nodded to us and walked away.

Yellow tape cordoned off the back yard, but Kasi and I had caught a glimpse of it—plastic sheeting covered a large area—I didn't have to ask why it was there. I found it difficult to walk away—to do anything but stand where we were. I put an arm around Kasi's shoulder. There seemed no place for us to be anymore.

The ringing in my ears had just begun to diminish when I heard the roar of jet engines. Directly overhead was a massive, twin-engine, wide-bodied jet, flaps full, landing gear down. It was majestic, stunning—it was why people looked at the sky—but in its slipstream lay the memory of Palmer, of Taggart, of my sister— maybe the 273 who died on Memorial Day weekend a lifetime before, and even the woman who followed a year later.

I looked away even before it descended beyond the trees, but I heard the reverse thrusters, envisioned the fire hoses, imagined Mullins's speech and the undeserved applause.

You have to make it end, Kasi had said. How?

We lost track of Carmichael and Mallory by late afternoon, Kasi and I. We were told to stay in the area for depositions and such, but we were going to anyway. Palmer's funeral had been scheduled for the next day—it already seemed like a century ago when he'd been killed—but when we inquired about Taggart, there seemed no one willing to take charge. We knew that he and my sister had friends, but we didn't know where to look.

In the vacuum Kasi took over. She assumed that if Eveline had declined cremation, perhaps Taggart would have also. She made some calls, handled all the minutiae I'd have never even thought about. There'd be a short service in the funeral home the day after Palmer's somewhat larger one.

It was after dark before I drove Kasi back to the hotel. Mallory followed us— she wasn't convinced either one of us could handle a car. Nor was she convinced, apparently, that we would have the sense to eat something.

"Let's get some food for you two," she said.

Nobody was hungry, including Mallory, but it was obvious she didn't want to let us out of her sight. Something in Kasi's expression—and undoubtedly in mine too—said we belonged in a trauma ward more than a hotel. But we dutifully ordered food, I picked at a few fries, had a few bites of a cheeseburger, then drank enough vodka to take the edge off things. Mallory was a good counsellor, saying little but letting us talk. Several times Kasi teared up, and each time Mallory acted as if it were no big deal—another life event that would pass.

Kasi and I wound up closing the place. Rather I did, finishing my last drink while Kasi dozed on the other side of the booth. When I nudged her awake and walked her to her room, I had the feeling she was about to ask me in. I know it because I was about to ask something similar. Shared mortality had left us in need of human contact, of reassurance that we were alive in every way. But linking that to sex would have ruined that particular pleasure forever. We said goodnight. I waited and watched her enter her room, as usual.

Next morning, slightly hungover, we attended Palmer's funeral. He had made countless friends over the years with his illegal agricultural endeavors, and every pothead in northern Connecticut, it seemed, stopped by to pay respects. Our hangovers went unnoticed.

And we met Lena, a girlfriend—or a girl *friend*, I wasn't sure. She was tough, plain-spoken, and funny: her eulogy was as close to a stand-up act as I'd ever heard, including one inappropriately uproarious tale about trying to graft a marijuana plant with a tomato. Of course she was high—why wouldn't she be? She and Ben must have had great times together. Kasi and I never introduced ourselves to her because, at some level, we both felt if we had let him be, he might still be alive.

Kasi was fretting over Taggart's funeral when a phone call took her off the hook. Lon's parents had arrived.

"They'll take it from here," she said. I thought I denoted some regret mixed with the relief.

"You wanted to be part of it, didn't you?"

"I owe him," she said, "but his parents need to do this more than I do. I hope people come."

I couldn't imagine a big crowd, and certainly the service that morning was much quieter. But Carmichael and Mallory came, so did Weber and a few uniforms. We talked for a bit, not about anything in particular. Nobody mentioned Walsh—he was apparently in the wind. I cared, but I had no taste for revenge.

Some other people my sister's age came in—neighbors maybe, book club readers. An older man stood close to the closed casket with a statuesque woman and a tall, neatly dressed young man from the funeral staff.

"Taggart's father," Carmichael said. "Came from Evanston. Half hour from you. Weird, huh?"

When he moved on, Kasi took my arm. "You should say something to them."
"What could I possibly say?"

"Tell them he was your friend. Let them know he didn't die without one."

"They know—look at all the people."

"Not the same," she said. "Say something."

I had the chance—everyone was milling about, waiting for the service to begin. I knew if I hesitated I'd talk myself out of it.

"You're Lon's dad," I said to the man. "I'm Daniel Blaine. I'm so sorry about your son."

"Eveline's brother," he said and took me by the arm. "I'm David, and this is my friend Nan. We felt awful about your sister. I didn't think Lon would get through it."

So they'd also been at Eveline's funeral, probably wondering where her asshole of a brother was—hey, didn't she have a brother?—where does he live?—is he dead?—how long does he plan to be an asshole?

I was afraid he would ask how I knew Lon when I never spoke to my sister, but he was eminently discreet, giving me the chance to confess at my own pace.

"My sister and I, Eveline," I said. "We were, I guess, estranged."

"It happens in families," Mr. Taggart said. "But you're here now. Being here for Lon is like being here for your sister, isn't it?"

"Not really," I said. "It's nice of you to say it, but it's not the same. I'm glad you were there though when Eveline died."

"Lon needed us. Knowing it was going to happen didn't make it any easier. Your sister…I mean we asked if we should call…but…."

"No, no," I said. "I understand why she didn't want me there. We were probably honest with each other all our lives—that would have spoiled it. I just wanted to let you know—Lon was a really good guy."

"He always was. He always had empathy—you can't teach it, but some people just have it."

"And so smart," the woman said. "He loved knowing stuff, not necessarily applying it."

"He did some applying a few days ago, saved a lot of lives. I know we throw the term around too much these days, but he was a hero."

His father smiled "When he was young he was so outgoing and entertaining—we thought he'd be a comedian. The last few years he's been, I don't know, different. But in a positive way. Eveline was good for him."

"For me too," I said. I was beginning to believe it. "I wish…I think your son and I would have been good friends. We were, sort of."

"Near-in-laws who like each other. That would have been refreshing."

For a moment or two we talked about the flowers, the service, even the weather. It had rained earlier, but the skies had brightened. They asked who had begun making arrangements and I told them Kasi. I looked around but didn't see her."

"Thank her for us," he said. "It was a big help."

I told him I would and he shook my hand. I held it for a beat or two.

"You know, I work in Chicago. I went to Northwestern." I paused and smiled. "I should stop telling you things you already know, right?"

"Nothing wrong with conversation," he said.

"We should meet sometime, have dinner, see a game maybe, just talk."

"We would love that, or you can just come by. Nan is an unbelievable cook and I'm an unbelievable buyer of expensive wine. Come and share."

I gave them each my business card and they promised to be in touch. If the father kept promises the way his son did, I can expect a call. Or maybe I can slip out of character for a change and call them.

I started to walk away, turned around again.

"Ember," I said, "their yellow Lab. What's going to happen to her?"

"Already in a shelter," he said. "Yellow labs have no trouble finding homes."

"Uh huh, well that's settled anyway." Something about my expression must have changed.

"Are you okay," Mr. Taggart asked. "Oh, yes. Just curious, what shelter?"

He fumbled through his jacket pocket and pulled out a receipt from a place in Southwick.

"Massachusetts," he said.

"How far? Which way?"

"Ten minutes. If I'd known you were interested…."

"Never even gave it a thought, and my place isn't really suitable, you know…." I was babbling.

"You should call now," he said. "They're popular animals."

I went outside immediately and dialed the number. A woman answered.

"You have a yellow Lab that was brought in today," I said. "Is she still there?"

The woman's voice on the other end was hesitant. She must have thought I was an escapee from a different kind of shelter. I'm sure I sounded like one.

"Who is this?"

"It was a mistake," I said. "I'll bring in the receipt that you gave to…um…David Taggart. He wanted me to have it and then he was…he was killed in an accident."

"The man who was just here?"

"No, his son. It was his son's dog. Lon. That's the son's name. He never wrote it down and I…his father will vouch for me."

I was talking too fast, grasping for anything credible. The poor woman on the other end, who probably hadn't signed up for grief-counseling that day, seemed as flustered as I was.

"We'll certainly hold her for you," she said. "We're a shelter. We don't have people queued up and waiting."

"I can be there by noon. I just didn't want her to be put down. It's a she."

"I'm aware. And we don't put down our animals."

"Of course. I knew that. It's Ember. She answers to that."

"*Answers* to it?"

"Responds. I'll be there by noon." I clicked off.

So dogs don't answer? They respond? What else should I know about dogs before I try to prove that someone wanted me to have one?

I came back into the viewing area and Kasi greeted me. "What happened to you? You're sweating."

"Right now there's a woman in an animal shelter probably calling the police. But I have a dog," I said.

"You look like you were chasing one."

"I was, sort of."

"Yellow lab?"

"Responds to Ember."

She squeezed my hand just as the funeral director asked us to take seats. I sat down near the back, but Kasi didn't take the seat next to me. Instead, she strode to the front of the room and stood by the casket. Carmichael caught my eye, silently mouthed *what?*

I faked surprise, but I knew. Earlier Kasi had asked if she could say a few words and the family agreed. Even delivering the eulogy she was the casual young woman in the floral hat, even when she wasn't wearing one. She spoke softly in a room that went silent in response. She was brief but eloquent, spoke as if Lon Taggart had been a childhood friend, not a man she's met a few days before.

"He was a good and decent man," she said. "And brilliant. And funny." She recounted a number of clever things he'd said and made us all feel a little better, but then she talked about his devotion to Eveline and how such sacrifice is unusual these days. Kasi would never indirectly aim a barb at me, but it was difficult not to contrast Taggart's devotion with my estrangement. She was giving the speech I should have given. Twice.

"This is one of the great honors of my life," she said. "Sometimes, losing someone the way he did makes it easy to give up on everything. He never did. Hundreds of people are alive today because of that. I'm alive today because of that."

She stepped away and returned to the seat next to mine. Her eyes were dry. Mine weren't.

"That was…just…wonderful. It could not have been easy."

"The words came easy. Saying them never is."

We were silent for the remainder of the service. Afterwards Carmichael cornered me standing alone.

"I'm speechless. Where did that come from?"

"You mean Kasi."

"Of course I mean Kasi. Jesus, I mean still waters and all that, but even so."

"People surprise us. He saved her life."

"Okay, look, you have to do me a favor. I want her to speak at my funeral." I smiled. "If you could guarantee it would be soon, she might accept."

"I'm serious. I want you to ask her."

"Shouldn't you do that?" I said, and waved Kasi over. She hesitated, of course, her natural aversion to Carmichael still evident.

"I know what you're going to say," she said. "Someone from the family should have done the eulogy."

"That's not it," I said. "Alex needs a favor. He wants you to speak at his funeral."

At first she thought I was kidding, but when she realized I wasn't, I think her first response was anger.

"I'm not entertainment at events," she said. "And what I said about Lon Taggart was all true."

"And that's what I want," Carmichael said. "I don't want someone from the Bureau saying how dedicated I was, how determined, how clever—I want someone to tell the truth. I know who I am. Someone should tell the truth."

"Warts and all," she said. "Warts especially."

Her face twisted into some look of skepticism, but Carmichael pushed ahead. "You don't have to decide today, but I figure you and Danny Boy—you'll at

least be Facebook friends, and then I can join in. When I go, you'll know. Hey, that sounds like some Internet funeral home slogan, doesn't it?"

"This is serious," she said. "Death is not a joke, and I hardly know you."

"We know each other from war. From danger. From almost dying together. From saving God knows how many lives. You know me just fine. Think about it."

Then he turned to me.

"She may hate *me*," he said, loud enough for Kasi to hear, "but she's a keeper. Don't you fuck this up."

I assured him I wouldn't, then added quietly for no discernible reason, "I have a dog now."

CHAPTER 37

Among the mourners was Kenneth Mullins. I'd hoped he would look a little more chastened, but he exchanged greetings with a few, shook hands with Lon's parents, then took a seat in back. I had met him only that once, but I couldn't very well ignore him.

"Daniel Blaine," I said. "We met a few days ago."

"I remember," he said. "I was cleaning out the office. Next Monday someone else will be in it."

"So everything went all right?"

"The ceremony was fine, lots of people saying insincere things to disguise the fact that I'd suddenly become useless. When you retire someday, and you're at a dinner, and someone says 'now he'll be able to golf every day,' I want you to stand up and say 'Fuck you, I don't want to play golf every day.' "

"Is that what you did?"

"No. I laughed. Your brother-in-law, he saved a life, huh?"

"At least one, maybe hundreds."

"The eulogy your friend gave was beautiful. Tell her for me."

"You can tell her."

"No. If I'm going to retire, I want to retire from Flight 191 too. It's enough. Tell her, please."

"I will."

"Did your sister have a charity or anything?"

The proper answer was no—if her life was a canvas, that crash consumed every square inch of it. But saying that would prolong the agony, and we were—every one of us—far past the point where we thought that would help.

"You can send a check in their name to the Southwick Pet Shelter. They'd appreciate it."

"I will," he said, and tapped some words on his phone. He might have been tapping "no way" but I don't think so.

"Listen, Daniel, I kept that crash picture on the wall for a reason. And I must have told the story to everyone who ever worked for me. Anyway, I'm going to ask something of you and you can feel free to say no."

"Which means I probably will."

"Hear me out though. An airline trade magazine is sending a reporter to interview me for a feature story. Something like 1500 words which means longer than any sane person would want to read. I'd like to use that as a forum to talk about 191 and the…well, the ripple effects of negligence and cruelty. I'd like to make your name available as a contact. I know the reporter and I've read his work. He's good, not sensational, not maudlin. What do you think?"

"I think if a reporter has an angle and you have a different one, the reporter wins. But yes, you can give him my name. But I have to tell you something first…just so you know. I had a visitor the other day. Christina Oakes."

"I'm not surprised."

"Her story, is it true?"

"Yes. I delivered the check and told no one. My wife knows, and some execs who thought this was a good idea probably know. Many of them are dead."

"And if a reporter asks me to be candid?"

"Be candid. That money helped the Oakes family, and in the end the story of the shoddy maintenance came out anyway."

"It was bribery," I said.

"I was dishonest—it was unforgivable. A reporter might see it as a small blotch on a perfect record or an indicator of a life of dishonesty. But as for you, say what you think is appropriate."

"Were there more incidents like that?"

"Payoffs? Yes. Not involving me, but there had to be. That hasn't changed much in forty years. Tina Oakes—is she okay?"

"She is. So are the kids."

"Good. And the agent, Carmichael, what about him?"

"What do you mean?"

"Why was his wife here?"

"At the ceremony? Just now?"

He looked around, then pointed. "By the door."

I looked. It was Carmichael with a woman, a tall, graying, frail-looking woman whose navy blue dress spoke more of winter than fall. I wanted to ask Mullins if he was sure the woman was Carmichael's wife, but that would have been a concession to Kasi's belief in Carmichael's philandering.

"Elise," Mullins said. "I met her once before. You should go over and say hello."

He smoothed the jacket of his dark gray suit. He was ready to leave, took a half step away, then stopped.

"That photograph from my office," he said, pointing to a table near the casket. "I put it down over there. Maybe it can be buried with him—end this once and for all."

"His folks may not go for it."

"Then you take it, but don't hang it in your house."

I know what he meant, but there was a magazine article ahead—I wondered if anything ever really ends.

Kasi was in a group with Mallory and a few other agents. I pulled her aside, but when I told her Carmichael was with his wife, she laughed.

"You're a funny man," she said.

"By the door. Over there. Mullins said it was her." She looked. Her astonishment was hard to conceal.

"That *is* her," she said. "But why? Why here? Why now?"

"I have no idea. Do we, you know, say hello?"

"I think we do," she said. "She looks…bad. Is she sick?"

We moved through the emptying room and saw Elise walking toward us. "Kasi Brennan," the woman said, barely above a whisper. "Your eulogy was beautiful."

"Mrs. Carmichael, I didn't expect to see you."

"Foliage," she said. "I always wanted to see a New England covered bridge in the fall. So we did, two days ago. Vermont. Near a town called Wilmington. Know it?"

"No, I don't."

"You should go. It's so transient—not the bridge, of course, but the leaves, the time. So fragile."

She looked at me. "You're Daniel Blaine. We haven't met but Alex talked about you—about the both of you. He said you did some good work. He doesn't give out many compliments so I'd write it down and maybe frame it."

"Pleasure to meet you, Mrs. Carmichael."

"Elise," she said. "My pleasure. Gotta freshen up a bit, but Alex is right over there."

She moved off.

"She's not right," Kasi said. "When did you last see her?"

"It's been years, but even so. She's not right."

"And you blame her husband."

"I don't know," she said. "It's more than that. Where is he anyway?" We found him in a far corner with a cup of water in his hand.

"I met your wife," I said, interrupting him. "She's very nice."

"I like her too."

"No, really, I mean…she's been here for a while?"

"All week."

"You never said anything. She could have had dinner with us."

"She doesn't…she's sometimes uncomfortable with a lot of strangers."

"She just sat in her room all day?"

"Hardly. I took her to some aquarium down near New London, some old village in Sturbridge…."

"I think it's called Old Sturbridge Village," I said.

"Well," he said, with an unaccustomed smile, "I had all the words right. We also hit a few casinos, or they hit us. She had a nice couple of weeks."

"And the foliage."

"Her dream, all her life, a covered bridge in the fall. Like a calendar, she said, so I took her."

Kasi was struggling for the right response, but was saved by Elise's return. "Ah, the three heroes—you should take a selfie."

Carmichael shook his head. "What happened to handing a stranger your camera and asking him to take a picture?"

"Too many stolen cameras, right honey?" Elise said, and we all laughed.

"I suppose," he said, "but let's not go overboard on the hero thing. These two were more like assistant heroes."

"Of course," she said, and took his arm, leaning on him a little. "Like I said, stingy with the praise. Alex, what was the name of that town in Vermont?"

"Wilmington," he said.

"Yes," she said, then turned to Kasi and me and was just about to say something when she stopped herself. It was an effort: I'd never seen anyone do that before.

And Kasi took my arm.

"I doubt if we're going to see any covered bridges in Vermont," I said. "We have flights to Chicago. No covered bridges out there."

"Sorry but you're wrong. There are a half dozen or so out in Iowa," she said. "I'll have Alex send you a list. And don't wait to see them," she said, then looked blankly at her husband.

"Elise and I are going to have to head out," Carmichael said.

We made our standard goodbyes and some blurred promises to keep in touch, then watched the two of them say something to a few agents at the door, Mallory among them, and then leave. The conversation in the group seemed somber.

We converged on Mallory as soon as she was free. "She's dying," Kasi said. "Elise is dying, isn't she?" Mallory didn't respond. Kasi pushed on.

"I met her before. That's not the same person." No response again from Mallory.

"She doesn't have to be dying," I said. "She could just be ill. She looked sort of okay."

"Her words," Kasi said. "She's marking time, trying to fill it up, trying to remember to…remember. She's barely fifty."

"She's not dying," Mallory said. "Not for a while. She could live another thirty years."

"And slowly deteriorate," I said. "So it's Alzheimer's."

Mallory, as expected knew everything. Elise had been diagnosed about a year before—some inexplicable confusion, some inability to concentrate, a lot of seemingly unrelated behavioral differences that led her to a doctor, to a specialist, and finally to some new, promising, but uncertain medication. Mallory wasn't sure if anyone else in the Bureau knew, but the fact that he'd been able to take his wife along on a somewhat important assignment led her to think that maybe Carmichael had called in a few favors.

"I talked to Elise," Mallory said. "She said she didn't want to be one of those women on a tour bus with other victims staring at the Grand Canyon or a redwood forest and not being able to share it. This is her way of avoiding that."

Mallory was angry, and I was hesitant to ask, but I had to know. "How much time does she have?"

"Ten weeks? Ten years? But don't call it time. It's existence, nothing more."

"You said experimental drugs?"

"All kinds of meds out there. She's signed up for a study after the first of the year. Something may take—maybe next year she'll be back to her old self—and her husband will be the asshole we know and love."

Kasi had been quiet through it all. I knew what she was thinking, of course: her thoughts were similar to mine.

"Guess I was wrong," Kasi said.

Mallory took her hand. "All the flirting, the bombast, the arrogance—that was never him. That doesn't excuse it, but it does explain why you didn't like him. He wasn't interested in being likable. He just wanted to do his job."

"And be with his wife," I said.

Mallory agreed. "Funny, even the most complex people want the simplest things. You guys might want to keep Alex in your thoughts—give him a call once in a while, email, something."

"Of course," Kasi said. "I never even knew where he lives."

"Outside D.C., a Maryland suburb. You can always reach him through the Bureau."

"I will," she said. "Those pills he takes, are they anti-depressants? I mean he takes them with alcohol."

"Antacids, mostly. He's trying not to hover—to give Elise some space. But then he worries himself sick. I wish I didn't feel so angry. I'm no Pollyanna, but life should be a little fairer."

Kasi agreed, then excused herself to "freshen up." Mallory grabbed my arm.

"Give her a minute or five," she said.

"Kasi is tough," I said. "That bomb, the abduction...."

"This is different. This is a different kind of personal. Give her some time."

I did. When she returned, reassembled and steady, we mingled for a while longer, said a few more words to the Taggarts, and headed out.

Just as we got to the car, though, Mallory caught up with us. "Walsh is dead," she said.

"What? How?"

"Marty Hendricks."

"He's in protective custody."

"He was until he escaped."

"That's nuts," I said. "You don't escape protective custody. The reason you're in protective custody...."

"I understand the principle," Mallory said, "but Hendricks had a mission, and he knew more than he let on. He didn't get there in time to stop the launch, but he nailed Walsh trying to escape."

"And shot him?" I asked.

"Beat him to death with a branch and turned himself in." Kasi was stunned. "Beat him to death? God!"

"It was personal," Mallory said. "He'll go to jail of course, but there's going to be a mental component to any trial. He's not a danger to anybody. Not to sound flip, but he killed the only person he's a danger to."

"I don't think that's going to be a defense strategy," I said, but these days, who knows?"

Mallory agreed, but she was still FBI.

"With that semi-anarchist past—I don't know. I want criminals brought to justice, but in Walsh's case, this may be the happiest of endings. And at least you two can leave knowing that things are settled."

Given all that had gone down since Sunday, her assessment seemed absurdly sanguine, but there'd have been no reason to argue. Not then.

CHAPTER 38

Kasi and I purchased the world's largest pet carrier in the world's most expensive pet shop, made our way to pick up Ember, learned that Lon's father had called ahead and greased the skids a bit, drove back to the airport, found out there was such a thing as an airport pet-sitter and hired her for the afternoon, dropped off the rental, checked to see if the flight was still on time (it was) , then went up to our rooms to pack and check out.

Hectic as it was, I thought we had done pretty well—until I found Weber waiting in my room. Harris tweed again, a grayish blue shade this time.

"Looks like breaking and entering. Should I call a cop?" I said.
"I know a few—let me take care of it. I wanted to catch you before you left. Carmichael says you did good."

"Cut a piece of leather with a scissors. Not to belabor it, but couldn't you have waited in the lobby?"

"I was a witness."

"To what?"

"To…to Taggart. I was watching the house. There were a few of us."

"You know what? I don't have to know."

"Yes you do. You want to know if he threw the bomb, because if he didn't, you won't be happy."

"No, not if he killed himself. Did he?"

"Kill himself? No. He just ran out of time—heaved it and turned and it went off. I know he told you he had seven seconds, but I'm not sure if he did. I counted two from the time he stepped out of the house. Maybe two to get there, another second to throw it, he should have had two left."

"I'll never shake that image. No reason Kasi has to have it too."

"She's a big girl. She used to investigate plane crashes."

"Then you tell her. I'd just as soon let her imagine that Taggart overestimated his ability to escape. And even if she knows, she doesn't know people saw it. That would only make it worse."

He meant well, in a kind of paternalistic way. It's what Carmichael might have done. But Kasi knew the odds, knew what five seconds meant, or seven. She had to know that the odds against Taggart were great, that even extricating her from the device long enough to save her was a feat. I didn't tell Weber any of that—he was trying to be a good guy, and with what I'd encountered with Devin Walsh, there was no harm in it.

He was about to leave when I remembered something totally unrelated.

"You know, I meant to tell you, Palmer told me about his wife, the accident that killed her, and how you people rallied behind her. He never forgot that."

"Right up the street. Yeah, I remember. He told you about the judge we ran out of town?"

"He did. He was grateful."

"In his own psychotropic manner."

"But he was, Lieutenant."

"We knew. Tell you what," he said with a smile, "we could have busted Palmer every day. But we weren't going to let some scumbag take away his wife, then when the law failed him, hassle him over some bullshit."

"Small town America," I said. "Sometimes it still works."

"And you're lucky it does," Weber said, with a stern grin. "Impersonating a…a…whatever you were impersonating and conducting your own investigation with absolutely no authority. Try that in Chicago, see how long you stay out of the system."

I laughed, but not too hard. I was afraid he'd change his mind about putting me in it.

I asked him if he felt cheated with Walsh being killed.

"No. No trial. No prison. No circus. No bleeding-heart judge or lunatic juror who wants to see exhibit 809 one more time, no chance for him to spew any more bullshit. You give Kasi my best. You and her…something? Nothing?

"Maybe something. Probably nothing. Can I ask you something? The jackets. How many do you own?"

"Sports jackets?"

"Yeah."

"Eleven."

"Wow. Patched sleeves on any?"

"Two."

"Kind of mid-twentieth century, isn't it?"

"Kind of. Shall I tell my wife you don't approve?"

"Does she approve?"

"Very much, my man. Very much. Anything else?"

"Yeah. Thanks, Detective. I owe you."

"For?"

"Not arresting me."

He frowned. "Which time?"

*****

When my life had returned to a semblance of midwestern normality, maybe a week or so before Thanksgiving, I got an email from Ken Mullins. He and his wife were at a golf resort in Arizona—as good a place as any to spend the winter, he said. I'm not sure what happened to *fuck you I don't want to play golf*, but maybe retirement gave him a new perspective, or maybe not staring at that photo of a doomed plane every day altered his thinking. If so, and if it took forty years to get there, then that was a big chunk of his life wasted trying to undo what couldn't be undone. Maybe that's everyone's story—my sister's, mine, maybe even my mother's, though she was either weaker than everyone else or stronger—able to understand that she would never recover but strong enough to leave life behind. I'm not sure where on that continuum Mullins fit, and the Oakes story with the $100,000 payoff still bothered me, but he attached the article on which I'd been consulted—a big word for a ten-minute phone conversation. The piece was good, fair, even considerate: Lon Taggart was portrayed as a flawed but selfless hero, and my sister as a justifiably tortured soul. But it was about Mullins.

He had been right about the author. When things calm down further and I regain some objectivity, I may contact him. Eveline's story is a hell of a lot more interesting than Mullins's, and even though I would fine with it. When wind up as nothing other than the villain of the piece, something that memorializes her struggles deserves at least as much ink as those of some airport executive.

I read the article twice, a fact that cut into Ember's take-me-for-a-walk time. She was probably unhappy, but I was I returned to Chicago in October, I relished these little jaunts—a new dog owner—kind of cool, trendy. But that was two months ago. December in Chicago really sucks. There's no polite way to put it. The wind blows in off the Lake, circles around buildings, slithers through side streets, and blasts into your face no matter which way you're pointed. Not even the suburbs are safe. The grass in the nearby park is concrete, and the river is solid. Ember seems less keen about venturing out—it's hard to blame her. I did find a dog-walker, so there's some exercise every day, even when I have late meetings or after-hours dinners I can't get out of.

On those nights, I get the Ember evil eye, but I keep telling her she's lucky—that I saved her from a life of misery with a family of cat people. She looks at me as if I'm crazy, as if I've forgotten that she already had two really good owners.

I've talked to Kasi a few times and struck up a semi-relationship with a woman named Patty Landreau, a colleague in Acquisitions whom I've known for years. We have fun together, but there's not much going on beneath the surface. Ember likes her well enough but gets a little antsy on the nights when Patty stays. Ember's hesitancy is not a deal-breaker, but *my* getting antsy certainly is.

Work—well it's been a grind since I got back, though it's the same work. The company is doing well, but everything seems bland and uninspiring. I gave myself some time to reacclimate, but I'm not getting better. Crozier, my supervisor, called me in one day just to talk. He doesn't do that, so I knew my change in attitude must have been noticeable. He asked if I wanted the week off between Christmas and New Years'. I said no, but then I had an idea and called him back. I took the offer, then I called Kasi. I had spoken to her only once since the funeral—a conversation about an episode of *Air Disasters* where I thought I'd seen her.

"Sorry, "she said. "I wasn't on that one. Now you watch *Air Disasters*?"

"Have to carry on the Blaine tradition."

"And when *that one* comes on?"

"An extra bourbon will get me through."

"Alex's drink of choice."

"I'm developing a taste for it. Reason I called—I'm coming to DesMoines for the holidays, if you're going to be around."

"What if I'm not?"

"I'll be there anyway. I already booked the flight and reserved a room."

"Last time you drove."

"Don't trust the weather. I'll be there three nights, see my aunt and uncle. Then I want you to go somewhere with me."

"The Twisted Bean? I still have credit there."

"Someplace warmer."

"It's warm in the Twisted Bean. You must mean an island. I've always wanted to see Barbados."

"How about Dallas," I said.

"That's not an island. That's not even a…Dallas? Why?"

"I have business there and you have your old buddy Jake. What do you say?"

"Is this a getaway, an extended date, two old friends visiting another old friend?"

"The last one, I guess."

"And Bethany will be joining us. I take it you dumped the woman in work and now you're married?"

"Bethany will not be joining us. What do you say?"

Her *why not?* was lukewarm at best, but I didn't worry about it. On this particular trip, her presence was desirable but not integral.

For the purpose of full disclosure, I have an embarrassing confession. When we left Connecticut after the funeral, I was so traumatized by the prospects of Ember traveling in the baggage compartment that I begged Kasi to ask Jake Moss to pull some strings. As a result, the three of us, two human, flew to Midway in a Learjet. I paid for the fuel, then took out a loan to avoid going to jail. During the flight Kasi and I had some wine; Ember slept. This is how the filthy rich live—except for the taking-out-a-loan part. If Mallory had driven us to the airport in her Lexus, the picture would have been complete, but she'd already left for Boston.

Kasi may not have been integral this time, but Jake Moss was. He didn't know why I was coming, and maybe if I'd told him he would have laughed. I was looking for a new job. Yes, sometimes I laugh too.

I'm forty years old and settled with a good job. I can work fifteen more years and walk away with lots and lots of money, or stay longer and make even more. But I have responsibilities now. I have a dog. Okay, that's a joke, but Ember ties me to my sister in more than a symbolic sense. We both remember her in our way, and when we reminisce (usually after a few bourbons and water—just water for Ember) we both get a little weepy. I think my old life is dragging both of us down. Which brings me to my plan: the closest NTSB regional office is Denver—not exactly "central" in my book, but that's where I'll be if I follow through, if Jake thinks I'm the right fit, and if I can convince Kasi to give the organization another chance.

I've done some prep work, even got a hesitant recommendation from Alex

Carmichael and a somewhat more literate one from Mallory. That's her *last* name, by the way. I'm sorry I learned that—she was more of an enigma before, so I've decided she'll always be Mallory. Just Mallory. She even called to talk one day, mostly about Alex's wife. Some of those miracle treatments seemed to be helping her. He wasn't doing field work, but he had been at the office every day until taking another sabbatical right through the holidays to do some more traveling with her before she gets involved in that study.

"Time is precious," Mallory said. I couldn't tell if she was reminding me of the time I'd wasted or the limits on the time still to come.

"My sister would have a good laugh over this," I said. "But do this for yourself, not for her."

"Of course," I said. I didn't want to explain that it was for both of us.

Just before Thanksgiving I Face-timed Carmichael. He seemed in good spirits, and Elise remembered me from the funeral parlor. I think she actually did—I read that Alzheimer's victims don't fake remembering: it's not a function of the illness. We laughed because Kasi had called him the day before. He asked if the two of us were engaged yet. When I said no, he repeated a previous kernel of wisdom from his vast trove. "She's a keeper," he had said at Lon's funeral. "Don't fuck it up."

Elise poked her head into the frame once more. "We're trying to get Alex to open up more, you know, say what he means."

"It's certainly working, keep at it."

They were off to Greece in a few days on what they both referred to as their End-of-Days tour."

When I didn't laugh they seemed disappointed.

"You never did have much of a sense of humor, Blaine," Carmichael said. "We'll call you when we get back. I'll try to come up with a funny story."

"Maybe you think this as grim," Elise said "but we prefer to call it apocalyptic."

They weren't going to feel sorry for themselves, so I wouldn't either. I promised to keep in touch, and planned to keep the promise. When I told Kasi we had spoken, she told me again how much she hated being wrong about people.

"It happens," I said.

"Not on that scale," she said.

"Really? When you make a thirty-year error, we'll talk."

*****

I arrived in Dallas with the two written recommendations for Jake Moss. There are a lot of ifs, but the world looks different to me these days. Some nights I wake up because I've felt the house shake as it did when that bomb went off; other times I see Taggart trying to free Kasi, but he's already a ghost and he can't help her; and my father turns up in dreams so often that I actually feel as if I knew him. I don't want the rest of my life defined by the events of a Friday in May before I was even born. It happened to my sister, and no sympathetic magazine article could undo the life she chose.

The first tentative step to changing things was the trip to Dallas. But the evening before I was set to leave, Bethany came by. I'd called her when I got back from Connecticut, but she couldn't talk and never returned the call. Then that evening she did.

"I'll come by," she said. "Don't go straightening up."

"Not an issue," I said. I tried to sound nonchalant and probably failed. When she knocked on the door, Ember proffered her usual single bark. "It's open," I yelled.

She stood in the doorway with her mouth agape. "What the fuck…you have a dog?"

"I just…you know…yeah, just the one."

"Just the one? How many are you supposed to have?"

"I just mean I have one dog."

"And you hate dogs."

"That's not true," I said, earnestly enough so that not only Bethany but Ember would believe me. I hope Ember did; Bethany didn't.

"You said they were useless and annoying. Remember I said we would get one someday. And what were your words?"

"Please, not in front of the d-o-g. Besides, you also said you'd marry me."

"But I was serious about the dog."

She got down on one knee and, complaisant like me, Ember trotted over to her, allowed herself to be petted. Bethany looked up at me.

"You said they were needy, and now you have one. That's good, you know, being able to satisfy needs. Kind of puts you out there in the world. What's her name?"

"Ember."

"Cool. A little irony. How old is she?"

"About five, not really sure."

She stood, smiled, put both hands on my shoulders.

"How on God's green earth do you have a dog? And don't tell me it's just one dog again. I need answers."

I gave her some. When she started crying, I bypassed the paper towels and went right for the Kleenex. I'm nothing if not trainable. Like Ember. I don't know about a dog putting me out there in the world: I've never been reclusive. But it does provide unfocused moments with some clarity.

After Bethany's emotions were back in tow, we spent a pleasant hour—it was less stressful than our interactions had been for a long time. I told her about my NTSB plans. She asked if there was a girl, and I didn't know how to answer. There was, of course, but not that way. Not yet anyway. I thought of the first days when Bethany and I were just beginning to be a thing. It was like that.

"So you're going to Dallas," she said. "What about Ember?"

"I have a walker, but I'm boarding her. Dropping her off in the morning. Of course I'm sick about it, but…"

"You're not boarding this dog," Bethany said, calling Ember again and gently tapping her side. "I'm off for a few days. I can come over and feed her, walk her, whatever. I won't steal anything, I won't even smoke your stash."

"Very funny. I'll be gone a week, you know."

"You got a coffeemaker and wi-fi, I'm working from home. Call the kennel and just cancel. Jesus, Danny, why didn't you tell me you had a dog?"

"It…uh…never came up?"

"Bad answer."

"One thing—I don't want this dog barking f-bombs after a week with you, got it?"

"I'd laugh," she said, "but I think you're serious." I was.

I canceled the kennel, and of course Bethany still had a key—or I should say always had a key. Ember seemed to like her well enough. Of course my sister liked Bethany too, and although I don't consider myself a spiritual guy, I wasn't that quick to dismiss the possibility that some kind of electric chain held my sister, Bethany, and me together, and that the current came by way of a yellow lab.

If Kasi and I do wind up together in Denver—it's not beyond the realm of possibility—then we might also be working together, a situation rife with pitfalls. But while I can easily envision her in the field again—the job she misses—I don't see myself picking through wreckage and interviewing witnesses. Give me a desk and some words and some figures and let me go to work. I speak the language as a result of my *useless* English degree, and I have many years' experience in the Chicago business world. Kasi can file reports and make breakthroughs—I can type them up. And Ember, uprooted from a quiet New England town to Sandburg's "City of the Big Shoulders" might welcome the move—to the mountains. I think it's worth the risk.

"Do something," Carmichael had said that day, when he was riding with Elise singing along to the CD he'd stolen.

Good advice.

(I did eventually find out what song that was too, and was disappointed: *Do Something*. That was the title—I'd hoped for advice a bit more profound, though I like the song.)

Regardless, flying to Dallas was *something*. Whether it's the right something for me—and for Eveline—I hope I'll figure out in time. A lot depends on Kasi and just where this relationship is headed. It's all very slow, but so much time has passed just to get to this point that I can't allow myself to become impatient. Not now.

So it's just Ember and me.

But Kasi is flying in from DesMoines the weekend after next on the promise of an actual Chicago deep dish pizza. I can't possibly stick her in a hotel after something that sublime, and I won't have her freezing on Michigan Avenue in winter. Besides, my place is large enough for us both to feel comfortable whatever the situation, though I'll have to monitor Ember's behavior. She was Eveline's dog. If she doesn't get antsy with Kasi around, it would be a good thing.

Acknowledgments

First to my wife, Deanie, for the patient proofreading of course, but also for the suggestions on how to manage a story that took forty years to develop, twenty years to write, one week to "happen," and three- hundred pages to narrate.

To my dependable first reader and long-time friend, Tom Ward, on whom I can always count to close-read a novel in a day or two and tell me if it holds together...and also tell me where it doesn't.

To my sister-in-law Cindy Satagaj-Radda who, with an artist's eye, scratched out the original cover design in a few seconds one evening in September, and then helped polish it over the months to come.

To my children, Jennifer and Christopher, once again put upon to "read something their father wrote." (He appreciates it.)

To my Chimney Crest writing partners David Fortier and Dawn Leger for their encouragement and patience–they first saw this story in much different form more than ten years ago. I'm sure they're glad to be rid of it.

Finally, a special recognition to an uncle, gone now nearly fifty years. John Fabale, a musician and teacher, captained B-25s during World War II, survived a crash in New Guinea, led his crew to safety, and became a decorated hero. His story, though he seldom repeated it, became family lore–one of the first tales I can remember being told. As years passed, airplanes–in all their glory (as in *Dark Time*) and tragedy (as in *Thirty-One Seconds*)– became my obsession too.

Lefora Publishing

Our mission is to publish new literature, including fiction, poetry, memoir, and criticism, with a focus on contributions that best serve to enhance and represent the intellectual life of the New England region.

Lefora seeks to support a vibrant community of writers... by stewarding writers through the editorial and marketing process,

by working with emerging talent as well as seasoned writers, by sharing in the development of their careers,

by hosting an online journal, by sponsoring writing contests,

by offering speaking opportunities,

and we will do each of these as we create the Lefora Publishing legacy.